ABOUT THE AUTHOR

David Nunan has been an expatriate for much of his professional life. For the last twenty-five years, he has lived in Hong Kong, where he is Professor Emeritus at the University of Hong Kong. He has published over thirty scholarly books on language, culture and education, as well as textbooks for young learners. His series *Go For It* is a market leader with worldwide sales exceeding four billion copies. Creative non-fiction books include a memoir, a travel book based on his experiences on author speaking tours, and a book of stories on expatriate lives in Hong Kong.

Other works by the author

<u>Creative non-fiction</u>

When Rupert Murdoch Came to Tea
Roadshow: A Personal Odyssey
Other Voices, Other Eye: Expatriate Lives in Hong Kong

<u>Selected books on language, culture and education</u>

What is This Thing Called Language?
Practical English Grammar
Introducing Discourse Analysis
Research Methods in Language Learning
Selected Works on Applied Linguistics
Learner-Centered English Language Education: The Selected
Works of David Nunan
Language and Culture: Reflective Narratives and the Emergence
of Identity (With J. Choi)
Learners' Stories (with P. Benson)
Knowledge and Discourse: Towards an Ecology of Language
(with c. Barron and N. Bruce)
Voices from the Language Classroom (with K. Bailey)

<u>Textbook series for language learners</u>

Go For It
Our Discovery Island
ATLAS
Speak Out
Listen In
Expressions

THE INFIDELS NEXT DOOR

DAVID NUNAN

THE INFIDELS NEXT DOOR

Vanguard Press

VANGUARD PAPERBACK

A CIP catalogue record for this title is
available from the British Library.

ISBN 978 1 78465 883 0

*Vanguard Press is an imprint of
Pegasus Elliot MacKenzie Publishers Ltd.*

www.pegasuspublishers.com

First Published in 2020

**Vanguard Press
Sheraton House Castle Park
Cambridge England**

Printed & Bound in Great Britain

Dedication

To Margaret and Chris Krutli whose research and data verification skills made this book possible.

Acknowledgements

With thanks to the team at Pegasus.

Prologue

At nine o'clock on a bleak winter morning in July 1934, a prominent local businessman rises to his feet in the magistrates' court of a provincial Australian city. Impeccably dressed in a dark-brown pin-striped suit and white shirt with starched collar and tie, he listens calmly to the clerk of the court read out the charge against him: that on the night of Thursday, 28 June, he had discharged a handgun at one Edward Francis Inman, with intent to murder. The plaintiff, a rough–hewn miner, sits on the other side of the court. He wears an ill-fitting, borrowed jacket. In contrast to the defendant, he is highly agitated, clasping and unclasping his hands and shooting angry looks at the defendant.

Although the public gallery overflows with curious spectators, there is no sign of the accused's wife and daughters. He faces the attempted murder charge alone, accompanied only by his lawyer and the lawyer's clerk. The businessman is Frank "Dodger" Price.

What had impelled him to commit this act? He was a justice of the peace, and a respected figure from one of the most prominent families in the town. The man he had allegedly attempted to kill was a younger, ill-educated manual worker.

Having heard arguments from the prosecutor as well as Dodger's lawyer, the magistrate turns to the defendant and says, "I deem it a case to call upon you. Frank Price. You are now charged with having on June 28 shot at Edward Francis Inman with intent to murder. Do you have anything to say?"

Calmly, and in a clear, measured voice, Dodger replies, "I am not guilty, and I reserve my defence."

Why had Price risked his reputation, his fortune, his business, and most of all his family, by attempting to kill Inman? The failure of his family, in particular his wife Violet, to appear in court to lend him moral support, was a clear indication of his guilt to those in the public gallery.

Chapter I
The House That Annie Built

Family and neighbours stand about eyeing the gleaming monster parked in the yard adjacent to the house. Some eye it warily, some with admiration, and some with outright envy. Little Paulie, a small boy in overalls, clambers onto the running board and stretches in vain for the door handle above his head. His father immediately and unceremoniously hauls him off and dumps him in the cracker-dust driveway where he squats, picking his nose and staring myopically at the adults through a pair of grubby glasses secured to his head with a piece of string. Mary laughs at the minor misfortune to her younger cousin. "Can we go for a ride, Daddy?" she asks her own father.

"Not now," he replies shortly. It's time for tea.

It's the last of the truly majestic models, fit for the transportation of cabinet ministers and captains of industry. In addition to running boards, it has massive, bug-eyed headlamps, and of course, the snarling silver jaguar frozen in flight on the bonnet. Nothing like it has been seen before in Railway Town, and probably rarely before in the whole of the isolated city. One or two of its ilk may be garaged in the enclave where the mine managers and other company bigwigs reside, but that part of the town is strictly off-limits to the residents of Railway Town.

The two brothers stand a little apart from the others. They roll cigarettes, scratch their heads, and wonder what to do with this unexpected gift.

"You'd better take it, Bill," says the younger man, somewhat reluctantly. He has his own car, a dun-coloured Ford Customline. He also has access to the ex-army trucks parked against the corrugated iron fence on the far side of the yard. His brother has no car. Like most working men, he relies on an ancient pushbike to get himself to and from work.

"I dunno, Jimmy," replies his brother. "I can't afford to run a motor like that." With the arrival of the new baby, he now had five mouths to feed. "How did she get the money to buy it?"

"Blowed if I know," says Jimmy, "but it's a bloody beauty, that's for sure."

As the prospect of a ride around the block in the beast fades, most of the neighbours drift away, and the extended family, along with a favoured few, head into the house for tea, as the evening meal is called: never "supper" or "dinner," terms that belong to the genteel. On this side of the tracks, "tea" means sausages and beer.

Along with her sisters, Babs and Yvonne, Bet had been born and raised in the Old House. Apart from the years of her father's disgrace, when along with her mother and younger sister, Yvonne, she had fled to Adelaide, it had been her home. When she married Bill, she moved to his house a few short blocks away. But her real home would always be the rambling, and by the 1950s, ramshackle dwelling built by her grandmother in the 1890s: a sanctuary and bulwark against the rumours and whispers that had driven the family from the city. She knew all of its quirks and most of its secrets. It was here that births, deaths, and marriages took place, and from here that funeral corteges departed. Here, many family dramas had played out over more than sixty years. And it was here that she had kept vigil beside Dodger's coffin during the long night before they buried him.

In keeping with most Broken Hill dwellings, the Old House was built of corrugated iron, a material she detested. The houses were cheap and easy to erect. They were also freezing in the winter, and hellishly hot in summer. During heatwaves, it was impossible to sleep indoors, so locals slept on canvas stretchers in the backyard under the stars. As a young woman, the large block on which the house sat allowed her to indulge in her passion for gardening. To mask the vulgarity of the corrugated iron, she encouraged creeping vines to embrace the exterior.

She had adored her grandmother, the matriarchal Annie Forbes, and the feeling was reciprocated. As she grew up, she learned the story of the Old House. The extensive plot of land came about because, when Annie and Uncle Tom escaped to Broken Hill from the scandals that had enveloped them in Adelaide, she acquired two blocks on the western edge of the town. She had the house constructed astride the boundary of the two blocks, thereby ensuring that no one else could build close enough to threaten their privacy.

Why did they build the house from such ugly material? Well, the cost was one thing, Annie said, but another was that corrugated iron could be easily added to, and Annie added to the Old House with great enthusiasm. In effect, it became two houses. The main structure, which faced the dirt road posing as a street, was fronted by a sleep-out. Enmeshed in mosquito wire, it became an additional bedroom, contested in summer, and shunned in winter. A corridor led from the verandah, past a number of bedrooms, to a large dining cum lounge room spanning the width of the house.

As a child, apart from the kitchen (always the social hub of homes in the bush), Bet loved the lounge room most of all. In winter, two fireplaces, one at each end of the room, burned non-stop and kept the room cosy. A massive sofa and armchairs into which a diminutive child could disappear sat solidly in front of the fireplaces. These had seen better days. Clumps of horsehair escaped through rents in the leather, but that mattered not at all to a six-year-old. The clumps were kept in check by one of the kangaroo-skin rugs that were in abundance throughout the house, thanks to the shooting expeditions that Uncle Tom and Dodger took to the Pinnacles.

Bet has just put the baby in its bassinet, when she hears chatter from the knot of people approaching the house, eager for sausages and beer after the excitement of the black, four-wheeled beast in the front yard. Her mother is hunched on the sagging sofa on the dark side of the living room, a room cluttered with bric-a-brac and exotica: an embossed Victorian coal scuttle and Oriental curiosities brought back from Shanghai by Aunt Babs after her years in the East as a vaudeville artist. Violet, her mother, lifts her eyes and grants Bet a vacant smile. What will be her disposition today? She knows her mother better than most, has observed her using her mental condition as a shield against the world. She tries a question on Violet. "Why did you do it, Mother?"

"You need a car, Bet. With the new baby, you need a car."

"Where did you get the money?"

Violet avoids her question, abandoning her temporary lucidity and retreating into vacancy. Bet would like to sit with her mother in this large room with its fretworked archways and ornate ceiling, but Yvonne calls her to come and help with the food. Even on the sunniest of days, this room is cast in eternal twilight thanks to the creeping vines she had planted as a teenager. The vines ran amok over the entire front of the house and, as the Old House succumbed to the heat of summer and the winter winds and rain, were probably responsible for keeping it upright.

She steers Violet through the cramped antechamber separating the bedrooms and living room from the back section of the house. This had served as Dodger's office cum study, although it lacked the intimacy of a proper study. Despite what he had done to her, after his violent death, Violet never allowed it to be touched. The large oak desk where Dodger had done his bookkeeping and his plotting dominates the narrow space and still displays the items that had sat there on the day he died: an antique inkwell, a pen set, a large sheet of blotting paper in a leather frame, and a solid silver case containing tobacco, now turned to dust.

The back section of the house, consisting of kitchen, pantry, storeroom, and laundry, is united to the front by a corrugated iron and mosquito wired cloister that looks on to the creeper-covered courtyard Bet had created years before. Attached to the inner wall of the cloister is a hand-operated pump for drawing water from the covered well behind the house. As children, they had been strictly forbidden from going near the well. In her teenage years, and prone to asking awkward questions, she had pestered Violet to reveal the secret of the well. What danger lurked there, when even as girls they'd had access to hunting knives and guns. It was due to your grandmother, she was told. The matriarchal Annie had been informed by a fortune-teller that one of her progeny would die by drowning. As a gullible teenager, she accepted this account. As an adult, she had her doubts. Her grandmother carried a handgun and wasn't afraid to use it. She was a confirmed atheist and a member of the Secular Society. The notion of her seeking counsel from a fortune-teller failed to fit the narrative of Annie's life.

As she leads Violet along the cloister, she remembers a traumatic incident that occurred in her childhood. Skipping along the cloister on her way to the kitchen, her path was blocked by a deadly black snake that appeared from nowhere. Frozen with fear she screamed to her mother. Violet rushed from the rear of the house and decapitated the snake with the blade of a shovel. It is hard to believe that the fragile creature on her arm was once capable of such decisive and violent action.

In in the kitchen, she finds family, relatives and friends who have gathered there after viewing the beast. The kids are loading up on sausages drowning in tomato sauce, mashed potato, and lumps of white bread smeared with yellow butter. The adults are loading up on beer and picking at the congealing sausages provided by Stevo, the family butcher from up the street. Portly Stevo is sitting at the end of the table drinking beer and avoiding the sausages.

She handles her mother onto the couch between the Aga range and the door to the cellar. There Violet sits, alone, silent, and barely visible, peering through rimless spectacles and smiling in a distant, queenly way, as family members thank her for her improbable gift.

The door to the cellar on her mother's right is locked. As children, they had been warned never to venture into the cellar because it hosted poisonous snakes and spiders. Of course, they immediately wanted to explore it, which they eventually managed to do one day when a careless adult left the key in the lock. Led by Yvonne, her more impetuous younger sister, she entered the forbidden and forbidding space. While redback spiders in abundance quivered on their webs, they searched in vain for the promised deadly snakes. What they found instead was something infinitely more enticing than snakes and spiders.

With the instinct of feral night creatures, Bet's sons and nephews sniff the air and keep their distance from Violet. When ordered to "give Nan a kiss," they do so reluctantly, avoiding the whiskered chin and swiping the kiss away with the back of a hand. Paulie, her second son holds back. "She smells, Mummy," he whines. "Just do it," hisses Bet, lips drawn taut across her teeth. Her son is right. Her mother smells faintly of old age, body odour, and stale flowers, which the handkerchief doused in violet water and tucked into the sleeve of her dressing gown fails to mask. A common symptom of her condition is an aversion to water, and each morning she fiercely resists her daughter's efforts to coax her into the bath.

She and Yvonne, known within the family as Yon, attempt to get their mother to eat, but she waves the food away. Pencil-thin, Violet exists on air. As family and friends eat and drink, she sinks further into the couch. Her dressing gown is pulled tight across her chest, a thin shield against a world that has been harsh to her. She sits there, alone. Just the way she likes it, thinks Bet, casting an occasional look in her mother's direction. She and Yon sit at a corner of the table. After two glasses of beer, she has switched to a pot of tea. Yon continues to drink beer.

"What are we going to do about the car?"

"The men will sort it out," replies Yon, nodding at their husbands at the far end of the room. "Jim says you should have it. No point in us having two. And you have none. With the baby and all…"

"It's too fancy for the neighbourhood. We'll stick out like sore thumbs."

"I thought you didn't care what people think."

"I don't want people to know my business when it's none of theirs. They'll think we've got tickets on ourselves. Worse, they'll think we've got money. But to be honest, I'm more worried about what we're to do about Mother. She isn't getting any better."

"You needn't tell me about that. She does live here with us, after all. It's time you took her for a while, Bet. We've talked about this."

"I'm not trying to shirk my responsibility. When you were going out with Jim, I did all the work of looking after her, and when you got married and Jim moved in here, I was the one who continued to look after her as well as running the house." Unmarried, there were times when Bet thought of herself as an unpaid domestic servant.

"You did. But we were running the business."

"I'm not saying it wasn't fair. I'm just saying I did my bit. And I did my bit after Father was killed—got my licence and drove one of the delivery trucks."

"Anyway, when you've got the car, you'll be in a better position to look after her."

"Let's see whether Bill decides to take the car. Won't be cheap to run, and now we have three children under five to feed…" The departure of the remaining guests provides an opportunity to leave unfinished a comment that was heading in the unacceptable direction of a complaint. The Price clan never complained and never explained: rarely to each other, and certainly never to outsiders. While she has her views on the car, it's her husband and his brother who will decide.

After the last of the guests have left, she and Yon are washing up in the pantry behind the kitchen. She keeps an eye on Violet, who had nodded off on the sofa. With the guests gone, her husband and brother-in-law subside onto hard-backed chairs at the table. She wonders, not for the first time, why it's considered unmanly to be seen sitting down. In the war years, when she had driven trucks for T. J. Price and Son, Fruit and Vegetable Merchants by day, and pulled beer in the front bar of the Grand at night, she had been struck by this male ritual. Even the inebriated refused to sit. They stood, staggered as the drinking session proceeded, and finally fell to the ground.

Her younger son is asleep on the floor in front of the Aga, a bunny rug bunched under his head. Of her older son, David, and Yon's two sons, there is no sign. "Can you keep an eye on Paulie?" she asks Bill. "I'm going take Mother to bed and collect the baby. Then I think we should be getting home. Tomorrow is a school day." She eases her mother out of the sofa and escorts her to the front of the house. She settles her mother, gently removes the sleeping baby from the bassinet and is about to head back to the kitchen, when she hears a noise from the master bedroom. Crossing the corridor, she pushes the door with her toe. The master bedroom is another space of secrets with the smell of ages. This is Jimmy and Yon's domain. Although it's strictly off-limits to children, she discovers her elder son and two nephews on the rug beside the bed. Robert, oldest and boldest of the trio, has pulled one of his father's gun cases from under the bed and is in the process of showing off the new shotgun, a beautiful piece with an intricately carved stock. Guns are an integral part of the culture. Most households have at least one. They serve a range of functions: from providing food for the house, to settling disputes, to ending the misery of a diseased family pet, and not infrequently to ending the misery of its owner. At one time, Broken Hill had the unenviable reputation of being the suicide capital of the country.

As she was growing up, guns were a constant presence in the Price household: her grandparents, father, and even her mother, the gentle Violet, possessed rifles and handguns. Annie had used her own handgun to shoot her drunken husband, the detestable Harry Dearmer. Dodger never left home without a pistol in the pocket of his overcoat. She had no time for the things. They were the root cause of all of the family's problems, and she refuses to have one anywhere near her own house.

"Put that away at once," she says in her sternest voice. "You know you're not allowed to play with guns." The three boys jump at the sound of her voice. Their heads swivel, and Robert drops the shotgun.

"It isn't loaded," he says.

"Just do as you're told." She turns to her son. "Get to the kitchen. We're going home soon."

"But you said I could sleep over." The three cousins, thick as thieves, frequently slept at each other's houses.

"I've changed my mind. Now just do as you're told."

"Isn't fair."

"If you won't do as I say, I'll fetch your father, and he can deal with you."

The threat has him on his feet in an instant. He follows her through to the kitchen, whining the whole way at the injustice. Back in the kitchen, the issue of what to do with the car has been settled—temporarily at least. They would take it.

The night is cold and clear, the sky crowded out with stars. In the demonization of Broken Hill, the fearsome beauty of the bush is never mentioned. She sits on the soft leather seat holding the baby as her husband drives them home in the car they can't afford. The two boys have fallen instantly asleep on the rear seat. She will have to wake them to prepare them for bed. They have stayed out far too late, and her elder son has to be up early for school.

They have no garage, so the car is parked in the side street where it sits, luxurious and incongruous in the moonlight. The children don't stir as they are ferried from the car to the house. She decides not to rouse them, but dumps them on their beds fully clothed, removes their shoes, and pulls an eiderdown over each small, supine body, kisses each with a "Mummy loves you," and, stepping carefully around the creaking floorboards, makes her way to the front room to breastfeed the baby. Her husband has retreated to their bedroom, but she has household chores to do. It will be after midnight before she gets to bed.

When she finally gets to bed, she is exhausted, but sleep won't come. What are they to do with mother—the fading Violet? Earlier, she had overheard a conversation between her precocious nephew Robert and his mother. "Why doesn't Nan know who we are?" he had wanted to know. "Why do you say that?" Yon had asked. "She doesn't know our names," Robert had replied. And he was right.

So, even the children were beginning to notice. Tomorrow she would make a trunk call to Babs in Newcastle—cost be hanged. Ask her to come as a matter of urgency. Despite the lingering resentment Babs had towards their mother, she had to be part of the solution.

Chapter 2
To the End of the Earth

They'd been promised one of the new generation clipper ships, capable of covering 250 sea miles a day, and were not disappointed. On the 19th day of February in 1852, having made the tedious trip from Wales with their baby son, they boarded the *Phoebe Dunbar* in Plymouth, and headed out of the harbour, into the English Channel, bound for South Australia. Built in 1850 by renowned shipping magnate Duncan Dunbar, it was making its second voyage to the Antipodes. The ship was named after Dunbar's younger daughter, whose face and figure graced the prow of the ship as it headed into open waters. On subsequent trips, it was to join a fleet of 11 other ships owned by Dunbar for transporting convicts to Australia.

Leaving her young son William in the care of her husband, Mary made her way onto the deck and watched the English coastline recede. She pulled her coat tight and turned her back to the bitter wind coming off the water. Enervated by the trip from Wales to Plymouth, she wondered how she would fare on this long sea voyage to the end of the earth. When William Henry informed her of the position in the newly established copper mining industry in South Australia, she had doubts, but kept them to herself. At just 23 years of age, she had led a sheltered life, she had a baby, and was devoted to her family. It had been upheaval enough, when, shortly after their marriage, her husband had moved them from their hometown of Gelligaer in county Glamorgan to the mining community of Bedwellty where he took a position as assayer and then junior manager of one of the mines. Given his passion for mining, his inquiring mind, and a restless spirit, his decision to accept the position in South Australia was hardly surprising. Being a kind, considerate husband, he had consulted her, but in the end the decision was his. Although she and her mother both shed tears, knowing she would be lost to her family forever, her mother had no doubts. "Your duty is to your husband," she said. And that was that.

Her mild-mannered husband's reasoning was impeccable, and she was left with not an argumentative leg to stand on. The mining industry in Wales was in decline. Many of the mines were nearing the end of their natural lives. The equipment and methods were antiquated. Australia was a brave new world offering limitless opportunities for an ambitious young engineer. In the United Kingdom, rumours abounded about the discovery of extensive goldfields in the colony of Victoria. "The biggest in the world, they say," William Henry reported to Mary.

As Britain receded and finally disappeared from view altogether, she was in no doubt that she would never see her parents and siblings again. What she didn't know was that her husband was destined to become a key figure in the establishment and development of the Australian mining industry.

She knew her husband had a second reason for abandoning the Old Country. His first was professional, his second, deeply personal. He had been born to John Price and Sarah Elizabeth Andrews on January 2, 1827 in Gelligaer. As a child, he attended chapel with his parents, but the roots of Christianity were never embedded deeply enough in his soul to withstand the doubts of his inquiring mind. As a young adult, he read and reasoned his way out of organized religion. His religions were rationality and science. A rift between William Henry and his parents developed, deepened, and never healed. The move from Gelligaer to Bedwellty afforded temporary relief from the condemnation of his home community, but it wasn't enough. The offer of a job in the New World was compelling. Mary did not leave Wales to escape religious oppression. The love of her husband, the words of her mother, and the fact that she had no choice were reasons enough for her not to question her husband's decision to abandon the country of their birth. She left Wales still committed to Christianity but arrived in Australia with doubts that in the course of time led her to secularism.

When the *Phoebe Dunbar* docked at Port Adelaide on June 7, 1852, the passenger list showed that it carried, among other passengers: Price, Henry Francis, 23; Mary, 22; and William, 1. Mary never asked her husband why he altered his name from William Henry and their ages for the duration of the journey, and he never explained. Was the alteration to their ages a clerical error, perhaps? On disembarking, he resumed his real name and retained it for the rest of his life.

Unlike the vast majority of their fellow countrymen, they arrived as free settlers in a free state. Between the first shipload of convicts to Australia in 1788 and their arrival, almost 2,000 Welsh convicts had been transported to Australia. Many spoke only Welsh and were unable to communicate with the majority of their fellow English-speaking convicts. A considerable number were transported, not for crimes (petty or otherwise), but for their political and religious views. They included trade unionists, free thinkers and political radicals. Over the next twenty years, William Henry and Mary would befriend many of those who shared their views.

On disembarking, they were met by a representative of the Burra Copper Mine who transported them and their possessions to a boarding house a short distance from the docks. They would have a week in Port Adelaide, where the Burra Copper Mine had an office. It was from here that the copper ore was dispatched by ship for processing in the Cornwall smelters. Once settled in the boarding house, William Henry returned to the docks to make himself known to the management. Having unpacked the few possessions, they would need during their short stay in Adelaide, Mary wrapped herself in a woollen shawl, and took baby William onto the verandah. It was colder than she had expected it to be, and she was slightly unnerved by the fact that it was winter in June. Clearly, there was a great deal that she would have to adjust to: the rough-hewn dwellings, the muddy streets, the terrifying screeches of the native birds, the clatter of rain on the iron roof, the lemon-scented eucalypt by the stables at the back of the boarding house—all were unfamiliar.

She had no great expectations of Adelaide. In the months prior to their departure, William Henry, ever the scholar, had obtained such books as were available on the colony. One of these, *Travels and Adventures in South Australia* by W. H. Leigh, she read on the voyage. Leigh arrived in Adelaide as ship's surgeon aboard the *South Australian*, a barque designed to carry emigrants to the colony. First impressions were not favourable. Through a piece of navigational mismanagement, the captain missed the Port River, and sailed up a creek. When the boat got stuck in mud flats and could go no further, the passengers and crew were forced to abandon ship and trek three muddy miles along a bullock track to the city.

The "city" proved to be a great disappointment to Leigh who had apparently expected a substantial colonial settlement but found, instead, a shantytown. Colonel Light's grand vision remained just that—a vision. Accounts such as the following left Mary under no illusion about what to expect on arriving in Adelaide. Leigh wrote:

> I had read, a few days ago, of the various names of the streets—such high sounding names!—this square and that square—east-end and west-end—such a terrace and such a street—that I could not but fancy that my sight was suddenly failing me, when I strained my eyes in vain to see either square, terrace, street, house, or even anything to lead me to the conclusion of there ever having been any. There was no volcanic matter; not even a stone could be found to indulge in the benevolent propensity of throwing it at a dog; and two or three people were jogging along together talking calmly of bullocks, when one would have expected to have beheld them at public thanksgiving for their own preservation from the mighty earthquake which had doubtless suddenly swallowed up the once-noble city of Adelaide.[1]

When William Henry returned to the boarding house and suggested an excursion into Adelaide, she was not enthusiastic. Little William had come down with a cold and was miserable. As usual, however, she went along with her husband's suggestion. She wrapped the boy up warmly and they took a bullock wagon into the centre of the settlement. With a population barely in excess of 14,000, it could hardly be dignified as a city. However, it was a considerable improvement on what she had expected, given Leigh's description. They made their way to North Adelaide and looked down on the embryonic city bound on one side by the River Torrens (in actuality, little more than a creek), and on the other three by open expanses which Colonel Light, the first Surveyor-General of the colony had determined would be parklands. "Yes," thought Mary,

---

[1] Leigh, W.H. (1839) *Travels and Adventures in South Australia 1836 – 1838*. London: Smith, Elder and Co. Cornhill

"I could settle here." Within a week, however, she would be forced to endure the hardship of a hundred-mile trek by bullock wagon to the settlement of Burra Burra north-east of Adelaide.

On the fourth morning after their arrival in Australia, having dressed and fed the child, Mary looked about for William Henry. However, he was nowhere to be found. She concluded that he must have gone to the office. It was odd that he had taken himself off without saying anything to her. He returned just before lunch. She heard a dray pulling up at the front of the boarding house, and when she stepped onto the verandah, found her husband hauling a large wooden case off the dray. He lugged the case across the verandah and into the front room which served as their bedroom. Setting it on the floor, he flipped open the brass clasps, raised the lid and hauled out a wooden box-like structure.

"What is that?" she asked.

"It's a camera," replied William Henry. "The company provided it. It will be useful in my work."

William Henry was a quiet, gentle man, not given to excessive displays of emotion. Mary thought she had come to know him well, particularly during the long and arduous sea voyage to the end of the earth, but he continued to surprise her with his unexpected interests. He had never spoken of cameras, and she had never been this close to one. They had only been in existence for a few years and were considered mysterious—magical almost—in their ability to capture the human image, if not the human spirit: not that William Henry and Mary believed in anything as irrational as magic. Given William Henry's devotion to science, she should not have been surprised at his turning up with this rather alarming object.

"Do you know how to use such a thing?" she asked, restraining little William who seemed to think that the camera was a toy and therefore his.

"I have a book on the subject," replied William Henry, fiddling to extend the lens. A great believer in books, he had been put out to learn he would only be allowed one sea chest of his precious collection for the voyage to Australia. The rest were disposed of at a second-hand bookshop in London.

As an engineer, William Henry had a practical side. Apart from technical knowledge, the essential quality of an engineer was an ability to solve problems. But problem-solving involved more than applying technical knowledge to the challenge at hand. Each challenge was different, and required creativity and imagination, qualities William Henry also possessed in abundance. In the early days of their marriage, Mary had marvelled at her husband's ability to bring his technical knowledge, creativity and imagination to solving domestic problems which, to Mary, had seemed unsolvable. His gifts were also apparent in his leisure activities, which included writing poetry and painting. She had no doubt that once he had mastered the technicalities of the camera, he would use it for artistic as well as scientific purposes.

Mary assumed that what passed for civilization in South Australia would extend at least a little further than the outskirts of Adelaide. Her assumption was confounded as the bullock wagon creaked and strained its way along the Port Road, skirted the city, and followed the line of the Torrens River before joining a line of other bullock wagons heading north-east along the Great North Road towards the township of Gawler. To the colonists, particularly those who had ventured into the interior looking for pastoral land to settle, or mineral deposits to excavate, the countryside north of Adelaide may have seemed civilized, but to a young woman from the Welsh Valleys with their soft green curves, their castles and their ancient ways, it seemed as though they were heading into a land as alien as the moon.

They were comparatively lucky with the weather on that first day of travel. Although locals might have shivered, for Mary the temperature in the low 50s was almost balmy. The sun shone for most of the day, and the sky was blue—an unsettling blue after the comforting grey skies of her homeland. By mid-afternoon a cold wind sprang up. Little William woke from a sleep and began to whimper. She pulled him to her, wrapped a rough woollen blanket around them both and held him tight. Her back ached from the unyielding bench on which they sat, and she wondered how much longer she would have to endure the jolting of the bullock wagon. But endure she did without complaint. What good would it do to complain?

After three interminable days on what she considered to be the sadly misnamed "Great" North Road, she arrived with her husband and child at their destination, Burra Burra, at last. Despite onboard privations, the trip by bullock wagon had seemed longer than the journey from England. Burra Burra was a rapidly developing township nestled on Burra Burra Creek in the lee of high rolling hills, the tail end of the Mt. Lofty Ranges, which provided a welcome backdrop to the mundane Adelaide Plains. Having finally arrived, she never wanted to see another bullock again, but in the days before a railway system began to snake across the state, bullock wagons and camel trains were the principal means of transporting people and goods from one place to another. She didn't know it at the time, but the bullock wagon was to be a permanent feature of her life as William Henry took mining jobs from one end of the state to the other.

Although she would never have said so to her husband, Mary had expected to find a colonial backwater as the bullock wagon finally creaked into Burra Burra. Instead, she found a thriving community of 5,000 inhabitants as well as several copper mines. She learned that the Burra Burra Copper Mine was popularly known as the "Monster Mine," the nickname reflecting its status as the largest mineral mine in Australia. Why was she not surprised? William Henry always based practical decisions on thorough research. Although naturally reserved, he was also ambitious. He would never have come to the end of the earth to work with a bunch of colonials scratching around in the ground for a living. While there were plenty of rough-hewn colonials (or "Native Sons" as they called themselves), Burra Burra was also populated with a multicultural mix of people from many different parts of the world. There were the Celts of course, the Cornish, Welsh and Scots, but there were also immigrants from a range of European countries, particularly the Germans, who would become an important part of South Australia's social identity. These people brought with them their cultures, customs, foods, and religions, adapting these to the strangeness of the Australian hinterland.

Mary also discovered that the township was a collection of different settlements. Each had its own cultural identity, which was reflected in their name: Redruth for the Cornish, Llwchwr for the Welsh, and Aberdeen for the Scots. Each also had its own mine and community amenities, shops, pubs, and churches, reflecting the cultures of the inhabitants. The Price family was housed in Kooringa, adjacent to and owned by the Monster Mine. This was the first company town in Australia.

On first sight Mary was dismayed by the shabby nature of the dwelling to which they had been assigned. It had been hastily constructed and smelled of damp. However, it was *their* house, and while William Henry took up his position as a mining engineer in the smelters of the copper mine, she set about turning the house into a home. Although household basics such as pots, pans, bedding and kitchenware were readily available, choices in the shops were even more restricted than in Adelaide. This was to be expected, and Mary made the best of it. Well, what choice did she have? She had no ambition other than to support her husband and raise a family. As there were no banks in the town, she, like the other residents, put her purchases on credit with the shopkeepers. She learned that in the local lingo this practice was referred to as shopping "on tick." The mine management paid the bills and deducted the amount from William Henry's wages.

As she familiarized herself with the geography of the town, she realized that she wasn't so badly off after all. Everything was relative. One day, when her housework was done, she took little William for a stroll down to the pretty creek that meandered through the town. There, she was shocked to discover families living like animals in dugouts along the banks of the creek. When William Henry came home from work that evening, she told him of her shocking discovery. Of course, he already knew about it. "One third of the population lives like that," he said.

Near tragedy struck one day. It was warm and sunny, so she opened the front door and let William outside to play on the verandah while she finished washing the sheets. "Don't wander off," she said. But being a two-year-old, and having inherited his father's curiosity, that's exactly what he did. Oddly enough, she had been woken in the night by the mournful cawing of some native creature in a tree at the back of the house. The sound gave her an uneasy feeling, and she had difficulty returning to sleep. Her unease returned when she woke. She said nothing to William Henry. His rationalism boarded on the extreme, and he had no truck with premonitions. So, putting her unease and memory of the night behind her, she got on with her domestic duties.

Washing sheets was a laborious business. You had to light a fire under a large copper pot and when the water was boiling, put in the sheets along with soap flakes, and turn them constantly with a long wooden stick. When the sheets were clean, you removed and rinsed them, then put them through a hand-turned mangle. They were then strung over a line that ran from the back of the house to a gum tree at the end of the yard. Once the sheets had been stretched taut to eliminate wrinkles and the necessity for ironing, a long, forked tree branch was wedged under the line, and with much heaving and grunting, the line and its contents were hoisted well clear of the ground and wedged there by the branch.

Mary had just finished hoisting the line aloft when she heard a woman screaming some distance front of the house. With a mother's instinct, she dropped her washing basket and rushed through the house into the street. "Don't let this be", she muttered to herself. "I should never have left him unattended." A cluster of neighbours, mainly women, given the time of day, had gathered around William, who lay on the ground, his blond curls mired by muck. Blowflies, attracted by the blood on his cheek, hovered over his head. A young man on a skittish horse caught her eye as she bent to scoop the child from the ground. William's eyes fluttered briefly before closing again. As she lifted him, his left leg flopped at an impossible angle. A sense of unreality swept over her. She had got him safely all the way from Wales, and now this. It happened in an instant. One minute he was playing happily by the side of the road and now he was unconscious, possibly dying. All she had wanted was to give him a temporary reprieve from the cold, dank house. "It weren't my fault," the young man called to her retreating back. "He startled me horse, Missus. Shoulda look after ya kid, ya should."

And she knew he was right. She should have taken him through to the back yard with her to play with his favourite toy, a wooden horse on a string, fashioned by his father from a piece of sappy pine. Now she had to face his father. She knew that William Henry, being the man he was, would not blame her. "Please open your eyes, Little One," she whispered as she lowered him on to his bed. "All I want you to do is to open your eyes." She turned to the two women who had followed her into the house. "Please fetch his father. At once."

When William Henry arrived, he was accompanied by the mine doctor. Medical assistance was difficult to get in the bush, and those doctors who chose, for one reason or another, to work outside of the city, made sure that they were well recompensed. Most people had to rely on "bush doctors": men (invariably men) who had some rudimentary first aid training and had honed their skills "on the job." On first arriving in Burra, originally it was called Burra Burra, but at some point, it was called Burra, she had been relieved to learn that the Company provided a qualified medical officer for employees and their families. This was less out of concern for the welfare of the employees than for the efficient function of the mine. An injured or incapacitated miner could cost more in terms of lost production than the expense of providing medical care.

"This is Dr Barrow," said William Henry. Barrow nodded to her without speaking then turned his attention to the boy. When William heard his father's voice, he opened his eyes and then vomited. Mary was torn between going in search of a cloth and staying to hear what the doctor had to say. She cleaned up the mess as best as she could with her apron. While the doctor was examining the child, William Henry asked her what happened.

"He was trampled by a horse," she replied, then waited for the next inevitable question. What was he doing that close to a horse without her presence? But the question never came.

Having finished his examination, Barrow straightened up and turned to them. "He's badly concussed, but there's no fracture of the skull. He'll recover from the concussion with rest. The main problem is his left leg. You can see that it's badly shattered. By rights he should be taken to Adelaide to be treated by a surgeon, but the trip would be too much for him. We'll have to do it here." Mary left unsaid the questions running in circles around her brain. The men would make the decisions.

"Should we move him to the infirmary?" asked William Henry.

"In terms of straightening and setting the leg, that would be preferable, but because of the concussion, I don't think he should be moved."

Mary could no longer contain herself. "Is he going to be all right? He's so…"

"Precious?" Barrow's lips twitched—the semblance of a smile. "I think so. There are no internal injuries as far as I can tell. You never know, but I'd say he's been very lucky. Sit with him, while I get the things I need for setting the leg."

While Barrow was gone, she busied herself cleaning William up and making him comfortable. He dozed, waking twice to vomit and cry out in pain before lapsing back into sleep. She wished that William Henry would say something, but he remained silent, hovering watchfully in the background. What's he thinking? she asked herself. I wish he would say something. Just before Barrow returned, he took her hand and said, "It was not your fault."

Setting William's leg was messy, traumatic, and only partially successful. Despite the administration of a whiff of the newly discovered anaesthetic, ether, on a wad of cotton, he screamed his lungs out at Barrow's efforts to realign the broken tibia. Mary held the boy's hand and tried to soothe him, though every scream tore at her. William Henry paced up and down the room tugging at his beard. Eventually, Barrow straightened up. "That's the best I can do, I'm afraid," he said. He bound the leg in splints and departed. For the rest of what would turn out to be a very long life, William was only be able to walk with the aid of a crutch.

Once the tibia had knitted, albeit crookedly, William Henry fashioned the first of what would be many crutches, and they embarked on the tedious process of teaching him to walk all over again. Given the demands of William Henry's work, this job fell largely to Mary. Every time William fell, she had to stifle a cry and resist the urge to help him up. "The boy has to learn to cope with his affliction," said William Henry. In years to come, as she produced children who fell ill and died from a range of causes, she would look back on the suffering she felt for her firstborn and realize why Barrow had been so matter-of-fact. At this time, she discovered she was pregnant with her second child, and, on June 3, 1853, she duly presented William with another son. They called him Henry.

As the management of the Burra Copper Mine became aware of William Henry's skill as an assayer, his exceptional talents for other aspects of mining, and a capacity for hard work, he found himself being asked to take on more and more duties. Responsibility for managing the household and caring for the two boys fell largely to Mary. She took to the roles without complaint. Mary was no fool, and, in other circumstances, may have sought a career herself. She was good with figures, and for a time between school and marriage, she had kept books for one of the local shopkeepers in Gelligaer. She could have become an assistant, or, given her devotion to children, even a schoolteacher. But this was Burra Burra, not the Welsh Valleys, and she put all thoughts of a career aside. Her aim in life was to be the best wife and mother possible. She would live out her dreams of another life by supporting William Henry in his.

The family grew, and so did her duties. On August 21, 1854, she gave birth to a daughter and, at William Henry's insistence, they named her Mary Ann. There were murmurs among members of Burra's Welsh community when they failed to have her christened, but nothing was said. At Henry's birth, William Henry had been approached by a prominent member of the local community. Asked about his failure to have the boy christened, William Henry replied, "We do not subscribe to organized religion."

"Oh, so you're heathens."

"Heathens, atheists, infidels. There are conceptual differences, but if you want to label us, any one will do," said William Henry and turned away from the questioner. Their absence from Chapel had been noted. When the tut-tuts and mutterings of disapproval were ignored, the churchgoers took the hint. Later, on moving to Adelaide, William Henry would become active in organizing meetings among a small group of secularists, but if there were any atheists in Burra, they kept their views to themselves. In any case, he was fully occupied with his career. He developed his philosophy by writing pamphlets and tracts and rehearsing his views with Mary. "I plan to write a book one day," he said. "And when I do, these will be useful."

Over the next two years, Mary had several miscarriages. She was beginning to think that the number of offspring would stop at three, when in 1857, she carried a baby to full term. It was another boy. Having exhausted her husband's names on the first two boys, Mary suggested that they name the new arrival Thomas. As she had done with her other new born children, she held the tightly bundled baby in her arms and wondered what the future would bring him.

With four children under seven, Mary had her hands full. By now,

William Henry's career had advanced to the point where they were able to afford part-time help around the house. Pressure was also relieved by the fact that three days a week William attended a school group organized by the Chapel. (It would be another twenty years before the Burra Model School was established.) William was accepted at the Chapel school despite the fact that his parents were avowed atheists. One of her friends, whose son also attended the school, told Mary that the elders believed if they could turn the son, the parents might follow. In fact, William hardly needed school: he was quite capable of teaching himself. At the age of four, he astounded Mary by reading the labels on the canisters in the kitchen. "He's sight reading," said William Henry. "He has no systematic knowledge of the alphabet, but his awareness that there's a relationship between what he sees on the canisters and what he hears is extraordinary for a child his age." William Henry drilled him in the alphabet, taught him phonics, and wrote some basic stories which Mary helped her son master and which he devoured. Four mornings a week, crutch propped under his arm, and satchel slung across his shoulder, he limped off to the informal school. While the other children played games with wooden blocks, he sat in a corner and read the primers that formed the basis of a rudimentary library. At home, when she had time, Mary got him to tell her about his day. She turned his accounts into simple stories which she wrote on pieces of card in her tidy hand. William read these to her, and to anyone else who would listen. He then illustrated the stories with crayons his father had acquired from Adelaide. In this way he constructed his own private library. Over time, his self-constructed stories were augmented with precious birthday books from his parents. His passion for books and book collecting, a passion acquired from his father, was to stay with him for the rest of his long life.

William's pleasure in books was a comfort to Mary. His crippled leg prevented him from joining in street games with the other children. Through books, he cultivated an inner life. However, he was no sickly recluse. "I refuse to treat William as an invalid," she told friends and neighbours, "and I won't have you doing so." Although unable to play games, he was an active boy. On Sundays, when the rest of the townspeople were at church or in chapel, she packed him off with his father on long walks. On their first excursion, she watched from the front steps of the cottage as he scrambled after his father up the steep slopes that bound Burra into a community. These slopes were being rapidly denuded to feed the smelters of the Monster Mine and the other smaller copper mines that provided the township with a reason to exist.

On their walks, William Henry introduced his son to the natural world—the flora, the fauna, the geology of the region and how it had been formed. He learned the names of birds, butterflies, and, as he got older, their Latin names. Not surprisingly, given William Henry's profession and passion, he learned a great deal about the geography and geology of the region. His father would pick up a lump of rock and explain its significance. It wasn't any old piece of rock, to be kicked aside. This was an ore-bearing rock, containing minerals of great significance for the development of civilization, metamorphosed in the subterranean furnaces of the earth. That was a sedimentary rock, squeezed into being under the immensity of the earth's weight. Copper, which could be found in both igneous and sedimentary rock, was of particular significance, his father explained, not only because it provided the good people of Burra Burra with a living, but because it was the very first metal to be extracted and used by ancient civilizations.

One day, on reaching the summit of the highest hill, William Henry paused and swept his arm across the landscape. He explained to William that in a few short years the hills would be bare. Copper-bearing ores formed in the furnaces of the earth had to be subjected to the furnaces of man to yield their precious mineral. The furnaces, or smelters, were fired by the trees that covered the hills, but soon they would be gone. Even now, the wood-fired smelters could only process a fraction of the ore extracted from the ground.

The vast bulk of the ore had to be shipped back to Britain to the coal-fired Cornish smelters for processing. The copper was then transported to markets all over the world to meet the needs of the Empire on which the sun never set. India was particularly voracious in its appetite for Australian copper. From his father, William learned that through an ironic twist of geological fate, South Australia was blessed with an abundance of mineral-bearing ore, but lacked coal, the one resource that was essential for realizing the wealth embedded in the ore.

After their expeditions, William would hurry home to rehearse to his mother what he had learned. She listened indulgently as he told her things she already knew. She got deep maternal satisfaction from observing the relationship that had developed between William Henry and their son. He loved all his children, of course, but the first-born was special. She touched her belly. Another one was on the way.

As Mary suspected, William Henry pursued his passion for photography beyond his professional work. As their family grew, William Henry applied for, and was assigned a larger dwelling. He set up one of the rooms in the larger house as a dark room for developing film. One Sunday afternoon, he decided to take a family portrait. Although Thomas was only two and a half, William Henry hoped he would sit still long enough for the portrait to be successful. The family was joined by Dr Barrow, with whom William Henry had established a friendship. While Mary dressed the children in their best clothes and brushed their hair, Barrow and William Henry set up the equipment in the living room. A heavy drape was hung on the wall to serve as a backdrop to the portrait. Once dressed, Henry and Thomas scampered excitedly about the equipment, until William Henry, afraid that they would knock the camera off its stand, called on Mary to get them out of the way. Once the equipment had been set up, William Henry gave Barrow instructions on how to operate the camera. Barrow, as a man of science himself, was fascinated with the equipment. In compensation for his time, William Henry had offered to take a portrait of his own family.

Finally, preparations complete, the children were admitted back into the dining room. Although she refused to show it, in her own way Mary was as excited as the children. As they grew to adulthood, the portrait would act as a permanent record of their younger, innocent selves. She imagined a series of framed family portraits, taken as the years progressed, adorning the walls of a family home. In her mind, this would be one of the substantial stone villas she had seen being constructed along the Port Road in Adelaide.

William Henry asked Mary to arrange the children for the portrait. She sat the two older boys, dressed in jackets and knee breeches, on low chairs. Mary Ann, in a flowing dress, with ribbons in her ringlets, stood between her brothers, her left elbow resting artfully on William's good leg, her fist tucked under her chin. Thomas, the youngest, sat cross-legged on the floor. Dressed in a smock, with his shoulder-length hair and a ribbon tied in a bow at his throat, he looked more girl than boy. With the children composed to her satisfaction, Mary took her place, standing behind William with her hand on his shoulder. William Henry joined her. "Now," he said to the children in as stern a voice as he could muster, "it's very important that you keep perfectly still. Thomas, do you understand? All right, Barrow, I think we're ready for you."

"Wait," said Mary, and placed William's crutch beyond the range of the camera. Mary Ann and Henry giggled when the dour doctor disappeared beneath the large square of black velvet cloth. "Very still, now," came a muffled voice from beneath the cloth. To Mary, the minute it took for the film to be exposed to light seemed interminable, but at last William Henry gave the word. The portrait shoot was over. "Perhaps we should take another one, just to be safe," he said.

"Oh no," said Mary. "The children would never sit still for that long again."

Released, the older children were sent to their rooms to change.

"When will we be able to see it?" asked Mary.

"I'll develop it during the week," replied William Henry.

The following day, Mary asked Henry and Mary Ann to do some shopping for her. "Take Thomas with you," she said, handing Henry a note for the shopkeeper. Heavily pregnant, she was unable to rest with boisterous children running in and out of her room. It was a sparkling autumn day, but because of the chill in the air, she made them put on jackets before they set off. William, busy with his books, was reluctant to move from his spot by the fire, but Henry and Mary Ann were happy to vacate the house, Thomas trailed behind, calling out plaintively, "Wait for me."

At the end of the street, several of Henry's friends were playing an impromptu game with a leather ball stuffed with rags. They made the rules up as the game progressed, which resulted in frequent interruptions and disputes. Henry, as sporty as William was bookish, stopped the disputes and dominated the game. While the boys played, Mary Ann chatted with two of her own friends. If the boisterous game had rules and a purpose, they were beyond her comprehension. This is the way boys are, she had decided.

Red-faced and breathing heavily, Henry returned to Mary Ann. "We'd better get to the shop, Mare," he said. Then: "Where's Thomas?" They scanned the street, but Thomas was nowhere in sight. "Did you see my brother?" she asked her friends. The other girls shook their heads.

"Maybe he went home," said Henry. He and Mary Ann ran back down the street.

"Where's Thomas?" asked Mary as soon as they burst into the house.

"We don't know," said Henry. "We thought he might have come home."

Mary put a hand to her throat. She glanced at William. A dark fear descended as visions of that day, years before, came back. She struggled onto the verandah and began calling his name. Several neighbours appeared in the street. Hearing the news, they set off to scour the town.

He was found at the base of a small ravine that angled down towards the creek. His gorgeous golden locks were matted with blood, and he lay quite still. A neighbour helped Mary to the head of the ravine, and she watched, numb, as one of the men clambered down the rocks to the boy. "He's breathing," called the man. Several other men were summoned. They formed a human chain and handed the boy up the slippery rocks to his mother. When she had him in her arms, he opened him eyes and smiled at her. "Thank God," she said, the words spilling involuntarily from the lips of the avowed atheist.

Fortunately, William Henry was not on a field trip that day but in the assaying room. On receiving the news, he hurried home from the mine accompanied by Barrow. Mary had cleaned up the boy as best she could. There was a shallow indentation in the right side of his skull where his head had struck the rock. The wound seeped blood where the skin had broken. It was less copious than she might have expected from a head wound, and she took this as a hopeful sign. When the men arrived, Mary told the children to move away from the bed to give the doctor room. They clustered by the door, eyes fixed on the doctor as he bent over the boy.

"Hello, little man," said Barrow, "What have you done to yourself?"

"Hewwo," replied Thomas.

"Why does his voice sound like that?" asked Mary Ann, her lower lip quivering. "It doesn't sound right. Why can't he say hello?"

"Hush," replied her mother. "Let Doctor do his work."

When Barrow eventually straightened up, Thomas lifted his head from the pillow. "No, Laddie," said Barrow. "You have to lie still."

"Want to ger up," Thomas, appealed to his mother, slurring his words like a drunk.

"No, no," said Mary. "Do what Doctor says." He was going to be fine. He'd had a nasty knock to the head, but he was wide awake. Although he was slurring badly, he could talk. He was going to be all right. So why was she filled with dread?

"Send the younger ones to their room," Barrow said to Mary. "William, come here." William limped to the bedside. "Sit here and make sure your brother keeps still. Can you do that?" William nodded. "Good lad. And wake him if he goes to sleep." Turning to William Henry and Mary, Barron said, "Can we go to the kitchen?"

Mary's heart thumped uncontrollably. She couldn't help herself. "What is it?" she burst out.

William Henry took her by the arm and led her into the kitchen. Barrow followed and shut the door behind him. Mary turned to him. "What is it?" she asked again. "He's going to be all right, surely. He's awake. He's talking."

"Sit down," said Barrow in his kindly brogue.

"I don't want to sit down." The three of them remained standing. William Henry put an arm around his wife.

"The prognosis is not good," said Barrow. "He has a depressed fracture of the skull. The bone is pressing on his brain. This is why his speech is slurred."

"What's to be done?" asked William Henry.

Barrow shook his head. "Very little, I'm afraid. I haven't the necessary equipment to elevate the bone off the brain. In Adelaide there would be a fifty percent chance that his life might be saved."

"But we can get him to Adelaide, surely," said Mary.

"He'd never survive the journey." Even though the road between Adelaide and Burra Burra had improved greatly in the years since they had made the trek north, it still took well over a day to reach the city.

"So, there's no hope," said William Henry.

'You have to prepare yourself for the worst. And the other children."

On April 22, 1860, two days after the accident, Thomas died in his mother's arms after a brain seizure. He was two years and eight months old. After a civil ceremony led by his father, he was interred in the Burra cemetery in an unmarked grave, as was the secular way. The church authorities were good enough to allow the child to be buried within the stone walls of the graveyard, rather than in the un-consecrated rocky hillside beyond the church yard.

William Henry's words rang in Mary's ears. Her flaxen-haired boy would not be "going to God and glory." God was the concoction of man—an excuse for his imperfections. Thomas would return to the earth. "Dust unto dust"—that biblical phrase was one of the few that carried truth. The mourners who had turned out on a bleak morning listened stony-faced. Who was going to contradict a father in his time of grief? The words gave Mary no comfort at all.

A week after the funeral, Mary asked William Henry to develop the film of the family portrait. "It's all I'll have to remember him by," she said. That and the lock of hair she had snipped from his head before they had taken him away from her. But when William Henry developed the film, all that could be seen of Thomas was a white smudge. Apparently, during the exposure, he just couldn't keep still. Mary put the photograph face-down in a drawer where it lay until she destroyed it before the family moved to Adelaide.

The small picket fence Mary had insisted be erected around Thomas's grave is long gone, and his remains are in an unmarked space along with dozens of other infants and small children who had died in those harsh, early Burra days. Mary's flaxen-haired boy is, as his father had said, nothing but dust.

Five weeks later, on June 1, Mary gave birth to her fifth child; another boy. In memory of their recently deceased son, whose flesh and bones were decomposing on the hill, they named him Thomas, adding a second name, John, to differentiate him from the brother he would never know. Holding the newborn baby, Mary, for the first time, refused to speculate on what life would hold for him. For his dead brother, her whispered words had been a curse. She was not to know that this tiny child would live a long, adventurous life and become a central figure in the Price family saga.

It had weighed on her from the day of the funeral. Each day, as she struggled to emerge from the grief that caused her to break down and sob uncontrollably at the most unexpected moments, and she prepared herself for the birth of her next child, the belief grew into certainty. She thought the unthinkable. But she lacked the words and the will to tell her husband. Finally, several weeks after Thomas John's birth, she could no longer keep it to herself. She had endured enough of this harsh, unforgiving land. She longed for the soft hills of Wales and the comfort of her family. She wanted to go home.

When she told him, it sounded so prosaic, so matter-of-fact. As always, he was understanding and sympathetic, but he urged her to be patient. While returning to Wales was unthinkable, he would do his best to secure a return to Adelaide, where at least there would not be the graveyard reminding her daily of her loss. However, the time was not yet right. She had to endure for the sake of the children. And endure she did. In fact, it would be another eighteen months before a position came up in keeping with William Henry's experience and status within the company and they were relocated to the Burra Copper Mine offices in Port Adelaide.

Chapter 3
The Burden of Existence

William Henry knew the burden of existing in Burra was crushing the spirit out of Mary. Every corner of the house triggered memories of the child who was lost to them forever. Forever. The chilling finality of the word. Friends and neighbours told him of sightings in the graveyard. He had informed Henry Roach, the captain of the Burra Mine, of his desire to move back to Adelaide, and while he was sympathetic, Henry Ayers in Adelaide was not. Ayers, one of South Australia's leading political figures and businessmen began as secretary of the mine, but quickly became manager, ruling from his offices in Adelaide and leaving the day-to-day operations to Roach. A stalwart Cornishman, Roach preferred to employ his fellow countrymen, but he had a soft spot as well as great respect for William Henry. When first approached by William Henry about moving back to the city, Roach said he would "put it to the Big Man." The word was not long in coming back. It didn't suit the company to move him from Burra at this time. Ayers was a hard man. He was to run the "Monster Mine" for nearly fifty years, even during his years as Premier of the State, and made his fortune from it. He had no intention of disrupting operations simply because one of his employees had lost a child. Ayers was a big man in every way, and when, in 1873, the largest rock in the world was discovered in Central Australia by the explorer William Gosse, he named it after Ayers.

William Henry knew that Mary had lost hope of ever getting away from Burra, but then in 1862, eighteen months after the death of his son, Roach informed William Henry that a position had fallen vacant at the mine's operation in Adelaide. The position was head of operations at the dock facilities in Port Adelaide. He would be in charge of loading ships with ore to be transported to the smelting works in Cornwall. Did he want the job? Although carrying a higher salary, it was not a job that was of any real interest to him. The Adelaide position was a managerial desk job, one he knew would give him little, if any, professional satisfaction. As a practitioner, he felt most at home in the field, where he could use his technical knowledge and skills as a prospector, assayer and engineer for the benefit of the company. Roach would be aware of this and would doubtless be counting on William Henry turning the position down. However, he only hesitated for a minute before accepting. It was the least he could do for Mary. With a population of 14,000, Adelaide could hardly be dignified as a city, but it had a cathedral and was entitled to be designated as such. In fact, it was barely three times the size of Burra, this despite the fact that Burra's population had declined as miners were lured east, by the prospect of greater wealth on the N.S.W. and Victorian gold fields. On their arrival back in Adelaide, William Henry detected an immediate lift in Mary's spirits. This was more than adequate compensation for the decline in his own.

Gentle in nature and optimistic by inclination, William Henry compensated for the disappointing turn his career had taken by devoting more time to his family. He acquired a substantial stone house, with ample rooms for their growing family a large rear yard containing stables and an orchard. The house was within walking distance of his office, and most days, unless otherwise required, he came home for lunch. As Mary was again with child, he also acquired a housekeeper.

"I wouldn't be surprised if you had twins," he said, casting a scientist's eye up and down her frame, on one luncheon visit.

"Nonsense," replied Mary. She was not in the habit of contradicting him, but on this occasion couldn't resist. "There are no twins on my side of the family. Nor on yours."

The move back to Adelaide brought with it another major benefit. It enabled those children who were of school age to receive a conventional education. This was particularly helpful for William who, at the age of 11, briefly attended the Dallison and King School, established by Thomas Dallison, before completing his elementary education at the Port Adelaide Grammar School. From there, in 1868, he gained admission to St. Peter's College, where he was made a prefect, and would go on to garner numerous prizes including the prestigious Westminster Scholarship. His younger brother Thomas John would one day follow in his footsteps.

William Henry was proud of all his children, but William held a special place in his heart. The boy's cheerful acceptance of his lifelong disability and his devotion to scholarship particularly endeared him to his father. Passionate about education, in sending his boys to St Peter's, an Anglican institution, William Henry put aside his aversion to organized religion. The school was acknowledged as the top educational institution of the day, not only for the rigor and excellence of its education, but also for its commitment to building character. The best education affordable was the greatest gift he could give his children. Equipped with the ability to reason, they could make up their own minds on the matter of religion. It was unthinkable that he should place his own professional ambitions above the needs of his children. Didn't he have his books, wide-ranging interests, including the exploration, mapping and documentation of the flora, fauna, and geological features of South Australia, and other diversions, including photography and membership of the Secular Association, compensating somewhat for the disappointment of a desk job?

Although in his own mind he was little more than a glorified clerk, he maintained contact with colleagues who continued to create a platform for the future wealth of an embryonic nation. One evening he turned into the Port Dock Hotel for a drink before heading home. He ignored the stink of beer-soaked sawdust, and elbowed his way past a knot of dockworkers to the bar. It was unusual for him to drink midweek, but a fatality earlier in the day had unsettled him. A stevedore had slipped and fallen into the hold of the ship which was being loaded with copper ore. Although not killed outright, he had been badly crushed by the ore, which continued to pour into the hold. William Henry was no stranger to serious mining accidents, but this one had upset him. He made a point of getting to know the men who worked for him, and he knew that this stevedore's wife was expecting their first child. Manhandled from the hold, the young man slipped into unconsciousness just as William Henry arrived at the dock and died before a doctor could be summoned. It fell to William Henry to inform the heavily pregnant wife that she was now a widow. She had stared at him uncomprehendingly, the news only sinking in after he had taken her hands in his and repeated the news. He was no good at this: incapable even of invoking the name of the Lord to offer small comfort. He had abandoned her when she collapsed on a hard, wooden bench in the rude workman's cottage, returned to his office, and had a cleric sent to offer the solace he had been incapable of giving.

The barman had just passed him a whisky and water when he heard someone call his name. At the far end of the bar, he saw a familiar face from his early Burra days. Alfred Jenkins had been captain, not at the Burra Burra Copper Mine, but at the smaller Llwchwr Mine. He had been drawn to Jenkins by a mutual interest in prospecting the Burra hills for new copper-bearing lodes. Jenkins beckoned to him. He picked up his glass and edged along the bar. He hadn't seen or heard of Jenkins for some years, and was surprised that the older man recognized him. Jenkins had the gnarled hands of a miner, and as they shook, he felt a slight shame at his own office-softened hands. He looked at the man who stood at Jenkins' left shoulder. He was strongly built with thinning red curls and a complexion that spoke of years under the Australian sun.

"Do you know this fellow?" asked Jenkins. From his tone and expression, it was clear to William Henry that he expected the answer to be yes.

William Henry shook his head. "I'm afraid we've never met."

The stranger extended his hand. "John McLeod. Pleased to meet you," he said. His hand was as weathered as Jenkins', his Scottish brogue as rough as William Henry's Welsh lilt was soft. He wondered what Jenkins had been up to since abandoning the Burra mine, what brought him to Port Adelaide, and what he was doing with the Scotsman who was clearly part of the mining fraternity. He thought he knew the whole of the South Australian mining community but had not met McLeod. The name was familiar, but then it was a common one.

"You may not know me, Mr. Price, but I most surely know you. It's an honour to make your acquaintance."

"Finish your drink, and I'll get another round," said Jenkins. "We've got a story to tell you, and I reckon it's one you'll be interested in."

It had been his intention to have only one drink and then get back to Mary, who was coping with a difficult pregnancy. However, intrigued by Jenkins' comment, he accepted the offer of another whisky.

"It's your story, John. Why don't you tell it?"

"Surely. As you might have guessed, I'm in the same game as you.

But not quite. I don't work for a mining company. Brother Donald and me, we're prospectors. Came out from the Isle of Skye to join the gold rush. By the time we got here, the big goldfields in Victoria and New South Wales had been pretty well picked over, so we decided to head west. Got to Adelaide, and then headed south, down Cape Jervis way. You familiar with that neck of the woods?"

"Well, I've been there," said William Henry. "But I couldn't claim any sort of intimacy." His passion for exploration had led him to most of the settled parts of the State as well as to the inhospitable interior. "It's pretty rugged once you get down south."

"And the further down you go, the more rugged it gets. Me and Donald, we had to hack our own trails through the bush once we got off the beaten track. Just to get that far south, we had to take a boat from Glenelg to the whaling station at Fishery Bay."

"Did you have any success?" William Henry had his doubts. From what he had seen, that part of the state offered little promise of gold.

McLeod confirmed his doubts with a shake of the head. "There were no gold seams," he said.

"But there was something else," said Jenkins, re-joining the conversation with another round of drinks.

"And what was that?"

"We came across an outcrop of ore that looked promising. We knew it wasn't copper, which is all that most prospectors seem to find in this State."

"I'd guess silver and lead," said William Henry.

McLeod was impressed. He knew William Henry by reputation but was yet to discover the depths of his knowledge, gleaned from extensive reading as well as years of prospecting.

"Silver and lead, indeed. We collected samples from the seam which was over half a yard wide and, as far as we could tell, ran for about fifty yards. When the assay results came back, they indicated rich deposits of silver and lead. We applied for a lease, naming it Talisker of Scotland after our home on the Isle of Skye."

"When do you expect to hear the outcome of the application?" asked William Henry.

"We heard today. That's what I've been doing in Adelaide. We have a fourteen-year lease." His already florid face became even more flushed. Raising his glass, he proclaimed, "To Talisker of Scotland."

"Talisker of Scotland," echoed Jenkins and William Henry.

"Next steps?" asked William Henry. The stevedores at the bar were becoming ever more raucous, and he had to raise his voice to be heard.

"I'll let Alf answer that," replied McLeod.

Jenkins drained his whisky in a single motion, thumped his glass onto the bar and announced, in a voice loud enough to rise above the din of the surrounding drinkers, "John and the shareholders have been generous enough to offer me the position of Mine Captain. I have accepted. Next week, I leave in a cutter for Fishery Bay with a full complement of Cornish miners and ample supplies. Half of the men will begin construction of offices and lodgings—initially we'll be accommodated in tents. The rest of the detail will begin immediately breaking the ore into small pieces and bagging it for transportation by bullock wagon to Fishery Bay. There it will be shipped to England to be smelted. As you well know, William, shareholders are always impatient for a return on their investment, and I propose to show them a return by the end of the year."

William Henry listened to this rather self-serving speech with interest. Silver and lead would add to the wealth of the colony which, until that point, had relied almost exclusively on copper.

"With that said," continued Jenkins, "we come to the real purpose of our presence here in Port Adelaide, which was to seek you out."

"Seek me out?" He made no attempt to mask his surprise.

"Indeed. In fact, we visited your offices earlier, but learned you had gone to the dock to deal with an unfortunate incident. We retreated to this good hostelry to celebrate the granting of the lease with a view to seeking you out at a later time. Your appearance here was most happenstantial, not to say propitious."

"But what purpose do you have with me, Captain?" asked William Henry.

"As soon as we have ore shipments flowing to England, we plan to construct a smelter onsite at Talisker. We need to have a competent and experienced engineer to oversee the construction of the smelter and to supervise its operation. That man is you, William."

"Am I to understand that you are offering me a position at this Talisker mine?"

"Indeed, we are," beamed Jenkins, waving to the bartender for another round.

William Henry walked home his head hunched deep into his overcoat. It had been a long and emotional day. He was tired and slightly dizzy from the consumption of an unaccustomed amount of alcohol. A confusion of thoughts cluttered his head. The Talisker job would free him from his dreaded office desk and get him back into the field. It would envelop him in the risks and excitement of a new mining venture: and mining, he felt in his bones, would make the Australia to come a nation to be reckoned with in the new Century. But what of his pregnant wife? His beloved children? What of William's education? The boy was brilliant, according to his teachers. What of his own growing importance to the Secular Association?

He had told Jenkins and McLeod he would give them his answer the following afternoon. They would meet at a reception in the imposing mansion of Henry Ayers on North Terrace, a reception to thank those who had financially supported one of South Australia's favourite sons, John McDouall Stuart. Several weeks earlier, McDouall Stuart had, after a number of failures, set off on one last attempt to conquer the continent. If he succeeded, he would be first to cross the country from south to north. William Henry knew both men: Ayers, from his years at the Burra Copper Mine. McDouall Stuart he knew less well. He had been invited by the explorer to advise the present, as well as a previous expedition on the types of geological specimens that should be collected as he traversed the continent. Although the previous expedition failed to make it to the Gulf of Carpentaria, the specimens they brought back reinforced William Henry's belief in the rich possibilities that lay beneath the surface of the continent.

The reception at Ayers' House was a lavish affair. The host was one of the wealthiest, if not the wealthiest citizen in the colony. He was also one of its most influential politicians. In 1857, he was elected to the first South Australian Legislative Assembly: its youngest member by a several years. Some months prior to the reception, he had been lobbied to take over the premiership of the colony, an overture he declined, but

William Henry predicted it wouldn't be long before he ascended to the premiership. His prediction was to prove correct when Ayers became premier the following year.

As guests arrived, they were greeted by uniformed waiters and offered champagne. A palm court orchestra jammed into a corner of the room laboured out light classics. William Henry asked for a glass of water and looked around for Jenkins and McLeod, but it was soon apparent that they were yet to arrive. Ayers circulated among the guests with a personal assistant trailing behind.

The amount of time that Ayers spent with each guest was an indication of the esteem in which they were held, or his assessment of their potential usefulness. William Henry received a perfunctory handshake. "Good of you to come," he said. "I trust that Mrs. Price and the children are well." He passed on to the next guest without waiting for a response. At that point, Jenkins and McLeod appeared, the former looking dishevelled and bleary-eyed. Clearly, their celebrations of the previous evening had extended well beyond William Henry's departure from the hotel. Jenkins' hangover had transformed his bonhomie of the previous evening into belligerence. Without wasting time on pleasantries, he accosted William Henry with a gruff "Well, what's your decision?" William Henry was nonplussed. In the few years they had spent together in Burra, Jenkins had been the soul of sanguinity. Before he could respond, Ayers called the assembly to order by rapping insistently on an empty champagne glass with a silver spoon. Although not unhandsome, he made himself a figure of slight ridicule by allowing mutton chop sideburns to descend below his jawline until they brushed his collar. In the years prior to his death in 1897 he encouraged their continued growth until the met under his chin.

"Gentlemen," he said. "I thank you for taking time out from your busy day to visit my humble abode (muffled laugher and snorts) to celebrate six months since the stalwart, not to say, heroic, McDouall Stuart set off on his sixth attempt to cross the continent. Despite your various accomplishments and contributions to our colony, you have one thing in common, you all contributed to the expedition—well, most of you at least." He paused to allow for appreciative titters. Is he looking at me? wondered William Henry. He may not have given money, but he had contributed in other ways, most notably in his geological knowledge and skill assaying the ore samples brought back to Adelaide by the fifth failed expedition.

"We have had no word from the expedition since they left the settled districts quite a few weeks ago, but being optimists, we believe that no news is good news. We think of the five previous expeditions, which all ended without reaching the Top End, not as failures but as training exercises. (Another pause for muffled applause)."

Would those creatures, both animal and human, have thought of them as "training exercises?" William Henry wondered.

"We think of the tragic end to the Burke and Wills expedition, not yet two years past. Although much of our great country has been explored and its potential mining riches have been exposed, one great challenge remains—and that is to cross the country from bottom to top, uncovering what there is to be uncovered in the unknown heart of this great land mass. Ignorant people over East refer to the 'Dead Heart.' Let me tell you Gentlemen, there is nothing dead at the heart of our State.

"But make no mistake, despite the tragedy of the Burke and Wills expedition, we are locked in a competition, nay, even a battle here. In this battle, we are the minnows. Investors in the Burke and Wills adventure outspent us ten-to-one. Their coffers groaned with the spoils from the gold rush. The Victorians thought they could win the race by throwing money at it. No less than twenty-four camels were imported from India to overcome a major challenge in crossing the continent—a serious lack of water. However, the expedition met with one disaster after another. So, what went wrong? They picked the wrong man for the job— an Irish policeman who didn't know the country and wouldn't listen to those of his men who did. Robert O'Hara Burke was unquestionably a brave man, but he was headstrong. He thought he knew best when he didn't, and that led to the death of most of the expedition in the middle of the continent, including Burke himself, and Wills, his second-in-command.

"Why do we believe that our much more modestly funded expedition is likely to succeed where the Victorian circus failed? Our hope rests in the man we have picked for the job—McDouall Stuart. Those of you who are acquainted with him know he is the right man for the job. His five failed attempts are not a sign of shortcoming but of strength—he knows when to turn back and regroup, and when he brought his men back with him (he paused to dramatize the effect of his words) he brought them back alive."

William Henry listened to the speech with interest. He knew that it was more than a speech, but a call to financial arms. There was no doubt that Ayers regretted the demise of the Victorian expedition. But it also provided the South Australians, the underfunded minnows, the opportunity to emerge as victors. Ayers also conveniently overlooked the fact that, according to the journal kept by Wills, the Burke and Wills expedition had successfully traversed the continent. Unfortunately, however, they had not managed to sight the open sea. Even more unfortunately, they failed to make it back.

As Ayers spoke, the uniformed attendants circulated, replenishing the champagne glasses. He concluded his speech by proposing a toast to the successful return of McDouall Stuart and his men, and then added, "Notwithstanding your previous generosity, we are in need of additional funds to bring the expedition successfully back to Adelaide once they have reached the settled districts to our north. Your generosity in this regard will be much appreciated and will not go unnoticed by a future Legislative Council." This last comment was nothing short of an outright bribe. William Henry and the rest of the men in the room knew he was alluding to his expected elevation to the premiership, and the fact that, when it happened, those who dug deep into their pockets could expect to be granted favours by the new colonial administration.

As soon as Ayers had finished speaking, Jenkins and McLeod reappeared in front of William Henry. It was clear that they had imbibed the liberally flowing champagne, if not wisely, then too well, and that the bubbles had improved Jenkins' humour considerably. William Henry told them of his decision. While the invitation was tempting, allowing him to return to the field and the work he loved most, at this point in time he had to put his family first, most particularly his wife, Mary, who was heavy with child. McLeod took the rebuff in good part. He wished William Henry luck, and said that when his domestic situation had changed, other possibilities at Talisker might avail themselves.

At seven o'clock on the morning of June 22, 1862, Mary went into labour. After summoning the midwife, and Alice, their toothless housekeeper, William Henry went to his office. It was not seemly for the husband to be present while his wife endured the agony of giving birth to his child. At the direction of the midwife, Alice boiled water, and spread sheets on the dining table in preparation for the delivery. At four o'clock, when there had been no word, William Henry returned home to be there when his three older children came back from school. No sooner had he entered the house, than Mary gave birth to a baby girl. Defying convention, he entered the dining room. He held a damp cloth to Mary's forehead and looked on as the midwife slapped the tiny child to make it cry. She then cleaned the baby up, and bound it tightly in a cotton cloth.

"There's another to come," she said. William Henry had been correct in conjecturing that Mary might be carrying twins. The second child was a boy, but in keeping with the tradition of the times, the boy was deemed to have been born first. Once the child had been cleaned up, William Henry took him in his arms.

"Is the child all right?" asked Mary.

"He's very small," replied William Henry.

They named the boy Benjamin, and the girl Sarah Elizabeth after William Henry's mother.

Interest in the McDouall Stuart expedition was kept alive by stories in the local newspapers about the leader and other members of the expedition. However, with no word from the expedition, these stories contained little in the way of substance. The whole population of Adelaide was on tenterhooks. Had the explorers made it to the Top End, or had they perished in the desert on this sixth attempt? There was simply no way of knowing. At one point, several prominent members of the business community lobbied Ayers to raise a second expedition to go in search of McDouall Stuart and his men. But Ayers, steadfast in his belief in McDouall Stuart's skill and judgment, refused.

After the birth of the twins, William Henry had little time to spend on speculating about the expedition. Benjamin, the smaller of the twins had been born sickly, and faced a struggle to survive. On several occasions, he was admitted to hospital and the doctors warned William

Henry and Mary to prepare for the worst. On each occasion, he rallied, and they brought him home. On one such occasion on a blustery, late August day, having seen Mary and the baby back to their house, William Henry made his way to his office. On his desk, one of his staff had placed a copy of the *South Australian Register*. Splashed across the front page was a report of the successful crossing of the continent by the McDouall Stuart expedition. The explorer had planted the Union Jack on Australia's northern shore on the afternoon of July 21, 1862. It had taken him nine months to complete the two-thousand-mile journey, and it almost cost him his life. The newspaper account reported that after resting for a week in an attempt to recover his failing health and giving his horses time to regain their strength, the expedition began the long trek home. However, McDouall Stuart's health continued to decline, and his horses began to fall, one by one. Within a couple of weeks of beginning his return, he was in such poor shape that his men began to doubt that he would live to see Australia's southern shores again. He had scurvy and was rapidly losing his sight. He was unable to use his right hand and had to dictate his journal to a subordinate. Eventually, the pain of riding became so unbearable that his men had to rig up a stretcher and carry him. At last, the expedition reached the settlement of Mount Margaret where they rested and sent world to Adelaide that they had succeeded in their quest to cross the continent. Miraculously, although many of their horses had perished, all members of the expedition survived.

William Henry read the various accounts of the expedition—its travails and triumphs. There were some dark whispers that McDouall Stuart had massacred a group of aborigines at what was to become Alice Springs, but these rumours were dismissed by his admirers, of which William Henry was one. He joined that large crowd which gathered along North Terrace to welcome the explorer, victorious at last in his quest to traverse the continent. With a population of little more than 15,000, Adelaide was hardly larger than a country town, and it seemed that everyone had turned out to see him. Although McDouall Stuart had returned alive, he came back a broken man. William Henry was shocked by his appearance. His once ruddy face was gaunt, his luxuriant black beard was streaked with grey, and he looked much older than his 37 years. He was given a substantial government reward and a thousand acres of prime pastoral land, but he chose to return to England where he died two years later.

When it was published, William Henry obtained a copy of McDouall Stuart's journal, documenting his trek to the Gulf of Carpentaria. Of particular interest were descriptions of the geological formations of the interior, as well as the samples of rock brought back by the expedition. Clearly, large swathes of the interior consisted of massive iron ore deposits. "One day, these will make the country rich," he said to anyone who would listen. On those weekends when there was nothing pressing to be done at home, he would ride out from the city, and indulge in his passion for surveying and prospecting. Although he came across several small lodes, there was nothing worth staking a claim for. But at that time, the substantial lodes within striking distance of the city had all been claimed. On those occasions when his son William was not busy with his schoolwork, he would accompany his father as he had done as a lad in Burra. He was an excellent horseman. His crippled leg was no impediment, and riding became one of his favourite forms of exercise.

Not long after McDouall Stuart's return, baby Benjamin lost his struggle for life. He died on October 7 at just fifteen weeks of age. The death certificate recorded the cause of death as "general debility." Less than two months later, Sarah also died from an acute bout of diarrhoea in the middle of an outbreak of typhoid. At the time, Port Adelaide was notorious for epidemics because it was where immigrants disembarked carrying deadly maladies from the disease-ridden ships that brought them from Europe. William Henry grieved for the two lost babies, who had lived long enough to become part of the family. But most of all he grieved for his wife and her profound suffering. Without the delusional comfort of religious faith, they only had each other, along with their surviving children, to sustain them. The knowledge that, at the time of Sarah's death, she was in the early stages of yet another pregnancy, was of little comfort to Mary. She set her face against William Henry's attempts to console her with the thought of another child to come. "I have brought seven children into this world," she said to him. "Three of them are dead, and William was extremely fortunate to survive. What sad fate awaits the child I am now carrying? My friends tell me it is God's will. I remind them that there is no God, but if there were, he would be a cruel and vengeful being—sparing this child, taking that with neither rhyme nor reason."

Their eighth child, another girl, was born on July 26, 1863. They called her Rebecca. She was a healthy child, and some solace to Mary who was still struggling to come to terms with the death of the twins. A week after the birth, William Henry was on the Port Adelaide dock supervising the loading of a shipment of ore when he saw a familiar figure approaching from the direction of his office. It was John McLeod. The two men shook hands, and McLeod asked if William Henry could spare him a few minutes of his time. They crossed the street to William Henry's office which was little more than a cubicle in the corner of a warehouse. William Henry offered the Scotsman a seat and eyed him curiously. He had given little thought to McLeod since they had met the previous year. McLeod filled him in on all that had happened on the Peninsula. The Talisker mine was doing very well. In fact, it had exceeded the expectations of the McLeod brothers and the shareholders. The township of Silverton, established to house the miners and their families, was also being developed. In addition to the dwellings, there were plans for a hotel, a school and a post office. Earlier in the year, a facility had been constructed at Fishery Bay to crush and dress the ore that was hauled by bullock drays down to the bay from the mine.

William Henry listened attentively, wondering where this was leading. McLeod finally got to the point. "Although things are going very well, Jenkins has decided to leave. His health is poor, and he plans to return to Britain. So, not to put too fine a point on it, I've been authorized by the shareholders to approach you about the possibility of taking over as Captain."

William Henry scratched at his beard. The offer was tempting. To be captain of a thriving mine would be the high point of his career, and it would get him out of a job that had become stultifying.

"Many thanks, Mr. McLeod, your offer is extremely generous," he said. "I'm flattered you think I might be well suited to the position."

"You have a good name within the mining community, and Jenkins thinks highly of you. He was very disappointed with your decision to turn us down last year."

"I'll have to consult my wife," said William Henry.

"Of course. I'll come back tomorrow," said McLeod, and took his leave.

The following day, when McLeod returned for an answer, William Henry said that after discussing the offer with his wife, he had decided to accept. It would take him a month or two to settle his affairs in Adelaide, but he would be able to take up the position before the year was out. His wife and children would remain in Adelaide until he was settled in Silverton, and then his wife and youngest child would join him.

The two men shook hands on the agreement. McLeod suggested he come down to Talisker for a few days to acquaint himself with the mine, its operation, and the men who would be under his command.

Chapter 4
Talisker

As a small child, William had arrived in Port Adelaide with his parents aboard the *Phoebe Dunbar*. Now, over a decade later, he was on a coastal schooner carrying him away from the Port Adelaide dock to visit his father. It was a magnificent high summer day in the middle of January 1864. The heatwave ushering in the new year had relented, and a cooling ocean breeze kept it that way. Although the ocean swell made him unsteady on his feet, he decided to stay on the deck where he was better able to take in the coastal settlements of Glenelg and Noarlunga. He jammed his crutch into his shoulder and took a firm grip on the ship's railing. With the wind at their back, they made good time down the coast. Once they had left the settled district behind, the Adelaide Plains gave way to high rolling hills that ended abruptly at the coast. This was the southern extremity of the Mt. Lofty Ranges, which ran all the way from Burra in the mid-North to the Fleurieu Peninsula, encircling the nascent city of Adelaide at its mid-point.

He had accepted with alacrity his father's suggestion that he make the trip. Having settled into Talisker in November, William Henry had returned to Adelaide to spend the Christmas and New Year period with his wife and children. He also took the opportunity to order some equipment for the mine, including a small steam engine and boiler which would be needed for the treatment works and smelting plant he planned to build on the mine site. This equipment was in the hold under the deck on which William stood. His father had shared with him ambitious plans to build a sizeable township and a significant mine on the Talisker site.

When they arrived at Fishery Bay, the coastal schooner dropped anchor offshore, and William and the equipment for the Talisker Mine were ferried ashore by barge. William Henry was waiting with three men he took to be miners beside a wagon pulled by two bullocks yoked together. He greeted his father warmly, and shook hands with the miners.

Two were older men, with creased faces and work-worn hands. The third was much younger, just a few years older than William himself. He introduced himself as Cadan. All three men had strong West Country accents.

The men looked curiously at his crippled leg. He knew what they were thinking. How would this maimed youngster cope with the rough and rocky terrain that encompassed the mine? In addition to the mining equipment, William had brought one of his father's brass-bound boxes of books along with a satchel of his own school books. Although it was the summer break, and all the schools were closed, William planned to spend his time at Talisker studying. He climbed into the wagon and sat on a bench at the rear. The men loaded the equipment and trunk, then Cadan leaped nimbly into the wagon and took up a seat next to William. He wondered whether the lad was showing off, comparing his own fleet-footedness with William's clumsy scramble into the wagon. He soon learned that it was not in Cadan's nature to show off. As the bullocks were whipped into motion, Cadan told his story. The eldest of seven children, four of whom survived, he had emigrated with his family as part of the great Cornish diaspora that followed the decline in the mining industry in south-west England. On arriving in South Australia, they were among the first wave of Cornish immigrants to head to the Copper Triangle north of Adelaide, settling near Kadina. So many Cornish immigrants were to move to the area that it became known as "Little Cornwall." While his father found work immediately, things were different for Cadan. As he was fourteen, he was expected to get a job and help support the family. However, barely literate, with little education and no experience, this was not easy. He found piecemeal work on a neighbouring farm, but the wages were poor. Then, through a contact of his father, he was introduced to Captain Jenkins, and was offered more stable work at Talisker, not as a miner, but as a general rouseabout. Although he was slightly built, and the work was physically demanding, he enjoyed life at Talisker. He also looked up to Captain Price, who was "like a farver to me." Once the schoolhouse was completed, William Henry said he would arrange after-school classes for Cadan and any of the younger men who wanted to learn to read and write. This was Cadan's dream—to get an "edercation." William was naturally pleased to hear the kind words spoken about his father. He warmed to Cadan's open-faced innocence, and said that he'd be happy, if time allowed in the evenings, to give Cadan some lessons. William noticed that when addressing his father directly, the men called him "Captain." When talking about him among themselves, they referred to him as "WH."

An unseasonal shower of rain had passed through the Peninsula earlier in the day, leaving the eucalypts fresh and bright. The lemon-scented gums gave off a spicy fragrance that William found pleasing. At the top of the ridge, the bullock wagon turned left, and followed a broader path before plunging back into the heavily wooded hillside and on into Silverton. They stopped at the manager's house, where William and his father clambered down from the wagon and the men unloaded the trunk of books along with a suitcase and some photographic equipment which WH had requested.

The mine buzzed with activity. William was impressed with what had already been achieved. He unpacked his possessions in the front bedroom opposite his father's, arranging his books on a small oak table that would serve as his desk. Then he wandered through to the kitchen and made himself a cup of tea while waiting for his father to return from unloading the pump engine and boiler. His father made no secret of his pleasure at having been liberated from his desk job, and to be back at the work he loved.

When WH returned, he gave his son a guided tour of the land, which was more extensive than William had imagined. At least half the miners seemed to be engaged in construction work. One team was building the Silverton Hotel, a school house, and post office, two others were laying the foundations for the treatment plant and smelting works. When completed, these would greatly improve the efficiency with which the ore could be processed for transportation to Cornwall. In the beginning, the ore was dug directly from the ground, but as soon as the surface rock was depleted, it was necessary to sink a main shaft to follow the line of lode underground. This required a winding house and poppet head to haul the ore to the surface.

WH led his son along a small bush track that led away from the main shaft. Telling his son to keep an eye out for snakes, WH parted the bushes and led him to a clearing in the scrub where the rocky ground had been broken up.

"What is this?" asked William.

"This is a new ore lode. I discovered it shortly after I arrived here." William couldn't help noticing the pride in his father's voice. He was a modest man, not given to boasting, and William was slightly surprised by this note in his voice.

"The full assay results are not in yet, but I have great hopes for it. This could be the saving of the mine," he said. "I doubt that McLeod's lode is as extensive as the brothers originally thought. We've reaching 150 feet with the main shaft, and we're already encountering water. Below a certain depth, the engines we have will struggle coping with the volume of water. Also, as we get deeper, the quality of the ore will begin to deteriorate." The sun was now high in the sky, and as there was no cooling ocean breeze up here on the ridge, WH suggested that they return to the house.

The following morning, William was woken at dawn by a cacophony from kookaburras sitting high in the eucalypts that ringed the settlement. Birds, wallabies, and other native animals were abundant in the bushland surrounding the mine. As a youngster in Burra, he had learned to name most bird by their call. Now, he identified the harsh screech of the sulphur-crested cockatoos, wheeling up the valley to alight on the ghost gums behind the hotel and the liquid warble of the South Australian magpies, squabbling and scratching on the corrugated iron roof of the house. From the kitchen, he could hear the muffled voices of his father and Mrs. Abernathy, the housekeeper who arrived early to get the fire going and prepare food for the day. William joined them and accepted a cup of tea from the housekeeper.

WH spent most of his day at the mine site, supervising the construction of the new buildings or directing mining operations. The contingent of fifty miners recruited by Jenkins were highly experienced, and once WH had issued instructions to the foreman, he was able to get on with the work that really interested him—surveying, prospecting, doing some rudimentary assaying and meeting the daily engineering challenges that had to be overcome in the course of constructing the mining shafts and drives, hacking the ore into compliant chunks, and hauling it to the surface. On this, his first morning at Talisker, William accompanied his father to the loading area. One of the bullock wagons was being jockeyed into position to be loaded with samples from a promising new lode some distance from the new Price Shaft. WH wanted the samples to be sent off for more detailed analysis than was possible on site. It would be transported north to Port Adelaide on the coastal schooner that had carried William south the previous day.

While his father spoke to the supervisor of the bullock team about one of the animals, which was reluctant to be put into harness, William explored the immediate environs of the mine. The miners who stood waiting to load the ore samples marvelled at how nimbly, with the aid of a crutch, the young cripple was able to negotiate the loose rocks and scree that was scattered about parts of the site. When investors and other visitors with fully functioning limbs visited the mine, it was not uncommon for them to stumble over the unstable ground, but the boy had no trouble at all.

William's head jerked up at the scream, which echoed down the valley. A wheel had come off the bullock wagon as it was being loaded pinning one of the men under the axle. He saw his father running from the engine room. Grabbing his crutch, which he had placed on the ground while inspecting the ore samples, William scuttled across the rough ground towards the loading area. The pinned man was screaming, "Get it off. Get it off," in a high-pitched, almost girlish voice. As he drew near to the scene of the accident, he saw to his horror that the victim was the lad who had befriended him on the ride up from Fishery Bay the previous day. The sun had crested the eastern ridge, and was beating into the camp. It was going to be a hot day. A solitary crow alighted on the roof of the new engine house and started up its desolate caw. The men who had been loading the wagon were joined by several others and were attempting to raise the wagon and free Cadan whose screams and cries of "Get it off" were heart-rending. William wanted the cries to stop. When his father ordered the men not to raise the wagon, William looked at him in astonishment. Surely, he wanted to alleviate Cadan's agony. "The axle has pierced the femoral artery. If you lift the wagon and release the pressure, he'll bleed to death in minutes." He ordered one of the men to fetch a length of cord and a stick, and then turned to William. "Run to the house and ask Mrs. Abernathy for a bottle of whisky—a full one." William carried out his father's instruction at a speed which surprised the miners.

"What's happened?" asked Mrs. Abernathy as he entered the kitchen. Like everyone else in the settlement, she had heard the screams.

"There's been an accident," said William. "I need a bottle of whisky. A full one." Mrs. Abernathy bustled into the small parlour off the kitchen and fetched a bottle, which William dropped into the satchel he always carried slung across his shoulder. He hurried back to the scene of the accident. By the time he got back, his father had cut off Cadan's trousers and was fixing a tourniquet around his thigh above the wound, tying the cord around the leg and using a stick to tighten the cord until it cut deep into the boy's flesh. Cadan's cries were weaker now, fear and pain having exhausted him. WH took the whisky bottle from William and forced it between Cadan's lips. The raw spirit made him choke, but his father kept forcing the spirit into him until a good third of the bottle had been consumed. Cadan lapsed into unconsciousness, and WH gave the order to raise the wagon and release the boy.

Another wagon was quickly prepared. One of the men was ordered to ride ahead to alert the captain of the schooner. As they prepared to lift the boy into the wagon, WH said, "Leave the ore samples. And don't leave until I return." WH was generally a leisurely, even laconic, walker, but now he sprinted to the manager's house, returning minutes later with an envelope in his hand. "Impress upon the captain that the boy has to be got to Adelaide with all speed," said WH. He handed the whisky bottle to one of the men in the back of the wagon. "If he comes to, make him drink more of this." He gave the envelope to the driver of the wagon. "Give this to the captain, and make sure he gets it to Head Office in Hindley Street."

William found it impossible to settle down to his books that morning. When the steel shaft had been removed from Cadan's leg, the thigh muscle had flopped open. It looked less like a human leg than a lump of meat on a butcher's chopping board. His father had cleaned it up as best he could, pushing the flesh back around the shattered bone, and securing it with a piece of clean cloth that had been soaked in whisky. His response to William's anxious question if Cadan would be all right was to put an arm around his son's shoulder and then turn away.

The wagon came creaking into the mining settlement late in the afternoon. Although the sun was sliding towards its rendezvous with the ocean, the heat was as intense as it had been at midday. They had wrapped him in a makeshift shroud fashioned from a square of sailcloth.

William looked up from his books. After lunch he had forced himself back to his desk in attempt to use study to drive from his head the images of the morning. Through the little window, he watched the three men climb down from the wagon and make their way down the incline to the manager's house. He heard their footsteps on the stone verandah, the creak of the front door, and the sound of WH's voice. The men settled themselves in the parlour next to William's room. Through the flimsy wall, he listened to snatches of conversation.

"The tourniquet worked loose on the ride down to the Bay. He bled out before we could do anything. In the end, he wasn't in pain. He didn't regain consciousness."

"Put the body in the engine house, and make sure it's securely locked. We don't want dingoes getting at it in the night. Given the heat, he'll have to be buried in the morning. Get a work detail to prepare a plot at once."

Into the suffocating night, William listened to the clash of shovels on stony ground as the detail prepared Cadan's grave in the area designated as the Silvertown cemetery. Two other mounds already existed on the spot. Both contained children, and, at the top of both were crude wooden crosses with the names, ages, and dates of death of the children. While WH was a committed atheist who presented his views with vigour, he did not impose these on others, and didn't interfere with the families who placed the crosses.

It was going to be another hot day. At eight o'clock, before the sun was too high in the sky, the whole community gathered at the gravesite. WH had decreed that no work would be done that day. William had experienced his father's grief at the death of his siblings, but had never seen him so visibly affected by the death of someone outside the family. He could take no solace in the notion that Cadan was residing in the arms of the Lord. He was unrelievedly and irredeemably dead and gone forever.

Four men carried the corpse, still wrapped in its sailcloth, on a canvas stretcher, from the engine house, up the hill to the cemetery and lowered it into the hastily prepared grave. WH then said a few words.

"This is a sad day. It has been a matter of pride to me that we have not had a work-related fatality in what is a very dangerous profession. It was bound to happen someday, but that it should happen to a young man who was just setting out to make his way in life is profoundly sad. In the short time I knew him, I came to respect his honestly, his capacity for hard work, his cheerful nature, and, most of all, his desire to better himself. It is now my sad duty to consign his body to the earth and to inform his parents of his death."

Several members of the gathering said amen. WH then signalled to the men standing by with long-handled shovels to fill in the grave. As they toiled to shovel the stony rubble into the grave the crow that had appeared the previous day landed in a tree on the edge of the graveside and began to caw mournfully—an ominous sign to the more superstitious individuals gathered at the grave site.

Some months after William had returned to Adelaide, construction of several buildings, including the Silverton Hotel, the Post Office and the school, were completed. Silverton was in the process of becoming a significant settlement on the southern tip of the Peninsula. In Adelaide the directors decided to organize a gala weekend to celebrate these various landmarks. WH made a trip to Adelaide for a meeting with the directors to discuss the gala among other things. As usual, he stayed at the family home.

For some time, WH had wanted Mary and the family to relocate to Talisker. It was about time they were reunited. Mary's preference was for life in Port Adelaide. She had her circle of friends, as did her older children. She had a comfortable life. She had done her time in the hardship bush post of Burra. While this city was her preference, her duty was to follow her husband. Another husband would simply have directed her to follow him, but it was not in WH's nature, and had never been his practice, to order her about. Although he had not consulted her on the decision to emigrate to Australia, things changed once they reached

South Australia. He realized that all they had were each other and the baby William and refashioned their relationship on the decidedly modern principle of equality which fitted snugly into his intellectual cosmology that encompassed secularism and humanism. On Mary's part, although William Henry made no demand, if it were her husband's wish, then she would follow. She made an initial foray to Silverton for the gala event. It was her first time to venture south of Adelaide, and would give her an opportunity to take its measure. She had a good idea of the geography and culture of the place from her husband's descriptions, along with the photographs he had taken to document the development of the settlement., but she wanted to see it for herself. This was not to decide whether or not to relocate—that she would do, but to decide when to relocate and what she needed to bring with her. William Henry (she refused to use the nickname given him by his Talisker colleagues) had already embarked on extending the manager's house, and once the extensions were completed there would be no shortage of accommodation for the whole family. A teacher had already been recruited for the school, and while educational opportunities would be more limited in the one-room schoolhouse than in the city, she and William Henry could compensate, as they always had, with any perceived shortcomings in their children's schoolings.

The gala weekend went off well. All of the company directors and most of their wives attended and were accommodated at the new Silverton Hotel. Mary had to act as hostess, ensuring that the needs of the wives were met. The retiring Mary was uncomfortable with this role but carried it off competently. Each of the new buildings was subject to a short ceremony. The engine house, which had acted as a temporary morgue for the hapless Cadan, was inaugurated, and the engine started, in a traditional Cornish ceremony. An outdoor luncheon was held on level ground at the front of the hotel. Food and drink were placed on long trestle tables, an impromptu brass band played with enthusiasm, if not a particularly high degree of skill. After lunch, the directors, and several of the more adventurous wives were treated to a tour of the underground workings of the safer parts of the main mine. The day concluded with a group photo taken by WH, the only challenge being to get those men who had imbibed, not wisely but too well, to stand still long enough to be captured on the photographic plate. As the sun set over the mine, Mary received many compliments. The consensus was that the day had been a success. She wasn't sure what she had done to deserve the praise, but accepted it with good grace, a smile and a tilt of the head.

On the day following the gala, with the guests gone, she took herself off for a walk beyond the immediate environs of the manager's dwelling. The warmth with which she had been greeted at the gala had given her confidence along with an unaccustomed courage. She found herself on the rough path that wound its way up to the burial ground. There she contemplated the two small graves that were marked by crosses, and the larger, unmarked mound. Over the years, the mound itself would be gone and there would be nothing to mark the fleeting time on earth of the young man called Cadan. She thought of her own dead children, Thomas interred in the Burra cemetery, the twins in Adelaide, and was overcome by a fleeting grief for a boy she had never known who was turning to dust beneath her feet. The burial ground afforded splendid views across the heavily forested valley. It was curious that the dead generally got the best views. It had been the same in her native Wales: churches and their accompanying burial ground almost invariably occupied the highest ground.

Due to a hold up in the completion of the extensions to the manager's house, Mary and the children didn't relocate from Adelaide to Talisker until the end of 1864, almost a year after WH had taken up residence there. She was accompanied by her four youngest children—Henry, now 11, Mary Ann, 10, Thomas John, 7, and Rebecca, who had just turned 1. William, now 14, remained in Adelaide in the care of the housekeeper, to pursue his studies. Mary had been upset when William Henry suggested this. She wanted all of the children to be reunited with their father. Their father, however, pointed to William's academic and intellectual gifts, which would be best served by his remaining in Adelaide. He told Mary he had already made discreet enquiries at the top private school in Adelaide for his son's entry there to finish his education.

The three older children attended the one-room school at Talisker. As the offspring of Captain WH Price, they were at first treated as curiosities by the other children. Most of these children were the first in their family to attend school. Their parents were either illiterate, or barely literate. When construction of the school had been completed, WH told Mary he'd had a challenge convincing some parents of the value of school. Some wanted their children, particularly the daughters, to go into domestic service until they were old enough to get decent-paying jobs and contribute to the household income. But WH was adamant. The greatest gift they could give their children was an education. While many parents agreed on the potential of education to transform lives, it came down to a matter of priorities, and putting food on the table came first.

At 11 years of age, quiet, practical Henry was the oldest child in the school. Eleven was the normal leaving age for those children who actually got to school. However, WH prevailed upon the teacher, who went by the teacherly name of Charles Goodenough, to keep Henry on. WH and Mary would augment at home the instruction Goodenough provided at school. Pretty Mary Ann was popular. However, it was the irrepressibly energetic Thomas John who attracted most of the attention. He made friends easily, flirted with the snotty-nosed girls in their shabby pinafores, and within weeks of arriving at the school had press-ganged some of the more pliant pupils, including his sister, into an impromptu concert. Mary Ann sang, Thomas John performed magic tricks, one pupil played the penny whistle, and four other others acted in a short play that was written and directed by Thomas John. Their concert was staged on a Sunday afternoon, and was well attended apart from some of the more religious members of the community who thought it improper, if not downright blasphemous, to stage such an entertainment on the Sabbath. It was an unfamiliar event to most of the curious miners and their families. However, they were charmed by Thomas John, who acted as MC, and entertained by the other children.

Mary marvelled at the diversity of human life. Each of her children was different in their talents and dispositions. William was gentle of spirit and scholarly. Henry, no scholar, had inherited his father's practical problem-solving skills. Mary Ann loved children, and, Mary guessed, would be a teacher or a nurse. Thomas John, the showman, artist and leader of others, also possessed a reflective nature. What sort of child would the infant Rebecca grow into? What unique gifts would she present to the world? Inevitably her thoughts turned to those who were no longer with them. What gifts had been lost to the world with their premature deaths? Whenever she shared her darker thoughts with William Henry, he urged her to put them aside. He quoted to her from a book of poems he had recently received from England: "The moving finger writes, and, having writ, moves on: nor all thy piety nor wit shall lure it back to cancel half a line. Nor all thy tears wash out a word of it. We too must move on, my dear," he said.

Shortly after the family settled in Talisker, the company approved WH's request to begin mining the line of ore that he had discovered earlier in the year. The Main Shaft had been extremely productive and had consumed all of the company's resources for most of 1864. It had also produced healthy returns for the shareholders, who agreed to put their faith and additional funds into the Talisker venture. One weekend, a handful of the company directors arrived by coastal steamer for a ground-breaking ceremony. The event was not as lavish as the gala that Mary had participated in earlier in the year, but was propitious, nonetheless. Having broken the ground with a new ceremonial pick, the Chairman of Directors embarrassed WH by handing him the pick and declaiming, "I declare this the Price Shaft in honour of William Henry Price, a leader of men, and pioneer in establishing the mining industry in this great state." WH later told Mary that he had no time for such things. She replied that there was no shame in accepting an honour that was so thoroughly deserved.

WH's reputation grew, and his name began to spread, not just within the mining fraternity, but also with the general public. His monthly reports to the directors and shareholders on the developments at Talisker were published in the local press. On visits to head office in Hindley Street he sometimes made public speeches, which were also reported. These were measured, sober speeches, devoid of political hyperbole. However, he made no secret of his belief that it was on mining as much as agriculture that the prosperity of the colony would rest. He urged politicians to support the development of infrastructure to enable the development of the colony beyond the confines of Adelaide. "If the colony is to be more than a city-state, the hinterland has to be developed," he said.

1865 was probably the high point for WH as Captain of the Talisker mine. In May, another lode was discovered. All the mining operation building had been completed and a reservoir was constructed. Interest in the mine was high, and the Silverton Hotel had frequently to turn away visitors who had not booked accommodation in advance. Visitors were not always benign. Silverton was a frontier settlement, and attracted prospectors, explorers and soldiers of fortune. Fights broke out in the front bar of the hotel, and on occasion shots were fired. There were times when WH himself had to produce his handgun to quell a disturbance. With a young family, these disturbances bothered Mary deeply, and she would draw the children into the house when violence erupted.

One evening in September, Mary made sure that the children were in bed and settled. Mrs. Trethewey, who had replaced WH's first housekeeper, having made tea and set the oats to soak overnight for the morning breakfast, had taken herself off to her lodgings. WH was chairing a small and nascent secular group in a meeting room at the rear of the hotel. Even though not all of the community members were churchgoers, not all nonbelievers were prepared to profess their lack of faith by joining the gathering of secularists. WH told Mary that there were only three or four men, five at most, who turned up. Apart from anything else, the participants had to have reasonable literacy skills, as the meeting discussed pamphlets and tracts, some written by WH himself, that were circulated prior to the meeting.

Mary settled herself in the parlour with a cup of tea, and waited for her husband to return. She had some news for him. Presently she heard the creak of the kitchen door. Ever considerate, he never entered by the front door when the children were sleeping. She listening to him pouring a cup of tea, adding hot water to the pot to freshen the brew. He then joined her in the parlour. She asked him about the meeting. Only two other members of the group turned up. They spent the evening discussing a pamphlet written by a member of the British secular association which documented a string of logical and logistical fallacies in the New Testament, such as the impossibility of Jesus having been born in Bethlehem, and the omission of any mention of David, brother of Jesus.

Mary had heard all of this before. She listened patiently, before sharing her news. Despite her vow, following the death of the twins, that she would bear him no more children, she was, once more, with child. WH took her hands and reassured her. By the standards of the day, they were very old to be parents: he was about to turn 40, and Mary would be 38 by the time the child was born. But age, of itself was no reason for pessimism. They would take things as they came, as they had always done. Mary gently withdrew her hands from his and folded them on the table. If this child were to meet with misfortune, she doubted that she herself would survive.

With the assistance of one of the Silverton women who had some experience as a midwife, in June of 1866 Mary gave birth to another daughter. In keeping with the practice of the day, the dining table provided the platform for the arrival of the baby. To the parents' relief, the child was born healthy. All its limbs were present and accounted for. They named her Sarah Elizabeth in honour of her dead sibling. Mary held the child, which had set up a thin wail in protest at being torn from the comfort and security of the womb. WH lifted the tiny thing from its mother's breast. With the discovery, some months before, of yet another promising seam, and now the birth of a healthy child, 1866 promised to be even better than the previous year.

William made the now-familiar trip by coastal steamer to Fishery Bay to visit his family, including baby sister Sarah Elizabeth, who was now three months old. It was early spring, and a bitter wind, which whipped up white-capped waves, drove him off his preferred spot on the deck. He perched on a stool next to Captain Jones. They had become friends of a sort over the course of many such trips. As they neared Cape Jervois, the captain pointed to a shoal of rocks where another coastal schooner had gone down the previous month with the loss of all on board.

It was good to get away, if only for a long weekend. He had outgrown the Port Adelaide school, where he was the oldest pupil by several years. Academically, he had also outgrown the teachers. When he pointed out an arithmetic error made by one of them, the teacher asked him if it weren't time for him to leave school and get a real job.

During the visit, he marvelled at Mary Ann's prettiness, was treated to an impromptu family concert organized by Thomas John and cradled the baby while he worked at his books. He had embarked on the study of

Welsh, and had stuttering conversations with his parents over supper. On the last day of his visit, his father led him through the bush to view the recently discovered ore seam. On the way back to the Manager's residence, situated on a hill, inside the mining lease, WH informed William that he would be accompanying him back to Adelaide. He had a meeting with the company directors. He had other news. William would not be returning to Port Adelaide School.

Relieved, but also shocked, William asked, "So what will I do?" Was his father going to consign him to the world of work?

"I have arranged an appointment with the headmaster of St. Peter's College."

St. Peter's was the preeminent school in the colony. It was also staunchly Anglican. Before William could ask the obvious question, his father went on, "Given your scholarly gifts, St. Peter's is unquestionably the best place for you. I have encouraged you to think for yourself. You know where I stand on matters of religion. Where you stand, or come to stand, is up to you."

The minute they entered the headmaster's office, William's first thought was, "This is where I belong." The floor-to-ceiling, book-lined shelves, the smell of beeswax, the floor, so highly polished that it reflected his own highly polished shoes: he had never been in such a room, but it possessed an uncanny familiarity. He had entered a parallel universe, "I've been here before," he said to himself. As they were ushered into the office, the Reverend F. Williams, M.A., rose from his immense mahogany desk and strode across the room to greet them. He directed them to leather armchairs surrounding a low table piled with papers and books. After the introductions, he interviewed William, while WH scanned the bookshelves. "You can take the measure of a man," William used to hear him say, "by the books on his shelves."

To William, it felt less like an interview than a conversation with a distant, kindly relative. What were his interests and accomplishments? More importantly, what were his values? At points in the conversation, William looked uncertainly at his father, but WH kept his eyes steadily focused on the bookshelf above William's head. At the end of the interview, the headmaster made a short speech which might have been, and probably was, rehearsed. In addition to its focus on academic excellence, the school was committed to building the character and values of its students. They would leave the college with courage, integrity, morality and honour. They would use the knowledge and the gifts that had been honed at the school, not to advance themselves, but to serve the community.

"You are an admirable candidate," he said. "All that is left is for you to go through the formality of sitting the entrance test. This can be done immediately under the supervision of the head prefect, Mr. Borthwick."

Given the Reverend Williams' enthusiasm for William and his prospects for entry to St. Peter's, it came as an unwelcome surprise to both father and son, to discover, on returning to the College later that afternoon that William had not done as well on the entry test as had been expected. "It was the Latin paper that let him down," the headmaster reported to a crestfallen WH. "But with some concentrated study in that direction, I would expect him to pass on a re-sit. Would you be in a position to assist with some private tuition?"

"Of course," replied WH without hesitating.

"Excellent. I shall consult the head of Classics, who, I am sure, will be able to arrange tutorial sessions. I will contact you once the arrangements have been made." They shook hands, and father and son departed.

William was devastated by this setback. He set high standards for himself and was his own harshest critic. He felt that he had let his parents down, his father in particular. Most sons his age would have left school at the age of eleven, if they had attended school at all, and entered the world of work in order to help support the family. His father had never wavered when it came to his scholarly ambitions. On the contrary, in his father, he found his greatest champion, and he appreciated WH's efforts to console him on this setback.

You are no stranger to adversity, William was reminded. He had struggled with his physical affliction from the age of two, at a time when society viewed debility of any kind as a condemnation from above. The course of his life would not always run true. The ebb and flow of success and failure were part of the tapestry of life. The key was persistence in the face of adversity. In relation to his physical health, he had learned this lesson early in life. But it was a lesson that applied equally, if not more so, to the interior life. To this point, he had attended schools where he had excelled in comparison with his peers: in fact, he was largely self-taught. Now he was seeking admission to an institution devoted to serious scholarship. It was to his credit, WH reminded him, that he had come so close to passing the entrance examination without private tutoring.

Sitting in the study cum office his father maintained in their Port Adelaide home, William half-listened to WH's well-meaning homilies. In the kitchen, the housekeeper clattered about preparing their evening meal. He loved learning for its own sake. He would do the necessary cramming required for entry to St. Peter's, but would not let rote learning redefine his scholarly life. ß

With the assistance of a tutor, William turned his considerable talents to mastering Latin while also extending his knowledge of the other subjects at which he excelled. He was determined to pass the entrance examination and earn entry to St. Peter's at the beginning of the spring term. His tutor and the Reverend Williams decided that he would be able to re-sit the examination by the end of May. However, early in May, he received a message from Talisker. He was to return to the Peninsula with the utmost urgency. Although there was no indication of the nature of the crisis, he knew that his father would not have recalled him for anything less than a major disaster which could only concern a member of the family. Packing his bag, and dispatching a note to the Reverend Williams, he left for Talisker the following morning. The day was overcast. A bank of black clouds gathering on the horizon promised rain.

His apprehension grew as the barge that ferried him from the schooner approached the shore. The bullock dray and driver were waiting for him, but there was no sign of his father. He threw his bag into the dray and scrambled abroad.

"What's happened?" he asked. "Where's my father?"

"He's waiting for you," replied the driver, but would say no more.

When the bullock dray drew up to the manager's house, his father emerged. He handed his bag to his father and clambered down. "It's the baby," he said. "She been having teething problems, and two days ago came down with an infection. The nurse hasn't been able to bring her temperature down. She's had two convulsions, and another one could be her last." After the death of the Cornish lad, WH had insisted that the mine's directors provide funds for the construction of an infirmary. Although he had no success in attracting a doctor to work in such a remote place, he managed to employ an experienced nurse who was able to deal with most routine accidents and maladies.

William looked around for his brothers and sisters. "They're at the school," said his father. "It's the best place for them right now."

He followed his father into the house. His mother sat in a darkened bedroom holding Sarah Elizabeth in her arms. The nurse hovered nearby, handing Mary damp cloths to swab the baby in an attempt to reduce her fever. William had only seen his little sister three times. His heart went out to the little child as well as to his mother. Fear and anxiety had etched deep lines into her face. She looked much older than her 38 years.

The child had another violent convulsion an hour after William had arrived. This one was too much for her tiny frame. She died a short time later. Henry, Mary Ann, Tom and Rebecca were fetched from the school. The family gathered around the tiny body that had been laid in its cot and covered in a cotton blanket. Mary sat next to the cot looking at her dead baby. Her hands were folded in her lap, and she seemed oblivious to her other children.

Three years earlier, William had listened to shovels striking on earth as miners excavated a grave for Cadan, the Cornish lad. Now he listened as a similar hole was prepared for his baby sister. Then, he had stood, head bowed in the stifling heat as the corpse was lowered into the grave. Now, as the child was interred, he and WH supported his mother, who was close to collapse. A short distance away, Cadan's grave was marked with a crude cross containing his name and date of birth. In keeping with WH's views, Sarah Elizabeth, like her three dead siblings, was buried in an unmarked grave. He had listened as Mary pleaded in vain for a simple plaque to mark the spot where their daughter lay, but WH would hear none of it. His father had made a short speech at Cadan's interment. Now, overcome with grief, he said nothing.

William was deeply affected by Sarah Elizabeth's death. He was not completely wedded to his father's philosophy and had observed the comfort that belief in a higher power brought to those who had lost a loved one. He had been encouraged by WH to read the Bible and various religious tracts. "To counteract the mistaken beliefs and false arguments of Christianity, you need to know their works better than they know them themselves." William was inclined to agree with his father's assessment of the King James' version as a magnificent world of literature, but was less sure of the assertion that, as such, it was a work of fiction. In fact, the blueprint for living set out in the New Testament was very much in line with his own growing convictions about how to live a good life in harmony with his fellow man. The factual anomalies in the Bible, such as the fact that Jesus could not have been born in Bethlehem, and that he was not an only child but had siblings, were of little importance to William. There were higher truths: putting aside violence, loving one's neighbour as oneself, educating children. These truths resonated strongly with William.

After the internment, Mary took to her bed. William sat in the darkened room that smelled of camphor and soap and held her hand. He learned that after the death of the twins, she had determined that she would bring no more children into the world. She repeated her vow to him, and this time she meant it. "There will be no more children," she said. And she was right.

Late one afternoon, as dusk descended on the city, William was limping along North Terrace, having finished his final Latin tutorial before re-sitting the examination for entry to St. Peter's College. Close to Ayer's House, where WH had initially rejected the overture to work at Talisker, his eye was caught by the warm glow of gas lights from a hall that looked oddly out of place on what was meant to be Adelaide's most elegant street. His natural curiosity led him towards the light. Entering the hall, he encountered a group of well-dressed men and women being addressed by a tall, besuited speaker with a shock of white hair. This was no group of working-class rabble-rousers.

William stood at the rear of the hall and listened to the speech. He had attended several meetings of the Secular Association in the company of his father, and at first, he thought that he had stumbled into such a meeting. The speaker's tone and cadence were identical to that of the secularists he had met. However, as he tuned in to the speaker's theme, he realized that this was a meeting of a very different kind. The speaker addressed social issues with which the secularists were in sympathy. The man's voice rose as he called for women's suffrage, and for the protection of women and children in factories where the children in particular were treated as slaves and forced to endure unspeakable conditions. The physical abuse of women and children was far more widespread than was commonly perceived, and the need to expose the abuse, both in the home and the workplace was critical. William listened to the speech with interest as it resonated with his own sympathy for social justice, a sympathy born partly out of his struggle against discrimination, partly from his upbringing, and partly out of natural inclination.

The speaker then took aim at the root cause of the violence: alcohol was the source of the moral and social ills of the day, and nothing short of a total legislated ban was acceptable. As he rehearsed facts and figures to support his argument, several younger men circulated through the sizeable audience handing out pamphlets. One of them handed a pamphlet to William and drew him aside. "I haven't seen you here before," he said. There was a pronounced Welsh lilt to his voice. William admitted that this was his first meeting.

At the end of the meeting, he left the hall and was making his way along North Terrace when the young man caught up and fell into step beside him. He introduced himself as Gwyn Walker, and asked if William would be joining them the following week. "I'm working on establishing a branch of the Band of Hope, here in Adelaide," said Walker, "and I'm looking for young people such as yourself to join me."

"I would need to know more," replied William cautiously.

"You will find basic information in the pamphlet. I can answer any questions you might have after you have read it."

As he waited for the Port Adelaide cab, William felt a slight sense of unease. Like his siblings, he had been raised as an atheist. Members of the meeting he had stumbled into were clearly anything but. The banner pinned to the wall behind the speaker's head read "International Order of Rechabites." He had never heard of the organization, although he knew that the Rechabites were an ancient Jewish tribe that foreswore alcohol among other things.

From the pamphlet, he learned that the Band of Hope was born out of the Christian temperance movement. Its mission was to educate children about the evils of alcohol. In order to join the Band of Hope, it was necessary to sign a pledge foreswearing the use of alcohol in any form. That would be no problem for William, who had no need or desire for any substances stronger than tea. What interested him was the mission to work with children. Once he had finished high school, it was his intention to become a teacher. At the end of his third meeting at the Rechabite hall, he signed the pledge and began working as a Band of Hope volunteer under the guidance of Gwyn Walker. He also had the temperance pledge tattooed on his left arm in Indian ink. In a short time, William's enthusiasm for the work saw him elevated to organizer. Although WH had always insisted that William and his siblings should make up their own minds on moral issues, he was concerned about the reaction of his father when he learned of William's conversion to the Christian cause.

When WH returned to Adelaide for meetings with the mine shareholders and to facilitate William's entry into St. Peter's College, he immediately noticed the tattoo which William made no attempt to hide by wearing a shirt or jacket: that would have been cowardice. William noticed the flicker of confusion and disappointment on WH's face, but his father said nothing at that time.

William settled quickly into school life. Because of his physical affliction, he was unable to take part in sports, which were highly valued in the college with its ethos of a healthy mind in a healthy body. His maturity, gentle nature, and commitment to his studies earned him the respect of the teachers and the admiration of his fellow students. He studied a wide range of subjects and was particularly fond of languages. While the other students were on the playing field, he taught himself French, German, and Welsh, and made a serious assault on Latin, the subject that had held up his entry to the college. His work was so outstanding that he was awarded the prestigious Westminster Scholarship, His father attended the award ceremony, and looked on proudly, even as Bishop Short handed him the Westminster Scholarship with a "God Bless you."

On graduating, he did what he always intended to do—joined the Board of Education. And his first posting was to the Talisker school. Rather than moving in with his parents, he took a room in the Silverton Hotel. After the regular school day, he ran voluntary temperance classes for young people, and in the evening offered literacy classes for those miners who wanted to learn to read and write.

In 1870, the year that William began his career as a teacher at Talisker school, WH had grim news for the directors of the Company. As usual, he travelled to the head office in Hindley Street to deliver his annual report. He didn't beat around the bush. All of the shallow reserves of ore had been exhausted. While the main shaft was still productive, the quality of the ore deteriorated the deeper they excavated. "We've reached the water table, and the pumping engine is having difficulty removing the volume of water required to continue operations. I've suspended smelting, and most of the miners have been redeployed to doing development work on the surface."

"How long do you give the mine?" asked the chairman.

"Two years at best," replied WH.

"Is there any chance that another seam might be found?"

WH shook his head. He had surveyed the accessible land up to a mile from the existing site. There were no other seams in the area.

"Gentlemen, we must be prepared for the closure of the mine," said the chairman.

It was no satisfaction to WH when, exactly two years later, his prediction came true. At an extraordinary general meeting, the directors and shareholders voted to close the mine. By this time, only fifty miners remained. They had received no wages for two months. WH negotiated for them to be offered alternative employment at one of the company's other mines in the Copper Triangle north-west of Adelaide. WH himself was offered and accepted the position of captain at the New Cornwall Mine at Kadina.

On his return to Talisker, WH had the melancholy duty of announcing the closure of the mine to the inhabitants of Silverton. The news came as a shock to no one. He noticed his son, William, standing on the periphery of the group. He had already informed his son of the closure, and the fact that he would have to find another position.

William's reply had surprised him. He had written to the Board of Education and had been offered a teaching post at the Ebenezer Chapel School, in Rundle Street.

The following night, WH was woken from a restless sleep by a loud commotion in the centre of the settlement. Pulling trousers and a jacket over his pyjamas, he rushed outside and was horrified to see flames leaping from the upper floor of the Silverton Hotel. His first thought was for William and was relieved to see him standing with a knot of other residents in a clearing some distance from the blaze. There was nothing to be done, and within a very short time the hotel was reduced to a pile of smouldering rubble. The destruction of the dwelling was eerily emblematic of the demise of the mines themselves. When news of the fire reached head office in Adelaide, the chairman asked WH if it could have been arson on the part of disaffected miners. WH refused to countenance such a notion. His men were completely loyal to him and that company. Had they not continued working at the mine without wages?

WH was concerned about the effect of the move on his wife. Mary had never fully recovered from the death of Sarah Elizabeth, and her physical and mental health continued to deteriorate. On a given day, she didn't want to leave Talisker, the next she couldn't wait to get away. Only nine-year-old Rebecca would accompany them to Kadina. William's career as a teacher was assured, and with his appointment to a school in Adelaide, he would reside in the family home in Port Adelaide. Eighteen-year-old Mary Ann, who had taken up nursing, was already living in the house. Henry, who was nineteen, had left Talisker two years before and was working for a farmer on Kangaroo Island. Particularly pleasing to WH was the fact that Thomas John had been accepted as a pupil at St. Peter's College.

In 1873, the year that Captain Price, Mary and Rebecca moved to the Copper Triangle, the area was second only to Adelaide in terms of population. After Talisker, it seemed a major metropolis. The year was a busy one for WH. He reopened the New Cornwall Mine at Moonta at the beginning of the year. In April he was also appointed as superintendent of the Great Britain Mine. He made regular trips to Adelaide to report to the directors of the mines as well as to check on William, Mary Ann and

Thomas John. The trips also gave him an opportunity to attend meetings of the Secular Association, which he had helped to establish some years before.

As the year progressed, Mary seemed to settle into life in Kadina. Her physical health improved, and she developed an interest in gardening. She even made some friends. The young woman he had loved and married in Wales had come back to him, he thought. In all ways but one. They slept in separate rooms, as they had done since the death of their daughter at Talisker. Mary had meant it when she told her eldest son that there would be "no more children."

In the middle of April in 1874, he travelled to Adelaide to present his annual report to the Board. The city-based directors were pleased with the healthy financial state of the mines that WH ran. The chairman proposed he be granted a generous bonus, and the Board unanimously agreed. He returned to Kadina in a buoyant mood. However, as dusk descended, he entered the house to find that all was not well.

"It's Mother," said Rebecca.

WH strode to Mary's room. He found his wife writhing on the bed. Mrs. Trethewey, the elderly housekeeper who had accompanied the family from Talisker, was cleaning up traces of vomit.

"She's been like this for most of the day. We were waiting for you to come home."

"Fetch Dr Fisk," said WH, removing the towel from the housekeeper. He tried speaking to Mary, but she didn't respond.

When the doctor arrived, he asked WH to leave the room while he examined Mary. Twenty minutes later, he came out and told Rebecca to go to her mother. When the girl had left the room, Fisk said, "She has an internal rupture. It could be a tumour, but because it came on suddenly, I suspect it's a ruptured appendix."

"What's to be done?" asked WH.

Fisk shook his head. "Just keep her as comfortable as possible. I've given her morphine, and I've left a bottle in the room. There's nothing else can be done. Get your children here as soon as you can. And don't stint on the morphine. It's all that can be done for her now."

Two days later, on April 16, Mary passed away. She was surrounded by her husband and children. Little Rebecca, distraught with grief, flung herself on her mother's corpse, crying out, "Mama, Mama, wake up." She had to be physically removed from the bed and carried from the room. As his siblings filed from the room, William lingered behind. He looked at his father, who nodded. "If it will give you comfort. But you know you mother's views." When WH left the room and pulled the door to, William bowed his head and prayed for his mother. The following day, in keeping with WH's principles and her own wishes, Mary was buried in an unmarked grave in an un-consecrated section of the Kadina cemetery.

Several weeks after his mother's death, William returned from the Ebenezer school to find his father and sister Rebecca sitting in the kitchen of their Port Adelaide home. He was surprised to learn that WH had resigned as mining superintendent at the Great Britain mine and decided to return to the city. He would be working for his former employers, prospecting for ore in the Adelaide Hills and adjacent districts.

William detected a change in his father's demeanour. Clearly deeply affected by his wife's death, he appeared withdrawn and somewhat remote. He would go off for days at a time on prospecting expeditions leaving the children, including eleven-year-old Rebecca, to fend for themselves. When he was not off prospecting, he would bury himself in his books or attend meetings of the Secular Association.

Then, at the beginning of June, WH surprised his children by announcing that he had been offered, and accepted, the position of Captain at the newly established Mount Coova mine in the interior of Queensland. He would leave South Australia by ship the following week. Apart from the occasional postcard and letter, they heard little from their father for over a year. Then, at the beginning of December 1875, he returned to Adelaide, his reappearance being as sudden and unexpected as his departure. Towards the end of his very long life, William occasionally reflected on the fact that his father's return set off a chain of events that was to have a profound impact on all of their lives.

Chapter 5
Land of Eternal Sunshine

Oh, the delicious joy of seeing Aberdeen, grim city of her childhood, disappear into the banks of rolling mist. She, her parents and siblings are on a small passenger ship heading down the coast to London where they will board the brand-new clipper ship, the *Patriarch,* Aberdeen-built it is reckoned to be one of the fastest in the world. The passenger ship struggles through the oily waters as though it is as anxious as she to put the city behind her: a city in decline with the demise, first of the textile, and then the whaling industries. Shipbuilding is all the city has left, or so her father said. At fifteen, Annie knew next to nothing about commerce and industry, and nor did she care. They are bound for Australia, the Bright New World. Bound for a land of eternal sunshine, where freezing fogs and the dank stink of a once magnificent, but now crumbling industrial city, were unknown

In school, she had been told to be proud of her name. The Forbes clan was one of the oldest and largest in Scotland. Well, the teacher would say that, being a member of the clan herself. Annie had been born on August 7, 1855, eldest daughter to Alexander Forbes and Helen Muirden. Seven siblings followed. And now they were on their way to a new life in a new world.

They were emigrating to Australia because her father had been offered a position as overseer of a new cannery at the Australian Meat Company in northern New South Wales. Despite the name, the company was solidly English, having been launched in London by Charles Grant Tindal who had extensive holdings of land in Australia as well as his native England. "One of the wealthiest men in the Empire," her father had said.

Leaving London on the *Patriarch,* Annie stayed on deck. As she braced herself against the wind, she sensed an eye on her back. She turned and confronted a stocky young man standing several feet away with a coil of rope slung over his shoulder. He was one of the crew. He grinned at her.

"Don't fall in," he said in an accent very different from her own. "We can't turn back to fetch you."

"Don't fall in yourself," she replied at once.

"What's your name?"

"Who wants to know?"

"Harry."

"Well, Harry, do you not have a job to do?"

"Well, you're a bold young wench, aren't you?"

"Watch your mouth."

He laughed. "For someone so young, you have a lot to say for yourself."

"You're not so old yourself."

"Older than you. And I reckon I know a lot more, too."

"Reckon as much as you like."

"Want to see the ship? I can show you below deck."

Looking past him, she noticed her father standing a short distance away.

"I have to go," she said, pushing past the young sailor.

"Well, take care of yourself—Mystery Miss."

"Who was that?" her father asked when she joined him.

"Just a deckhand."

"Well, keep away from him and his like."

Five days out from London, the clipper ran into a massive storm. The sails were furled to save the masts, and the ship was tossed about as though it were a toy. Passengers were told there was nothing to be done but ride it out. The passengers huddled in their cramped quarters and prayed. Many were sick, and rivulets of vile liquid slopped back and forth. She would rather be up on deck than stuck down here like a trapped animal. She alone was unafraid. What was the point of fear? It wouldn't make the storm abate. Her father did his best to comfort his wife and the younger children, but she could tell from his voice that he, like the others, was afraid. When night fell, the cabin was plunged into a darkness so intense she felt its weight like a black shroud. The shrieks, the vomiting and the entreaties to the Lord were the only indications that they were not alone.

As dawn broke, the storm relented, and she, along with the rest of the passengers, rushed onto the deck to be greeted by a gentle ocean and a sky so startlingly blue that it hurt her eyes.

Several of the passengers had sustained injuries from being thrown about and had to be treated by the ship's surgeon. One elderly man had died, presumably from a heart attack, and was buried at sea. Annie, along with a knot of other passengers, observed the simple ceremony. The captain said a brief prayer, and then the weighted shroud was bundled over the side by three deckhands, including Harry. It was the first time she had seen him since their encounter at the beginning of the journey. As he turned away from the ocean, he caught her eye and gave her an insolent wink.

For several days after the storm they were practically becalmed. The captain told Alexander that the clipper ship, which could reach twenty knots an hour, was barely making five. Bored, she took her box of painting materials onto the deck and settled down to her favourite pastime. But very soon even that grew boring. Spending endless hours painting an endless ocean and populating the sky with imaginary gulls could hold her lively imagination for just so long.

"Pretty work there, Annie."

Startled, she swivelled her head. How had Harry discovered her name? Later, she realized that it would not have been difficult. If he could read, and it seemed that he could, a scan of the passenger manifest which contained the names and ages of all on board would have told him what he wanted to know.

The following day, she decided to explore parts of the ship that she hadn't yet seen. In the aft hold, one of the doors that had been locked on a previous excursion yielded to her touch. She knew that this part of the ship was off limits to passengers, but she entered the hold without a second thought. The space held brass-bound passenger trunks, crates of dry goods for consumption on the journey, and barrels of water. The musty air smelled strongly of tar. A rat scuttled across her feet, making her jump. There was nothing of interest for her here. Disappointed, she turned away, and was about to leave when he came through the door.

"Well, well, well," he said, mocking her accent. "The beautiful

Aberdeen Annie. What could she be doing down here where she don't belong? Waiting for Harry perchance?"

She was about to dismiss his comment on her looks: beautiful she was not. As she matured, she had been called a handsome young lady by friends of her father, but never a beauty. Before she could reply, he stepped forward, pushed her back against a crate, and kissed her roughly on the mouth. She was too surprised to respond. The rum on his breath was as alien as his tongue. His calloused hand held her head firmly to his muscular arms made escape impossible. She had never been kissed, had never even been touched by an unfamiliar male. Strangely, although the act was alien, it was not entirely repugnant. Her heart pounded, partly from shock, and partly from something else. And the fluttering sensation in her stomach—that was entirely new. He finally pulled away, leaving her dazed and confused. He turned and walked wordlessly from the hold, leaving her leaning against the crate wondering what had just happened.

Finally, she left the hold, made her way upstairs and paced the deck. It was a beautiful day, with a brisk breeze speeding the ship towards the equator, although they were not yet far enough south to feel any real warmth in the sun. She thought of nothing in particular, but realized that occasionally her eyes wandered surreptitiously in search of Harry Dearmer. Harry, however, was nowhere to be seen. The tedium that had overtaken her as the trip progressed had been replaced by an emotion of a different sort. Harry represented danger, that she knew. But his presence also promised an antidote to the enervating boredom of shipboard life, and the hint of danger was not entirely unwelcome.

Two mornings later, she returned to the aft hold and was disappointed to find the door securely locked. She returned to the deck, intending to spend the morning contemplating the ocean, but after an hour found herself drawn again into the bowels of the ship. Finding the hold still securely locked she began retracing her steps, when Harry appeared. He took her hand and led her back to the door, which he unlocked, hurried her inside, and locked it behind them. This time a forceful hand on the back of her head was unnecessary, but was free to roam over her neck and face. Again, she tasted the rum on his tongue, and inhaled his male scent. The scent, which she might once have found repugnant, excited her. Wilful and headstrong, it never occurred to her to wonder what she was getting herself into. It would be some years before she came to regret, the day she had ever set eyes on Harry Dearmer.

They agreed to vary the times at which they met to minimize the chances of being caught. Alexander was no fool, and he had already warned her off Harry. Harry would nominate a time when it suited his schedule. The trysts broke the monotony of her day, and she was disappointed, if not outright hurt, on those occasions when he failed to show up because his duties had been changed. One day, as she approached the door at the hour they had agreed upon, she found a work detail in the storeroom removing crates of provisions for the galley. One of them spotted Annie. "You're not supposed to be down here, Miss," he said.

"Sorry," she replied, and retreated.

Several days later, Harry failed to turn up at the appointed time. She sat on a barrel for twenty minutes, then dejectedly headed for the door, when it was flung open, and Harry strode in. He was unsteady on his feet, and she could tell at once that he had been drinking more heavily than usual. Instead of returning her smile, he took her by the shoulders and propelled her backwards across the room. She was too shocked to protest. He pushed her skirts above her waist and shoved her onto a crate. Her knees buckled when they struck the edge of the crate, and her exposed buttocks landed heavily on the splintered top. Although she made no attempt to struggle, he held her down with one hand while he unbuckled himself with the other. Then he lifted her legs, fumbled and poked, and finally managed to enter her. When she gasped at the sharp pain, he shoved his calloused hand across her mouth. Despite her precocity in other areas of life, she was innocent in the ways of sex. It had shocked her when she began to menstruate at the age of thirteen and had to be reassured by her mother that she was not bleeding to death from some internal malady. She had giggled with her school friend Tess, when told of what happened to Tess's older sister on her wedding night. Now she was experiencing it at first hand, not on her wedding night, but on a packing crate in the hold of a clipper ship.

Her buttocks were bruised by the cruel planks as he continued to shove himself in and out of her. She hadn't seen it, but could feel its bulk. Her only sightings of the male appendage were those of her younger brothers. She had no idea that those shrivelled pink sausages could grow to such proportions. The pounding seemed to go on for an age, each thrust deeper and more painful than the one before. Finally, he gave a groan as though it was he, who had been penetrated, shuddered, and rolled away. As he stood up, she glimpsed the thing that had penetrated her. It had shrunk, but still dangled ominously as he moved about.

He shoved a piece of rag between her legs before pulling down her skirts. "Better keep that there for a while," he said gruffly. Then, more gently, "I did what I had to do. I needed that."

She was thankful none of the family was below deck when she returned to their quarters. When she inspected herself, she was horrified to find the rag covered in blood, and quickly replaced it with a rag she used when menstruating. Lying there, she thought about what he had said—that he needed her. She was certain that's what she heard. Did that make it all right? She wasn't sure. What she did know for certain was that it would never happen that way again. Next time, if there were ever a next time, it would be on her terms.

She was lying on her bunk with her face to the bulkhead when she heard her mother and two of the younger children return. Feigning sleep, she listened as her mother, noticing the bloody rag on the floor, scooped it up and dispensed with it as she always did on those occasions when Annie carelessly left her rags lying in view of her younger siblings.

For a week she kept to herself. When at last she allowed herself to be seen on deck, he fell into step beside her. He had been waiting for her to reappear. "This afternoon," he said, before disappearing through a side door. She continued her slow stroll around the ship, nodding to the other passengers as if nothing had happened, as if her life hadn't changed forever.

That afternoon, she returned to the hold. The storeroom door was unlocked. Inside, he lounged on a crate. He grinned at her, certain in the knowledge that she would come. He rose to his feet as she approached. She let him kiss her and stroke her cheek, but when he reached to lift her skirts, she drew back and slapped his face with all the strength she could muster. He reeled back, shocked. The battle line had been drawn.

Alexander Forbes was keenly aware that he and his family were part of the great mid-to-late-century diaspora from the British Isles. In 1870, the year they abandoned their homeland, more than 300,000 people left Britain, a disproportionate number of them Celts. Few of them, the Forbes family included, would ever return. Alexander was a measured, kindly man. Some even called him timid. He knew that. Yes, he was a member of the Forbes clan, but got no particular satisfaction from that. In fact, he had sprung from humbler stock, his father and grandfather being crofters and fishermen and had no contact with the aristocratic Baron Forbes who resided in Castle Forbes, the family seat 25 miles west of Aberdeen. Married at 20, he worked initially as a clerk, but worked his way into management in the manufacturing industry. He felt no guilt at abandoning clan and country, just the usual trepidation at the challenge of transporting his family safely to the end of the earth.

The long journey he had made to Hampshire to meet Charles Tindal bore fruit in the form of a letter inviting him to travel to Australia and take up the position of overseer of Tindal's new meat processing plant in northern New South Wales: the latest addition to the Australian Meat Company which had been established five years earlier. It would be a challenging position, and the canning operation would require the slaughter and processing of some 35,000 head of cattle annually. The canned product would provide a significant source of protein for the British nation. He was an engineer and knew next to nothing about the cattle industry. What he did know about, and why he got the job, was canning in general, and the revolutionary Liebig canning process in particular. Liebig refined the process invented by the French to get food to Napoleon's troops without it having to be salted. It enabled food produced in one place, such as beef in Australia, to be transported vast distances to consumers in Britain.

There were good reasons for taking on the challenge of transporting his reclusive wife and clutch of children from the once fine city of Aberdeen to a land rumoured to be festering with deadly snakes, spiders and other insects as well as a fractious indigenous population. "The only good Aborigine is a dead one," he had been told by a colleague who had been to the Antipodes and lived to tell stories about it. The Aberdeen of Alexander's childhood was not the Aberdeen of today. He saw no future for his children in the city of his growing years.

He worried particularly about his headstrong eldest daughter. Although not conventionally pretty, Annie was outgoing and vivacious. At fifteen, she was already turning heads in Aberdeen: another reason for leaving the place. But they hadn't been on board the *Patriarch* five minutes before heads swivelled in her direction. An observant man, and no fool, he was aware of the temptation she offered to the single male passengers as well as the ship's crew. One in particular, a burly young crewman called Harry Dearmer, was persistent in his attentions. Alexander could sense trouble in other men, and Harry reeked of it. On several occasions he had warned Annie not to encourage the sailor, but his words had had little effect. No good could come of this relationship: he felt it in his bones. But short of pushing Harry overboard, there was nothing he could do.

When the *Patriarch* entered Sydney Heads, everyone was on deck. It was a splendid introduction to the most spectacular harbour on Earth. They arrived on a morning in early January 1871. The sun, high in an azure sky, was benign on this particular day. How disorienting it was to encounter high summer in January. The sheer, sandstone cliffs guarding the entrance to the Harbour were topped with alien, olive-leaved trees. Birds wheeled over the ship's masts, emitting raucous screeches that frightened the children. On the water, vessels of many shapes and sizes ferried people and goods from one end of the Harbour to the other. Surely, there could be no greater contrast between the sight of Aberdeen slipping into history, and the one that greeted them as, aided by a stiff nor' easterly breeze, the *Patriarch* sailed between the heads. Making its way slowly into Sydney Harbour, the clipper passed Circular Quay, site of the original settlement of Sydney, and now its main commercial hub. It rounded a headland, and dropped anchor in the adjacent Darling Harbour.

Darling Harbour was a confusion of activity, serving both as a commercial port and a passenger terminal. In addition to the *Patriarch*, two other clippers had recently arrived. A brig flying the flag of the United States was at anchor a short distance away. Barges, lighters, and other smaller vessels bustled around the larger ships like supplicants as passengers and goods were disgorged.

As soon as they had disembarked and been processed through the arrival shed, Alexander arranged for the onward transportation of their possessions to their new home at Ramornie Station, situated on the Clarence River, northwest of Grafton. The Forbes family would travel to Ramornie the following week. In the interim, they would stay at a hotel in Darling Harbour. He had been assured by his new employer that despite its location, the hotel was "perfectly respectable."

Once they had settled into their rooms, Annie asked to speak to her father in private. In a parlour on the ground floor, she made the announcement he had feared. She would not be coming with them but would stay with Harry in Sydney. Alexander knew that she had continued seeing the deckhand during the course of the voyage, and that a deep attachment had formed, but had no idea it had come to this. Normally a mild-mannered man, he rose from his chair. "I forbid it," he thundered. "This nonsense has gone on long enough." He should have been more forthright on the ship. Had it out with Dearmer. Gone to the captain. "Get back upstairs at once. You're still a child. That scoundrel has turned your head." He had never spoken to anyone like this before—certainly never one of his children. His anger stemmed from grief and a deep sense of guilt. He had let his headstrong daughter have her way from childhood because he feared her indomitable will. He had failed in his duty as a father, and now he risked losing her altogether. He fell back into his chair and put a hand to his head.

His words had rattled her, and a flicker of uncertainty crossed her face, but then she picked up the calico bag at her feet, and headed, not for the stairs, but the door. By the time he had regained his feet, she was gone. He rushed from the hotel, searched the bustling streets in vain, and then returned slowly to the hotel to inform his wife that their child had been lost to them. Poor, timid Helen collapsed on hearing the news. The smaller children were utterly confused. Where was the big sister they adored? Fourteen-year-old Helena was particularly distraught. Her sister was precious to her. Helena was more like her mother in temperament and admired Annie's wild streak as well as her compassion. She could never be that sister to the younger siblings. Turning her face to the wall, she let her grief tumble in streams to the pillow.

When they finalised their plans, several days out from Sydney, Harry had suggested she leave a note for her parents and slip away. That way she could avoid complications, such as the possibility that her father might contact the law—or what passed for the law in that part of the world. She shook her head. Sneaking away was not in her nature. Now sixteen, and mature for her age, she was practically an adult. She was capable of making decisions about the direction of her own life. She loved her parents, and her parents loved her. Her father was a rational man. She would speak to him. He would see reason and talk her mother around.

It was a shock to discover that, when it came to her future, her father was neither as rational nor as reasonable as she had thought. When they finalized their plans for being together, Harry had given her clear instructions on how to find him. It was simple, he said. Once she left the hotel in Darling Harbour, all she had to do was follow the line of the harbour around to the adjacent Circular Quay. He would be waiting for her in an area bounding the western edge of the Quay. "Ask for me here," he said, thrusting a piece of paper into her hand. In his surprisingly neat hand was written: *The Seaman's Mission, George Street, The Rocks*. The last words he said to her before they parted were, "Just make sure you're there before night falls." He had told her that this was his maiden voyage to the Antipodes, but his easy familiarity with the topography of Sydney caused her to doubt this.

She had not expected her new home to be a Little Britain, but neither had she expected it to be so foreign. The sights, smells, and sounds were utterly unfamiliar. With the exception of one or two males who were well-tailored, most of the people she passed were shabbily dressed. While most of the accents were recognizably English—she even heard some Scots—others were an uncouth variety she took to be Australian. Many individuals were clearly foreign. At one point she passed a shop filled with Chinese men and caught a snatch of their high-pitched, sing-song language. It was her first sight of members of the Asiatic race, and although she knew it was rude, she couldn't help staring at their feminine-looking gowns, their pigtails, and their long-stemmed pipes. Little could she guess that one day far into the future she would move to Shanghai, where she would take to smoking a similar pipe.

The bustling street she hurried along ran parallel to the harbour.

While she couldn't see the water, the masts of the tall ships protruding above the warehouses lining the waterfront reassured her that she was on the right track. After about half a mile, she lost sight of the masts, and realized she must have reached the western limit of the harbour. She turned left off the thoroughfare and found herself in a maze of smaller streets lined with crudely constructed workers cottages. Ancient dogs lying in the dirt bared their teeth as she passed. An invisible rooster crowed somewhere in the distance. Women stared at her from open doorways. She realized that she was hopelessly lost.

It was now mid-afternoon, and the day was heating up. The bag on her shoulder grew heavy. There was no shade in the street, and the sun bit into the back of her neck. She stopped to address an older woman lounging in a doorway. Despite the heat of the day, the woman had a ragged shawl pulled around her shoulders. "Excuse me," said Annie, "I seem to be lost. Could you kindly give me directions to George Street?" The woman squinted at her, pulled the shawl more firmly around her shoulders, withdrew in the dim recess of the room, and slammed the door.

Stung by the woman's hostility, Annie had no option but to continue on her way. It was not only the woman's hostility that upset her, but also her refusal to even acknowledge Annie's existence. So much for Harry's breezy assertion that finding one's way about Sydney was easy. She came to a small square where several streets converged. The square looked a little more civilized than the warren she had just exited. It contained several two-storey, stone buildings, a couple of shops and a pub. In the centre of the square stood a scribbly eucalyptus tree. She rested for a moment under its shade. The leaves gave off a pleasant, spicy smell. She had just about worked up the courage to enter one of the shops to ask for directions, when two men came out of the pub. They were better dressed than the people she had encountered to this point in her trek. Seeing her, one of them said, "You look lost, my dear."

"I am," she replied, forcing a smile.

"Just off the boat, are we?" said the other man, on hearing her accent.

"That I am."

"If you're trying to find your way back to Darling Harbour, you're heading in the wrong direction," said the first man, hitching his thumbs into his open waistcoat.

"I've just come from there. I'm looking for George Street."

"Well you won't find it wandering around here. We're heading that way. Why don't you tag along?"

Both men had flat nasal drawls. She didn't find the accent at all pleasing to the ear but understood it well enough. By "tag along" she assumed she was being invited to accompany them. She fell in beside them. They crossed the square and entered a narrow street at right angles to the one from which she had entered the square. She hoped it hadn't been a mistake to go with the men.

"Where do you hail from?" asked the first, and more talkative of the men.

"Scotland. Aberdeen," she replied.

"Aberdeen," he echoed, mocking her accent by flapping his tongue on the 'r' and elongating the 'ee.'

Leaving the narrow street, they turned left onto a broad thoroughfare that she recognized as the one she'd originally been on. She'd been walking in circles in the maze of workmen's cottages. They made their way westward for a block, then the two men stopped in front of an office.

"This is us," said the talkative one. "Just keep on along this street to the end. You'll run into George Street. Where exactly do you need to get to?" For an answer, she fished out Harry's note. The man read the address, grinned and handed it to his companion, who gave a snort. "Reckon she's a pup?"

"Wouldn't think so—not a nicely dressed, well-mannered young woman like this. But you never can tell."

Annie's face reddened. She had no idea what "pup" referred to but knew it couldn't be a compliment. Her conclusion was correct. She later learned it was a slang term for prostitute. She was annoyed at their talking so openly about her rather than to her. She snatched the piece of paper out of the stranger's hand.

"Now, why would a nice young lady like you be going to the Sailors' Mission? You, fresh off the boat and all—or so you say."

"Mind your own business," she replied. Her cheeks burned, which added to her annoyance. "If you must know, I'm going to meet my fiancé."

For some reason, this amused the men greatly. "Well, dear, you'd better run along. You wouldn't want to keep your 'fiancé' waiting, now, would you?"

She fell into Harry's arms, less from emotion than exhaustion. He hurried her into the street away from the curious eyes of the other sailors. It was almost dark by the time he got her into the room he had taken a short distance from the Sailors' Mission. It was more a doss house than a hotel, but at least they had a room to themselves. It was the first time they had seen each other completely naked. His torso was heavily muscled, but she couldn't help noticing the thickening of his waist as he pushed her down. It was luxurious, sex for the first time on a bed rather than a splintered crate. Two things that hadn't changed: the rum on his breath, and his hunger for her.

Later, they ventured into the street for food. He knew of a tavern not far from the Mission that was safe. He took her arm and walked her down the centre of the street. "I told you to get here before nightfall," he said.

"And I did," she replied.

"Only just."

She decided not to argue, not on this night. For once he was right. It was not a safe place. You could smell danger in the shadows. When they were just short of the tavern, a tremendous wind began gusting from the south. She heard a distant rumbling, then a sharp crack as a sheet of lightning split the evening sky. Fat drops of rain spattered on the road. The rain quickly turned to a torrent, and they had to sprint the short distance to their destination.

The tavern was small and dark. It reeked of tobacco, alcohol and men. Although she had little appetite, she chewed on a lump of the mutton that was shoved at them on a tin plate. Harry drank pints of beer with rum chasers. He pressed on her a glass of rum diluted with warm water. It was her first experience of alcohol. It was sweeter than she had expected but burned the back of her throat. After several sips, she felt dizzy and pushed it aside. Harry struck up a conversation with one of the other patrons whom he had met during a day of drinking. She half-listened to the conversation and tried not to think of her family, particularly her younger sister Helena. When Helena's image came to mind, her resolve came close to crumbling

Once the storm abated, they made their way back to the hotel. On the way, she was startled by a drunk who lurched at them out of the blackness. Harry shoved him hard in the chest, and he fell into the mud, cursing them. "It's not the drunks you need to worry about," said Harry, who was a little unsteady himself, having topped up what he'd consumed during the day with several pints of beer and numerous shots of rum.

Despite the emotional and physical exhaustion of the day, she slept poorly. Harry did what he wanted with her, and fell into a heavy sleep, sprawled on his back, snoring heavily. She had never been one for regrets. Now, in the dark, she fended off mosquitoes just as she fended off the worm of doubt that worked its way into her mind. Where to from here? It was as though she had leapt from the deck of the *Patriarch*, but was yet to hit the water. Two overwhelming impulses, the romantic and the practical, went to war in her head. Harry had money for now, having been paid off by the shipping company, but the money wouldn't last long given the amount he spent on alcohol. They needed money, and they needed somewhere to live. As light began to seep through the rag that served as a curtain, she fell asleep, waking only when Harry reached for her.

The summer storm of the previous evening, referred to by locals as a "Southerly Buster," had cleared the oppressive heat and humidity of the previous day. Even the Rocks put on its best face as they stepped out into the fresh mid-morning day. She would come to look back on that first full day together as the best their relationship ever had.

Harry steered her straight to the tavern, which had quickly become his home from home, and seemed to operate twenty-four hours a day. They drank mugs of black tea, Harry's of course laced with rum, and gnawed at a rustic loaf smeared with jam. Annie, who was fond of food, and who would, in time, become an accomplished cook, only ate the bread because it filled a hole in her stomach. She craved protein: eggs and salt beef came to mind. Even the rancid mutton, rejected the previous evening, would have been welcome. Hopefully, they would be able to find something more substantial later in the day.

After they had consumed the rudimentary breakfast, Harry purchased a pint of rum which he shoved into his pocket, then led Annie down a flight of stone steps that ran beside the tavern. These took them to a dock lined with tall ships on the western side of Circular Quay. The quayside hummed with activity. Soldiers, whose scarlet tunics had faded to a dirty pink under the sun, strolled around pretending to keep order. Horse-drawn carriages bullied their way through the people on foot. Wagons, dodging street vendors, ferried goods from ships to warehouses and bond stores in the Rocks. Intoxicated with love and the exoticism of the place, she inhaled the confusion.

The colour and movement provided Annie with a distraction from the concerns of the night. Worrying comes naturally to the human mind but is ultimately futile. Today, she would put aside her concerns and enjoy herself. Making their way toward the eastern side of the Quay, they encountered a street market. Harry was happy to let her buy food. She drifted from one stall to the next, picking up a lump of cheese here, salted beef there. A loaf of bread. Ripe tomatoes from the market gardens to the west of the settlement. Harry took a pull on his pint of rum and handed over cash for the purchases.

They left the Quay and made their way further east, clinging as close as they could to the water without tumbling in. Eventually, they came to a high wall, constructed of Sydney sandstone, as were all of the substantial buildings they had passed. Entering a wrought-iron gate, they found themselves in a large public garden filled with an astonishing variety of exotic trees, plants and shrubs. In addition to the spicy eucalypts that were becoming familiar to her, the pathways were lined with shrubs bearing large scarlet leaves. As they descended the slope leading to the water, they passed a clump of stately palm trees, their branchless limbs reaching skyward and topped with spiky leaves. Who owns this magnificent garden? she wondered. They weren't trespassing, surely. The gate was open, and other members of the public were sauntering the paths.

The garden ended in a sea wall that separated it from a small cove, bounded on one side by the stores and warehouses of Circular Quay, and on the other by a wooded headland. Anne removed her shawl and placed it on the wall. She laid out their provisions, breaking the lump of cheese and loaf of bread into chunks. They ate without speaking, listening to the raucous screeching of the local birds that strolled about a short distance from them. She ate hungrily. By her side, Harry picked at the food and pulled on his rapidly depleting bottle of rum. On the water, a clipper ship accompanied by smaller craft, made its way toward its berth. This was the Australia she had imagined in the grim Aberdeen winter that preceded their departure.

The spell broke when Harry, his pint bottle now empty, decided it was time to return to the hotel by way of the tavern. He tossed the bottle into the Harbour where it bobbed for some time before sinking. He took her by the arm and steered her firmly back to the Rocks. She wanted to discover more of the garden's secrets and delights but realized by the firmness of his grip that he had other things in mind. It was of no great moment. There would be time enough to explore the gardens in the weeks and months to come—or so she thought.

By the time they got back to the tavern, the sun was low in the western sky. A crimson-stained bank of clouds was building on the horizon. As he had done the previous evening, Harry drank several pints of beer accompanied by rum chasers. He began in a buoyant mood, but when she suggested they return to the hotel his face turned ugly. In the short time they had been together, she had noticed how he could switch in a second from amiable, even affectionate lover, to hostile stranger. What seemed to her an innocent comment or a trivial incident could ignite him. He rarely shouted but seethed with a rage that was almost visible. Not wanting to ruin the day, she resisted her natural instinct to speak her mind. Finally, he signalled to the bartender to bring him a pint of rum, took her arm, and led her back to the hotel.

She thought of defying him, as she had at times on the ship when his behaviour displeased her or she wanted to remind him that she wasn't chattel. On this occasion, she submitted. And she was glad that she did. He displayed a rare tenderness, almost a sweetness, towards her. An hour passed. She fell into a deep sleep in his arms and slept the night through.

The previous day had ended well, and so in the morning, she decided she would tread lightly no longer. She would discuss their future together. She would not ask him what his plan was. The decisions had to be mutual: the relationship had to be a partnership. He listened in silence, then, when he spoke, his response shocked her profoundly. In order to finish his apprenticeship, he would be sailing with the *Patriarch* when it left Sydney. The sailor's life was the one he had chosen when he had been disowned by his parents. What did she expect? he demanded with a flash of aggression. How were they going to live? Did she want a life of servitude, she a domestic servant and he as handyman to some wealthy family?

And what did he expect her to do? she retorted. The answer shocked her even more. Go to Clarence River with her family. Settle at Ramornie Station and wait for him. When he had finished his apprenticeship, he would come for her. "I will marry you," he said. "And now," he said, waving the now-empty pint bottle, "I'm going out." When he returned an hour later, alcohol befuddled but looking forward to her arms and soft breasts, she had gone.

On Annie's abrupt departure, Alexander's wife had taken to her bed, and could not be persuaded out of it. "If you hadn't taken this position, this would never have happened," was all she said, and turned her head away from him. He was no less distraught, but being of a practical bent (he was, after all, an engineer, and a Scot to boot), he was determined to continue down the path on which they had embarked. He would not squander his emotional energy on events he could not control.

Having failed to comfort his wife, Alexander left the younger children in Helena's charge and made his way to the Australian Meat Company offices at Circular Quay. He was not to know it, but was following in his daughter's footsteps. Annie had passed this way not an hour before.

William Morris, a red-face, non-nonsense Englishman in charge of the Sydney operation, greeted him warmly. "We've been waiting for you," he said. "We're extremely anxious to see the cannery in operation. It will bring affordable meat to the people back Home." Alexander would get used to Great Britain being referred to as "Home." It was a term widely used throughout the country, even by some Native Sons who had never been north of the equator.

Morris showed him over the warehouse and explained the procedures for getting the preserved meat and other by-products of the industry such as tallow, artificial manure, hides and pelts, from Ramornie to Sydney, then onto ships bound for England. Alexander was impressed.

Despite Helen's accusatory comment, he felt that the decision to uproot his family had been the right one. They returned to Morris's office and finalized the arrangements for transporting the family from Sydney to northern New South Wales. They parted with a firm handshake. As well as acquiring a colleague, Alexander felt that he had made a friend.

"Could you spare the time to come by tomorrow? I'll have some paperwork drawn up which I need you to sign."

"Of course," replied Alexander.

The following morning, he did his best to coax Helen out of bed. With the window shut, and the curtains drawn, the room was stifling, although Helen didn't seem to notice. She sat up in bed, accepted a cup of tea, but refused to leave the bed.

"I have to go to the office," he said. "I won't be long." All he received in return was a sniff.

As it happened, he was gone longer than expected. Having dealt with the paperwork, William Morris said, "And now, I would say that it is about time for a spot of lunch. My club is just behind the Customs House. We'll go there." Although Alexander was anxious to get back to the family, it would be undiplomatic to turn down the luncheon invitation. In any case, Morris struck him as a man who would never take no for an answer. After lunch, they returned to the office as Morris wanted to double check the paperwork. He frowned and set several documents aside.

"Is there something wrong?" asked Alexander.

"Oh, it's just a minor formality. These documents have to be signed and sealed by the public notary. Unfortunately, that can't be don't today. I'm afraid that can't be done today. Would it be possible for you to come back tomorrow?"

"Certainly. I'm now officially an employee of the company. I can be here by 10 o'clock."

"Excellent."

The two men shook hand. Alexander returned to the hotel. The family had already eaten and retired to their rooms, so he had a a solitary meal, a whisky in the parlour, and retired to his own room. He tried to engage Helen in conversation, to tell her about his day, but she lay stiffly on the bed and refused to answer his questions.

It was mid-afternoon the following day by the time he returned to the hotel. As he walked down the cramped corridor towards their rooms, Helena rushed at him in a highly agitated state.

"What's happened?" he asked in alarm. "Is it Mother?"

Helena flung her arms around her father, something she had never done before, as Alexander discouraged excessive displays of emotion. She ignored his question. "She's back, she's back," she cried. "Oh, Father, she's back."

Chapter 6
Annie Gets a Gun

Ramornie Station offered comfortable accommodation to the family. The manager's house, a sprawling homestead with wide verandahs and spacious rooms, was situated on a rise well out of sight and sound of the slaughterhouse and canning works. Her father undoubtedly had a busy and stressful life, but for her mother and siblings, existence was easy. Dark-skinned servants padded barefoot across the wooden floor. Her mother taught them the correct way to fold the linen, dust the furniture and polish the silver. They listened and watched attentively and then, to her mother's mild exasperation, went back to the ways they had always done things. She had occasional sightings of the aboriginal stockmen from a distance. Their job, so she learned, was to muster the cattle. This meant they had to round them up and herd them into the enclosures where they would be slaughtered. One day, roaming beyond the confines of the homestead, she encountered two of the stockmen up close. They stared unblinking down at her from their horses as though she were a creature from an alien world—which in fact she was.

For Annie, Ramornie was stultifying. There was nothing for her here. Her father gave her a horse and she learned to ride. She also learned to shoot and discovered that she was good at it. She immersed herself in her watercolour painting, turning out faintly praiseworthy landscapes. She raided Alexander's library, and read everything else she could get her hands on. But it was not enough, it was never enough.

She sat in the shade of the verandah as the sun slid across the sky and thought about her relationship with Harry. Love was not the right sort of word. She was addicted to the danger Harry represented. She simultaneously hated and was thrilled by his unpredictability. She had an urge to write to him, but this was impossible. She had no idea where in the world he was, or if he would ever keep his promise and come back to her. So, she started a diary in which she described the trivia of her days.

How her father's foreman, Les, called her "Dead-eye Annie" when she was in the back paddock blasting spoiled meat cans off logs. She woke one night, thinking there were abandoned babies wailing in the dark, later to learn they were bats, or flying foxes. She documented the most thrilling event since her arrival: a subtropical cyclone which flooded the Clarence Valley, cutting them off from the nearby township of Grafton. She also wrote about more deeply personal matters, such as her miscarriage, and how she would have bled to death if her mother hadn't found her. She kept the diary under lock and key in her room, away from Helena's prying eye.

As her competence as a rider developed, she ventured further from the confines of the homestead. Late one morning in early autumn, she followed a trail along the riverbank and came across the camp where the natives lived. At that time of day, the able-bodied blacks were working up at the station, and the camp was occupied by old men and women, who squatted in the dirt and kept a watchful eye on the young children, most of whom were naked. Several native dogs were curled up on the riverbank. One looked up and bared its teeth. Their humpies were constructed of sheets of bark from the tall eucalypts that lined the riverbank and corrugated iron scrounged from the station. Despite the heat, a substantial fire formed the centrepiece of the camp. Not far from the fire was a mound of rubbish, including animal bones and rotting carcasses. As she sat on her horse, transfixed by the scene, an old woman emerged from one of the humpies holding a small marsupial by its hind leg. She threw it on to the fire, nauseating Annie with the stench of singeing fur and flesh. She wheeled her horse and headed back to the homestead. She had observed poverty in the slums of Aberdeen, but had never witnessed anything that came close to the sight on the riverbank. Back at the homestead, she looked at the young women who washed her clothes and made her bed with fresh eyes. It seemed impossible that they could inhabit the parallel universes of the squatter camp and the homestead.

In her diary. she wrote about her father's efforts to improve the condition of the blacks under his charge. He pressured them to attend the Sunday church service he established on the property. Annie, who had stopped attending church herself, disapproved of this effort to "civilize" the black, although she said nothing to her father. He built a wooden barrack down by the river for the senior stockmen and their families. However, the barrack didn't last long. The natives pulled it down for firewood.

One day in late May a letter postmarked Cape Town arrived for her. It contained nothing of much consequence. This didn't matter. The fact that he had written to her was enough. She had been surprised to learn that he was literate. He told her that his ability to read and write was due to his maternal grandparents, who were French, and who had provided for his education. Their plans for him did not include a life on the ocean. He had run away to sea to escape from his abusive father. One notable omission from his letter was any mention of his intention to return to Australia.

Every few months a letter would arrive. Then, early in the New Year, came the one she had been waiting for. She was to make her way, not to Sydney, but to Melbourne and she was to be there by the beginning of March at the latest.

She left Ramornie Station early on the morning of February 20, 1874. Her mother cried, and her father allowed her a hug. When she kissed Helena, her sister whispered to her, "I'll always be here for you." As she took her leave, Alexander pressed a letter into her hand. She had requested the letter several times but had given up all hope that her father would provide it. She stuffed the letter into her bag, left, and never looked back.

The marriage certificate shows that on March 17, Harry Edward Dearmer, 22, seaman, married Ann Forbes, 18, domestic, "by licence" at the manse of the Presbyterian Church, by Rev. Robert Hamilton, in Fitzroy, an inner-city suburb of Melbourne. The document also stated that the ceremony was carried out "With the written consent of Alexander Forbes, the bride's father." It also showed Harry's residence as Dromana, and Annie's as Rosebud, both pretty townships on the Mornington Peninsula where they had entered into domestic service with wealthy families in the region.

Several weeks after their marriage, at Harry's insistence, they relocated from the Mornington Peninsula to Melbourne. If you had to be anywhere in the colony, he said, the city was the place to be. It hummed with wealth from the gold rush, although that wealth was not evenly distributed. Evidence of the wealth was to be seen in the stately Victorian buildings dotted about the city square. Collins Street was arguably the most elegant street in Australia. Although no rival to the great industrial cities in Britain, Melbourne was described as the finest Victorian city in all of the British colonies. For a time, it was the richest city in the world as well as one of the largest.

Despite its wealth, Melbourne in the 1870s was a violent city, and an expensive one as well. On arriving from the country, Harry and Annie's most pressing need was for shelter. Harry had money, having been paid off by the shipping company along with some living expenses to tide him over until the ship made its return leg home. The company was unaware that Harry, newly married, had no intention of returning to Britain. One of his shipmates advised him to look around the eastern part of the city bounded by Little Bourke Street and Flinders Lane. "That's where your money will last longest, Mate—unless you lose it by other means," said his companion, tapping his nose. Annie was impressed with the buildings along Collins Street, although they were no finer than similar buildings in her native Aberdeen. Slipping between the long row of horse-drawn vehicles that occupied the centre of the street, they turned into a narrow lane and continued eastward. After crossing Russell Street, the neighbourhood deteriorated. The two-storey dwellings were solid looking enough, but poverty was in the air: the people were shabbily dressed, and the buildings poorly maintained. Harry steered Annie into a tavern with a low-slung ceiling. The walls were smoke-stained, and the room reeked of alcohol and sweat. The few patrons standing at the bar or sitting at low tables turned to stare at the interlopers. Annie locked eyes with one young woman sitting at a table with three men. The woman was as young as Annie, possibly even younger. Annie put an elbow on the bar and stared the woman down while Harry bought drinks—a beer with a rum chaser for him and a rum and water for her. They took their drinks to a table in the corner. Harry quickly downed his beer and rum chaser. Annie was not much of a drinker. In fact, she had not tasted alcohol in the year they had been apart. She had hardly touched the glass to her lips when Harry finished his. "Wait here," he said, getting to his feet. "I'll see what's around."

After he left, she toyed with her drink and engaged in another staring contest with the young woman. She felt again the sensation in her belly. She was yet to say anything to Harry: it was far too soon but she would have to tell him eventually. The young woman at the table across the room rose, pulled her tattered shawl around her shoulders, and departed with one of the men. Annie received a baleful look. "You're in my territory," it said. The two other men at the table ignored her and continued with their drinking and smoking.

She thought about her family and the pain she had caused, but then pushed the thought aside. What was done was done. As a young, confident woman, she considered regretting past actions a waste of time and emotional energy. The only member of her family she kept contact with was Helena. When the time was right, she had that channel to her parents.

Men had always been attracted to her. She knew she was handsome, in the Scottish manner, rather than conventionally beautiful, and also knew that it was her vitality and boldness that attracted them. Harry was the first one she had allowed into her heart, an impulse that, with maturity, she would come to regret, and one that would haunt her in the years ahead. For now, sitting in that low tavern, she was happy. She had done her time at Ramornie Station and was free to live her life the way she wanted.

The young woman returned alone shortly ahead of Harry. She looked slightly dishevelled and gave Ann another stare before returning to the two remaining men on the far side of the room. When Harry came back, he fetched himself another drink from the bar before joining her. "I've found a place," he said. The "place" was a room on the ground floor of a two-story residential building in Punch Lane, not far from Parliament House. "It's half the price of the other places I looked at."

Punch Lane ran off Little Bourke Street in the "contaminated" quarter of the city, a place of prostitutes and criminals. She was soon to discover why the room represented such extraordinary value. Several days after they moved in, Annie bumped into a young woman who occupied the room upstairs. She introduced herself as Polly. Harry, as usual, was out. Polly was similar in age to the girl who gave her the evil eye in the bar, but her demeanour was completely different. Her cheeks dimpled when she smiled, and she had kind eyes. During the day, when Harry was out, she would bring Annie cake and they would chat. At night, she would leave the dwelling at dusk and make her way up Punch Lane. In the early hours of the morning, Annie would sometimes wake and hear Polly climbing the stairs to her room., She quickly realized that, despite her sweetness, Polly and the bar girl were in the same game.

One morning, Polly brought Annie a newspaper cutting. It was from *The Melbourne Herald* dated August 21, 1872. The girl was illiterate. She knew of the events that were documented in the article, but wanted Annie to read it to her. Annie, hard edged, but basically soft at heart, was shocked. The first paragraph read:

HORRIBLE MURDER OF A WOMAN IN MELBOURNE YESTERDAY MORNING

In the chief centre of the city of Melbourne—close to that Parliament which rules and governs and guides the moralities and immoralities of the people, within a few feet of Bourke Street east, and in the vicinity of that contaminated "black spot" Little Bourke Street, running from Stephen to Spring Streets, halfway up on the left-hand side, and when Melbourne proper, with it philanthropists for the reclamation of fallen women, larrikins and sanctimonious criminals from Pentridge [prison], are supposed to be enjoying the slumbers of innocence and repentance—at 2 o'clock in the morning one of the most horrible murders recorded for years past was perpetuated, the victim being an unfortunate woman, named Mary O'Rourke, alias Hewitt, aged about forty years and recently arrived from County Cork. (*The Herald, Wednesday, 21 August 1872)*[2]

The newspaper cutting went on to describe the murderer, a pretty young Irish woman called Margaret O'Donohoe, not long herself arrived from County Cork. Like her victim, she worked as a prostitute out of the house in Punch Lane. She smashed in the head of her housemate, Mary

[2] Leigh, W.H. (1839) *Travels and Adventures in South Australia 1836 – 1838.* London: Smith, Elder and Co. Cornhill

O'Rourke, with the blunt edge of an axe for insulting Margaret's mother—ironically, for calling Margaret the daughter of a whore. Shortly after the event, she turned herself in at the Bourke Street police station, where she had trouble getting the police to take her story seriously.

The room in Punch Lane would bear witness to the first of many beatings inflicted on Annie by her drunken husband. However, they were not to be compared to the bloody slaying of Mary O'Rourke. When Annie learned of the murder in the very room where she put up with Harry's beatings, she was shocked and not a little afraid that the same fate might await her. But what was she to do? Jobless and penniless, she was effectively enslaved by her husband. She didn't know it at the time, but the slaying was to presage the violence that would pursue her and her offspring for much of her early adult life.

While not as harsh as Aberdeen, Melbourne's weather in August was not quite what she had expected from Australia. It differed dramatically from the more benign weather of northern New South Wales: hard rain and biting wind one minute, astonishingly blue skies with a sun that provided little heat the next. There were times when she thought that Melbourne in winter was not so different from Aberdeen in summer.

Harry spent a lot of his time away from Punch Lane, and she soon realized why he had been keen to move from the country. The underbelly of the city was his natural habitat. She grew bored and wanted to explore her new home beyond the confines of the slums. However, without money, it was only possible to venture as far as her feet would carry her. Dressed in clothing that grew shabbier by the day, she received dismissive looks and the occasional proposition as she made her way down Spring Street past the neoclassical Parliament House. She ignored both the stares and the propositions. If the weather looked reasonable, she liked to walk in the gardens behind Parliament House. But with her active mind and independent spirit, there was only so much time she could spend wandering penniless through the city streets.

The first real confrontation came when she asked Harry for money. His dismissiveness irritated her and she let him know. His answer was to walk out the door. Her response was to ransack their room looking for his cash. She found something more ominous: a handgun wrapped in cloth and stuffed under the mattress on his side of the bed. As she was the one who made the bed every day, she was surprised to find it there. Either he had only just acquired it or had planned to be in for the evening until their argument prompted him to rush out without thinking of the gun. When he returned an hour later, somewhat inebriated but not excessively so, he was confronted by the barrel of his own handgun pointing steadily at his breastbone. After staring him down, she lowered the gun and returned to its place under the mattress, only this time, it was on her side of the bed. For the rest of her long life she kept a handgun close at hand.

The day would come when Annie would shoot Harry Dearmer, but that day was a distant prospect. On this evening, her intention was to put a metaphorical warning shot across his bow. She might have given herself to him, but she was not his chattel: she was every bit his equal. Thus, began an enduring battle between the wily Harry Dearmer and the headstrong Annie Forbes. The altercation ended where many other would for years to come: in bed. And it was on this night, while he stroked her and showed the sweet side of the man she had married, that she told him of the child in her belly. With a child on the way, and tiring of the violence and squalor of the inner city, she convinced Harry to move back to the Mornington Peninsula. She also made another decision. She would no longer refer to herself as Annie. She would exchange the childish diminutive for the grown-up Ann, for, with an embryo in her belly, and despite the fact that she was still in her teenage years, in her own mind, she was fully a woman.

She was a complex character. At the age of fifteen, she was seduced by an English sailor. She married the sailor, bore him children and would one day be involved in a shoot-out with him in which he would come off second best. Working as a housekeeper, she would bear children out of wedlock to her employer and one of his sons. She had a passion for painting, and her landscapes were admired by family and friends. Although she came from Calvinist stock, she was a committed atheist and dismissed as anachronistic nonsense the notion that bearing children out of wedlock was a sin. She took no nonsense from the men in her life, kept a revolver handy, and wasn't afraid to use it.

She was an independent woman, born before her time. In a later century, she would have been called a feminist—a label she would have loathed.

On February 14, 1875, Ann Forbes gave birth to the first of her numerous children, a boy, at Dromana, on the Mornington Peninsula. She registered him as Alexander Frederick Dearmer. In naming him after her father, she hoped to breach the gap that had opened up after she had fled from the family. It worked, putting the seal on a reconciliation that had been initiated by her sister. The boy and his grandfather would grow up to be very close. Naming the child Alexander was an explicit declaration of her commitment to her family. Shortly after the birth of the child, she had to return to her work as a housekeeper in the house of a wealthy Dromana family. Harry had lost his job again and was unable to find another. His drinking, violent nature, and predilection for walking off with his employers' possessions rendered him unemployable in Dromana.

Chapter 7
Bound for South Australia

Every so often Alexander Forbes noted the letters addressed to Helena in the hand of his estranged daughter. Then, one morning a letter arrived addressed to him informing them that she was with child. After the birth of the boy, he was pleased to learn that it bore his name. He wrote back to her expressing his pleasure and saying how much he and her mother looked forward eventually to seeing their grandson. At Helena's instruction, he addressed the letter care of her Dromana employer. From Helena, he learned that not all was harmonious in the marital home due to Harry's drinking and violence. Although the news that Harry was mistreating Ann distressed him, particularly coming so soon after the birth of his first grandchild, it was hardly surprising. From their first encounter on the ship from London, he harboured doubts about Harry's character, and subsequent actions on the part of his now son-in-law had only confirmed his original assessment. It would not do for Harry to intercept and read any of their correspondence, so sending them care of her employer was a useful solution.

He told Ann that the family was leaving Ramornie. They were moving to Angaston, a township in the Barossa Valley north of Adelaide where he had been appointed head of the South Australian Canned Fruit Company. Despite its name, it, like the Australian Meat Company, was owned by British interests. He had developed a solid reputation in the food processing industry, and throughout the 1880s and 1890s, would go on to manage and own a succession of food processing and canning companies in Adelaide, the Barossa Valley, and several other fruit-producing areas in different parts of the colony.

Through subsequent correspondence after the move, Ann learned that her parents were delighted with the Barossa Valley. Despite the eucalypts and native vegetation, the Valley had a distinctly European feel. The native brush was rapidly giving way to grazing pastures, orchards and vineyards. Townships, their main streets lined with public buildings made of local stone, dotted the landscape. A number carried European names, such as Seppeltsfield, named after Joseph Seppelt, a migrant from Lower Silesia, Germany.

Alexander purchased a rambling homestead on the outskirts of Angaston, originally known as German Pass, but renamed after George Fife Angas, a wealthy English businessman who was one of the founders of South Australia. It was Angas who arranged for shiploads of Lutherans to emigrate to South Australia to escape persecution by the Prussian King and who provided land in the Barossa for them to settle.

Alexander threw himself into the task of establishing the cannery. He met George Angas, then in his late 80s, but still actively managing his property on the outskirts of the township named after him. Angus introduced him to community leaders and prominent settlers in the Barossa, and he became well-known throughout the district. Once they had become established, he wrote to Ann with a proposition. If she, Harry and baby Alexander would move to South Australia, he would provide financial support for the child's upbringing. He would also find work for Harry at the cannery on condition that he moderated his drinking.

The letter from her father presented Ann with a dilemma. Alexander's suggestion provided a solution to their financial difficulties. With Harry out of work, they relied exclusively on Ann's meagre wage as a housekeeper. Little Alexander was a sickly child, and medical treatment was expensive. Although he no longer brought any money to the household, Harry continued to drink. Moving to South Australia would also bring her back to her family and give her parents the opportunity to bond with their grandson.

She had to pick her moment to put the proposition to Harry. It was crucial to catch him at a time when he was sober. When she eventually broached the subject, his reaction was disappointingly predictable. There was no way that he would work for her father. Nor did he want to be surrounded by her family. Although an alcoholic, Harry was no fool. While her father had given approval for their marriage, he would only tolerate Harry for the sake of his daughter and grandson. She knew this was true. On those occasions when Alexander and Harry had encountered each other on the clipper ship from London, the antipathy between them was profound.

As Harry warmed to his theme, he raised his voice. "Keep your voice down," said Ann, "you'll wake the baby." But it was too late. She got to the baby before Harry did and picked him up. On several occasions when the baby had cried, Harry had picked him up and shaken him so violently that she thought his neck might snap.

"I'm getting out of here," said Harry abruptly.

She was relieved. "Where are you going?" she asked.

"That's none of your business," he snapped, but then relented. "Up to Melbourne. I need money."

"Well, you know where it is. Just go!"

He didn't return until the following day when the late Autumn sun was low in the sky. She was trying to get Alexander to sleep in their bedroom, when she heard him banging around in the kitchen. She slipped her handgun into the pocket in her pinafore, Once the baby had settled, she walked into the kitchen. He was sitting at the kitchen table drinking rum from the bottle. He looked terrible. It was clear from his appearance that he had been on a two-day drinking spree. However, uncharacteristically, he was not aggressive. And he had news for that surprised her. They would go to South Australia, not to the Barossa Valley, but to Port Adelaide. There, she would be close enough to her family to see them regularly, but they would not be close enough for Harry to be sucked into the vortex of Forbes family life. During the drinking spree, he had met up with a former shipmate who had just returned from South Australia. The shipmate, like Harry, had abandoned the clipper ship company that employed him and taken work on a coastal schooner that ran goods and passengers up and down the South Australian coastline. Port Adelaide was the place for them. He planned on returning to his previous occupation as a sailor, and she would have no trouble getting work as a housekeeper.

This was an entirely unexpected turn of events. Yes, of course she would go. Pretty as it was, and as kind as her employer was, there was nothing in Dromana for either of them. But what about the cost of uprooting themselves from Melbourne and getting to Adelaide? For an answer, he reached into his coat pocket and dumped a wad of banknotes on the table. She had better sense than to ask where the money came from.

The prospect of escaping the stultifying smugness of the Mornington Peninsula, where Harry had a reputation as a drunk and a petty thief, improved his mood. In Port Adelaide he could slip into the shady anonymity of the docklands. It was an environment he knew. There, he would find like-minded characters whose interests and habits mirrored his own.

Ann knew that Harry's equanimity wouldn't last, but while it did, she was content. He was far from the model husband: there were occasional flashes of his violent temper, and he still drank, but the drinking wasn't quite as constant. And for a while the physical abuse stopped.

Harry would go to Port Adelaide ahead of her to look for work and secure accommodation. She would finish up her service in Dromana and join him when her employer had found a suitable replacement. On her last day of service, her employer gave her an unexpected severance bonus, a reference that spoke so highly of her housekeeping skills that she was hard put to recognize herself, and a letter of introduction. The letter was to a former business associate, an "honourable, upstanding gentleman," a widower, who might need a housekeeper.

And so it was, that several days after moving from Dromana to the colony of South Australia, she found herself nervously approaching the Price family home in Port Adelaide. The pretty teenage girl who answered the front doorbell informed her that Captain Price was not at home but would be in that evening if she cared to return.

The cottage that Harry had found, located conveniently, as it would turn out, around the corner from the much more substantial Price house, was small and dark and would require Harry's skills as a handyman to be made habitable. Harry's mood remained positive. He wasn't exactly jovial, but flashes of temper were rare. As anticipated, Port Adelaide was much more to his liking than the genteel Mornington Peninsula. By the time she arrived, he had acquired a circle of drinking companions, and was becoming a familiar face in the Port Adelaide pubs. Inability to find employment as a sailor was a major disappointment and he had to settle for dock work as a stevedore. All things considered, however, the move to Port Adelaide had been a positive one for both of them.

WH's life had slipped into a comfortable pattern following his return from Queensland. Now almost fifty years of age, with grown children and no wife, he continued working in the industry to which he had devoted his life. Rather than being employed by a single company, he worked as an independent mining consultant to several, carrying out surveys for possible mining sites. He had made his mark and amassed enough money to keep him comfortable financially. He had a solid stone house in Port Adelaide, which was large enough to accommodate those of his children who chose to live with him. The house stood on a block of land large enough to accommodate a pleasant garden, including an orchard of stone-fruit trees, and stables at the rear.

Of the five children who survived to adulthood, only Thomas John and Rebecca, both still at school, lived with their father. William had established himself as a teacher. The second son, Henry, worked as a farmer on Kangaroo Island. Quiet and practical, he rarely visited Adelaide. Thomas John visited the farm when his studies allowed and brought back news of Henry. He was "keeping company" with a young woman from Rapid Bay called Mary Benkenstein.

When William Henry returned from Queensland, Mary Ann, his eldest daughter, announced her engagement to Samuel Tyzack. Her fiancé came from wealthy English stock. One of his uncles, after whom he was named, owned numerous businesses including a factory in Glasgow and a colliery in Durham. When his uncle died, Samuel learned that he had inherited the colliery. After their marriage, in March 1876, he and Mary Ann moved to England where he claimed his inheritance. Three years later, Mary Ann converted to Christianity, and was baptized at Bishop-Wearmouth, in Durham. Rebecca eventually also moved to England to be with her sister. She, too, became a Christian, and was also baptized at Bishop-Wearmouth, in Durham in 1884. And so it was that of the five surviving children from the union of the committed secularists, William Henry and Mary, only Thomas John, and possibly Henry, remained true to the principles on which they had been raised.

As his stature within the mining community continued to grow, WH became an advocate for the industry. Shortly after returning from

Queensland, he was commissioned by a Melbourne-based mining company to explore for mineral deposits in South Australia. His prospecting revealed significant copper lodes in the Blinman region north of Port Augusta which he reported to the directors. The company was reluctant to invest in the area due to its remoteness and the difficulty of getting the ore to the smelters down south. They asked WH to lobby the colonial government in Adelaide to extend the railway line being planned to link Adelaide to Port Augusta out to Blinman. WH and a colleague, Captain Matthews, did their best to convince the state politicians, but their words fell on deaf ears. After months of unsuccessful lobbying, they went public with the following letter to the *S.A. Register*.

THE FAR NORTH. MINES.
TO THE EDITOR,

Sir—Public attention is again being directed to the rich mineral lands lying to the north of Port Augusta, and now that the Port Augusta Railway Bill is passed it is likely we shall soon hear more about them. We thought the number and richness of the copper lodes in that part of the country were so well known that we were surprised to find two members of Parliament (one in each House) rising up to cast doubts upon the fact. They go to work to attack the correctness of the account given of the mines in a book lately printed by the Government, and which we understand was prepared by Mr. Harcus by order of the Government to give the best information about the colony for persons in England and America. We have read the chapter on the mines, and if our testimony can help, we shall be most happy to give it as to the truth of the statements it contains. It was written by Mr. J. B. Austin, who travelled all through the mines in the North. We have been engaged in prospecting and mining in the North off and on for the past 14 years, and we are practical miners. We can assure you, Sir, there are lodes of ore in the North enough to astonish any person. You might in some places break ore off the surface that would go 70 per cent of copper. We know of one place where there were horizontal layers of ore covering about four acres that appear as if it had been thrown off from the main lode. We have worked on one of the latest discoveries where over a large space of ground there is a great quantity of fine green carbonates mixed in the soil. This can be dug out and easily dressed by puddling to a high percentage of copper. We have worked on the Sliding Rock, where there is a wonderful deposit of malleable copper, in little pieces like coarse grains about the size of blasting powder, mixed with the clay. This stuff can be brought up to 70 and 80 per cent by puddling. One of the undersigned, Captain Matthews, knows a place in the North where with 200 good miners he could turn out 1,000 tons of ore a week that would give about 10 per cent of copper. Then, Sir, look at the quantity of copper raked from the Blinman and Yudnamutana Mines. Why it did not pay them unless they could send away ore averaging 30 per cent, because of the high price of cartage, and for a long time the ore they sent down to Port Augusta averaged 35 per cent. Then there are the Daly and Stanley Mines giving bismuth as well as rich copper, the Mount Rosa and Mount Lyndhurst, Mount Deception and Warrioota, and many others we could name. These mines could all be profitably worked if there was a railway to take away the ore. We think it is both wrong and foolish for members of Parliament, or any person else, to try and injure an important industry like mining in this colony. We can't think what can be their motive. There may have been some mistakes, but where would the colony have been without its mines! We are, Sir, etc, T. MATTHEWS, Mining Captain, W. H. PRICE, Mining Engineer. *S.A. Register Saturday 8 July 1876*[3]

However, not even this public appeal was enough to convince the parliament. WH returned to Melbourne to report on his failure to sway the politicians. Their reluctance to invest in infrastructure to support the development of the mining industry in the state was a mystery, he told them. But then South Australian society had always moved in mysterious ways: an odd assemblage of economic timidity, religious conservatism and social progressivism.

[3] *S.A. Register* Saturday 8 July 1876, p.3

The front doorbell jangled at seven o'clock one evening just as he had settled at his desk with a whisky and water, to work on an address he was to give to the Secular Association the following evening. Rebecca had mentioned that earlier in the day someone had come by looking for him. On opening the door, he was confronted by a young woman who could not have been more than eighteen years of age. She was neatly dressed, but hatless, and her black hair was pulled into a severe bun, accentuating her high cheekbones and striking eyes. In a pronounced Scottish brogue, she introduced herself as Ann Forbes, and apologized for disturbing him at home. Curious, he showed her through to his study and offered her a chair, which she politely refused. Her upright bearing made her seem taller than she really was.

"I'll come straight to the point, Sir," she said, handing him her reference and letter of introduction. "I want to know if you would have any use for an experienced and hard-working housekeeper. If you are, then I would like to offer myself for your service." He was impressed by the clarity of her diction, and the way she held her head high and looked him in the eye. Despite her youth, she came across as a proud woman with a strong sense of self and the typical forthrightness of a Scot. There was nothing obsequious or grovelling in her manner. She sought work. If he needed a housekeeper, she would be happy to take on the task. As it happened, her timing was impeccable. The woman who had looked after the household during his time in Queensland had given notice the previous week. He read the letter of introduction and glanced at her reference. "Ah, Mr. Holland," he said. "Is he enjoying his retirement?" He hadn't seen the company director since he had retired. It was a long way from Collins Street to the Morning Peninsula, and WH's trips to Melbourne to provide consulting reports were short.

"Yes," replied Ann. "He's very well."

WH was anxious to get back to his address. "Can you start tomorrow?"

"Yes," she replied, slightly taken aback, but pleased. Neither of them had the slightest inkling that his offer, and her acceptance, would change both of their lives.

"I won't he back until late tomorrow, but my daughter Rebecca will be here, and she can answer any questions you might have."

He moved to show her to the door when she said, "There is something, Sir."

"Yes?"

"I have a small child. I'll have to bring him here when I work."

"That's fine," replied WH.

"And another one on the way."

"Congratulations," said WH, and showed her out.

She settled quickly into her work. Rebecca liked her and so did he. She was calm and efficient, and if there was anything that she didn't know, she asked.

Three days after she had started work, she came to him with a request. Her husband, who worked on the docks, had been laid off. Would there be work for him at the Price household? He had worked as a handyman and Jack-of-all-trades on the Mornington Peninsula. She couldn't help noticing the repairs that were needed around the house. The yard also needed work.

Her request could have been considered impertinent, but WH didn't take offense. He agreed to speak to Harry. Only much later did he learn that Harry had been dismissed from the docks for threatening his supervisor with a handgun, and that he had been dismissed from a number of positions in Victoria for theft. Had he known, he might have had second thoughts about employing him. If he had known how entangled Ann and her family would become with his own, he might have turned them both away.

Tom's father and sister had retired to their rooms by the time he got home that Friday night after five days with his brother on Kangaroo Island. The crossing had been delayed by a malfunction on the vessel that was to ferry them to the mainland. The delay had bothered him less than some of the other passengers. Pencil and notepad in hand, he made notes about the school play his class would perform at the end of the term. He had been pleased, but not flattered, by the headmaster's invitation. False modesty was not part of his makeup, and he was the natural choice to produce the play.

It wasn't the silence that disturbed him as he entered the darkened house; it was the feeling that things had been rearranged in some indefinable way. Too exhausted to be concerned by the unsettling sensation, he retired to his room. In addition to his studies at St. Peter's College, he had a part-time job as a porter in the East End produce market, and on Saturdays, his working day began at dawn, loading sacks of potatoes, carrots and onions, and crates of more perishable items such as tomatoes and lettuces, onto horse-drawn drays for the delivery of produce to grocery stores in the city and surrounding suburbs.

The following morning, the house was in darkness as he left and made his way down Port Road to the East End of the city. He returned in the middle of the afternoon to find a stranger, a stocky but strongly built man dressed in dungarees and singlet, splitting wood by the stables. Tom scratched his head and eyed the man with suspicion. The man paused, straightened, and turned to face him. He held the axe in his left hand as if to demonstrate his strength, looked the boy up and down, and then resumed chopping.

The instant and mutual antipathy between man and boy was to last as long as they were to have anything to do with each other, and would, at a distant point in the future, come perilously close to costing both their lives.

Unsettled by the hostility in the stranger's demeanour, Tom entered the house from the rear. Inside, there was another surprise. A young woman in her late teens or early twenties was folding clothing at the kitchen table. At her feet was a basket containing a sleeping baby. From the way she carried herself, it looked as though there might be another on the way.

"Who are you?" he asked less intimidated by her than by the stranger with the axe. His father had said nothing about employing a new housekeeper.

"Ann," she said looking him over. "You must be Thomas John." Her Scottish burr was not unpleasant, but not as kind on the ear as the softer Welsh of his father. Calmly, she turned back to the pile of washing on the table. Feeling slightly awkward, Tom put the kettle on the hob to boil water for tea.

"Would you like me to do that for you?" she asked.

"No, thank you," he replied.

When the kettle boiled, he poured the water into a pot, then waited for the leaves to steep. The baby stirred, opened its eyes and began to whine.

"What's the baby's name?"

"Alexander," she replied.

"So, you're here to work for my father."

"That I am."

"And who is he?" asked Tom, jerking his thumb toward the back yard.

"That's Harry. He's my husband."

Tom poured tea into a cup and then removed himself to the front of the house. Ann watched his retreating back. He was smaller than Harry by half a head, still little more than a boy, but there was a wiriness and confidence about him. His shoulders were broad. The physical work in the East End markets was turning the boy into a man. She felt comfortable in this household. In the short time she had worked there, she had never heard her employer raise his voice. Her major concern was Harry, whose behaviour had become increasingly erratic. Two nights before, when he had come back late having been out most of the day, he had slapped her across the face when she questioned where he had been. Were it not for the boy in the basket, and another baby on the way, she'd have gathered her things together and left. However, encumbered with offspring, she was trapped, and only felt secure in William Henry's house.

The years between 1876 and 1880 were difficult ones for Ann. She continued to be employed by William Henry and worked hard to keep her marriage stable. Dearmer was a violent man who, when frustrated, resorted to violence against Ann and the children. It was not in her nature to put up with such treatment, but she did so for the sake of her son and her new baby, whose arrival was imminent. On September 5, she went into labour. On the morning of September 6, the baby, another boy, was born. As was the custom at the time, the delivery took place on the dining table of their cramped cottage around the corner from the Price house. The midwife, a friend of Ann's, bound the baby tightly in a cotton cloth and handed him to Ann. She named him Percy. Despite her exhaustion, she experienced a piercing joy as she attached the baby to her breast.

The birth was the only bright spot in a dismal period in her life. Several weeks after the birth, Tom returned from school and observed Harry removing a set of tools from the workshop that abutted the stables. Several minutes later, Harry left the premises with a hessian sack slung over his shoulder. Harry reported what he had seen to his father who, on inspecting the workshop, discovered that some of his expensive prospecting tools were missing. The following day, when Harry turned up for work, WH confronted him and dismissed him. Ann was mortified and ashamed. She apologised to WH for bringing her husband into their lives. WH did his best to comfort her. It was not her fault, and he did not hold her responsible in any way. "If you ever need sanctuary from your husband, just come to me." That night, Harry returned home drunk. She confronted him, and a row erupted between them. Alexander cowered in a corner of the room, whimpering. He wanted to run far away but it was night, and he was almost as afraid of the dark as he was of his father. The row ended with a beating for Ann, which she endured. When he turned on Alexander, she rushed from the kitchen and returned with her revolver. She levelled it at him. "Get out of here," she said, in a low voice. He could see from the look in her eye that she would not hesitate to fire, and that she would not miss. He lurched from the house and did not return for several days.

On Friday, November 3, 1876, exactly two months after the birth of Percy, the following report appeared in the *Adelaide Express and Telegraph*.

An instance of shocking brutality on the part of a father towards a child came before Messrs. J. Henderson and H.C.E. Muecke, at the Police Court, Port Adelaide, on Friday, November 3, when Harry Edward Dearmer was charged with assaulting Alexander Frederick Dearmer, his son, aged one year and nine months. The information had been laid at the insistence of Mr. Charles Hains, who stated that on the previous day his attention was called to the child's condition by some women. The child's face was bruised and his lips were swollen, while his body bore the marks of having been thrashed with a piece of rope in a fearful manner. Sarah Wasley, a neighbour, stated that she heard the screams of the child on the day, mentioned in the information, but she did not witness the assault. She had seen the father, on previous occasions, beat the child, who was in the habit of running into the witness's house when he saw the defendant coming. Sergeant Innes said the mother had taken the child away with her, and could not be found. The bench regretted that the evidence against the defendant was not stronger, but they had no doubt he had been guilty of grossly ill-treating the child. They ordered him to enter into recognisance in the sum of 30 pounds, and to find two sureties of 15 pounds each, to keep the peace. The bench thanked Mr. Hains for taking the matter up.[4]

Ann was not at the police court to testify against her husband, because, after the beating, she fled to her parents' home at Angasten. She left Alexander with them before returning to Adelaide with the baby. Alexander would live principally with his grandparents for much of his childhood.

One November evening in 1876, almost a year after he had employed Ann and Harry, and a month after he dismissed Harry for the theft of gardening tools, WH returned from work, retreated to his study with his evening water and whisky, and leafed through the *Adelaide Express and Telegraph*. On the inside page was the court report of the assault on Alexander. A mild and gentle man, the report shocked WH. That such brutality could go on under his nose infuriated him. He was almost as angry with himself as with Harry. How could he have been so blind?

The account explained certain facts, in particular Ann's request for a substantial loan, to be repaid from her wages, and the sudden absence of Alexander who had been a constant presence in the house. For the last few days, she had come to work accompanied only by her new baby. It was two years since the death of his wife, and as his grief settled into a dull ache, his fondness for Ann, now twenty-one, grew.

The following morning, he stayed at home. When he heard movements in the kitchen, he called her into his study. She appeared, the baby on her hip. He placed the newspaper before her.

---

[4] The *Adelaide Express and Telegraph* Friday, November 3, 1876, p.2

"Why did you not speak to me of this matter?" he asked.

She paused before speaking. "It was not of your making. I am responsible for my life and the lives of my children."

"Where is your son? What has become of him?"

"He is in a safe place now."

Her answer alarmed him. "What does that mean?" he asked.

"He is with my parents."

"But you and the baby, you are not safe."

"I can take care of myself."

"I am not so sure that you can. There is a room here for you."

He noted the startled look on her face at his offer. She shook her head. "That would not be right. I can take care of myself," she repeated. He had no option but to free her to get on with her work.

Although Ann and Harry lived a short distance away, Harry had effectively disappeared from WH's life. There had been only one sighting since he had dismissed Harry. One evening, when he was walking home from a meeting at the Port Adelaide docks, he came across a fracas outside a pub. From the other side of the street, he observed Harry laying into another man with a lump of wood. Several other men grabbed him from behind and restrained him until two police officers arrived. He continued on his way home. He would not see Harry again until a violent confrontation took place at his own house when Ann finally sought refuge from Harry's abuse. The only evidence of Harry's continued presence in Port Adelaide were the occasional bruises on Ann's arms and face.

Apart from her children, the only thing that gave Ann solace was her work. She treasured her days at the Price household, just as she dreaded the nights at her own. Occasionally, she was able to visit her parents in the Barossa Valley, or meet her sister Helena in the city. The rhythm of her life was punctuated by births, deaths and the trials and tribulations of her husband. Did life have to be like this? For each year she lived, she felt she aged five. She had a miscarriage, her third. Then, two years after Percy's birth, she had a third son and named him John William Hector Dearmer. Giving him her employer's name was an act of rebellion: and it earned her a beating, but there was nothing he could do, as it was, she who had registered the child. Ann's growing attachment to her employer infuriated Harry and led to increasingly violent behaviour towards her and the children. On several occasions, she had to produce her handgun in order to fend him off. In the months following his birth, John William Hector grew increasingly emaciated. The doctor who attended him was mystified by his condition and was unable to offer a remedy. On March 31, 1879, just ten months after his birth, the baby died. An autopsy revealed that he had died of marasmus, a nutritional deficiency brought about by a lack of breast milk. Ann was grief-stricken. The baby had died because of her inability to provided him with the nutrition he needed. Already carrying her fourth child, Ann buried him in the large cemetery on the city's western edge. Five months later she gave birth to another son, Sydney Dearmer.

One afternoon in 1878, as she was finishing her work for the day and preparing to leave, Thomas John came home and began packing up his possessions. "I'm moving out," he said, in reply to her question. Having finished school, he had decided to follow his eldest brother into the teaching profession. He had taken rooms in a boarding house in St Peters not far from his former school, and close to the primary school where he would work. He would also be continuing his education at the newly established University of Adelaide.

She felt a pang at the thought the he would no longer be around. She would miss his easy charm and winning smile. Once he moved out, she rarely saw him as he generally visited the house on Sunday, the one day of the week when she transferred her housekeeping skills from the Price household to her own. Then one day in 1879, there he was on East Terrace sauntering past a line of drays being loaded with sacks and boxes. Having left his part-time job as a porter at the market, it was his habit to drop by the market to chat with former workmates and bring home a bag of fruit and vegetables. On this day, he carried a shoulder bag loaded with market goods. She caught up with him, and took his arm. "Ann!" he said in delight.

Almost twenty now, the boy that he was had become a man. She noted the beginnings of a moustache—presumably an attempt to look older. Unlike her husband, he had a gentleness of spirit and a genuine warmth, and he had always treated her as a human being rather than a servant. He asked after her and the children but made no mention of Harry. They went for tea in rooms adjacent to the market.

Too soon, the time passed. She had her own market shopping to do but agreed to meet him the following week at the same time and place. When she arrived, he had already seated himself at the rear of the tearoom and was making notes in a pocketbook. He closed the book as she sat down.

'What are you writing?" she asked.

"My father has asked me to address the Secular Association next week, and I'm assembling my thoughts."

In her time as housekeeper for the family, she had grown increasingly interested in secularism, an interest WH encouraged. "What will you speak about?"

"The Bible, and its myths," he replied. "I'm calling my address 'Know thy enemy'."

At the end of their time together, she produced a small watercolour from her bag and handed it to him. It was an impressionistic rendering of the kitchen garden at Ramornie. She smiled at the look of surprise on his face.

"I never knew you had artistic talent," he said. "Do you still paint?"

She shook her head. "There's no time," she replied. "And it isn't encouraged."

The following week, he presented her with a photograph, a self-portrait he had taken with the camera his father had given him as a graduation gift.

On the fourth, and, as it would turn out, last of their clandestine meetings, she wore an irregularly shaped bruise on her left cheek, just below the eye. She had attempted to disguise it, but the welt was clearly visible. She was grateful to him for making no mention of the bruise. He had to cut short their meeting to collect a document from his rooms for his father. When she suggested accompanying him, he seemed pleased, and they strolled along the river for a short while before catching a horse drawn tram to St. Peters.

Although on the surface the boarding house had seen better days, it was still a substantial dwelling: a classic Adelaide bluestone, with a return verandah and a garden at the rear. Surprised and delighted by the house, she sat on a bench on the verandah and looked at the trees marking the course of the distant river while Tom collected his papers. Although she cared nothing for social conventions, it would not have done to enter his rooms, She had no inkling that, many years into the future, it would be from this very house on Eighth Avenue that a double funeral cortege would carry both her and Tom to their final resting place.

That evening, Harry went too far. He returned home drunk as usual, but even more than usually belligerent. Ann had made up a bed in the kitchen, for the baby, Sydney, who was out of sorts with a fever, and wailing loudly.

"Shut him up," says Harry. "If you don't, I will, and I'll shut him up for good."

"You can hit me all you want," said Ann, "But lay a finger on the head of one of my children again and I will kill you." She meant it, and he knew it, so, taking her at her word, he beat her black and blue. Then he went to the bedroom, fell fully clothed onto the bed and began snoring loudly. On an impulse, she snatched up the children and ran from the house.

After parting from Ann, Tom made his way to Port Adelaide, all the while thinking of Ann and the unspoken complications in her life. It might have been coincidence, or it might have been fate that prompted him to stay the night at his father's house. At ten o'clock, his usual time for turning in, there came a loud bashing and calling at the kitchen door. As soon as he opened the door, she rushed in, dragging the children with her. "He's coming for me," she said. Even in the subdued light, he could see that she had been badly beaten.

WH emerged from his room disturbed by the commotion. "What is it?" he asked.

"Dearmer," replied Tom. "You look after Ann and the children. I'll take care of Dearmer." Her husband's name had not been mentioned since he had been dismissed from the household. Tom collected a cricket bat from his room and stood by the front door. He knew that Dearmer was unlikely to come creeping to the back door to retrieve his wife and children. He was right. Within minutes, Harry was pounding on the front door.

"Open up," called Dearmer. Tom opened the door. He confronted the bulky man, blocking his entry to the house. Dearmer eyed the cricket bat with contempt. Although unsteady on his feet, he would have no difficulty disarming Tom, but there was a look in the younger man's eyes that made him pause. Tom knew that Dearmer had a gun, but tonight he appeared to have come empty handed.

"My wife," he said, "I know she's here."

"She's staying here."

"Let me speak to the bitch."

"Not tonight."

WH appeared at Tom's shoulder with his own revolver in his hand. Dearmer stood his ground for a minute, but saw the older man was just as determined as his son. "You're welcome to the bitch," he said, then turned and shuffled away.

One evening in late 1880, as had become her nightly custom, Ann brought a whisky and water to him as he sat at his writing desk. As she set the tumbler down, her hand brushed his. It was only a light touch, but it sent a tingle shooting up his arm. Without pausing to consider the consequences, he held the hand, then stood and took her in his arms. She pressed herself to him as though she had been waiting for the gesture. Neither spoke. When he led her from the study, she followed without hesitation.

Despite the thirty-year gap in their age, the liaison was not entirely unexpected. Ann was a handsome young woman who had been abandoned by an abusive husband. She was not the sort to sit around and mope. WH was a lonely widower, a man of substance, financially secure, highly thought of in the community, and a respected figure within the mining industry in South Australia and beyond. Taking up with him offered Ann and her children the financial and physical security she never had with Dearmer. Concrete evidence of the relationship appeared in the form of a baby son on 27 November 1881. Although WH and Ann had little regard for the proprieties demanded by Victorian society, they registered the child as Frank Dearmer, and Dearmer, who had not been seen after being turned away from the Price household the previous year, was named on the birth certificate as the father. As Frank began to grow there were whispers that he bore an uncanny resemblance to Tom who had left for a teaching post in the country exactly nine months before the birth of the child. William, the only godly male member of the family, had also left Adelaide to take up a position as a teacher on Kangaroo Island, at the Kingscote Area School, which claimed to be the very first school in South Australia.

Chapter 8
A Crime of Passion

In March 1881, Tom completed his studies and accepted a teaching position at the Wallaroo Mines School about 5 miles from the centre of the small rural town of Kadina. He knew Kadina well, having been a frequent visitor to the area when his parents lived there a decade earlier. Wallaroo was a pretty port town on Yorke Peninsula north-west of Adelaide. Along with the neighbouring towns of Kadina and Moonta, it made up an area known as the Copper Triangle because all three towns drew their wealth from the rich copper deposits in the region. The area was also known as Little Cornwall because of the number of Cornish miners who settled there in the nineteenth century. In fact, in the mid-1880s, half of all immigrants to South Australia came from Cornwall, most of them to work in the mining industry.

Tom had mixed emotions about leaving Adelaide. His feelings for Ann had continued to grow, and he knew they were reciprocated despite the fact that she had established a relationship with his father that was anything but platonic. Despite the pain it caused him, Tom wished his father well. He deserved the companionship and comfort that Ann gave him. Tom, four years younger than Ann, and just beginning to make his way in the world, had neither the physical nor financial resources to support Ann and her children. Moving to Kadina would give him the distance he needed to deal with his feelings. When, months later, he learned of the birth of WH and Ann's first child, he could not help wondering at the possibility that the child might be his. He pushed the thought aside, but it was one that haunted him for the rest of his life.

On arriving in Kadina, Tom took a room in a boarding house recommended by the headmaster. It was conveniently located in a back street halfway between the centre of the town and the school. The boarding house, the largest in town with ten boarders, was owned and run by Mrs. Ellen Opie who told him she was a widow, although it wasn't long before he discovered that her husband had run off with a young woman who had been employed as a maid at the boarding house.

Mrs. Opie had two children: a son, Owen, who was a year or two younger than Tom, and an eleven-year-old daughter, Caroline. Caroline Opie looked older than her eleven years. She was already maturing into a woman and was clearly destined to become a beauty. When the housekeeper ran off with her husband, Mrs. Opie made her daughter leave school and take on housekeeping duties.

Tom was captivated by the girl and, as the weeks lengthened into months grew close to her. He encouraged her to study in what little spare time was available to her and lent her books on subjects he thought might be of interest. One weekend, when her mother was visiting her sister in Adelaide, he set up his camera and took a photographic portrait of her. He had her dress in the one decent outfit she possessed, instructed her on how to arrange her long brunette locks, and how to hold herself while he threw the black cloth over his head and exposed the plate that would capture her image. Later, when the photo had been developed, he presented it to her as a postcard inscribed with the words *To Dearest Carry, with fondest wishes, Thomas.*

Occasionally, when her domestic duties allowed, she would slip from under her mother's watchful eye and visit him in his room to sit with him while he painted. He also recited poetry to her from the pocketbook he carried with him at all times. She was playful and headstrong, qualities he admired in a woman, and he had to admit that, although a decade younger, she reminded him of Ann—not in looks, but in her independence of spirit. She teased him about his poetry.

"I don't know what they mean," she said to him one evening as he sat in the drawing room after the other boarding house residents had retreated to their rooms.

"Poetry has a meaning of a different kind," he replied.

"And I don't know what that means."

"One day you will. You're still young."

"I know more than you think I do," she said. He let the provocation pass.

He returned to Adelaide when the school closed in December for the Christmas break. The Port Adelaide house hummed with humanity. He shared a room with his brothers, William and Henry, who arrived from Kingcote. His sisters shared another room. Ann's parents came to visit from the Barossa, bringing Alexander, Ann's firstborn, with them. He held the newborn Frank in his arms for the first time and an odd sensation stirred within him. Ann's constant presence stirred emotions of a different kind. No opportunity presented itself for them to converse privately. She held herself apart from him, or so he thought. It was with relief and regret that he returned to Kadina earlier than planned. The school was yet to reopen, and with time on his hands, he gave himself over to his favourite pursuits—reading, writing, painting, and taking early morning walks beyond the town before the sun unleashed its heat.

His visits to Adelaide became less frequent. During school holidays, he travelled to Kangaroo Island where he spent time with his older brothers, William, in Kingscote, and Henry on his farm a short distance out of town. One summer, he returned to Kadina a week before school was due to resume. The region was in the grip of a heat wave, and in the afternoons, he sought refuge from the heat on the side verandah, which was shaded by a vine-covered trellis. It was there while he was reading late one afternoon and enjoying the fragrance of a potted lavender bush, that he was confronted by Mrs. Opie. The landlady thrust at him the postcard with the photographic portrait he had taken of Caroline two years earlier.

"What is the meaning of this, Mr. Price?" she demanded.

He was startled by her aggression. He had heard arguments between her and her daughter, arguments that he was not meant to hear, and more than once the sharp slap that Caroline received when she answered back, but this was the first time she had unleashed her aggression on him.

"It is an innocent likeness of your daughter, Mrs. Opie," he replied, doing his best to remain calm in the face of her anger. "There is no 'other meaning,' as you say. It was taken some time ago."

"Innocent? *Dearest Carry*? *Fondest wishes*? These are not innocent words, Mr. Price. This is no way to address a child. I know the ways of men. You stay away from my daughter, do you hear?" She tore the postcard in two and threw it into his lap, then, without waiting for a response, turned and marched into the house. Minutes later, he listened to the cries and protestations as Caroline received a beating from her mother.

For several days after the confrontation, Caroline kept her distance. Then, one afternoon when her mother was out, she knocked on his door and slipped into his room. He rose from his desk and embraced her.

"I'm sorry," he said. "I wanted to be a good thing in your life."

"You are," she replied. "You are the only good thing in my life."

Caroline was now fourteen. For three years, Tom had kept in check the infatuation which had grown as the girl had bloomed into womanhood. The embrace was their first physical contact. He kissed her and she let him.

"We have to take care," she said. "Owen is aware of the situation and has warned me off. If he knew what you just did, he would do you harm." Her brother lived and worked in the neighbouring town of Moonta, and only visited his mother and sister on weekends. His interactions with Owen were infrequent, and their relationship was distant. Tom's private assessment of her brother, which of course he did not share with her, was that he was a dullard, and possibly a bit of a thug.

Tom's infatuation with Caroline continued to grow, and seeing her going about her domestic duties without acknowledging his presence at the boarding house tormented him. When she was not working, she retreated to her room and, if the opportunity arose, he would sneak into the room and take her in his arms. He knew the risk he was taking but was powerless to resist the direction in which his legs carried him. On her fifteenth birthday, which fell on Boxing Day 1884, he presented her with a brooch. Early in the new year, Ellen Opie noticed the broach on her daughter's dressing table and confronted Caroline, who denied that it had come from Tom. Not believing her, Mrs. Opie waited until Tom came home and followed him to his room. His refusal to either confirm or deny her accusation infuriated her. Once more, she demanded that he stay away from her daughter. Tom heard her out. When she had finished, he said to her, "I'm terribly sorry that I appear to have upset you, Mrs. Opie, but now I have work to do." He spoke politely, and then turned away. Shaking with anger, the boarding-house keeper left the room.

Tom's response to Mrs. Opie's confrontation was typical. He devised a secret code, which he taught to Caroline. They no longer had any physical contact at the boarding house but used the code to exchange messages and met in a secluded bushland park on the edge of town. Shortly after they had begun their assignations, he sent her a note proposing marriage. He would wait the ten months until she turned sixteen, and then make a formal proposal to her mother.

His passion for the stage made him a natural choice for organizing the annual Christmas performance at the school. The headmaster and other teachers who, with one or two exceptions, viewed this as a chore, were more than happy to leave the task to him. At the end of his first year at the school, when he happily accepted the assignment, the headmaster suggested that he follow his predecessor and put on a Nativity play. This made sense. It was what the parents would expect, and they had the costumes from previous years in a tea chest in the storeroom. Tom flatly refused. It was a courageous stand. From his first arrival in the town, he had made clear his views on organized religion: no surprise to those who remembered the views of his father a decade earlier. Despite his atheism, which cut against the grain of the community, he was generally well-liked, the exception being his landlady. "We'll have none of that talk around here," she had said when he broached the issue of religion with one of the other boarders. Teachers, like bank managers and ministers of religion, were respected by virtue of their profession. Tom was dedicated to the children in his care, and their parents, few of them who had formal education themselves, appreciated this. Through learning, you could better yourself, escape the inevitability of a short life in the mines or a somewhat longer one as a farm labourer.

In his second year in Kadina, when two miners were killed in an accident, he organized a variety concert to raise money for the bereaved families. Although the amount raised was not substantial, it added to the esteem in which he was held in the town. The only sour note came on the evening following the concert. On his way home from school, he called into a pub some blocks from the boarding house. This was unusual, as he was a moderate drinker. The pub was quiet at that early hour, the only other drinkers being a group of young farm labourers at the far end of the bar. He recognized one of them as Caroline's elder brother. As he entered, the men, who had been talking loudly, grew silent and turned to stare at him. Owen said something to his companions that he didn't catch. He ordered a whisky. The men began talking again in raised voices. As he sipped his whisky and tuned in to their conversation, he realized they were talking about him in terms that were anything but complimentary. He quickly downed his drink, dropped some coins onto the bar, and left. This was out of character. Tom had courage, and wasn't afraid of conflict, as he had shown in his confrontation with Harry Dearmer years before, but the animosity towards him in the bar was palpable, and he had no desire for a fight with Opie.

Several months after he had proposed to Caroline, another confrontation, and this a much more serious one, took place between Tom and her mother. He realized that she meant business when she burst into his room without knocking and asked him to explain the rumour that was circulating among her friends that he and her daughter were engaged.

"I don't know how this gossip got started, but I am asking you to contradict such a report. It is outrageous that such talk has started. My daughter is just a child."

Taken aback her outburst, Tom said nothing. Caroline must have shared this information, but with whom? Presumably with one of her former schoolfriends. This was a major setback to his plan to marry the girl. Now that Mrs. Opie knew, she would take measures to thwart him. He would say nothing until he had spoken to Caroline. For a good two minutes, they stared each other down before she abruptly turned and left the room. He knew that from now on he would be under surveillance, but he had to speak to Caroline. He waited until he thought he heard her mother moving about downstairs, and then crept along to her room.

On returning from school the following afternoon, Tom handed Mrs. Opie an envelope. It contained a letter giving notice of his departure with immediate effect along with two weeks' rent. Then he packed his possessions into a trunk and arranged them to be delivered to a hotel in a secluded part of town where he had taken a room. It was a temperance hotel which suited Tom because the rooms were cheap, and it would be quiet.

Mrs. Opie was relieved to see the back of him, although she realized it provided greater opportunities for him to pursue Caroline away from her watchful eye. Initially, he had seemed a pleasant young man with a decent education. While she had disapproved of the warmth of his affection for her daughter, it seemed innocent enough. As time passed, his eccentric views on religion and his dandy ways caused tensions. She formed the opinion that he thought far too much of himself. As Caroline grew into womanhood, and his affections intensified into infatuation, her disapproval hardened into an intense dislike.

Things came to a head one day when Tom was at school and Caroline was out shopping, Mrs. Opie went through her room and came across a note penned in what she recognized as Tom's distinctive handwriting. Caroline returned to find her mother waiting for her, note in hand. She had been unable to decipher the code and demanded that Caroline tell her what it said. Caroline refused. She asked her mother for a few days to think about it, and Mrs. Opie, knowing full-well how headstrong and stubborn her daughter could be, gave her a week.

The following day was a Saturday and at the earliest opportunity Caroline slipped away from the boarding house and made her way to Tom's hotel. She knew he spent most free Saturdays at the school conducting art classes for those of his pupils who were interested but was certain to be in his room during the morning. She slipped unnoticed in the rear entrance of the hotel and made her way up the stairs to his room.

At her knock, he came to the door paintbrush in hand and was surprised and delighted to see her. She let him kiss her, then sat on the edge of the bed and told him what had happened.

She finished her account by saying, "I just don't know what to do."

"You have to leave. It will only get worse," he said.

"All I want to do is to get away. It's all I've wanted for a long time, and I have told my mother, so how is that possible? I have no money and nowhere to go."

"I will work something out," replied Tom. "I'll leave a note for you at the hotel desk on Tuesday. If you agree with my plan, then leave a note saying so."

On Tuesday, Caroline gave her name to the girl at the front desk, a girl who, thankfully, was unknown to her. She read the encoded note, pocketed it, and asked the girl for a sheet of paper and an envelope. She wrote a single word reply on the notepaper, inserted it in the envelope, and wrote Tom's name on the front. At the end of the week, she refused to decode the note. She had to stall until Tom's plans had been set in place and asked for another week. With great reluctance, her mother allowed her one more week, but said, "That will be the end of it. If you refuse at the end of next week, I shall beat you, and it will be a beating you will not forget in a hurry." Thinking that the plans must sure be in place in the next few days, she readily agreed. However, during the week, she learned from Tom that the plan could not put into action until two days after her mother's deadline.

On the appointed day, her mother appeared in her room with the note in one hand and a thick piece of knotted rope in the other. When Caroline again refused, her mother lashed her across the shoulder with the knotted rope. Then, her anger getting the better of her, she rained blows indiscriminately on the shoulders, arms and across the face. As each blow cut into her, Caroline let out a shriek. The sounds only encouraged her mother to strike her even more forcefully. It was only when she collapsed on the bed that her mother dropped the rope. "Oh Caroline," she said, "how could you make me do this to you?"

She turned her face to the wall, a knot of anger hardening in her stomach. She heard her mother leave the room and close the door. That her mother could blame her for the pain she was now experiencing was beyond belief. A short time later, she heard the door open and felt the weight of her mother on the end of the bed. Her mother fumbled for her hand, but she pulled it away.

"What I did, I did for you. It was for your own good."

Caroline ignored this small offering. "I want to go away. I'm not staying here."

There was silence from the end of the bed. Then her mother said, "That may be a good idea. Take a week off. Stay with one of your friends and think about your future." She felt a light touch on her damaged shoulder. "Get some rest now, and we can talk later." She heard the faint note of triumph in her mother's voice. She thought that she had won.

Two days later, she left her mother's house, saying that she would go to her friend Daisy's place in Moonta. Her mother gave her money for the week along with her blessing. The week passed quickly. With Caroline gone, Ellen Opie had added the duties normally undertaken by her daughter to her own. When at the end of the week, Caroline failed to return, she summoned her son Owen. "Go to Moonta and get her back," she said. The following day, she grew increasingly concerned as the sky darkened and Owen hadn't returned. When he did was alarmed to see that he was alone.

"Where is she?"

"They don't know," her replied, handing her a note from Daisy's mother. From the note, Ellen Opie learned that Caroline was not in Moonta, and had not been there all week. She had left the boarding house the previous week and simply disappeared.

"What to do? I shall go to the police," she said, crumpling the note in her fist.

Owen was against the suggestion: of course he was. As a boy, he had frequently pitted himself against the law, and come off second best every time. He had other ideas. "I will handle this," he said. "The schoolteacher was paying attention to her. I'm sure he's behind her disappearance."

"After all I did to warn her off him. If this is true, things will have to change around here. But first we have to get her back."

"He has something to do with her disappearance—there's nothing more certain. Don't worry, I'll get her back."

In the four years that he had been at the Wallaroo Mines School, Tom had settled comfortably into rural life as well as into his profession. Unlike some of the other teachers, he knew each of his pupils well—their lives beyond the schoolyard as well as their interests and educational needs. He treated them in an adult manner, even though most of them were far from adulthood, achieving discipline through reason, not the strap, and finished each day by reading aloud a chapter from a book he brought from home. These books were very different from the primers that were a staple of the classroom library. Each day, he ended the reading at a suspenseful point in the story. The children would beg him to read on, which he never did, snapping the book shut and telling pupils that if they wanted to know what happened next, they had to turn up the following day and be good students. The pupils weren't perfect, and he dealt with misbehaviour by banishing the miscreant from the reading. This led to tears, entreaties and promises never to misbehave again. Tom was fair but firm, and the child had no choice but to swallow his medicine. (Tom sometimes mused on the fact that, while girls were just as capable of misbehaving as boys, it was only ever the boys who got caught.) On those weekends when he had no other commitments, he was busy at the school, rehearsing an upcoming play with pupils, conducing sketching classes, or leading a group on a nature ramble on the outskirts of the town.

September 17, 1885 was a Thursday. A half-day for the pupils had been declared so teachers could tidy up the classrooms and the schoolyard. Those children who had no adults at home to look after them were kept at school to assist the teachers. Tom took a group to the art room, which acted as his "home" room, and set them to work washing down storage areas and benchtops, and re-shelving art equipment. By four o'clock, the work was completed. Tom dismissed the pupils and was gathering his things together when Mary Davey, one of the school assistants, appeared in the door of the art room. She told Tom that there was a messenger in the lobby with a telegram for him. Leaving his bag in the art room, Tom walked down the corridor to the lobby, where he was confronted by Owen Opie. Before he could speak, Opie swung a punch which caught him in the left eye and knocked him to the ground. Before he could scramble to his feet, his larger and stronger assailant was on him. He held Tom down with his left hand and pulled a revolver from his jacket pocket with his right. He pushed the muzzle into Tom's neck. Behind them, Tom heard a confusion of footsteps and then the voice of the headmaster, Robert Willshire, who had come from his office at the sound of the scuffle. "What's going on?"

Without releasing his grip on Tom, Opie twisted around and waved the pistol in Willshire's direction. "Stand back! If you interfere…" While he didn't complete his threat, his intention was clear.

"Just go, Mr. Willshire," called Tom. "Don't risk your own life."

Robert Willshire didn't need another excuse to retreat. He left the lobby, and pulled the door shut. The pistol exploded a shortly after the sound of the door slamming. It was followed by a second shot. Tom never knew whether the shot was intentional or whether Opie had instinctively pulled the trigger at the sound of the door. The sound deafened him, and he felt real fear for the first time.

The pistol shot brought Willshire, Mary Davey and her sister, Joanne, back into the lobby. "Don't be afraid, Mr, Willshire," cried Opie in a high-pitched voice, waving the pistol wildly in the air. "I will not hurt you or anyone else, except this wretched infidel." He spat the last word at Tom.

Willshire, an older man, remained calm. "I suggest that you give me the gun," he said.

"No, sir, I will not give up the gun," said Opie.

"Is there anything I can do to settle matters between you?"

"No. My little sister has been abducted by this scoundrel. You shall hear all about it after." Turning back to Price, he said, "Get on your feet, you infidel."

"Let me go. I'll go quietly," replied Tom, climbing to his feet.

"Yes, if you attempt to run, I'll shoot you dead."

"Will you allow Mr. Willshire to go with me?"

"Yes."

"I need to get my hat from my office," said Willshire.

"Put your hands on your head,"

Willshire did as he was told.

Now you can fetch your hat."

The minute the Headmaster vacated the lobby, Opie with the pistol still levelled at Tom, pushed him out of the lobby and across the schoolyard.

"Where are you taking me?" asked Tom.

"To my mother. You will tell her the whereabouts of my sister."

"What makes you think I know where your sister is?"

Tom spoke quietly but firmly. Opie was in a highly agitated state and had already demonstrated his willingness to fire the pistol. He had also threatened Tom's life in the presence of witnesses. However, Tom was determined to protect Caroline from further violence, and that meant keeping her location secret. As they entered the street, Opie concealed the pistol beneath his coat, and marched Tom briskly in the direction of the boarding house.

Having retrieved his hat from his office, Richard Willshire returned to the lobby to find it empty. "Where's Mr. Price?" he asked Joanne Davey who was in an adjacent classroom.

"They left," she replied. "I heard the man with the gun say they would go to his mother's house."

"Send Mary for the police," said Willshire. Despite his outward sanguinity, he had been badly shaken by what had taken place and was concerned for the wellbeing of young Price. He had been a friend of Tom's parents during the years that they had lived in the town, had known Tom since he was a boy, and had mentored him in his early years as an assistant teacher. The young man who had suddenly appeared on this sleepy September afternoon threatening murder and making wild accusations against Price was clearly unhinged. On first encountering Opie, Willshire feared for his own life as the young man waved the pistol in his direction. Now Price had been abducted at the point of the gun.

The light was turning when Mary returned with Constable George Farquhar from the Wallaroo Mines Police Station. Willshire corroborated Mary's account of the afternoon's drama. Farquhar searched the lobby and recovered two bullets from the door that separated the lobby from the verandah

"What next?" asked Wilshire. "I'm concerned for the safety of my teacher."

"I think I know something of this matter," replied Farquhar. "Secure the school and go home. And say nothing for the moment."

Tom sat in the kitchen of the boarding house, his anger and indignation tempered by fear of what Opie might do. At least, after a whispered conversation between Owen and his mother, the pistol had disappeared from the kitchen table. He sat at the long pinewood table, arms folded, left eye bruised and swollen from Opie's blow, refusing to answer any questions about Caroline: not about her whereabouts, nor about the marriage rumours that swirled about town. Given the presence of three other lodgers in the parlour adjacent to the kitchen, voices had to be tempered.

Any attempt at keeping events privy to those immediately involved evaporated when Constable Farquhar stomped onto the wooden verandah that framed the front of the boarding house and rapped sharply on the doorframe. He was admitted and led to the kitchen by Ellen Opie. Owen Opie was known to him, but he had never seen Tom before. Tom identified himself, then, before Farquhar could ask for an account of what happened, Tom pointed to Opie and said, "I wish to have that man charged with attempting to murder me."

Ellen Opie immediately added, "And I want this man arrested for the abduction of my child."

Farquhar ignored both demands. Under the watchful eye of Tom and Ellen Opie, he patted Owen down and removed ten bullets from his coat pocket.

'Where is the weapon?" asked Farquhar.

Again, there was no response from Opie.

"He went to his bedroom a little while ago," said Tom.

"Where is your bedroom?" asked Farquhar. Opie pointed at the corridor that ran the length of the boarding house.

"Show me."

Opie led him down the corridor. A short time later they returned, Farquhar carrying the pistol in his hand. The weapon had five chambers, two of which had been discharged. The bullets matched those Farquhar had found at the school.

"He had good reason for what he did," said Ellen Opie. "My daughter has gone, and we have reason to believe that Mr. Price is responsible for her disappearance." She repeated her demand for Tom to be arrested and charged with abduction.

"I shall have to ask both of you to accompany me to the station," Farquhar said. He led them in the direction of the Kadina Police Station, which was larger and better staffed. On the way, Opie, realizing the seriousness of the situation, spoke for the first time, "I did not want to hurt him, only to frighten him so that he would tell us what he has done with my sister." At the station, both men were handed over to the duty officer. Farquhar provided a brief account of the events of the afternoon and gave the pistol and bullets to the officer. Each prisoner was then taken to a separate cell.

"What's going to happen?" asked Tom as he was ushered into his cell by a constable barely older than Tom himself.

"You have to spend the night here."

"Why?"

"An accusation has been made against you. Tomorrow, you will be questioned, and a charge may be prepared. You will then have to face the Police Court to determine whether you have a case to answer."

"And if it is determined that there is a case to answer?"

"You will be tried in the Adelaide Supreme Court."

With these words, the constable left, locking the heavy steel door and opening a small aperture so that Tom could be checked on during the night. He then strode back to the relative comfort of the front desk. Tom sat on the thin mattress covering the concrete bench that served as a bed. The constable's chilling words brought home to him the reality of his situation. Hands clasped behind his head, he stared at the plaster wall which had been defaced with what looked to be the blade of a knife. Not three hours ago, he had been engaged in directing his pupils as they cleaned up the art room. Now he had been deprived of his liberty and faced the prospect of a prison sentence.

He could have sworn that he had not slept a wink, but shortly after daybreak was woken by the day desk sergeant, who had come on duty at dawn. The sergeant brought him tea in a chipped enamel mug and gave him an encouraging smile. His face was familiar. The it came to him. The sergeant's youngest son had been his pupil the previous year. He was a pleasant open-faced boy but struggled with his letters. For several months, Tom gave him reading and writing lessons after school. Although the boy never caught up with his fellow students, he made reasonable progress, and his parents were grateful to Tom.

The tea had long been consumed when he was escorted from the cell. He wondered what had taken them so long—presumably interrogating Opie. Tom was formally arrested and charged with the abduction of a minor. He was told that Opie had already been charged with attempted murder and was committed for trial in the Supreme Court in Adelaide. Given the evidence against him in the form of the pistol and ammunition, and Opie's own statement, there was no need for him to face the Police Court. The fact that he had a case to answer was transparent.

When asked to reveal Caroline's whereabouts, Tom refused. He would only answer questions in the presence of a lawyer. Although his stomach churned, on the surface he remained calm. The sergeant nodded. They would see to it. He was returned to his cell where he sat and stared at the disfigured wall. The day passed slowly. As evening approached, he was brought bread, cold meat, a mug of tea and a change of clothes that the police had fetched from his hotel.

The following day, a man was admitted to his cell by the duty officer. He introduced himself as John Uffendell, a local solicitor, who would represent him at the committal hearing. Uffendell was youthful-looking man with a pleasant face. He could not be more than thirty years old, which bothered Tom. The duty officer and Uffendell escorted him to the interrogation room. Again, he was asked to reveal Caroline's whereabouts. He looked at Uffendell who nodded. "You have to tell them," he said. "The arraignment cannot proceed until she is found." Somewhat reluctantly, he revealed that Caroline was staying with his brother Henry, at his farm on Kangaroo Island. Tom was remanded in custody pending the retrieval of Caroline from Kangaroo Island. He would then face the Kadina Magistrates' Court where it would be determined whether he had a case to answer.

On the day before the hearing Tom gave the desk sergeant a list of clothing items, he would like brought from his hotel room. Like his father, Tom dressed well. It was this that gave him the reputation in the country town of Kadina as a dandy. About town, he could be taken for a local businessman or doctor rather than a rural assistant schoolmaster. For his court appearance, he had instructed the sergeant to fetch his light grey suit with matching waistcoat, white shirt and bow tie.

Tom slept poorly and woke before dawn. While nervous, he was quietly confident that the case against him would be dismissed. He had right on his side. His actions were entirely admirable. He had rescued a young woman from a life of servitude and abuse. He had spent almost two days in the windowless cell. For someone with such a creative mind and lively curiosity, incarceration was an impossible proposition. It was inconceivable that the charge against him would be upheld.

An orderly, accompanied by a police constable, brought him bread, jam and tea. Mechanically, he chewed on his breakfast, changed into his suit, and sat on the bench fussing with his bow tie which, in retrospect had been a mistake. He should have gone for the sombre grey necktie, one that matched his suit, but it was too late for small regrets.

The constable came for him shortly before nine o'clock. Stepping from the eternal twilight of his cell into the startling sunshine of a spring morning was to step from one universe to another. He looked up at the sky and smelled the freshness in the air. As he was led the short distance from the police station to the courthouse, a reporter from the *Adelaide Register* tried to question him. The escorting officer fended off the reporter and guided him into the courtroom. Stories of the abduction and subsequent shooting, most with lurid embellishments, spread quickly, and half the town had turned up for the hearing. The gallery was packed, and members of the public spilled into the street. He was slightly ruffled to see Mrs. Opie sitting prominently in the section of courtroom reserved for the prosecution. She locked her black eyes on him as he entered, and he could feel them burning into his head during the hearing. He was seated next to John Uffendell and instructed to wait for the court officials to appear. Uffendell patted his knee and gave him an encouraging smile. As they waited, the solicitor assured him that he had nothing to worry about. Although this was Uffendell's first case, and he had not before risen to defend a client, he had been fully briefed by Tom and was convinced his client had no case to answer. He assured Tom that he would be back at school with his pupils the very next day. However, as the arraignment got under way, the hearing took a very different course from the one predicted by the young solicitor.

Tom looked curiously across the room to the Prosecutor, an army officer by the name of Lance-Corporal Bennett. Older than Uffendell, it would be his job to convince the court that Tom had a case to answer. After an intolerable delay, during which the gallery behind him grew restless, the presiding officers, two local Justices of the Peace, Joseph Guener and Clarence P. Styles, entered the room from a side door. "All rise," called the clerk of the court. When the Justices had settled themselves, the room was called to order and the hearing began.

Tom's facade cracked when Caroline was brought into the court by the prosecution. Wearing a simple, white dress, her hair in ribbons, she looked more a demure schoolgirl than the spirited young woman who had infatuated him. She gave him a brief glance, then allowed herself to be led into the witness box.

When asked to identify herself Caroline said she was the daughter of Mrs. Ellen Opie and resided in Kadina.

"Do you know the prisoner?" asked Bennett. Tom was startled to hear himself referred to as a prisoner. It seemed as though he had already been tried and found guilty.

"Yes, I have known Mr. Thomas John Price for nearly five years. For most of that time, he lived at my mother's boarding house."

Under examination, Caroline admitted that Tom had been paying attention to her for around a year.

"Were his intentions romantic?" asked the prosecutor.

When Caroline hesitated, Mr. Guener said, "Answer the question, please." Her answer came in the form of a nod.

"We need to hear the answer from your own lips."

"Yes," she replied, to gasps from the gallery.

"Was your mother aware of the attentions Mr. Price was paying you?" asked Bennett.

"Yes. She found some of the gifts he gave me—a brooch, an album, a handkerchief box."

"And she instructed you not to associate with an older man, as any good mother would do to a young, innocent daughter."

"Yes."

"Did you disobey her?"

Again, Caroline hesitated, and had to be prompted to answer the question.

"Yes."

Tom listened with increasing alarm as the narrative unfolded. He was being constructed as a designing, if not lecherous older man intent on luring her into a sordid, illegal relationship. In reality, he was only a few years older than Caroline. Although his feelings were intense, his intentions were honourable, his actions driven, not by lust, but by his love for her and a desire to rescue her from a life of exploitation and physical abuse. Why wasn't Uffendell objecting to the line of questioning?

"Is it true that the prisoner made a proposal of marriage to you?" More gasps from the gallery.

After another pause, Caroline answered in the affirmative.

"Please tell the court about the circumstances of the proposal."

"He made the proposal in a letter that was written in a code he taught me."

Bennett then took a note from the clerk of the court and held it up.

"Is this one of the letters you received from the prisoner?"

"Yes."

"What does the code at the top mean?"

"*My Dear Carry*."

"And at the bottom?"

"*I kiss you.* and *Your own Thomas*." The intimacy of the words simultaneously titillated and scandalized the gallery.

"And where is the proposal letter?"

"I burnt it."

"Why did you burn it?"

"I was afraid someone might read it."

"Would that someone be your mother?"

"Yes."

"But your mother was aware of Mr. Price's designs?"

"Yes. My mother cautioned me not to speak to the prisoner. More than once, I told the prisoner my mother forbad me to speak to him."

Why did she persist in referring to him as a prisoner? Why couldn't she refer to him by name? From the line of questioning, it seemed that he had manipulated Caroline into deceiving her mother.

"But you disobeyed her."

"I kept seeing him."

"What were the circumstances that led you to run away?"

"I was unhappy at home and had wanted to go away. Mr. Price knew I was unhappy and encouraged me to do so. About a fortnight ago, I received a letter from him saying I would be much happier far away and said I could go to his brother's farm on Kangaroo Island. I replied to that letter saying I would accept his proposal. For some time, I had determined to leave home whenever a chance came along. This was the first chance I had."

At this point, Bennett changed his line of questioning. Was it true that Mr. Price had paid her to leave Kadina?

Tom read the confusion on Caroline's face. It was true that he had given her money for the trip, but it was understood between them that this was a loan. The word "payment" had a sinister connotation and misrepresented the nature of the transaction. At long last Uffendell got to his feet and objected to the question, but he was overruled.

"Answer the question, please, Miss Opie," said Guener.

"Mr. Price gave me £3 on the Sunday before I went away."

"Did you understand that this was a gift or a loan?"

"Objection," said Uffendell.

"Overruled," replied Guener. "Answer the question, Miss Opie."

"Nothing was said when the money was placed in my hand," replied Caroline. No, nothing was said, thought Tom, but none was needed. The kiss and the embrace spoke volumes, but they could not be admitted as evidence into a court of law. She had offered to pay him back some time, but he had waved away the offer.

"How did you get away from your mother? Did Mr. Price aid you?"

"Objection," said Uffendell, who seemed to be growing in confidence, if not vocabulary.

"Overruled."

"Four days after I received the money from Mr. Price, I told my mother I was going to Moonta to stay with a friend."

"And did you go to Moonta?"

"I did not. I went to Wallaroo and took the train to Adelaide. Mrs. Harry Price met me at the Adelaide Railway Station and took me to Mrs. Price's sister, Mrs. Collins, at New Thebarton. I stayed two nights and one day, and then went to Kangaroo Island."

"What were you expecting?"

"I didn't know what to expect. I didn't know that the prisoner had written to his brother or anyone else, but I was treated with great kindness."

"And how were you treated by the prisoner?"

"The prisoner always behaved as a gentleman to me during the time that he lived at the boarding house. He helped me with my education, he gave me gifts, he gave me hope for the future."

"Please stick to the facts that are relevant to the hearing," interjected Styles, the other J.P. presiding over the hearing. Stick to the facts? What could be more relevant than his kindness? But, Tom realized, kindness had no place in the courtroom. It couldn't be seen, touched, tasted or weighed.

Bennett indicated that he had no further question. When asked if he had any questions for the witness, Uffendell declined. Tom was surprised by this decision. Did he lack the confidence to question Caroline, or did her want to save her further distress? Her time in the witness box had been lengthy and she was clearly affected by the ordeal.

The clerk of the court next called Mrs. Opie. She strode purposefully to the witness box, took the oath of office, and identified herself as Ellen Opie, keeper of a boarding house at 15 Frances Terrace, Kadina. She stated that she had a daughter called Caroline who was fifteen years of age. The clerk of the court tabled a birth certificate to verify Caroline's age. By the time Mrs. Opie had finished testifying and the presiding Justices had retired to consider their verdict, it was past 5 o'clock in the afternoon. It had been a long day, and only the hardiest spectators remained in the public gallery. At 5.30, the Justices returned, the court was instructed to rise, the Justices settled themselves, and Guener delivered their verdict.

"The Bench finds the prisoner guilty and commits him to stand trial at the next Criminal Sitting of the Supreme Court in Adelaide. Bail is allowed: payment of £50 by the prisoner on his own recognizance and two sureties of £25 each. The prisoner is remanded in custody until the bail is posted."

Numbed by the verdict, Tom was led back to his cell.

Chapter 9
A Close Call

Adelaide was agog with the news of the Kadina criminal cases. Like its better-established siblings, Sydney and Melbourne, the City of Churches had its own dark underbelly. While murder, actual or intended, was not unknown, the abduction of an attractive underage girl by a country schoolmaster, and the attempted murder of the perpetrator by her vengeful brother, brought a new twist to a familiar crime. In the weeks leading up to the trials of Owen Opie and Thomas John Price, the *Adelaide Advertiser, the South Australian Register* and the *Evening Journal* ran several pieces on the "Kadina Shooting Case" and the "Kadina Abduction Case" as they were called. Given the fact that both cases were linked, they were to be held in tandem.

Tom moved back into the Price family home in Port Adelaide in advance of his trial. The family knew of the case of course, given the newspaper coverage and the involvement of Henry and his wife. Not surprisingly, they accepted Tom's version of the story, that his action was prompted by a desire to rescue a vulnerable young woman from domestic abuse. The public was not so sure. The revelation that he had proposed marriage to the girl indicated that his action was driven by more than a humanitarian impulse to rescue her from domestic abuse.

For Tom, it was comforting to be surrounded by his family. Ann was a source of strength, and in the weeks leading up to the trial, the gap between them that had grown during his years in Kadina began to shrink. He also got to know his half-siblings, Frank, who was almost four, and Lilian, who had just turned one. He formed a close attachment to Frank, a bond that was to remain for the rest of his life.

When Tom told his father he would repay the bail WH had posted for his release, following the Kadina hearing, the offer was waived away. Their focus had to be on ensuring a "not guilty" verdict. Now a prominent member of the South Australian professional and business community,

WH secured the services of Charles Cameron Kingston to represent his son. A barrister and member of the Legislative Assembly for the seat of West Adelaide, Kingston was a formidable character—so formidable, that years into the future, he would be appointed, along with Alfred Deakin and Edmund Barton, to convince the British Parliament to grant independence to the Australian colonies. Over six feet tall, a champion sportsman, and possessing great strength, he dominated the courtrooms in which he appeared and was disliked by some members of the profession for his overbearing and bullying tactics. Ironically, given the charge against which he would defend Tom, the only blemish on his character was that he had seduced the younger sister of another prominent member of the South Australian business community. While Kingston was very different in character and disposition from WH and Tom, both agreed that after the disappointing Uffendell, they needed a lawyer with Kingston's experience and ability to dominate the trial. More important than his overbearing disposition were his radical, libertarian views which were very much in accord with those of WH and Tom.

As the trial date approached, from time to time at night Tom relived Ellen Opie's testimony at the arraignment. He wondered how much of it she would rehash at the trial to come, and what bearing it would have on the outcome. In pre-trial briefings, Kingston revealed to him that somehow the Opies had secured the services of W. V. Smith to defend Owen. "One of the few adversaries in the State for whom I have any time," he told Tom. This was of little comfort. It wasn't meant to be. Kingston did not see it as his job to leave his clients in any doubts as to the precariousness of their situation.

"Why would he be an adversary?" asked Tom. "He's not part of the prosecution at my trial.

Kingston smiled—rather patronizingly, Tom thought. He was told that in this game, everyone was an adversary. Smith would undoubtedly want to get Tom into the witness box. He would seek to reinvent Opie's character in the Supreme Court trial at the same time as attempting to blacken Tom's. Kingston predicted that Opie would not be found guilty of attempted murder. And that would place a heavy burden on Tom at his own trial. "Mr. Smith will not be a disinterested party to your trial. In fact, I heard just last night that he would be a co-prosecutor along with the Crown Solicitor."

Courts of law and the rituals surrounding criminal trials enacted within them are designed to intimidate. The intention is to reduce the accused to a cypher, to remind him constantly that he has no power. On the day that the twin trials began, Tom, rarely given to nerves and never subject to intimidation, was a wreck. As expected, his experience in the Kadina Police Court was a taste of things to come.

Opie's case was the first to be heard. The clerk read the charge: that Owen Richard Opie did discharge a loaded pistol at Thomas John Price with intent to murder him at Wallaroo Mines School on September 17. An alternative charge was also read—that the prisoner had fired the pistol with the intent to maim and do grievous bodily harm.

As Kingston had predicted, once the charges had been read Smith rose and signalled his intention to call Tom as a witness. Kingston immediately rose to his feet and objected. Given the intertwined nature of the two trials, the judge took his time in deciding whether to allow the request. Finally, he said, "I am inclined to allow Mr. Smith to ask some questions of Mr. Price concerning his past life. However, I wish it to be particularly understood that it must not be taken as a precedent. I shall observe Mr. Smith's questions and disallow any that I deem to be too remote. The answers provided by the witness are to be taken as they are, and no evidence can be called to refute them."

In the cross-examination, Tom stated that he had resided at the Opie boarding house for approximately four and a half years. There were audible gasps from the public gallery when Smith asked if he had boasted of performing acts of personal immorality with Miss Opie. Stunned, Tom shook his head. "Absolutely not," he replied.

"Do not pursue this line of questioning, Mr. Smith," said the judge. Smith withdrew the question, but in Tom's mind the damage had been done. He was then led through a series of questions concerning the events at the school and at the boarding house. Immediately after the headmaster had withdrawn from the lobby, he had grappled with Opie in an attempt to wrest the pistol from him. Two shots were discharged. He could not say whether they were accidental, but Opie's intention to see him dead was clear. He had then been taken at gunpoint to the boarding house. Constable Farquhar had knocked on the door of the boarding house about fifteen minutes later. After recovering the revolver from Opie's room, Farquhar had taken them to the police station where he had been incarcerated pending being charged with the abduction of a minor.

Tom was followed on the stand by a witness who identified himself as Clarence Sebastian Newman, an accountant at the National Bank of Australia at Kadina. On the afternoon of September 17, the accused had come into the bank at about three o'clock in the afternoon and said to him, "You have a pistol here. Will you lend it to me for a bit?" Newman agreed to the request and was getting the weapon from the teller's draw when the manager intervened, saying that the gun could not be removed from the premises. However, he would lend Opie his own weapon. He retrieved it from his desk and handed it over to Opie along with fifteen rounds of ammunition. Opie pocketed the gun. As he was leaving the bank, Newman asked him if he was going for an afternoon's shooting. "I surely am," he replied.

Smith concluded the hearing by saying that while his client had acted very foolishly, he had done so in the interests of his little sister. The most the jury could do was to find him guilty of common assault. If his client had meant to kill or maim Price, he had ample opportunity for doing so. The first discharge was caused by Price striking his hand, and the second by the ensuing struggle for the gun. His client had no intention of killing Price, merely to compel him to go to his mother's boarding house and reveal the whereabouts of his sister. The assault was of a most trivial nature, and the demands of justice would be fully satisfied by a fine of five shillings or thereabouts.

The judge took a rather different view. In his summing up to the jury, he dwelt upon the necessity of using the strong arm of the law to protect the community against acts of violence, which were becoming all too prevalent in society. He then pointed out the distinction between the different counts in the indictment. The key decision for the jury was to decide whether the prisoner intended to shoot Price, or merely to frighten him.

It took the jury less than fifteen minutes to return with their verdict. They found Owen Richard Opie guilty of common assault. The judge thanked the jury for their service, dismissed them, and announced that he would defer sentencing until the case against Price had been heard.

Tom was then called to the witness stand by the Clerk of the Court. As Kingston had predicted, prosecuting him were the Crown Solicitor and W. V. Smith. His trial had a tricky beginning which could have swung the case against him. The Clerk placed a Bible before him and intoned the standard formula. "On this Bible, do you swear to tell the truth, the whole truth, and nothing but the truth, so help me God?"

"I do not."

The gallery, crammed with members of the public who had been drawn by the scandalous nature of the accusation and the prospect of salacious revelations, gasped. "Did he say do *not*?" they whisper to one another. The Clerk of the court turned to the presiding judge who leaned toward Tom and said, "Explain yourself."

"It would be meaningless," replied Tom. "There is no God, and this book," he pointed to the Bible before him, "is a work of fiction." More gasps from the gallery.

The Judge peered at Tom over his spectacles. "Are you saying that you are an atheist?"

"I am," said Tom, "As, indeed are my father and other members of my family."

"In that case, before the trial can proceed, I ask you to affirm that you shall tell the truth, the whole truth, and nothing but the truth on your own recognizance."

"I so swear," replied Tom.

"I shall therefore allow the case to proceed. Should you make any statement which I judge to be false, you will be held in contempt and dealt with accordingly."

Reporters in the press gallery scribble down this exchange which was subsequently reported in the *Advertiser*.

The Clerk then read the indictment. "You are charged with having, at Kadina, on September 10 last, taken and caused to be taken Caroline Opie, an unmarried girl under 16 years of age, out of the possession and against the will of her mother, Ellen Opie. How do you plead?"

"Not guilty," replied Tom in a firm voice.

Ellen Opie was the first witness for the prosecution. She repeated the evidence she had given at the Kadina hearing. Nearly a year before, when Caroline had just turned 15, she had asked Tom to deny the rumours swirling about town that he and her daughter were engaged. "It was a hard thing for the mother of a child so young to be associated with the name of any man. I could not allow it."

"What was the defendant's response?" asked Smith.

"He made no reply."

She then stated that on September 10, she had given Caroline permission to travel to Moonta to stay with a friend. Instead, induced and financed by the accused, she had absconded to Kangaroo Island, where she had stayed with members of the accused's family.

Kingston then rose to cross-examine her. Was it not true that her daughter had run away from home following a severe beating with a knotted rope?

"It was not…" began the witness but the Judge intervened.

"Just answer the question. A 'yes' or 'no' will suffice."

"Yes."

Caroline was then called to the stand. She repeated what she had said at the Police Court. Smith then produced a cutting from the local Kadina newspaper. It contained a letter of apology written by Caroline following the court hearing. In the letter, she said she had made statements in court against her mother and other that were untrue.

Kingston, in cross-examining Caroline asked if her mother had been present when she wrote the letter.

"Was it written under duress?"

"Yes," she replied.

"It is clear that you were unhappy at home?"

"Yes."

"During the ten days that you spent with his family on Kangaroo Island, did you have any contact with the accused?"

"No. From the time I left home until I returned, I never saw him."

"How were you treated by him before you left home?"

"He always acted to me very respectfully and as a gentleman. When the defendant proposed marriage, he suggested that we should not be married until I was over eighteen years of age."

The final witness to be called was Owen Opie. Prompted by the Crown Solicitor, he recounted the events surrounding the assault at the Wallaroo Mines School and how he had taken the accused back to the boarding house at gunpoint.

"What took place there?"

"The defendant revealed the whereabouts of my sister. He said that he had done the wrong thing, that he was deeply apologetic for his actions. 'I will get down on my knees and apologise,'—those were his exact words."

At this, Kingston rose and made an objection. "My client's words were spoken under duress—at the point of a gun. They are not admissible."

The judge agreed and moved to have Opie's statement struck from the record. This concluded the case for the prosecution against Tom.

In his closing address to the Jury, Kingston said there was no evidence of abduction within the meaning of the Statute. No proof had been submitted of the girl being "taken" out of the mother's possession by the defendant. He alluded to the fact that no similar case where a conviction was obtained could be found in the history of English Law Courts.

"In this case," he went on, "it must be borne in mind that the girl now lives with her mother, and, if she coloured her evidence at all, it would be to the injury of the defendant. For some reason, the mother had developed a strong dislike to the defendant. Her statements were most unreliable and utterly untrustworthy as proved by other witnesses. The conduct of the defendant was not in any degree reprehensible, and he had acted with the purest motives towards the girl."

As there was no coercion, and Tom had not seen Caroline after she left Wallaroo, the abduction case against him was dismissed. However, it was a close call, as Kingston reminded him after the Jury, having done its duty, was dismissed. He was left in no doubt that it was Kingston's skilful summing up, emphasizing the nobility of Tom's cause and calling into question Ellen Opie's evidence that had resulted in the successful outcome. Had the decision gone the other way, Tom's reputation would have been in tatters and his teaching career ruined. His gratitude toward the court moved him to request that the sentence imposed on Opie be lenient. In his summing up, Prosecutor Smith had suggested that justice would be fully satisfied by a fine of five shillings or thereabouts. The judge had other ideas and imposed a sentence of six months in prison with hard labour.

Although Headmaster Willshire, who had provided a glowing character reference to the court, offered to reinstate Tom at the Wallaroo Mines School, Tom declined. He might have been exonerated by the court, but knew that public sentiment in the town was solidly against him. In the court of public opinion, he was guilty of encouraging and assisting an underage girl to abscond from her family and would not be welcomed back into the community.

Willshire fully understood Tom's reluctance to return to the Copper Triangle. Using his contacts within the Education Department, he helped Tom obtain a position as assistant teacher at Port Victoria, a pretty coastal township down the Peninsula from Kadina. Just before Christmas, and two months after the Adelaide trial, Tom wrote a long letter to Caroline reiterating his commitment to her and repeating his promise to wait for her until she turned eighteen. He asked Willshire to find some way of getting the letter to Caroline without her mother's knowledge. Willshire expressed misgivings but acceded to his young colleague's wish. Caroline never replied. Did she ever receive the letter? He had to wait until January to check with Willshire as the headmaster had left the district for the Christmas and New Year break. Willshire assured Tom that he had personally placed the letter into Caroline's hands. "Painful as I know it must be, for your own sake I urge you to put the business and the girl behind you," he said to Tom.

The year that unfolded was not a happy one. In the early months, he thought constantly of Caroline. It tortured him to think of her incarcerated in the boarding house just a few miles to the north. Taking Willshire's advice, he resisted the urge to contact her. Her retreating back as she left the Adelaide Supreme Court was the last sight he ever had of her.

His enthusiasm for teaching also waned. The headmaster at Port Victoria school was a martinet, demanding complete obedience from children and teachers alike. He made no secret of his distaste for the creative arts and would appear without warning in Tom's classroom to disrupt an art or music lesson by criticizing Tom in from of the pupils. He put a stop to Tom's practice of ending the school day by reading to the children. Tom's natural optimism and sunny disposition evaporated.

He did his best to remain cheerful in from of the pupils, but outside of his classroom, he became withdrawn.

Once it became known that the new assistant teacher was the central figure in the Kadina Child Abduction Case, the townspeople kept their distance. It mattered little that the charge against him had been dismissed. "Where there's smoke, there's fire," was a commonly expressed sentiment whenever his name came up. Suspicions solidified when it emerged that he was an atheist. Well he would be, wouldn't he? No God-fearing Christian would abduct a child. He endured the year, and then, when the school closed for the Christmas break, travelled to Adelaide to visit WH, Ann, and the children, and then made his way to Henry's place at Kingscote. He settled quickly into the rhythm of the sleepy township. It was such a relief to stroll down the street without the pressure of prying eyes. The locals either didn't know who he was or didn't care. He indulged in his favourite pursuits. He read, he painted, he wrote. Between Christmas and New Year, he endeared himself to would-be thespians as well as the cricketing fraternity by organizing an Amateur Theatre night at the Queenscliff Hotel to raise money for the local cricket club. A week before he was due back in Port Victoria for the new school year, he sent a telegram informing the headmaster of his resignation with immediate effect. He was more than welcome to stay on with Henry and his wife for as long as he liked, but eventually the insular country life palled, and he made his way back to Adelaide where a series of ever more dramatic events were to change his personal and professional lives forever.

Chapter 10
Love Triangle

At the age of twenty-five, Ann reflected on the turbulence of her life over the preceding decade: the shipboard seduction by Harry Dearmer, which was nothing short of rape; the stultification of Remornie followed by the insanity of existence with a drunken, violent husband, first in Melbourne and Mornington, and then in Port Adelaide; four sons born to Harry; the dramatic night in 1880 when she had sought refuge in the Price household from the ongoing cycle of violence in her own home; the treasured domesticity of caring for WH, her passion for Thomas John, and the four more children who arrived during this new phase in her life; the joy brought by those of her children who survived and the lingering grief left by those who had not. All this by the age of twenty-five. What, should she live so long, would the next quarter century bring?

From time to time, she wondered what had happened to Harry. For the first year of her life with WH she lived with the quiet fear that he could reappear at any time to reclaim her and his children. However, he had not been seen nor heard of since being turned away from the house by the gallant fifteen-year-old Tom and his cricket bat. Missing, presumed dead, she thought—and hoped.

Following the death of his wife, WH led a solitary, almost withdrawn life. When she entered into service, she noted the gentleness and affection he showed his children, a stark contrast to the treatment meted out by Harry to her and her children. From the start, he had treated her kindly and respectfully, and when she moved in, she felt less like a domestic servant, than a member of the family. With young children about the house again, he became less withdrawn. She was able to lighten his mood and make him laugh. The night his children were all away and her own sons tucked up in bed, when he took her by the hand and led her to his room, she went without a moment's hesitation.

When their first child was born on November, 27, 1881, he was registered as Frank Dearmer, and Harry was named on the birth certificate as the father. However, with Dearmer gone for well over a year, there was no room for doubt as to the parentage. Or was there?

From the first moment she set eyes on handsome, sweet-natured and engaging Thomas John, there was an unspoken, mutual sensation of recognition—as though they had known each other in some other time and space. He possessed his father's qualities of kindness, creativity and curiosity with the added attraction of boundless energy and enthusiasm. He treated her with friendship, respect, but also an easy familiarity. As the pressures of his studies grew, she saw less of him about the house, and when he moved away from home, she felt an unsettling sense of loss. Their chance encounter at the East End market had led to a rekindling of their relationship. Then came the day she accompanied him to his lodgings and sat on the verandah enjoying the sunshine while he completed a pencil sketch of her. That night, it was the discovery of the sketch, which she had carelessly left in her bag, that threw Harry into a drunken rage and set off baby Sydney's screams. She scooped up the baby, grabbed Percy, and fled, while Harry stumbled about searching for the revolver, she had hidden earlier that day: an act that undoubtedly saved her life as well as those of her children. A short time later, Tom saved her again, beating Harry off with nothing but a cricket bat.

She visited Tom at his lodgings in St. Peters in March 1881, having received a note from him that he had something to tell her. He had been offered and accepted a position as assistant teacher at the Wallaroo Mines School in the mid-North and would be leaving Adelaide. He wanted to tell her in person. She was unable to disguise her distress. She closed her eyes. Then he was holding her, comforting her. It happened quickly, and with a sense of inevitability that astonished her in retrospect. And then they parted, she to the life she established with his father, and he to his new life as a rural schoolteacher. They would see each other only sporadically over the next few years on his infrequent visits to Port Adelaide. During those visits, nothing was ever said about what had happened on that warm afternoon in St. Peters.

As the 1880s advanced, the man who gave her shelter, security and children spent increasing amounts of time away from home. He extended his reputation in the mining industry and consolidated his fortune by acting as a consultant and technical advisor to numerous firms. He made regular trips to other parts of the country, particularly to Melbourne, which was the financial capital of Australia. During these absences, she was mistress of the household. From her time in Melbourne, she knew that the head offices of companies, large, medium-sized, and small, were to be found along Collins Street, as were the captains of industry, and the money men. He shared with her the details of his work when she asked. He would carry out surveys of nascent mining sites and report on their potential to Melbourne. He would also provide assessments to shareholders on the financial health of existing mines. The life of a mine is finite, he told her. Once the line of load-bearing ore began to peter out, the mine was doomed. He used his expertise to forewarn shareholders of the health of the mines in which they were invested: which were robust, and which should either be put on life support or terminated. Companies that WH either managed or advised shareholders on during the 1880s included the eclectic South Australian Plaster of Paris, Cement, Salt & Chemical Manure Works Co., the Aclare Silver Mine, Callington, the Gilles Glen Osmond Silver-Lead Mining Co., the Hamlyn Gold Sections Mining Syndicate, and Scotts Creek Silver-Lead Mining Syndicate.

For his work, WH was well compensated, both in cash and shares, although money was not a primary or even a secondary consideration. He was immersed in his work, and she was more than happy to support him by managing the domestic side of his life. He was unfailingly kind and considerate to her, and loving to the children, regardless of whether they were his or Harry's. In 1883, they had a second son. He was registered on the birth certificate as Dearmer, and Harry was identified as the father despite the fact that he had not been sighted for over three years. Lest there be any doubt as to his real lineage, he was given the forenames William Henry Price. They never married, partly because of uncertainty as to whether Harry was still alive, and partly because neither she nor WH put much store on the institution of marriage. Although she observed conventional proprieties by registering her children in Harry's name, outside the house she grew confident enough to go by the name of Ann Price.

Sadly, four months after his birth, William Henry Price Dearmer died of marasmus, a lack of sufficient breast milk, the same cause that had led to the death of his half-brother, John William Hector, four years earlier. Battling her grief, she insisted that the surname on his death certificate be changed from Dearmer to Price, resulting in the rather bizarre name of William Henry Price Price. Just a few weeks later, tragedy struck again. Eight-year-old Percy, the second son of Harry and Ann, died of tuberculosis and meningitis, at the Children's Hospital in North Adelaide. William Henry and Percy were both buried next to their deceased siblings in the West Terrace cemetery.

Some solace from the untimely deaths of William Henry Price Price and Percy Dearmer came with the birth, eight months after Percy's death, of Lilian Theresa. Again, the child was named Dearmer on the birth certificate, and Harry was identified as the father.

It was a comfort and relief to Ann that her parents embraced her relationship with WH. WH and Alexander were about the same age, and it would have been understandable in any era, much less the Victorian, if her parents had been scandalized at her taking up with a prominent atheist almost thirty years her senior, and to bear his children out of wedlock. However, in WH, they recognized a man of principle, of standing in the business community, and, it must be admitted, a man of wealth, who offered Ann and her children the security and protection that had been denied by her husband. On visits to Adelaide, members of the Forbes family stayed at the Price house, or, if space was limited, in a nearby hotel. When work took WH out of the city, he stayed with Alexander and Helen at their capacious Angaston residence. WH and Alexander grew particularly close as the years passed.. WH had such trust in a contemporary who, in other circumstances would have been his father-in-law, that he named Alexander executor of his will.

WH was a modest man. While he had benefited from, and contributed to, the mining boom that was part of the fabric of Australia's development in the second half of the Nineteenth Century, he attributed this to being at the right place at the right time rather than to his engineering and surveying skills. In his early years, he saw the South Australian copper industry almost brought to its knees as miners and members of the general public, delirious with gold fever, rushed east to New South Wales and the newly established colony of Victoria where large gold deposits had been discovered. When a colleague at the Monster Copper Mine at Burra suggested they seek their fortune on the Ballarat goldfields, he rejected the invitation out of hand, replying that, "With copper, iron ore and coal, you can build a nation. What can you do with gold?" It was to be his mantra for the rest of his working life. He was well aware that his jaundiced view was not shared by others, and was bemused at the lust for gold that brought people, not only from across Australia, but from around the world, as word spread that the largest goldfields the world had ever known had been discovered in the Antipodes. To his mind, one long-term benefit to the country was that hitherto sparsely populated parts of the county became populated.

In his work, he interacted with a wide range of races and nationalities as people flooded in, not only from Britain, Europe and the United States, but also from Asia, especially from China. When he first arrived in South Australia, a colony that had been established as a business rather than a dumping ground for convicts, he noted with distress the discrimination that was experienced by the Celtic minorities, the Irish, the Cornish, the Welsh and the Scots. His distress stemmed, not from his own background as a Welshman, but from his adherence to the principles of humanism— a belief that all people were equal, regardless of their race. He escaped discrimination because of his membership of the professional class, but it disturbed him to see the thread of white racism that was being woven into the fabric of the young country. In 1855, the Victorian government enacted the Chinese Immigration Act, severely limiting the arrival by boat of newcomers from the north with their pigtails, incomprehensible language, strange-smelling food, and other cultural oddities. He applauded the ever-practical and resourceful Chinese, who circumvented this regulation by disembarking in South Australia and trekking hundreds of miles overland to the Victorian goldfields. He would not live to see racism enshrined into the very first piece of legislation passed by the Australian parliament. It would have saddened him to know that the legislation was championed and steered through parliament by Alfred Deakin, a man he knew and admired.

Although gold was the fashionable find of the day, it was by no means the only mineral that was sought. Manufacturing powerhouses in the Northern Hemisphere hungered for silver, copper, lead, zinc, and other minerals, and the mines that WH established and managed fed this hunger. By the 1880s when WH was at his peak professionally, Australia, although still twenty years from nationhood, was the richest country in the world. Development was powered by an unprecedented influx of foreign capital, although the ever-cautious WH warned directors and shareholders in Melbourne not to expect the flood of overseas funds to last forever. He got no satisfaction from seeing his prediction come to pass at the end of the decade when returns on investments failed to meet expectations, and investment declined dramatically with disastrous consequences for the entire country. The ensuing depression heralded cycles of boom-and-bust that would become a feature of the Australian economic landscape throughout the nineteenth and well into the twentieth century.

At the time of Tom's trial, WH had asked Ann why she alone of the Price clan refused to appear in the public gallery of the Adelaide Supreme Court to provide moral support for his son. Her reply confirmed, if confirmation were needed, what he had long suspected. *I do not wish to set eyes on the girl who has brought this upon him.*

In 1887, Tom gave up his career as a teacher. He came back to Adelaide from Port Victoria and took up residence in North Adelaide. His return coincided with the birth, on July 17, of Ann's last child. On the register, she was named as Viola Alice Dearmer, although the surname was misspelled as Dearmar. However, no father was named, either on the register or the birth certificate. The failure to assign paternity had a simple explanation. She admitted to WH that she could not be sure whether the child was his or Tom's.

Ann spent increasing amounts of time at Tom's house in North Adelaide, and toward the end of the year she left the Port Adelaide home with the children and moved in with him. His friends found it odd that WH bore her no ill-will: not toward his son, nor to his common-law wife. But then WH was unconventional in many ways. In fact, he encouraged the relationship. His health, not always robust, was beginning to fail, and Tom could be trusted to nurture Ann and the children. He told her nothing of his visits to the doctor. "Four to five years, if you're lucky," the doctor said. It wasn't the dust in his lungs that would carry him off. The dust would weaken him, leaving him vulnerable to tuberculosis or pneumonia. The doctor called these diseases the Miner's Friend, because they ended the agony of a slow death from dusting.

In May 1888, WH abruptly left the Wheal Terrell Mine, which he had managed for two years, and moved to the mining town of Broken Hill, 330 miles north east of Adelaide. Located in arid semi-desert, just across the New South Wales / South Australian border, it was an inhospitable place to live, although the drier climate would be kinder to his lungs than the cold, damp Adelaide winters. His health was not the primary reason for moving across the border. Broken Hill offered exciting professional prospects for someone with his experience and knowledge. Once there, he took on the management of two newly established mines, the South Extended Mine and the Rising Sun North Mine. On first moving to Broken Hill, he lived alone in a galvanized, corrugated iron shanty. These hastily erected houses were the standard miners' dwellings throughout Broken Hill, although more substantial stone houses also occasionally punctuated the streetscapes. Cheap and easy to erect, the corrugated iron houses were stifling hot in summer, and impossible to heat in winter.

In 1883, five years prior to WH's arrival, a rich seam, or lode, of silver, lead and zinc had been discovered in the area by a boundary rider called Charles Rasp. Remaining upright on a horse for twelve or more hours a day was physically if not mentally taxing. It was also a lonely existence. Rasp would spend two to three weeks at a time riding along the barbed wire fences that separated one sheep property from another, repairing breaks in the wire and replacing fence posts that had been uprooted by feral animals.

WH was aware of the folklore surrounding Rasp's find. One day, on a rocky outcrop, he had picked up several misshapen lumps of rock that glinted oddly in the sun and shoved them into his saddlebag. He subsequently handed the samples to his boss, George McCulloch, who had them assayed in Adelaide. When the results came back, McCulloch, along with six other men, including Rasp, formed the Broken Hill Proprietary Company Limited. The mines established on the broken hill were, as WH predicted, destined to become the richest silver, lead and zinc mines in the world. What he could not predict was that the Broken Hill Proprietary Company would become, and remain into the 21st Century, the largest resource company in the world.

Rasp, like many immigrants, was not what he seemed. In fact, Charles Rasp was not his real name. He had been born into an aristocratic Portuguese family in Saxony, Germany as Hieronymous Salvator Lopez von Pereira. On arriving in Australia, presumably out of deference to the Anglo colonists, he changed his name to the more prosaic and infinitely more pronounceable Charles Rasp. Rasp would be the only one of the original seven investors who held on to his shares in BHP, and by the turn of the century was worth more than a million pounds, a huge fortune in those days. WH got to know Rasp but never learned what ghosts had chased him out of Europe, nor what impelled him into the Back of Beyond. It wasn't the done thing, to inquire into someone's background. Australia was a land for reinvention, and many immigrants found their way to the colonies with the express purpose of erasing their past.

The Broken Hill of 1888 was harsh and uninviting, which bothered WH not at all. The moment he left Britain, much of his life entailed hardship: from the clipper ship voyage to Adelaide to the early years in Burra, from establishing the Talisker mining community to the south of Adelaide, to life in the mid-north. Years after his discovery of the line of lode, in a newspaper interview Rasp described life in Broken Hill in the following terms: "At the start it was very bad. There was no accommodation, water and provisions were scarce and the weather was very trying. It was an awfully dusty place. For 12 months it was really doubtful whether we would make anything out of it; I had unlimited faith in it right through. Of course, I did not think it would turn out as big as it has done, but I always thought it would be a fairly good thing." A "fairly good thing," was a considerable understatement, given its subsequent emergence as the richest mine in the world.

The challenges of running not one mine but two kept WH very busy. Trips to Adelaide to visit his children became less frequent, although he continued making trips to Melbourne to report to company directors and shareholders on the health of the mines he managed. He arranged these trips to coincide with meetings of the Secular Association presided over by the exiled British secularist and firebrand Joseph Symes. Like many people who share a philosophy, but have very different personalities, they became firm friends. At their second meeting, WH invited Symes to Broken Hill to address a small assembly of secularists which he had formed into a society.

In October 1889, almost eighteen months after he arrived in Broken Hill, WH was leaving the entrance to the mine and heading to a meeting of the Secular Association of which he was a founding member. It was just on dusk, but he noticed a figure in the shadows on the far side of the road. He nodded good evening to the gateman, and turned left, towards his destination. It wasn't long before he became aware that the figure on the other side of street was following him. He paused, crossed the road, and confronted the man who stood his ground as WH approached.

"Mr. Dearmer," he said. The younger man had aged and gained considerable bulk but was clearly recognizable. Although not rolling drunk, he was clearly alcohol affected. Unsteady on his feet, his fists clenched. and barrel chest pushed forward, he looked more ursine than human.

"I'm looking for my wife."

"How did you find me?"

Dearmer brushed the question aside. It wouldn't have been difficult to track WH down. As a prominent member of the mining community, his appointment as a manager to new mining and exploration ventures was frequently noted in the Adelaide and Melbourne newspapers.

"My wife, where is she?"

WH thought quickly. Harry had taken the trouble to make the arduous trek to Broken Hill from goodness-knows-where to find his wife. Broken Hill was a small place, and it wouldn't have taken him long to establish that she wasn't in the township. WH had no intention of telling the younger man that he and Ann had separated, and that she was now living in Adelaide with Tom along with the children she had borne to Dearmer and WH.

"I cannot help you, Mr. Dearmer," WH replied and resumed his walk. Although bicycles were the usual form of transport for most workers, WH, who could have afforded a horse and sulky, walked for the sake of his deteriorating health. His priority was to forewarn Tom and Anne that Harry was on their trail.

Chapter 11
The Past Returns

Since childhood, Tom had been passionate about the stage, and his return from rural South Australia to Adelaide gave him opportunities to become more involved in amateur theatricals than had been possible in either Kadina, Port Victoria or Kangaroo Island. It was an interest he was to pursue for the rest of his life, and one that eventually took him beyond the shores of Australia to Europe and the China. He infected his younger half-sisters with a passion for public performance. Outgoing Viola, known in the family as Babs, took to the stage as soon as she could toddle. The more introverted Lil also enjoyed performing, although she was happier at the kitchen table with her watercolours and crayons. In their teens, both girls would become involved in vaudeville and carve international careers on the stage.

Like his father, Tom was also active in the Secular Association and wrote tracts to the Adelaide newspapers challenging the privileged position of Christianity and questioning the veracity of the Bible. This was a courageous thing to do in a strongly religious state whose capital city was known as the City of Churches and his views didn't go unchallenged.

In a lengthy letter to the editor of the *Adelaide Advertiser* on 3 June 1889 captioned "HOW THE NEW TESTAMENT HAS COME TO US." he crossed swords with the Reverend William Fletcher, a Congregational minister and scholar. Originally from England, with B.A. and M.A. degrees from the University of London in mathematics, classics, moral and natural philosophy, and political economy, Fletcher, in addition to his duties in the church, was a lecturer and member of Council at the University of Adelaide. He had also served as vice chancellor of the University from 1883 to 1887. Although not known as an original thinker, he was a formidable adversary for a former rural schoolteacher. With characteristic boldness, Tom had no hesitation in taking on Fletcher and the religious establishment. In a lengthy critique, he wrote:

Sir—With a due deference to the Rev. W. R. Fletcher's scholastic attainments, I beg to offer that there is not one scintilla of evidence that the New Testament, Gospels, etc, as we now have them, were in existence within 120 years of the supposed birth of Christ. Mr. Fletcher refers to a very old manuscript in the Vatican library, but he omits telling us that there are grave differences between that and the present New Testament. Dean Alford, who states that he read this manuscript in the Vatican library, remarks— "A formidable list of passages might be given in which our version either has confusedly mis-rendered the original or has followed a form of the text now well-known not to have been an original form." The Rev. gentleman also mentions "another copy nearly as old" as the one at Rome. This is evidently Dr Lischendorf's discovery—a discovery so valuable that he kept it a secret for 15 years! He discovered this MS in the Convent of St Catherine at Sinai, but we know that a Dr Simonides also discovered some MSS at the same convent, of which the Westminster Review said— "We share the suspicions, to use the gentlest word which occurs to us, entertained, we believe, by all competent critics and antiquarians." So much for the trustworthiness of Sinaitic MS3. There is one fact of the greatest import which should always be born in mind when considering how the New Testament has come to be, and that is the extensive frauds and forgeries that were systematically practised by the early church. Professor Mosheim, the popular Christian historian, tells us that among the early Christian Fathers it was considered "an act of virtue to deceive and lie, when by that means the interests of the church might be promoted." And again, the pious Eusebius says— "I have reported whatever may rebound to the glory and suppressed all that could tend to the disgrace of our religion." ("Evangelical Preparations," book xii, c. 31). Bishop Fell admits that "'in the first ages of the Church, so extensive was the license of forging, so credulous were the people in believing, that the evidence of transactions was grievously obscured." Daille asserts that "the writings of the fathers are in great part forged;" and again says—

"They would forge whole books to serve the ends of the priesthood." Bishop Marsh states that the writings that have come down to us are either "entirely spurious, or so interpolated as not to be depended on." The Rev. Edward Evanson denounces the gospels of Matthew, Mark, and. John as "spurious fictions of the second century." The famous Trinitarian text (1 St. John v, 7), the Apostles' Creed, and the Athanasian Creed are all recognised by scholars as forgeries. Page after page of similar admissions of Christian writers can be given. Will Mr. Fletcher, in the face of such overwhelming testimony, still hold that there is no evidence that the New Testament has been tampered with? The Rev. gentleman refers to Origen, but his authority is extremely suspicious, for even Bishop Horsley stigmatised him as "not to be incapable of asserting in argument what he believed not, and that a strict regard to truth in disputation was not one of the virtues of his character." Origen often quotes the Protevangelion and other apocryphal books as scripture, and I hardly think Mr. Fletcher would accept him as an authority in that direction. Again, if Origen really believed certain Scriptures to be the word of God, how do you account for his final rejection of Christianity and acceptation of Paganism? We are then referred to Irenaeus. I am afraid the Rev. gentleman will find himself awkwardly placed if he accepts all that Irenaeus says. Irenaeus quotes Hermes as Scripture, and says that Matthew wrote in Hebrew, whereas the first Gospel has only existed in Greek. Irenaeus, too, flatly contradicts the Gospels by stating that Jesus' ministry extended over 10 years and that Jesus lived to be 50 years of age. (Vide "Against Heresies," book II. c. 22). And further, Irenaeus informs us that there are only four gospels, "because there are but four quarters of the world, and every cherub has four faces!" Perhaps Mr. Fletcher will inform us whether he concurs with Irenaeus on these points. It is worthy of note that Irenaeus was the first to mention the four canonical gospels, and he lived about 182 AD. He also mentions the gospel of Truth and the gospel of Judas. Professor Semler (the "immortal Semler," as Bishop Marsh designates him) maintains that the writings of Irenaeus are spurious. Clement, of Alexandria, is useless as an authority, inasmuch as he cites as Scripture documents which do not appear in the present New Testament. We are next informed that Clement, of Rome, quotes from the gospels and epistles. In opposition to this assertion I put the Rev. Canon Sanday's frank admission that "Clement is not quoting directly from our gospels." This is how Clement describes the Phoenix, a fabled bird — "There is a certain bird called the Phoenix; of this there is never but one at a time, and that lives 500 years. And when the time of its dissolution draws near that it must die, it makes itself a nest of frankincense and myrrh and other spices into which, when its time is fulfilled, it enters and dies. But its flesh putrefying breeds a certain worm, which being nourished with the juice of the dead bird brings forth feathers, and when it is grown to a perfect state it takes up the nest in which the bones of its parent lie, and carries it from Arabia into Egypt, to a city called Heliopolis." Does Mr. Fletcher accept Clement's evidence on the Phoenix? Can we place implicit trust in one who so readily believes such outrageous nonsense? Not everyone is aware that the 27 canonical books of the present New Testament are only a selection made from innumerable documents that were current in the early days of Christianity. There is no evidence as to where, when, or by whom this selection was made. I have by me the Apocryphal New Testament, which contains all the gospels and epistles which are not included in the present New Testament, but which were accepted as canonical during the first four centuries of the Christian era. There is nothing to distinguish these apocryphal gospels from the canonical writings, and many scholars such as Whiston, go so far as to state that many of the apocryphal gospels and epistles are equally inspired as those that are accepted at the present day. I am, &c., May 31, 1889. T. J. PRICE. (4) [5]

Fletcher had no interest in dignifying this tract from a young upstart, and a non-believer, to boot, with a response. However, Tom came under attack from other members of the Adelaide religious establishment. Two weeks after the publication of his letter, the following somewhat sarcastic rejoinder appeared.

[5] *Adelaide Advertiser* Thursday 3 June 1889, p.6

To the Editor. Sir, In the Advertiser of June 3 **"T. J. Price"** says that we have no proof the New Testament writings were in existence within 120 years of the time of Christ. On June 4, "Truth" writes— "We cannot go farther back than A.D. 170." I was surprised at reading these statements. Surely the above writer has been asleep for the last 20 years. It used to be thought that the earliest proof of the reception of New Testament writings was to be found about A.D. 180, but recent discoveries prove that even the Gospels had acquired such a reception more than half a century earlier. It is admitted by all really learned infidels, amongst them Baur, Renan, and Strauss, that four of Paul's epistles were written before the year 60, namely Romans, Galatians, and the first and second of Corinthians. These Epistles prove that within 25 years after the death of Christ, Christian societies had been established through the Roman Empire, from Jerusalem to Tome; they also prove that there was agreement in the reception of the doctrines of our present gospels as of Divine authority. These four Epistles prove that the creed taught by Paul and received by the Christian churches before the year 60 included all that the Christian creed of today embraces. It is an historic fact the Paul died under Nero before A.D. 68, also that he wrote the four Epistles I have named before Festus succeeded Felix in the government of Judea, A.D. 60. Paul was in prison in Caesarea two years before Festus succeeded Felix, so we thus carry the date up to A.D. 58. Christ was crucified about the year 34, so there is only left 24 years. In Galatians' 1st chapter, we read that Paul went down into Arabia and spent three years, 14 years after he went up to Jerusalem. Now, if you add the three to the 14 you obtain 17 years to take away from the 20 between A.D. 54, which is the date assigned when Galatians was written, and the Crucifixion of Christ, A.D. 34; and you have thus only three years remaining. Never since the apostolic age has Christianity stood so proudly on her rendered reasons in the field of historic research as at the present hour. — Am etc. R. Clisby.[6]

[6] *Adelaide Advertiser* Tuesday 18June 1889, p.3

Despite the flimsiness of his evidence (a disputed date "was admitted by learned infidels") Mr. Clisby got the last word. Tom would have made a meal of Mr. Clisby, as he had done of Fletcher, but he never got the chance. Clisby's letter is followed by a note from the editor of the *Advertiser* that "this correspondence is closed": no further correspondence on the subject would be entertained.

If nothing else, Tom's newspaper pieces reveal a lively intelligence, skills in scholarship, a detailed knowledge of the Bible and Bible history, and a passion for promulgating his own worldview. Many of his writings and speeches over the rest of his life as a committed atheist (he rather preferred the label "infidel," a term first applied to him by Owen Opie) were devoted to demonstrating that the Bible was largely a work of fiction. While admitting to his existence, he asserted that Jesus could not have been born in Bethlehem, that he had siblings and that he was a radical liberator rather than a messiah. Interestingly, over 100 years after Tom's attacks on the veracity of the Bible, the work of contemporary biblical scholars supports his view that significant parts of the Bible are fabrications.

Shortly after the public exchange of letters, Tom received a telegram from his father warning him and Ann that Harry Dearmer had turned up in Broken Hill looking for Ann and that he was on his way to Adelaide. They should expect a visit from him at the house they were occupying in North Adelaide.

It didn't take Harry long to locate Tom and Ann. In the early afternoon of November 6, 1889, there came a sharp rapping on the door of their lodgings. Having been forewarned by his father, Tom was prepared for the visit. As he advanced to the front door, their houseguest, Miss Westphall, a friend of Ann's and occasional babysitter, appeared from her room. Tom warned her to stay back before opening the door. He refused to admit the older man to the house, and rejected Harry's demand to see to Ann. If he wanted to speak to his wife, they would meet him at the office of Tom's lawyer, Mr. Charles Dashwood, the following day. He had no idea how Harry would react to this demand and was relieved when Harry grunted and turned away. He had aged markedly in the decade since their first confrontation and had gain considerable weight but had lost none of his belligerence.

The following morning, Harry and Ann met face-to-face for the first time since the traumatic evening almost a decade before when, beaten black and blue by her husband, she had sought refuge in the home of her employer. Harry was the first to speak, He wanted a reconciliation with Ann as well as access to his children. Ann cut him short with a derisory snort. A reconciliation was out of the question. She wanted a divorce. Inflamed at her words, he hauled himself to his feet. Fearing that Harry was about to attack Ann physically, Tom also began to rise, but Dashwood motioned him to stay in his chair. The lawyer then turned to Harry. In a firm but quiet voice, he instructed Harry to sit down. There would be no violence, physical or verbal, in his chambers.

Although never one to be intimidated by the law, Harry resumed his seat. He was disoriented and confused. This was not what he had expected. They may not have seen each other for ten years, but Ann was still his wife and the mother of his children. She had borne children to other men. She was cohabiting with this smug young man in the fancy suit on the other side of the room, someone he'd despised at first sight. If there was any divorcing to be done, then it would be done by him. They had money: it would cost them, and he wouldn't come cheap. He was the wronged party here, he said slapping the corner of the desk.

Without going into legal niceties, Dashwood pointed out that under progressive South Australian legislation, which he himself had drafted, women such as Ann, who had been forced to leave the marital home because of physical abuse, had the right, not only to a divorce, but also to financial compensation. Was Harry able to furnish any evidence that he had provided for his wife and children over the preceding decade? Dashwood thought not. At this point, Harry, still as incensed, but more confused than ever, got to his feet again and headed for the door, pausing only to hurl a curse and a threat back into the room. "I'll get you both," he said before leaving the chambers.

Dashwood smiled at Tom and Ann. "Empty threats. I'll track him down and have the papers served on your husband," he said. "His bluff has been called. You won't be troubled by him again." Charles Dashwood was one of South Australia's preeminent lawyers and lawmakers. In addition to practicing law, he was a member of the House of Assembly, representing the constituency of Noarlunga, and soon to be made a judge and Government Resident (effectively Governor) of the Northern Territory. When he made a prediction, he was rarely wrong. In this case, he was almost fatally wrong.

After leaving the lawyer's chambers on North Terrace, Harry made his way to a nearby bar. He sweated in the early heat and stewed over the humiliating encounter in the chambers. The smugness of Price, the superiority of Dashwood, and the calm assertiveness of his wife ate into him. When the aggression of the bully is blunted, he has recourse to only one other remedy. After several drinks, his rage subsided into a sullen knot in his stomach. Aided by the better part of a bottle of rum, an embryonic course of action hardened into the certainly of a plan. For the rest of the day, he drifted from bar to bar, drinking steadily as he searched for a place he remembered, from his years in Adelaide a decade before. It had relocated to a side street, and the name had changed, but it plied the same trade. Satisfied, he found a watering hole not far from the doss house on Hindley Street where he had taken a room and drank the rest of the day away. When night fell, he stumbled back to his room and fell fully dressed onto the bed.

Friday passed in a drunken blur. In order to execute his plan, he had to be reasonably sober, so he postponed the plan for a day. At mid-morning on Saturday, he returned to the bar on Rundle Street, downed three double rums to steady his hand, then made his way down the street towards the eastern end of the city. In the side street he had located two days before, he entered the small shop he had found after the altercation in Dashwood's office. Protective wire mesh covering its windows and shades darkened the interior. The larger shop opposite the Central Market would have afforded greater choice, but in this less obtrusive place, which had been managed by one of his drinking companions in earlier days, there would be no questions asked, and if they were, no answers would be forthcoming. Fifteen minutes later, he exited the shop with a cardboard box tucked under his left arm. He continued down to East Terrace, and, despite his earlier resolve, entered the first hotel he came to. Just to steady the hand, he told himself. It was another unseasonably warm day, suggesting a hot summer to come. Despite the heat, Harry wore a coat.

A steady stream of lunchtime drinkers trickled into the bar seeking liquid sustenance and refuge from the heat. Harry positioned himself at the end of the bar, with his back to the wall. He placed the box on the bar, ordered a beer in deference to the heat and a whisky chaser. Downing the drinks and resisting the urge to signal for a second round, he tossed coins on the bar, scooped up the box, and made his way to the lavatory in the alley behind the hotel. He transferred the contents of the box to his coat pocket and dropped it onto a pile of stinking rubbish on the lavatory floor.

Shortly after lunch, Harry arrived at the front door of the Price residence on the corner of Mann and Melbourne Streets. Remembering his lack of success in gaining entry to the house earlier in the week, he strode down the side of the house, and entered through the back door into the kitchen.

Miss Westphall, who was taking her customary post-luncheon rest, saw a figure passing her window and recognized it as the man who had had the altercation with Tom several days earlier. She walked down the passage to the kitchen and encountered the man standing by the kitchen table. It was clear, from the look in his eye and the smell on his breath, that he had taken alcohol. Before she could challenge him, he asked, "Is Mrs. Dearmer inside?"

Later, Miss. Westphall provided to police an account of what happened next:

"I said to him, 'Mrs. Price is in the drawing room.' He replied in a sarcastic voice, 'Oh, it's Mrs. Price then, if you like!' I asked if I should call her, but he said, 'Oh, never mind, I know where to go.' He went down the passage towards the front door and I went into my room. I heard a scuffle and a pistol report and jumped out of the window to raise the alarm."

When Harry arrived, Tom and Ann were painting in the front room. Tom was completing a landscape, while Ann worked on a portrait of baby Babs from a photograph taken by Tom. As soon as he heard the heavy tread of footsteps in the passage, Tom knew immediately who it was.

He stepped out of the room to confront the intruder, turning the key to lock the door as he did so. Harry drew the revolver from his coat pocket and took aim at Tom's chest. Instinctively, Tom lunged for the revolver, striking it down from his chest. This swift action saved his life. There was a sharp report, but the bullet entered his leg rather than his heart. Both men then scuffled up and down the passage, Tom trying to wrest the gun from Harry, and Harry doing his best to retain possession. The wound in Tom's leg bled profusely, and he feared he was going to faint. He clung on to Harry as they wrestled up and down the corridor. Tom noticed Frank and Lilian standing at the end of the passage. Unaware that she had already slipped out of the window to fetch the police, he called for Miss Westphall to get the children into the kitchen out of harm's way.

On hearing the gunshot, Ann rushed to the door but was unable to open it. She began beating on the door, and heard the key being turned in the lock. She grabbed her revolver from the bureau by the door, slipped off the safety catch, and rushed into the corridor. Horrified at the amount of blood that Tom had lost, she raised her pistol and screamed at Harry to drop his weapon and go. Harry had no intention of doing so. He raised his revolver towards her. Weak as he was, Tom managed to slip his index finger behind the trigger, preventing it from being discharged. Ann joined Tom in trying to wrest the weapon from Harry. In the struggle, her own gun was discharged. The bullet struck Harry in the abdomen. Confused, Harry dropped his revolver and clutched at his stomach. Tom reached for the gun, but then collapsed on the floor, weak from shock, loss of blood, and the agony of the bullet lodged deep in his calf. Now disarmed, and with a bullet in his abdomen, Harry stumbled past Frank and Lilian into the kitchen. There, he dropped portraits of himself and Alexander, tore up another of Ann, and shredded a letter which he had also been carrying. He then attempted to escape through the laundry which ran off the rear of the kitchen, but was confronted by a police officer and Miss Westphall.

"That's the one," said Miss Westphall, pointing at Harry.

When the officer grabbed him by the arm, Harry said, "I've been shot." The officer took him back into the kitchen and made him sit on a chair.

As soon as the disarmed Harry headed for the kitchen, Ann's

attention turned to Tom and the children. She half-carried, half-dragged Tom into the bedroom and got him onto the bed where he lost consciousness. She then hurried the children into Frank's room, reassuring them that everything would be all right.

The next few hours were chaotic. Neighbours fetched a doctor who dressed Tom's wound and gave him ether to relieve the pain. Harry had been taken from the kitchen to the front room. The doctor examined him there and found his injury to be a superficial flesh wound, his pendulous belly arresting the progress of the bullet to any of his vital organs. Ann sent Miss Westphall to fetch Henry Price's wife, who was staying with a relative in Port Adelaide, to come and collect the children. Both Frank and Lil had witnessed the shootings. She was concerned about the effect this experience might have on them and didn't want them questioned by the police constable. In the kitchen, she found the objects that Harry had dropped: portraits of himself and Alexander, a photo of her. The three photos had been torn in half. Also, on the floor was a letter which had been shredded. Did he destroy the photo and letters before the shooting, or as he was about to leave the house? It surprised her that for years he had carried mementos of the family. However, given the brutality with which he had treated them, she was unmoved by his apparent sentimentality.

Before she could piece the letter together, a senior police officer arrived. Leaving Tom in the care of a nurse, she agreed to give a statement Characteristically, Harry refused to co-operate with the police, and attempts to get a statement from him proved futile. However, Ann's account of what happened was sufficient for the police. She and Harry were both arrested, charged with attempted murder, and taken into custody leaving Tom to be cared for by the nurse and Miss Westphall.

The following day, a reporter from the *South Australian Register* arrived and sought an interview with Tom, who, aided by the ether, was still slipping in and out of sleep. Despite his ordeal and the fact that he was in considerable pain, Tom was anxious to make his account of the shooting public. His version, when it appeared the following day, shocked and titillated the Adelaide community.

Seeing that he was in such a state, the reporter was anxious to postpone the conversation, but the sufferer, hearing him at the door, asked who it was, and being told that it was a reporter asked the nurse to bring him in. The nurse had instructions from the doctors that Price was not to be allowed to talk, but the patient demanded that he should be allowed to see the reporter, who accordingly went into the bedroom. The poor fellow made some incoherent remarks, and several times the reporter attempted to leave the room to allow the sufferer to recover, but at each movement Price became restive. At last the journalist got out unobserved, but about a quarter of an hour later Price called him again, and then in quiet tones, with well-chosen words, made the following statement—"On Monday last I was to have gone to Broken Hill, but Dearmer having turned up there, father wired me to stay and protect Mrs. Price. I stopped home. Dearmer put in an appearance on Wednesday last and had an interview with Mrs. Price, who wished Dearmer to sue for a divorce. She said they had tried to live together but found it impossible owing to his persistent cruelty." The patient then seemed to lose recollection of what occurred, and took up his narrative thus: — "Dearmer turned up here yesterday at about 12.30. I was in the front room painting with Mrs. Price. As soon as I heard a man's footsteps in the passage, I guessed who it was, I stepped out of the room, and saw Dearmer coming up the passage. Directly he saw me he drew the revolver and pointed it at my chest. I immediately locked the door of the front room so that Dearmer could not push in, and then jumped at the hand which held the revolver. The revolver went off, but I had knocked it down, and I felt a bullet, which otherwise would have gone near my heart, enter the back of my right leg. I grappled with him to procure the revolver. We scuffled up and down the passage till, feeling faint, I turned the key in the door of the front room. Mrs. Price rushed out with a revolver in her hand. She urged Dearmer to go, but instead of doing so he tried to shoot her. I prevented him doing this by holding my fingers behind the trigger of his revolver. We all scuffled again and got towards the dining room, where the revolver held by Mrs. Price accidently went off and wounded Dearmer in the region of the abdomen. Then I wrenched the revolver from him, and directly his weapon was gone he cleared out of the back door. As he rushed out, he dropped the portraits of himself and his boy, and tore up one of his wife. On the back of the boy's portrait was written 'my boy,' and on the back of his own portrait 'his father.' He also tore up a letter, the pieces of which are in the possession of the police. Then I found I was wounded in the leg, and soon afterwards had the doctors probing it." *South Australian Register* Monday 11 November 1889(6)

Despite his befuddlement from the drugs and the pain, Tom was determined to get his and Ann's version of what happened into the public arena at the earliest opportunity; certainly, before the case came before the court. In particular, he wanted it known that Ann's revolver had been discharged accidentally. He had learned a valuable lesson at his abduction trial years before. A clever prosecutor could take a sequence of facts and artfully fashion a narrative that was nothing short of fiction. Ann had been charged with the serious crime of attempting to murder her husband. She was living in sin, had borne children out of wedlock, and could not legitimize them while her husband lived. This, a prosecutor could argue, was motive enough to want him dead.

Four days after the shooting, on November 13, Ann made her first court appearance. She was represented by the formidable Charles Cameron Kingston who had defended Tom so effectively in the very same court a few years earlier. His career had waxed in those years. He had been made a Queen's Counsel, and would go on to become Premier of South Australia and, on Federation, a member of the Australian House of Representatives. He still retained his views as a radical liberal lawyer which was as important to Ann as the honours bestowed on him by the political and legal establishment.

Presiding over the hearing was Mr. Samuel Beddome, Police Magistrate and Justice of the Peace. Just short of retirement, Beddome was a highly experienced member of the legal fraternity in the colony, having begun his career as a clerk of the Adelaide Police Court in 1845, and appointed Police Magistrate in 1856. In the early days of the colony, life was chaotic and maintaining order a challenge. Beddome was a founding figures who helped establish the rule of law. His appointment to the case was an indication of the seriousness with which the Attorney-General viewed the case.

"Beddome takes a very dim view of cases such as this," Kingston had told Ann. Noting the concern on her face, he added, "But it's very much to our advantage that your husband has refused legal assistance. It appears that he intends to represent himself."

Ann was formally charged with the attempted murder of her husband, Harry Dearmer. When ask how she pleaded, she replied, "Not guilty," in a firm voice. Her trembling hands, she kept pressed to her sides. Kingston immediately moved for an adjournment. He wanted to call Tom as a witness for the defence, but Tom had not recovered from his injury.

The case was adjourned for three days. When it resumed on November 26, Tom was still incapacitated. However, Beddome refused Kingston's application for a further adjournment.

"We shall hear the case for the prosecution, Mr. Kingston," he said. "Witnesses for the defence will not be required at this time."

Harry Dearmer was the first witness for the prosecution. Before he was called to the witness stand, the court was told that Harry, who had been remanded in custody, had steadfastly refused to answer any of the questions put to him related to the shooting. Harry had never been inclined to co-operate with the law and it was clear, once he was brought into the court, that he had no intention of doing so now. He belligerently refused to answer any of the questions put to him.

"Mr. Dearmer," said Beddome, "If you persist in your refusal, I shall have no option but to hold you in contempt."

Harry then opened him mouth for the first time. "I have something to say."

"Please go ahead."

What he said prompted gasps from the public gallery.

"I want the charge against my wife dismissed."

Ann was shocked. This was out of character - contrary to everything she knew about her husband. Why did he make this request? Was it out of a concern that, with Ann's incarceration, there would be no one to care for the children? Highly unlikely, thought Ann, given his past treatment of them, and the fact that he had had nothing to do with them for almost ten years. More likely was the possibility that if the charge against her were dropped, so too would the charge against him.

Beddome quickly quashed the request. "That is out of the question, Mr. Dearmer, as it is beyond this court's jurisdiction. The charge was brought by the Attorney-General, and only he can have it withdrawn. If you have nothing else to say, then you are dismissed."

After the court heard evidence from the police, the case was adjourned for a further twelve days, to the 28th. Kingston requested bail for Ann, which was granted. While she was grateful to her friend Jane Westphall for staying on to nurse Tom and look after the children, she couldn't bear the thought of spending another twelve days without seeing her family. A request by Harry for bail was denied.

Due to the slowness of Tom's recovery, a further extension was sought and granted. Harry and Ann finally faced Beddome again on December 5. Kingston immediately moved to have the charge against Ann dismissed on the grounds that the evidence against her was flimsy, that she had been protecting her children, and that the revolver had discharged accidentally in the course of a struggle with Dearmer. Beddome concurred, and the charges against Ann were dropped. She was a free woman and Tom was not required to testify, although he could have done so if necessary.

Harry did not get off so lightly. He was charged with the attempted murder of Thomas John Price. He entered a not guilty plea and was remanded in custody until December 19 when the formal arraignment took place. At the arraignment, medical evidence was given that Tom's wound was anything but superficial, and that he had come close to losing his leg. Dearmer was committed for trial in the South Australian Supreme Court, the trial to begin on February 5, 1890.

At the trial, Harry had the good sense to accept the offer of a defence counsel rather than continuing to represent himself. After Tom and Ann had provided evidence, counsel for the defence asked that the charge be downgraded from attempted murder to feloniously wounding with intent. The lesser charge was accepted by the court, Harry changed his plea to guilty, and was sentenced to three years with hard labour.

As Tom led her from the court, Ann said quietly, "I hope that's the last I ever have to see of him."

"There's the divorce proceedings," Tom reminded her.

Ann shook her head. "If it means having to deal with him, then I'm not interested." Tom knew better than to argue with her. He steered her into a bar on North Terrace opposite the newly constructed Parliament House to celebrate the happy end to an unhappy affair. As they entered the bar, they had to endure nods and whispers from the other patrons. Once seated, with a weak whisky and water before her, Ann said, "We have to get away from here."

Chapter 12
Death of the Patriarch

"Which one takes your fancy?" asked the land agent.

Ann cast her eye over the saltbush-covered sandhills that formed a natural backdrop to the two blocks of land. A crow perched on a rotting post marking the boundary between the properties passed a mournful verdict on both blocks. The sun burnt into the black stuff of her dress. It was as desolate a scene as you could possibly imagine, as unfinished and unfanciable as any tract of land could be in that parched corner of the interior. Her mind's eye took her back to the countryside around the Aberdeen of her childhood, and she was struck with wonder at where life could lead one—if you allowed it to. Most people, of course, had neither the resources nor the desire to be led anywhere. But in that, as in most regards, she and Tom were at one. Not that she was free of all regret, but living life in the rear-view mirror had never been her style. Her reverie was broken by a tugging at her sleeve. "It's hot," young Frank said. "You promised me a horse if we came out here, Mamma."

Turning to the land agent, she surprised herself as well as Tom by saying, "We'll take them both." As she inspected the blocks, an idea had taken shape in her mind. Her desire for privacy and the ability to conduct her family life as she wanted away from prying eyes would be solved by building the house squarely in the centre of the two blocks and then enclosing the entire property with a high fence of corrugated iron.

Tom was more than happy to leave the planning and construction of the house to Ann. He was fully occupied establishing a grocery business in the town. The townspeople needed a reliable supply of fresh fruit and vegetables, as well as dry goods, and Tom was able to draw on his contacts at the East End wholesale market in Adelaide to supply them. While he never imagined himself as a grocer, there were certain advantages to the decision. He knew the business, for which there was definite demand, had the resources and contacts to ensure success, and, best of all, he would be working for himself.

If establishing the business, constructing the house, and raising a family weren't enough to keep Tom and Ann occupied, they also threw themselves into amateur theatricals, as well as assisting his father run the Broken Hill branch of the Secular Association.

As a mine manager, one of WH's tasks was to recruit, not only miners, but tradesmen, including carpenters and masons, to carry out construction work on the mine sites he supervised. In 1890 he recruited tradesmen for both the Rising Sun Mine and the South Extended Mine. During slow periods, several of the men were redeployed to construct the house at 32 Ryan Street under Ann's direction. She was delighted to discover that one of older men was a master carpenter and had WH commission him to decorate the rooms and hallway in the main part of the house with picture rails and fretworked archways from rich, red cedar wood which the master carpenter sourced for her, although he wouldn't say where. "Fell off the back of a bullock wagon," he replied when she asked. Externally, although larger than average, the house looked much the same as its neighbours. Inside, however, the decorative woodwork, high ceilings made of pressed metal, well-proportioned rooms, and chandeliers gave it an elegance that was lacking in the cramped miners' houses that constituted the rest of the neighbourhood.

The men worked quickly and efficiently, and within months the house was habitable. With the house completed, the men constructed several outhouses: stables for the horses, chicken coops, and a zoo and aviary for the children. When William, a passionate naturalist like his father, moved to Broken Hill to take up a teaching post, he rescued and rehabilitated native animals from the surrounding bush: a wounded, baby wedge-tailed eagle, orphaned galahs and sulphur-crested cockatoos that Frank and Lil fed with boiled oatmeal, a couple of wallabies, a large turtle that mysteriously turned up in the garden where it would reside for many years, and a vicious, one-eyed emu. As well as tending the baby birds, Frank was entrusted with the chore of feeding the larger occupants of the zoo. William warned him to steer clear of the wedge-tailed eagle which was growing rapidly and to keep on the emu's blind side. "If he sees you coming, he'll take out your eye in revenge," he joked, but the ten-year-old took the threat seriously.

Although the house was generously proportioned, it was a lively place with the children, Tom, Ann and WH in permanent residence. His other children and friends from Adelaide and Melbourne were frequent visitors. William lived for a time at 32 Ryan Street when he first arrived to take up his teaching position. Occasionally, mining colleagues and other acquaintances would arrive from the mining communities where WH had worked, and sometimes from further afield. All were offered accommodation. Given the alternatives, the offers were invariably accepted.

One visitor, who was to have a significant impact on Tom and Ann, was Joseph Symes. WH had met Symes at a meeting of the Secular Association in Melbourne a year or two before. Despite their very different natures, the two men became firm friends, a friendship cemented by politics, not personality. WH invited him to Broken Hill to address the local branch of the Secular Association. The Society was very much a family affair, with WH its President, Tom its Chairman, and Ann a member of the committee. It held weekly meetings, at which Tom lectured the small but enthusiastic audience on the benefits to humanity of secularism, the pernicious influence of religion on education, and the Biblical fallacies upon which Christianity was founded.

WH learned that his internationally renowned friend had not always been a secularist. He was born in England in 1841 to a family of devout Wesleyans and at seventeen had entered a Wesleyan college to train for the ministry. His disenchantment with organized religion began with the proclamation within the Roman church of papal infallibility, and he was radicalized by involvement in a number of labour unions in the north of England. In 1876, he became a member of the National Secular Association, which had been formed ten years previously by Charles Bradlaugh, who, despite being elected a Member of Parliament by the voters of Northampton, was denied his seat because of his atheism. The mission of the Society was to fight for a separation between church and state. Although lip service came to be paid to this notion in Western democracies such as Britain, the United States and Australia, in none of these countries did it get further than the lips. Political leaders such as

Alfred Deakin, a Father of Federation, were devoutly Christian (although the eccentric Deakin also dabbled in spiritualism, and sought guidance, not only from God, but also from the dead through a Melbourne medium.)

Symes was an eloquent and passionate speaker, and his commitment and drive attracted many new members to the Society, although his ferocious denunciation of Christianity earned him enemies among the English establishment. When, in 1883, he was invited by the Victorian secularists to come to Melbourne as an organizer, he saw it as an opportunity to bring his brand of secularism and humanism to the colonies. He arrived there with his wife in early 1884. He wasted no time in establishing a paper, *The Liberator*, to take his message to those who were unable to hear him in person. In the following year, he chaired the Second Freethought Conference. However, his strident denunciations of the smugness, wowserism and cant, of colonial society led to the same problems in Victoria as it had in England, and resulted in several court prosecutions in which he defended himself with fiery denunciation of his detractors. In 1889, with moral and financial support from WH, he ran for the seat of Collingwood in the Legislative Assembly. His radical platform included land nationalization, progressive income tax for the redistribution of wealth, abolition of colonial titles, a free Sunday, legalized contraception, and the ending of discrimination against Chinese. This radical agenda was far too rich for the electors of Collingwood, and it came as no surprise to WH when his friend ran last in the election. He was also ejected from the Democratic Club where his radicalism was deemed to be the most extreme in the entire polity of nineteenth century Australia. He proudly shared with WH a newspaper cutting which carried this denunciation.

With his star on the wane in Melbourne, he accepted WH's invitation to address the Broken Hill Secular Association. He also accepted the offer of accommodation at 32 Ryan Street. Having deposited his Gladstone bag in the bedroom, which WH had graciously vacated for him, and having shaken out his old black frockcoat and arranged it over the back of an upright chair in the corner of the bedroom, he proceeded to the kitchen where WH, Tom and Ann sat at the long wooden table that dominated the room. He accepted Ann's offer of tea, but refused a chair, preferring to stride up and down the room on his spidery legs, holding forth in a loud hectoring voice on his detractors. He also frightened the wits out of the children by coruscating those who believe in ghosts. "I don't believe in ghosts," he declaimed. And then, rather contradictorily added, "I disapprove of them!" Lilian and Babs, who were cowering behind the pantry door very much believed in ghosts and looked fearfully into the darkened laundry that led off the pantry for signs of discontented spirits.

It was no accident that the kitchen was one of the largest rooms in the house. It, and the pantry attached to it, gave Ann the opportunity to engage in her passion for cooking. She was up early each morning to light the fire that had been set the night before, and prepare the substantial breakfast that Tom, in particular, enjoyed. On the morning after Symes' arrival, she was joined by WH. She poured him his customary cup of tea and asked what she should prepare for their famous guest.

WH had no idea. "You'll have to ask him yourself," he said.

When Symes appeared, she did just that.

"Porridge with a pinch of salt," he replied. "And a cup of strong black tea."

Slightly disappointed that she would not have a chance to display her culinary skills, she fetched the tea and porridge while WH and Symes sat at the table discussing the evening's event.

The Secular Association normally met in the Masonic Hall in Oxide Street, but on the occasion of this, Symes' first public speech in Broken Hill, Tom suggested a building he rented in Beryl Street. It was an attractive stone structure consisting of a hall surmounting a large cellar. The cellar served as an office and storeroom for his fruit and vegetable business. The hall did duty as a rehearsal space for the numerous benefit concerts that Tom organized as well as a venue for musical recitals. The hall was smaller than the Masonic Hall, and if the audience was modest as Tom expected, it would not be an embarrassment.

It was to this building that Joseph Symes was brought by WH, Tom and Ann, to give his speech to a small audience of committed secularists along with members of the general public who were curious to see this controversial and divisive "Atheist Evangelist," as he was known: a term in which he revelled. WH gave a fulsome introduction to Symes. It could have been a little more succinct, Tom thought; the audience had, after all, come to hear Symes. Symes rose from his chair and strode back and forth across the room tugging at his wispy beard as though assembling his thoughts. He then launched into a denunciation of the Victorian establishment which had sought to shut down his newspaper, *The Liberator*. "These muddle-headed hypocrites confuse freedom and lawlessness. My paper was founded in the interests of freedom, certainly, but not lawlessness, not licence. Freedom for everyone is consistent with the rights of all. Every man has a natural right, and should by this time also possess the political and social right to criticize any opinions known to the world. And yet, even today, men are sent to prison like felons for laughing at the superstition known as Christianity. Hundreds of lies and volumes of slander are incessantly used by Christians against their opponents and when they find an opportunity of doing us harm, they most devoutly embrace it." He paused to allow the audience to savour the irony of his adjective. "Is my paper a blasphemous publication? That depends on the nature of blasphemy. If blasphemy is the equivalent of fearless truth and the exposure of consecrated shams and pious imposture, our course is clear. We shall crowd our paper with all the blasphemy its pages can carry."

He spoke for almost an hour, and then, just as members of the audience were beginning to shift uncomfortably in their seats, he closed by roaring at them: "We prefer conscience to self, and will do what we deem our duty to mankind in spite of the bigots and hypocrites. We mean warfare, and quarter will neither be begged nor granted."

In the year before his visit to Broken Hill, Symes had been involved in an ugly split within the Australian Secularist Association. Some members, objecting to his extremist views, and autocratic and paranoid personality, attempted to wrest control from him. When a physical attempt to take over the ASA Hall in Fitzroy failed, the breakaway group took legal action. To Symes' horror, the court found in favour of the breakaway group, and he was ejected from the hall he had built.

Although Symes was undoubtedly a difficult character who had a gift for making enemies, Tom admired him for his views, and the eloquence and passion with which he pursued the secularist cause. They also had one quality in common: both men were fearless. Newspapers provided accounts of meetings Symes addressed in country towns being broken up by gangs of strong-arm Christians. But Symes never backed down in the face of physical violence. He had a will of iron and a thick skin. Tom's father clearly thought a lot of Symes and the feeling was reciprocated, so Tom kept his reservations about the firebrand to himself.

After the celebrated atheist left town, WH wrote to him thanking him for undertaking the arduous trip to the bush to bring an important message to the people who needed to hear it. Although at the hall meeting, he had been preaching largely to the converted, the main points in his speech had been published in the local press, and generated considerable and, in WH's word, "animated" discussion. Symes replied, thanking WH for the hospitality extended to him by the Price family and inviting WH to attend an upcoming meeting in Melbourne of the Freethought Conference. WH immediately replied, enthusiastically accepting the invitation, and began making notes on possible themes for his talk. The correspondence, thus begun, continued. It gave WH the intellectual nourishment that was lacking in Broken Hill, being largely confined to kitchen table conversations with Tom, Ann and a few close friends.

WH said nothing to his family, but as 1891 progressed, his health began to deteriorate. Tom and Ann both noticed his growing frailty. When he reluctantly decided to abandon plans to travel to Melbourne to address the Secular Association, they knew that something was definitely wrong. By October, his health had deteriorated to the point where he was forced to resign from his position as mine manager. Despite his ill health, he remained positive and optimistic. "This is a blessing in disguise," he told Tom. "I shall now have the time to write the book I always wanted to write—a history of secularism in the colonies, and a treatise on the development of my own philosophy." Mornings he spent writing at his desk. After lunch, he sat in the kitchen garden Ann had established in the courtyard behind the house adjacent to the covered well. There, he dozed in the sunshine, an open book on his knees.

One afternoon, Frank returned from school complaining of pains all through his body and difficulty in breathing. Within an hour, he began to burn with a dangerously high fever. The family doctor, Richard Korff, was summoned. Like most middle-class families, the Prices paid their family doctor an annual fee of ten guineas and for that he would attend them at home at any hour of the day or night. It only took Korff a minute to diagnose Frank. He had contracted influenza and bronchitis. "This is the third case I have diagnosed today," he told Ann and Tom. "I'm afraid we are in for an epidemic." Within days, the girls also came down with the disease. Next was Tom. Only Ann and WH escaped. WH abandoned his books and assisted Ann in nursing the family.

When he received word of WH's retirement and invalid state, Joseph Symes made plans to visit his friend and give a public speech to the Broken Hill Secular Association. Before he could get to Broken Hill, WH collapsed and had to be helped to his bed by Tom and Ann. Tom fetched Dr Korff who confirmed that he had also succumbed to the influenza and bronchitis epidemic. Given the perilous state of his lungs, he was an easy target. The family was devastated, Tom being particularly hard hit. "We should never have allowed him near the children," he said to Ann. Fearing the worst, he sent telegrams to William in Adelaide and Henry on Kangaroo Island alerting them to what had happened and urging that they come to Broken Hill immediately.

By the time Symes arrived, WH's condition was terminal. Symes was shocked at his physical appearance. He had aged a decade in less than a year. Symes gripped WH's emaciated wrist. "How are you, my friend?" he asked.

"I could be dying," joked WH, "but apart from that I'm remarkably well."

During the day, Tom and Ann took turns reading to him, and the children, now fully recovered, ran in and out of the room to see how he was. Although his condition was highly contagious, he received a constant stream of visitors. After the lunch that Ann insisted on preparing for him, Symes had a long conversation with WH. He should have been sleeping but wanted to discuss with Symes a tract that he planned to publish as soon as he was well enough to write. "There's too much to say, and too little time," he said.

"Well, if you don't get some rest, you'll never recover," replied Symes. "Right now, I have a meeting in town to discuss the details of my public lecture for the Secular Association."

"Good luck," said WH. "I would hope to attend but doubt that I will be recovered in time."

"Just rest, my friend." He left WH propped up on pillows, and smiled at the hand raised weakly to salute his departure.

When he returned, he was disturbed to be told WH's condition had declined dramatically. Tom had tried to contact Korff, but the doctor was in the neighbouring town of Silverton attending to a badly injured miner. He left word that Korff was to hasten to 32 Ryan Street immediately upon his return to Broken Hill.

Korff arrived at 10 a.m. the following morning. He examined WH, then led Tom and Ann to the kitchen. "There's nothing more to be done, I'm afraid," he said. "You must prepare yourselves for the worst." During the day, WH drifted in and out of sleep. As night fell, his condition continued to worsen. Symes stayed up with his friend along with Tom and Ann. At 3 a.m., Tom woke the children and brought them to pay their last respects to their father. Frank remained dry-eyed. Babs buried her face in her mother's skirts. It was the reserved Lil who was inconsolable. Next day, his friends and colleagues were shocked to learn that William Henry Price had died. Not 24 hours before, he had been propped up on pillows cheerfully receiving them. And now he was no more. He was laid out in the main room at 32 Ryan Street.

The fact that he had obituaries and tributes in newspapers across Australia, from the *West Australian* in Perth to the *Melbourne Argus* and *Sydney Morning Herald* in the east, is a tribute to William Henry's standing within the mining industry as well as his role in its establishment. *The Barrier Miner* provided the following report of his death.

Death of Mr. W. H. Price

THERE died at his residence, Ryan Street south, at between 8 and 9 o'clock this morning, **Mr. William H. Price**, the retiring manager of the South Extended and Rising Sun North mines, and one of the oldest mining managers in Australia, at the age of 63 years. **Mr. Price** had suffered from the prevailing epidemic, and bronchitis supervened; and it was from this latter affliction that he died. It was not thought even yesterday that **Mr. Price** was seriously ill, but during the night his condition became much worse, and Dr Korff was summoned. It was too late, however. Mr. Price had been in Australia for nearly 50 years, and had occupied many important offices. He was first engaged at the Burra smelting works in a responsible position. Then he managed the TALISKER silver mine, south of Adelaide; was at the Blinman copper mine and the New Cornwall, in the north of South Australia; went to Queensland as mine manager; returned to South Australia, where he managed the Wheal Tyrrell and other properties; and, between three and four years ago, was appointed to the management of the South Extended and Rising Sun North. On account of generally failing health he had recently resigned this appointment, and was just about handing over the management. He had the reputation of being an excellent miner, and scrupulously honest in his dealings with employers and employees alike. **Mr. Price** leaves a large family, including **Mr. T. J Price**, well-known locally. The funeral is to take place on Saturday next. The usual service at the grave will be dispensed with; for it there will be substituted an oration pronounced by Mr. Joseph Symes, of the Secularists' Association. **Barrier Miner Thursday 22 October 1891**(7)[7]

Two days later it was from 32 Ryan Street that the funeral procession left. Because of his atheism, he was buried in an unmarked grave in un-consecrated ground on the outskirts of the cemetery. The graveside oration was given by Symes. The *Barrier Miner* summarized Symes' oration. While he said some nice things about William Henry and the circumstances of his death, the main burden of the oration was a speech on atheism. Ever the Evangelical Atheist, he mounted a vigorous defence of the secularist's attitude to death and the myth of the afterlife.

THE funeral of **Captain W. H. Price**, late general manager of the South Extended No. 1 and Rising Sun North mines, took place this afternoon in the presence of a large number of friends, brother

[7] *The Barrier Miner* Thursday 22 October 1891, p.2

mining managers, and members of the Oddfellows' Lodge, to which he belonged. The funeral was conducted by the Secular Association, of which **Mr. Price** was an enthusiastic member, and the arrangements, perfect in every detail, were in the hands of Messrs. O'Connor, and Co., Argent Street. On the funeral cortège reaching the cemetery it was seen that a large number of people were already on the ground, attracted, some, perhaps, by curiosity to see how the secularists conducted their obsequies, but all with a feeling of genuine sympathy for the bereaved family. On the coffin being lowered to its last resting place, Mr. Joseph Syme, whose tall figure occupied a place at the head of the grave, said it was his painful duty to officiate at the funeral of their friend, Mr. Price. Secularists do not believe in any parade or show at times of burial. They do not believe in keeping up the grim worship of death. They rather thought it was their duty to repress everything in that line. At the same time, they wished to show all the respect possible for the memory of the departed and sympathy with the feelings of the relatives who survived. As secularists, they were total unbelievers in a future life; they believed the dead were really dead—that death was no mockery or mystery. As the Christians' Bible itself put it, "The dead know not anything." That was one portion of the book which secularists thoroughly believed. They had inquired into the proofs submitted of a future life, and found that there was no evidence at all of such a state. All that had been preached about the dead had been imagined or dreamt by living people who had never experienced death. They thought it honest to declare their belief before the world. They did not claim that other people should swallow their opinions; they only claimed their right to hold them. They lived holding these principles, and were satisfied to die with them, because they believed in their truth. They endeavoured to lead lives as useful, as pure, and as noble as their neighbours without prayer and without asking for divine aid. They were guided by the force of intelligence alone, and he considered their lives would bear as close scrutiny as others, though they had no superstitious belief to trouble them. They had solved the problem of how to meet death without fear and without horror. Certainly, they had no morbid desire to die, for they respected human ties and loved their kindred. But when death came, they were not afraid of some undefined punishment in a future state for having their own thoughts while they lived. They did not hope for an impossible heaven, neither did they dread an impossible hell. Referring to Mr. Price, the speaker said he had known him for three years, but that during the past fortnight their intercourse had been extremely close. In all Broken Hill no kinder parent or better husband could have been found. He had fallen a victim now, as much from his devotion to his relatives, as to the disease which had attacked him. When all his family were down with sickness, he had tended them most carefully, and so fallen sick himself. He had seen him during his last few conscious moments, and he had died as he had lived, a total unbeliever, and as cheerful as a man could be under the circumstances. At the face of that open grave it was well to remind those present that they had work to do, that they should make the most of their life not for themselves, but in making others happy. The hearty sympathy of all was asked for those who survived. They could do no more for the dead, "after life's fitful fever he slept well," but they could do much for the living. Let them fill up their lives with good thoughts, good motives, and good intentions, and they would meet death as calmly as he who rested beneath. Flowers were then plenteously bestowed on the coffin, and, as the mourners turned away from the open grave, many were visibly affected. *(Barrier Miner, Saturday, 24 October 1891)*[8]

That night, Symes donned his trademark long black coat and prepared to leave for town. When he asked if Tom would like to accompany him, the younger man hesitated.

"Just go," said Ann. "I will look after the children. He is no longer with us, and we now have to get on with our lives. It's what he would have wanted."

The lecture was held in the newly opened Town Hall, a splendid stone structure that dominated Argent Street and which had been constructed thanks to the generosity of the mining companies. The Price

[8] *The Barrier Miner* Saturday 24 October 1891, p.4

family had been intimately involved in the development of the hall. The massive foundation stone, which was laid by Sir Henry Parkes, came from one of WH's mines. At the ceremony, Ann was one of the local residents invited to lay one of the foundation stones.

Symes was in such command of his subject that he never needed notes. He was a fluent and forceful, if rather long-winded, speaker, and Tom never tired of listening to him, as much for his ability to hold an audience as for the message he delivered. His subject for the evening was "An Atheist's Views of Conscience and Duty: An Eye-Opener!" Despite the title, the talk was sparsely attended. Presumably most Broken Hill citizens were not interested in having their eyes opened by the acerbic Symes. Before launching into his speech, which according to a newspaper account "was the most rational Mr. Symes has delivered here, and made evident what has hitherto been wanting, viz, that the secular party actually has a mission," he paid tribute to his friend Mr. W.H. Price and the nature of his passing. He took the opportunity to castigate what he saw as the hypocrisy of his detractors. Christians were in the habit of saying very harsh and uncalled for things about the deathbeds of atheists and freethinkers, whereas if they could only attend on one of these occasions it might knock some of the superstitious beliefs out of them. He had seen Mr. Price at the time of his death, and the old gentleman passed away calmly and quietly. Secularists regretted the death of their friends as keenly as others, but they had one advantage—they had no fears as to their future, they were assured that they were suffering no sort of punishment.

Having captured the high moral ground, Symes then warmed easily to his theme of conscience and duty from an atheist's standpoint. He challenged the assertion that atheists had no morality, conscience or sense of duty, arguing that if this were the case, he would keep his atheism to himself and masquerade as a Christian. He then interrogated the logic of Christianity, arguing that they could not tell what morality was. Is something moral simply because God wills it, he asked, or does he will a thing that possesses morality prior to him willing it? If God was absolute, he could not be moral, because morality developed in societies through interaction. Morality simply meant adhering to the customs and norms of a given society. Manners or customs did not differ from morals, and they sprang up wherever there was society which was why what was considered moral differed from society to society. "Until you find a basis for morality," he thundered at the audience, "you cannot give an answer for the paradox I just posed to you."

"Hear! Hear!" called several members of the audience.

Symes concluded his address to generous applause. He then said he would entertain questions. He answered each question that was put to him promptly and, as one observer noted, "occasionally at considerable length."

After Symes had left for Melbourne, with a promise to return, Tom, Ann and the children adjusted to life without the patriarch. When WH's death certificate arrived, Tom pointed out to Ann that it contained at least two errors: his father had died, not of asthma, but of influenza and bronchitis, and he had fathered nine children, not ten.

"Should I have the record corrected?" he asked.

"Why bother?" replied Ann. "We know the facts. Who else is there to care?"

As already noted, the two offspring about whom comparatively little is known are Rebecca and Henry. It was eventually determined that Rebecca went to England to be with Mary, and was baptized there. No marriage or death certificated ever came to light. Somewhat more is known of Henry. His young adulthood was spent as a farmer on Kangaroo Island. During that time, he took in Caroline Opie when brother Tom spirited her away from Kadina to rescue her from physical abuse at the hands of her mother. After leaving Kangaroo Island, he worked as a miner, possibly in Broken Hill, Electoral rolls relate that by the time of Federation, he was living and working in Cobar. He was killed in a mining accident there on 30 November, 1912.

One notable omission from WH's death certificate are the names of the four children he had with Ann. This could be because they were registered as Dearmer's children. There is another possibility; that Thomas John, not WH, was the father.

DEATH CERTIFICATE OF WILLIAM HENRY PRICE

DATE & PLACE OF DEATH: 22 OCTOBER 1891, BROKEN HILL, NSW

NAME & OCCUPATION: WILLIAM HENRY PRICE, \
MINE MANAGER

SEX & AGE: MALE, 63 YEARS

CAUSE OF DEATH: ASTHMA

DURATION OF LAST ILLNESS: 1 WEEK

MEDICAL ATTENDANT: DR. KORFF

DATE HE LAST SAW DEC'D: 22 OCTOBER 1891

NAME OF FATHER: JOHN PRICE

OCCUPATION OF FATHER: GAMEKEEPER

NAME & MAIDEN SURNAME OF MOTHER: SARAH ELIZABETH ANDREWS

INFORMANT: THOMAS JOHN PRICE, SON, BROKEN HILL, NSW

WHEN & WHERE BURIED: 24 OCTOBER 1891, BROKEN HILL CEMETERY

UNDERTAKER: O'CONNOR & CO.

NAME & RELIGION OF MINISTER: JOSEPH SYMES, LECTURER

WITNESSES OF BURIAL: J. WRIGHT, C. F. NEWALL

WHERE BORN: WALES

HOW LONG IN AUSTRALASIAN COLONIES: ABOUT 42 YEARS

PLACE OF MARRIAGE, AGE & TO WHOM: WALES, 21, MARY WILLIAMS

CHILDREN OF MARRIAGE: WILLIAM, 42 YEARS,

HENRY, 39 YEARS

MARY, 37 YEARS

THOMAS JOHN, 32 YEARS

REBECCA, 26 YEARS

2 MALES, 3 FEMALES DECEASED

Chapter 13
A Sea Change

With his grocery business firmly established, and the wrenching sadness of his father's death settling into a dull ache that would fade with the passage of time, Tom spent less time doing the rounds of the fruit and vegetable merchants, and more on the interests that were closest to his heart. He took over WH's position as head of the Secular Association and, with it, the near-impossible challenge of converting the town to the cause of humanism and atheism. He also threw himself with even greater enthusiasm into to his real passion—the theatre. As he matured, so did his ability to cultivate hair on his upper lip, and he now boasted a fine moustache with waxed tips. This, along with a vigorous head of curling hair, gave him the look of a theatrical impresario: an impression that was by no means accidental.

In his early adult life, while working as a teacher, he had organized theatrical events to raise money for an unlikely assortment of causes, such as the Kangaroo Island Cricket Club. In Broken Hill, he stage-managed and promoted charitable events such as the Annual Shearers' Concert as well as performances to raise money for the families of miners killed in the course of their work. These events were usually family affairs involving not only Lil and Babs, but also Ann and, on occasion, Frank, who was more interested in the sporting field than the stage.

In 1888, Broken Hill's first newspaper, *The Barrier Miner*, made its appearance. In the 1950s it would be acquired along with a string of other country newspapers by a young newspaperman called Rupert Murdoch, who used these rural newspapers as the springboard for creating a national newspaper business that would eventually become a global media empire. *The Barrier Miner* documented the business and social life of the town for almost 100 years. The fortunes (and later misfortunes) of the Price family are featured prominently in its pages. In the early days, the family received favourable publicity and positive reviews for their contributions to the charitable and cultural life of the community. The first of many reports of their foray into show business, an account of the Annual Shearers' and Hospital Benefit at the Theatre Royal, was reported in 1892. Another event that was reported on in considerable detail was a minstrel and variety entertainment organized to raise money for the widow and orphans of a Mr. Charles Fellowes, who had been shot and killed at Wilcannia to the east of Broken Hill. The entertainment was staged at the newly erected Town Hall. *The Miner* rather enigmatically reports that

> The building was about three parts filled; and, although the prices of admission were small, a good sum must have been realised. The program as originally framed was very attractive; but at the last moment several of the leading performers disappointed the organisers of the entertainment. The audience was generous, however, and applauded the different items vociferously" (*Barrier Miner* Tuesday 23 January 1894).[9]

The number and variety of shows reported on by the paper was impressive. They included a "Grand Entertainment" given by "Price's Juvenile Surprise Party" in the Cosmopolitan Hall in aid of another family in financial distress; a Barrier Art Union to raise money for local artists; a Surprise Benefit Performance in Tait's Athenaeum in aid of another bereaved widow and her children. There was no shortage of venues for the events. Tom's favourite was the Theatre Royal, managed by his good friend Bert Sayers, but he also had at his disposal numerous other theatres and halls including the Town Hall, the Cosmopolitan Hall, Tait's Athenaeum, the Crystal Theatre, and the AMA Hall.

From the time of its establishment, Broken Hill was a rough, raw settlement situated in an inhospitable landscape. For many of its inhabitants, life was nasty, brutish, and short. Visitors were warned by the locals to take care: "There's a fight on every corner down Argent Street on a Saturday night," locals would proudly say. While Tom was not solely responsible for bringing culture to the bush, he did play a

---

[9] *The Barrier Miner* Tuesday 23 January 1894

leading role. In addition to theatrical events, he organized art shows, and with no hint of false modesty, mounted exhibitions of his own photography. His enthusiasm and genial nature made him a popular figure around town, although he did have a reputation as a bit of a toff, and behind their backs, the Prices were sometimes accused of thinking themselves a cut above the rest of the townsfolk. You'd expect that of a doctor or lawyer, but a grocer?

Tom not only organized the events and arranged the program, but also took part in the performances. He played various musical instruments including the bones, an eccentric but popular way of generating a rhythm by clicking animal bones together. He was also adept at singing, acting out skits and dramas, and presenting humorous monologues. Reviews in *The Barrier Miner* were effusive and illustrated the extent of his repertoire. Invariably described as Mr. T. J. Price, he was reported as appearing in "laughable Dutch vagaries." "The reporter covering the event presumably meant humorous rather than risible," he said to Ann when she read the review out to him. He "excited mirth" in burlesques such as *Little Biddy and the Flower Girl*, as well as "hitting the popular taste" with vaudeville songs of the day. Tom had no qualms about promoting his own family, and several shows were entirely family affairs:

> The Price Family gave an entertainment at the A.M.A. Hall, Thackaringa, on Saturday evening last. The hall was crowded, and the singing and acting of Mr. T. J. Price, Mrs. Price, Master Frank, Miss Lilian and little Viola interested and amused the audience for over two hours. Master Sid Carpenter also contributed two songs, each of which was encored. The dance was afterwards held and kept up until midnight. (*Barrier Miner* Wednesday 30 August 1899)[10]

Although he was a successful businessman, Tom's benefits demonstrate that he never lost the humanitarian and charitable side to his persona. Not only did he stage concerts to raise money for the bereaved families of townsmen killed on the mines, he also continued to support itinerant

[10] *The Barrier Miner* Wednesday 30 August 1899, p.2

shearers in the district. On one occasion, he even organized a concert to raise money for striking miners in the Newcastle coalfields seven hundred miles to the east of Broken Hill. The decade prior to Federation was an uncertain one for the country in general and for Broken Hill in particular. A major economic depression, initially brought about by the withdrawal of foreign capital and the collapse of some of Australia's largest banks, hit the mining industry hard. The price of silver, lead and zinc plummeted, which put the mines at risk. From its earliest days, Broken Hill had been a union town, and in 1892, when the mine managers attempted to reduce costs by importing cheap, non-union labour, the union leaders called a strike. The strike lasted four months, causing great hardship to the townspeople. It collapsed in September with the arrest in front of the town hall of the union leadership. During this time, Tom organized numerous concerts and extended lines of credit to those firms owing money to his wholesale fruit and vegetable business. This was in stark contrast to the actions taken against debtors by Frank during subsequent depressions, including the Great Depression of the 1930s.

Federation itself faced considerable headwinds. Proponents such as Deakin and Barton had to convince minnow states such as Western Australia and Tasmania that they would not be swallowed up by Victoria and New South Wales. There was no unanimity between the two largest states over issues such as free trade and protectionism. And over all, was the looming presence of the British parliament. Without its ratification, Federation would be doomed.

There are many unlikely events in the Price family chronicle, none more so than the stories of Viola (Babs) and Lilian, "The Two Prices" as they described themselves on their calling card. From a tough mining town in the far west of New South Wales, they went on to establish international careers for themselves, performing across Australia, and then in Europe and Asia. They started out as children performing Highland dance routines, singing, and doing simple conjuring tricks at charitable events orchestrated by Tom. Newspaper accounts never failed to praise their performances, albeit somewhat patronizingly. Typical comments included: "Little Viola met with a good reception in her Dutch impersonations." "*How They Do It*, by Little Lilian, was encored, and the clever little entertainer responded with the sailor's hornpipe in costume," "Little Lilian and Little Viola—were all successful in their songs, encores being the rule." "Miss Lilian and little Viola interested and amused the audience for over two hours." As they grew older, the sisters were greatly encouraged by these comments, as well as by Tom, and they developed loftier ambitions. Of the two, Babs was the more ambitious. One morning, at the breakfast table, she read aloud extracts lauding their performance from the night before. She and Lil giggled at extravagance of the praise.

"You'll always be 'Little Viola,' Babs," laughed Lil. "No matter how plump you are."

Babs folded the newspaper. "There's only one way to find out if we're as good as they say we are, Lil," she replied.

Lil eyed Babs. Her younger sister was far more impetuous, not to say more capricious, than she. What did she have in mind?

"We have to get out of here." She rested her elbow on the table and stared at the clock on the wall. "I listen to that clock, and think it's ticking our lives away. I have to get out of here. This is what I want to do with my life. I know that you and I are different. You have other interests— your painting and your books, but this is my passion."

Lil knew her sister better than to point out all the obstacles that would confront an eighteen-year-old who had led a sheltered life in the bush trying to succeed on the national stage.

"Have you spoken to Tom and Mamma?"

"Not yet. I wanted to tell you first."

Bab's announcement filled Lil with conflict. The four-year gap in their ages had created a special bond between them. There was none of the sibling rivalry that might have arisen had they been closer in age. She was protective of Babs, and was the only member of the family who could temper her impetuosity. While not opposed to travel, she had no great desire to leave home. Her own ambitions were vague and ill-formed: a husband, children, a home of her own. She would wait to see how their parents reacted to the proposal.

Tom was immediately enthusiastic. He had always encouraged the girls to hone their talents and pursue their passions. Ann also gave her blessing. Babs had inherited her own impetuosity and headstrong nature. It would be out of character for her to disapprove.

Tom threw himself into arranging Babs's departure. There would be a grand send-off in the form of a performance at the Crystal Theatre in which Babs would showcase her range of talents from conjuring and dance to music and song. His friend Bert Sayers would write an introduction for her to his contacts in the Melbourne theatre world. And for Lil? After a lengthy discussion with her mother, she agreed to accompany Babs. While she could try her luck on a larger stage, her principle role initially would be to keep a protective eye on her little sister. The word chaperone was never used, certainly not in Babs's presence, but that effectively was the role she would play. Tom took photographs of the girls. One was a formal portrait. Others featured them in costume doing a jig and the Sailor's Hornpipe. He had calling cards made. On the facing side was inscribed:

The Two Prices

Viola—Lilian

The verso contained the portrait, two snapshots of the girls in their stage costumes, and a photo of the House that Annie built—a symbolic reminder to the girls of their origins. Again, the text "(Viola) The Two Prices (Lilian)" served as a reminder of who was the preeminent performer.

Bas' send-off concert took place on 30 September 1904 and the ever-obliging *Barrier Miner* described it as a triumph, although her conjuring came in for some mild criticism.

Miss Viola Price, the talented young lady who for years past has favourably engaged the attention of Broken Hill audiences, has now decided to turn her gift for entertaining to some practical account, and with that end in view will shortly proceed to Melbourne. Miss Price has been known to the Broken Hill public chiefly as a clever dancer, and her skilfulness in that direction has enabled her to twice win the Caledonian Shield at the New Year's Day gatherings. More recently a natural expertness in sleight of hand led the little lady to give performances in conjuring and her success in that direction no doubt justifies her in adopting the profession of a lady conjuror and illusionist. Besides having a considerable amount of skill as a conjuror, Miss Price possesses what is perhaps an equally valuable consideration to the professional artist: an attractive personality and agreeable stage presence. Fortified with these and an unassuming manner, Miss Price's gifts as an illusionist will be greatly enhanced, and a little stage experience should give her great control over an audience. At the Theatre last night, a complimentary benefit concert was tendered under the patronage of the Caledonian Society and the Barrier Centre League of Wheelman. Several of the members of the Pipers Band were present, with Chief Stevenson and other prominent figures, and the kilted ladies gave an air of picturesqueness to the proceedings. There was a crowded house and Miss Price was accorded a flattering reception. "Viola the Sorceress," the stage title by which the beneficiary has elected to be known, performed some clever conjuring tricks, displaying a fair amount of dexterity and cleanness in manipulation, and astounded the audience by her illusions. From the depths of apparently empty pieces of piping Viola produced a weird menagerie of lizards, kittens, cages of canaries, seagulls, etc, and would have further mystified the audience in that direction but for the fact that her attendants were lax in their work. The resources of the lady's art were exploited to a sufficient extent by the addition of card tricks, palming and so on, to show that Miss Price has considerable possibilities of entertainment at her fingers' ends. But conjuring is an exacting art, now that so many wonder workers have appeared before the public, and Miss Price will have to work hard before becoming perfect. In a pleasing Dutch impersonation Miss Price displayed her versatility and her clogging was greatly appreciated. She also danced a capital Highland fling to the pipe music of Mr. H. Murray. At the termination of the entertainment Miss Viola Price was made the recipient of a handsome gold bracelet from friends and admirers. (*Barrier Miner* Saturday 1 October 1904)[11]

Initially, Tom had intended accompanying Babs to Melbourne to help

[11] *The Barrier Miner* Saturday 1 October 1904, p.5

her get settled and assist with introductions to impresarios. Bert Sayers provided a list of contacts and a letter of introduction which also acted as a brief letter of recommendation for Babs. Unfortunately, at the last minute, Tom had to cancel his plan and travel to Adelaide to sort out a minor crisis with his wholesale supplier at the East End market. Babs left Broken Hill, accompanied only by Lilian. She carried with her Bert Sayers' letter, which made no mention of Lilian. Clearly, her role was seen as chaperone rather than performer, but that was soon to change.

Crystal Theatre, Broken Hill, NSW
Bert Sayers Prop.
13/10/1904
To Whom it May Concern:

This will introduce Mr. T. Price who is desirous of introducing Miss Viola Price to the public as a Conjuror, Illusionist etc. She was tendered a most enthusiastic send off by the Broken Hill public, and I should confidently state that with stage experience she should become a decided acquisition in her special line as prestidigitator.

As a Scotch Dancer she is facile princeps, having won the Championship of the Barrier and I can truthfully recommend her as an all-round artist, dramatic and otherwise.

Bert Sayers
Prop. Broken Hill Theatre

The girls found accommodation in a boarding house in Melbourne's theatre district a stone's throw from Punch Lane where their mother had once lived. Armed with Bert Sayers' letter, they began doing the rounds of the theatres. After several auditions, they were both lucky enough to be scouted by Harry Rickards, the foremost impresario of the day, and were able to add "Under engagement to MR. HARRY RICKARDS" to their calling card. Becoming a member of the Rickards Troupe represented a significant step in a competitive field. Vaudeville was the most popular entertainment genre of the era, and the most accomplished artists were feted as film stars, as later pop singers, would become to succeeding generations. At its most popular at the turn of the century, it would survive until the 1930s, when it was overtaken by the burgeoning film industry.

From established members of the Troupe, they learned that Rickards' real name was Henry Benjamin Leete. Born into a middle-class family in London in 1843, he went against the wishes of his puritanical parents by selecting vaudeville as a career, becoming a singer, comedian and theatre owner. Having established his reputation in England as a baritone singer and music hall performer, he first came to Australia in 1871, appearing alternately in Melbourne and Sydney, and developed a troupe which he took Australia-wide. He told the girls that he had visited Broken Hill in the mid-1890s, and had a vague recollection of having been introduced to Tom at a social event organized by Bert Sayers.

Rickards was a restless character, performing in the United States as well as back in his native England. At one point he took a troupe of performers to South Africa. He brought many acts to Australia: acrobats, ventriloquists, instrumentalists, impersonators, singers and animal acts as well as celebrated stars of the stage, including the world-famous escape artist Harry Houdini. By 1904, when Viola and Lilian joined the troupe, Rickard had acquired a sizeable fortune—enough to purchase a mansion at Darling Point, Sydney's most exclusive suburb, and a country estate near Margate in England.

The Two Prices were constantly on the road, performing at venues across Australia. Babs took readily to the punishing schedule. With her outgoing personality and an appetite for new experiences, she was well suited to the life of the troubadour. Lil, quiet and introverted, disliked living out of a suitcase, although she was happy enough with the career that had been thrust upon her. By 1906, they were well-known across the country. In that year, Rickards added international engagements to their schedule. He also had them perform solo in addition to their act as a duo. In February, Lil performed in Sydney; in April, both girls travelled to New Zealand, and appeared together in Wellington, before Babs performed solo in Christchurch. From there she travelled to Tasmania, again performing solo in Hobart.

By September, Lil, initially the more reticent of the two, had secured engagements in Europe, appearing as a solo artist in London and Paris.

Although she had no engagements, Babs was not one to be left behind. She spent a month with her sister in Europe. Ever peripatetic, she then returned to the Southern Hemisphere to join a troupe on another tour of New Zealand.

Before they set out on their career, Tom had created a postcard for the girls. On the face of the postcard, he reproduced the portrait he had taken for their calling card. On the verso, was the return address:

Thomas John and Ann Price
32 Ryan Street
Broken Hill
New South Wales
Australia

He handed a packet of the cards to Lil with the injunction to keep in touch.

Lil extracted a card and turned it over. "Why have you printed 'Australia' on the address?" she asked.

"You will go far," replied Tom. "Your talents can't be confined to these shores." His words proved prescient. Lil, ever reliable, sent postcards weekly, punctuating these with longer letters. When the mood took her, Babs scrawled short notes at the end of the longer letters. Tom grew increasingly restless as the narrative of the girls' lives beyond Broken Hill unfolded in Lil's letters. In contrast, his own life as a wholesale grocer in the back-of-beyond was stultifying.

"Pack your bags," he said to Ann when he received the news of Lil's European engagements.

"Why?" asked Ann. "Where are we going?"

"Paris," he replied.

And, leaving the business in the hands of a manager, that's exactly what they did. Ann needed no second invitation. For some time, it had been clear to her that Tom had wearied of the pedestrian business of peddling fruit, vegetables and smallgoods around the town. His restless spirit and artistic temperament, taste for show business, and the success of the younger members of the family were all he needed to abandon the

Bush for the glitz and glamour of Paris.

When Tom suggested to Frank that he accompany them, he was sorely tempted. However, now in his 20s, his eye was caught by the beautiful Violet O'Keeffe and he had embarked on a campaign to reciprocate by capturing her heart. He bombarded her daily with postcards and letters. Postcards bearing a portrait of the sender were a common form of communication at the time. Over the course of three months, Violet received over 150 of these from her persistent suitor. The postcards were produced by Tom, and Frank had an unlimited supply.

Violet was no easy catch, and in 1907, several months after Tom and Ann had left for Europe, Frank turned up in Paris. In addition to a desire to see the city that had entranced his parents, he thought that his absence might engender in Violet a passion that the postcards had singularly failed to arouse. Absence is supposed to make the heart grow fonder, but this was a risky strategy on Frank's part, because he was not the only young man about town who had been captivated by Violet.

At the beginning of 1908, the family returned to Australia. After a short break, Lilian and Babs left for New Zealand to join a troupe in Auckland. Frank resumed his pursuit of Violet, inundating her with postcards. He informed her that he had over 1,000 of these and would use all of them if necessary. She wasn't sure if this was a boast or a threat. The daily postcards were also punctuated by long letters which must have consumed a great deal of his time although there was nothing earth-shattering in their content. Most detailed the trivia of Frank's daily life.

After his European adventure, Tom found it difficult to settle back into domestic life in Broken Hill. He handed responsibility for the business to Frank and put 32 Ryan Street on the market. A legal dispute arose over the fact that the house had been built on the boundary of two blocks of land, and he eventually withdrew the house from sale, However, the fact that he had attempted to sell it was a clear indication to the children that he and Ann had outgrown Broken Hill.

Chapter 14
An Oriental Adventure

In February 1912, the six-year-old emperor of China, Puyi, abdicated, ending 2,000 years of imperial rule. His abdication capped the chaos of the previous year and marked the end of the Qing dynasty. The Republic of China was declared under the leadership of Sun Yat Sen who had plotted the end of the monarchy from his base in Hong Kong. However, it did not bring stability. Rival warlords with their own private armies squabbled over the southern provinces. Shanghai, as usual, was in the thick of things.

It was in this roiling mess that the sisters Price found themselves. In October of the previous year, their manager, Harry Rickards, died unexpectedly of a stroke while on a visit to England. Following his wishes, his widow, a trapeze artist and acrobat, shipped his remains back to Sydney where he was interred in Waverley Cemetery. The Rickards' Troupe was acquired by the impresario and sports promoter Hugh McIntosh. Known as a "colourful theatrical identity," McIntosh had done many things in his life, not all of them on the right side of the law. Coincidentally, as a young teenager, he had run away from his home in Surry Hills, Sydney, which in those days was a slum, and ended up in Adelaide. From there, he made his way to Broken Hill where he worked as a child labourer for BHP. By the time he was a young adult, he had worked at a wide variety of occupations including a silversmith's apprentice, a barman, a surgeon's assistant and a pie-seller at sporting events. At the age of 19, he was drawn to the stage and appeared as a singer and dancer in pantomimes in Melbourne. Some years later, he made a brief return to Broken Hill and appeared in several of Tom's benefit concerts. In consequence, he knew the Price girls as child performers before they become internationally famous. Now he had acquired the adult versions, along with the rest of the troupe.

One evening at the end of a performance in Sydney, he invited Babs and Lil to supper. The Sydney show only had a week left to run, and Babs guessed that he wanted to discuss options for their next engagement. "Wouldn't it be wonderful if he had an opening for us in Europe? Paris would be perfect. You've performed there, Lil, but I never have."

Lil was not so sure she wanted another overseas tour. Although not wedded to Australia, she had never enjoyed living out of a steamer trunk as her younger sister did. "Let's just wait and see what he proposes," she replied.

"Shanghai," proclaimed McIntosh as though he had successfully negotiated the purchase of the city. "Pearl of the Orient." He raised his champagne glass in an extravagant toast. He was on his third glass. Babs was on her second. Lil was still toying with her first. She half listened to his rambling monologue. He was going to take their careers to the next level. They would have star billing at the new Apollo Theatre. He had used his connections to have them written up in the top variety magazines. With him, they would have more fame and financial security than they had ever dreamed of. "Shanghai is the place to be," he said. "Things happen there."

"Hyperbole," Lil said to herself. The one good thing about Hugh McIntosh, she thought as she toyed with her champagne, was that you didn't have to make an effort at conversation. Babs was enthralled at the prospect—she less so. All she wanted was to find a kindred heart and abandon this peripatetic life. Little did she know what was waiting for her in the eye of the oriental storm.

In March 1912, they sailed from Melbourne to Hong Kong. The trip from Australia was uneventful. Lil was able to get on with her reading and painting, while Babs amused herself in the bar, where she flirted with several of the eligible bachelors on board, and, Lil suspected, had a brief fling with a dashing newspaper correspondent who informed Babs he was on his way to cover the unrest in southern China. Unrest? McIntosh had said nothing to them of unrest.

Like other first-time visitors to the Far East (which, for Antipodeans, should be called the Near North, as Lil observed to Babs), they stood on the deck as the ship made its way into Victoria Harbour. They were suitably awed by the Peak, a barren rock which reared dramatically skyward from the Harbour foreshore, and admired the jumble of vessels vying for space on the crowded waterway. These were of every conceivable type, from naval warships and merchant ships flying flags of many different colours, to unstable Chinese junks bobbing uncertainly on the black water.

Once the ship was moored, they disembarked and were met by McIntosh. Ever on the move, he was on his way to America to negotiate with promoters the possibility of a world title bout for the promising young Australian boxer, Les Darcy. Although still in his teens, Darcy had fought several world-class American boxers in McIntosh's Rushcutters Bay stadium and was touted as a future world champion. McIntosh had made a fortune by staging international bouts in the stadium, including a world championship title fight between Americans Tommy Burns and Jack Johnson: both world heavyweight champions. He figured that he could make even more by bringing the young Australian champion to the United States. He was interrupting his trip to travel to Shanghai where there were "management issues" at the Apollo Theatre. "But don't worry," he reassured the sisters. "The show will go on."

He led them away from the Harbour through a puzzle of Hong Kong streets crowded with rickshaws; coolies wearing wide-brimmed woven hats ferrying all manner of strange-smelling foodstuffs, from sweetly-scented tropical fruits to pungent dried fish; ragged, barefoot urchins ducking and weaving between the ceaseless stream of human traffic; beggars with deformities that defied belief. The unfamiliar sights, noise and smells overwhelmed the young women.

"Where are we going?" asked Lil. "I thought you said you were taking us to our hotel."

McIntosh grinned. "I said that I was taking you to your accommodation," he replied. "I didn't say anything about a hotel."

"So, where is this accommodation?"

"Up there," replied McIntosh, lifting a finger to the Peak which was even more intimidating now that they had disembarked.

"How on earth do we get up there? Surely you don't expect us to walk."

For an answer, McIntosh laughed and assisted them into a rickshaw.

The barefoot and shirtless rickshaw coolie, reed-thin and burnt black by the sun, set off at a gallop along a narrow street that wound steeply upward.

"Poor fellow," said Babs. "Where does he get the strength?"

"Surely he isn't going to pull us all the way to the top," said Lil.

He wasn't. He came to a stop next to a two-story stone structure on the outskirts of the settlement and indicated that they should disembark. The Peak rose seemingly vertically skyward. McIntosh's rickshaw drew up beside them. He disembarked and led them into the base of the building.

"Welcome to the Peak Tram," he said.

They found themselves confronted by a funicular railway. McIntosh handled them into the carriage as though they were his baggage, which in a sense they were, and clambered in beside them. When all passengers were settled, the carriage jerked into motion. It ran horizontally for a few yards, and they abruptly began its upward ascent. Babs and Lil were thrust back in their seats. Lil looked ahead through a canopy of trees at the tracks that ran almost vertically up the hill. Parallel to the tram tracks was a trail which shortly diverged to the left and was lost in foliage. A line of barefoot coolies in broadbrimmed hats trudged slowly along the trail. Flexible bamboo poles supporting woven bamboo baskets bounced on their shoulders. McIntosh explained that the tram only carried human traffic—white traffic, of course. The locals were not permitted to ride the tram, nor to reside on the Peak. Food, furniture, household appliances and personal possessions had to be transported to the top by coolies. "Even your trunks," he said. "They'll arrive sometime this afternoon." Only Chinese who had a legitimate reason to do so—servants, coolies and houseboys—were permitted to venture past the Mid-levels.

When the Peak Tram levelled off and jolted to a halt, the passengers disembarked into a world that could not have contrasted more starkly than the one they had just left. Chaos was replaced by order. The incomprehensibility of the streetscape below was replaced by a reassuring Englishness. Solid bungalows and two-storey country homes were set in pleasing gardens with extensive lawns. However, one had only to look beyond the hedge to be reminded that you were in a world that differed in every conceivable respect from the one they had left.

McIntosh led them across a paved courtyard to a lookout bounded by a low stone balustrade. There, they were able to look down onto Victoria Harbour, to have pointed out to them the ship on which they had arrived from Melbourne, a shimmering lozenge on the water. Beyond the harbour, they could see Kowloon and the New Territories beyond.

"Is that China?" asked Babs, pointing at a line of hills in the distance.

"It was once, and is supposed to be again, when we are long dead, unless we can renegotiate the treaty we struck with the Chinese government of the day thirty years ago." By "we" he was referring to the British government. Like most who had been born and bred in Australia of British stock—he himself had been born in the slums of Surry Hill to a Scottish policeman—he referred to Britain as "Home."

Babs found it slightly ridiculous to be seated in a sedan chair, basically a woven wicket chair of the type you might find on an Australian veranda, with a canvas top to protect the incumbent from sun and rain, and long poles protruding front and rear. The poles were hoisted onto their shoulders by two coolies of indeterminate age. She was learning that when it came to age there was no telling with the Chinese. They were dressed in the coolie uniform—bare feet, ragged knee-length shorts, and wide-brimmed woven straw hats.

McIntosh's sedan chair led the way. She had no idea where they were going. McIntosh enjoyed surprising them and straightforward questions for information were more often than not rebuffed. Their destination turned out to be a substantial house set behind wrought iron gates on Mt. Kellet Road. She would soon learn that Mt. Kellet, which was a spur of land off Victoria Peak, was one of Hong Kong's premier addresses, noted in particular for its splendid views.

McIntosh referred to their host, retired Colonel Holmes, as "my associate," a suitably ambiguous term which gave the sisters no inkling of either his current profession or his relationship to their patron. They later learned that he was one of the investors in the Apollo Theatre and had "other dealings" in Shanghai. He greeted them warmly on their arrival and apologized for the absence of Mrs. Holmes as it was her bridge day. They learned that the Holmes adapted well to the local culture but drew the line at mah-jongg and other Chinese diversions. A uniformed housemaid showed them to their rooms while McIntosh and Holmes retreated to the study to drink whisky and discuss the Apollo issue, whatever that might be.

Their week in Hong Kong was uneventful. They made trips down from the Peak to explore the town. On the first occasion, while Lil sketched a street scene in her notepad, Babs wandered through what they were told was a wet market. She put a handkerchief to her nose to mask unfamiliar smells, and was repulsed at the sight of a pig being butchered on a concrete slab. She tried to make some sense of the language but was soundly defeated. There was one word she heard often enough for it to stick. Later she asked the colonel what it meant. "Oh, gweilo," he said. "Foreign devil. They were talking about you."

"Of all the nerve!" replied Babs. "There's nothing remotely devilish about me."

Returning to the Peak from their second expedition, the tram was enveloped in a thick, white mist. "Not much point in having the most spectacular view in the world if it can't be seen," noted the acerbic Lil.

On their last evening the Holmes arranged a supper party. Late in the afternoon, as they were having sundowners on the veranda, before dressing for dinner, Mrs. Holmes asked if the girls would entertain the guests with one of their song and dance routines once the brandy had been passed around.

"It would be our pleasure," said Babs.

Lil was not happy. As they retired to dress for dinner, she grumbled to Babs that they weren't performing bears.

"We've always had to sing for our supper," replied Babs. "In any case, we could hardly have refused."

The assault on their senses in Hong Kong barely prepared them for Shanghai. For all its exoticism, Hong Kong felt reassuringly British. Shanghai had an ominous edge. McIntosh arranged comfortable rooms for them on the second floor of a boarding house off Szechuan Road just around the corner from the newly constructed Apollo Theatre. The theatre was more than suitable for their act, and they were not disappointed to be allocated the largest of the dressing rooms at the rear of the stage, although they were somewhat concerned to learn that the manager had absconded with all the takings from the previous season's shows. This was the "issue" that had prompted McIntosh's detour to Shanghai. A temporary solution was found in the form of an Irishman of McIntosh's acquaintance. "What McCafferty knows about show business could be written on a postcard with a blunt pencil," he told the girls. "But he can be trusted. And no one will cross or double-cross him." They learned soon enough why. McCafferty had worked as a mercenary for at least two warlords in southern China and knew a thing or two about how to deal with double-crossers.

Once settled in Shanghai, they found that McIntosh was true to his earlier promises. They appeared at the top of the bill at the Apollo Theatre. The vaudeville publication, *The Mirror*, reported that Viola and Lilian Price, two Broken Hill girls, who had reached a high rung on the ladder in vaudeville, and who for some years were members of the Rickard troupe, were currently appearing at the new Apollo Theatre, Shanghai, China. The article spoke in glowing terms of their act, noting in particular that in Shanghai, the young ladies had succeeded in hitting the popular expatriate taste in their Scotch and Dutch specialties.

The girls kept in touch with Tom and Ann in their customary fashion, sending weekly postcards supplemented with the occasional longer letter accompanied by Lil's sketches and watercolours. These missives were hungrily devoured, particularly by Tom, who was fascinated by the descriptions and visual portraits of life in the Orient. They also frustrated him. "Why am I wasting my time selling sacks of onions to miners' wives in Broken Hill?" he complained to Ann.

McIntosh returned to Shanghai after an unsuccessful trip to America to secure a fight for Les Darcy. This was not because he was unable to find promoters willing to stage a fight for the young Australian boxer but because Darcy refused to sign up with McIntosh. Furious that he had wasted time and money in attempting to advance Darcy's career, McIntosh vowed that he would block any attempts by Darcy to fight in America. He managed to do this when Darcy eventually undertook the trip with another promoter. McIntosh used his influence with a number of state governors to have Darcy banned.

There was more bad news when he got to Shanghai. After a dispute with McCafferty about money, the Irishman promptly resigned and set up his own business smuggling guns and other supplies upriver from Shanghai to brigands who were attempting to overthrow one of the provincial governors. The Apollo was once more without a manager. "I've got the most splendid theatre in Shanghai, and the most talented performers in the whole of the Orient, but no one to rely on to manage the place," he complained to the girls.

"We might have a solution to your problem," Babs said to him.

In March, *The Barrier Miner* reported that Thomas John Price, fruit and vegetable merchant, late of Broken Hill, had been appointed manager of the Apollo Theatre, Shanghai. Leaving Frank in charge of the business, Tom and Ann sailed from Melbourne to Hong Kong, and from there to Shanghai. They took lodgings on Szechuan Road, a short distance from the theatre and close to Lil and Babs. Tom threw himself into the job of managing the theatre, feeling that he had found his true calling. Shanghai, a city electric with excitement and intrigue, was his kind of place. Doubts about his decision to reinvent himself began to grow only as civil unrest continued to spread throughout the city.

When they entered their dressing room at the end of their last performance of the season, Lil and Babs were confronted by a large bouquet of flowers. At first, they assume it must have been left by the management. It would have been typical of Tom to celebrate the ending of their highly successful season with a fine bouquet of flowers. Lil began changing into her street clothes, but Babs noticed the card that had been tucked in among the flowers. She plucked it out and read it to her sister.

"Would the Misses Price be so kind as to honour us with their presence at supper this evening? We await your pleasure, and hope for a positive response to this invitation. Sidney Gilbert & Walter Lockhart."

The names were unfamiliar to the girls. "Well, what do you think, Lil?"

"I don't know. It's been a long week." Although she could sense that

Babs was keen for some company and fun, Lil had been looking forward to getting back to their rooms and finishing the watercolour she had been working on.

Babs, ever impulsive, said "Oh, come on, Lil." Snatching up a pencil, she scrawled "*Accepted—VP*" at the bottom of the note, passed it to an attendant and then began changing into her street clothes. That single impulsively scrawled response would result in the next big change to their lives.

The men rose as Babs and Lil entered the club at the rear of the Apollo Theatre and approached their table. The shorter of the two took Babs's gloved hand and touched it to his lips. "Sidney Gilbert," he said. "So delighted that you accepted our invitation." Walter Lockhart, tall, dark, decent looking, but not quite as handsome as he had appeared from a distance, gave Lil's hand the same treatment. They had obviously decided in advance who would escort which sister in the event of the invitation being accepted. Both men were impeccably turned out in the fashion of the day, although Lockhart's attire was slightly more subdued than Gilbert's. There was a flamboyance in the cut and combination of Gilbert's suit, waistcoat and bow tie. There was something of the Dandy about him, thought Babs. He reminded her of their late, lamented mentor, Harry Rickards.

The girls were seated at the circular table between the two men. Although the cork had been extracted from the bottle of champagne standing in an ice bucket by Sidney Gilbert's elbow, it had not been broached. Etiquette demanded the men wait for their guests, although it seemed to Babs from the animation in his eye and the smell on his breath that Sidney had already taken a drink or two. He signalled to the waiter to attend to their glasses, and then proposed a toast. "To the Misses Price—Antipodean adornments to the Orient." He winked at her as he raised his glass.

"To the Misses Price," murmured Lockhart. Glasses were clinked. Lockhart and Lilian touched the glasses to their lips, but Sidney and Babs drained theirs. Gilbert immediately called for their glasses to be replenished.

"Steady on, Babs," said her sister.

Gilbert looked enquiringly from the elder sister to the younger. "Babs? Aren't you Viola? Am I mistaken here?" He feigned annoyance at the confusion. "Have I been deceived?" Another wink, just in case she missed the joke.

"There is no deception," replied Babs. "Viola is the name I was given at birth; Babs is the name my family and friends use."

"And what should I call you?"

"Well, most people call me Viola, but you can call me Your Ladyship—or Ma'am if you prefer. If I eventually decide to like you, I shall allow you to call me Babs"

Gilbert roared with laughter and raised his glass for another toast. "And most people call me Sidney, but you can call me Sid."

"If I decide to like you, I shall call you Sid. For now, you shall be Mr. Gilbert."

"And what if you decide you don't like me?"

"You will never see me again."

The animated accord struck up between the younger couple was not matched by Lockhart and Lilian. Barely a word had passed between them. Babs turned to the man on her left and asked, "And what brings you to China, Mr. Lockhart?"

"I work for Lever Brothers."

"Oh, the soap people," replied Babs.

"Indeed," interjected Gilbert. "Look at those pristine hands. He's here to improve the standard of hygiene of the Orientals. Has his work cut out, I must say."

"Are you here on a long-term basis, Mr. Lockhart?" asked Lilian.

"I came here six months ago to establish a presence in China. Originally, my tour was to be for a year, but I have extended for a year, so I'll be here for another eighteen months."

"Are you happy about that?"

Lockhart shrugged. "I do whatever the company requires of me—but I must say, I'll be happy to get back to Port Sunlight." He omitted to mention that the push by British and other European companies into China in the dying days of the Qing Dynasty was highly contentious. The bitterness of the Boxer Uprising a decade earlier in which a group of rebels calling themselves the Righteous and Harmonious Fists attempted to throw out the European and Japanese occupiers had not been forgotten, nor had the fact that the Chinese had to pay a large reparation and make significant concessions to foreign firms such as those represented by Gilbert and Lockhart.

"Ah, my erstwhile companion yearns for Port Sunlight, where the sun never shines!" said Gilbert.

"And you, Mr. Gilbert?" asked Babs.

"Sidney, please. I manage China for General Electric, and I'm here for the long haul. No immediate plans to return, not unless there's a war."

"War? Here in China?" asked Babs, looking alarmed.

"Well, war is always possible here," replied Sidney. "Just look at its history. But we're here to make money for Britain, not war. No, I was thinking of war in Europe. If that should happen, I shall return to fight for King and Country. But I highly doubt that there will be war in Europe." In fact, when, a couple of years later, Sidney's confident prediction turned out to be badly wrong with the beginning of the Great War, he did not return to fight at all, but stayed put in the Orient.

Supper was served. Lilian picked at her food, but Babs ate with gusto. Another bottle of champagne appeared. At the end of the meal, the orchestra, which had played quietly during the meal service, struck up a waltz, and several couples proceeded to the dance floor.

"Would you care to take to the floor, Your Ladyship?" asked Sidney in a mocking tone.

"That's a brave invitation, Gilbert," says Lockhart. "Proposing to step onto the dance floor with the most accomplished dancer in the whole of the Orient and possibly beyond. Brave indeed!"

"Perhaps your friend thinks he can help improve my technique. Or maybe he thinks I need more practice—after all, I was only on the stage for three hours this evening," said Babs.

"For a beautiful woman," replied Gilbert, "I've never been averse to making a fool of myself."

As they moved towards the dance floor, Lockhart felt obliged to ask Lilian if she would care to join them. Suspecting that he was only asking out of politeness, she declined. She lacked the energy of her younger sister, and the last thing she wanted at this stage of the evening was more physical activity. She thought wistfully of their comfortable rooms not far off North Szechuan Road. She watched Babs and Gilbert twirling from one end of the dance floor to the other. Gilbert acquitted himself well, although he was not in her sister's class. Other dancers paused to watch as, holding herself erect, she crossed back and forth across the floor as though she owned it.

"Has she always been as gifted?" asked Lockhart.

"Yes," replied Lilian without a hint of envy.

When Babs and Gilbert return from the dance floor, Babs flushed and animated, Gilbert smug with his small success, a bottle of brandy had appeared on the table. Lilian gathered her wrap about her and rose to her feet. "I think it's time for us to go," she said to Babs. "We've imposed on these gentlemen enough."

"Just stay for a nightcap," said Gilbert, indicating the brandy balloons, which had just been filled.

"Yes, please, Lil," said Babs, still glowing from her exertions and whatever it was that has passed between her and Gilbert on the dance floor.

Lil pursed her lips. Disagreements between her and her sister were rare. "No, I'm going."

"Well, I'm staying," replied Babs, drinking a glass of water, then picking up a brandy balloon and downing its contents.

"I'll walk with you," said Lockhart getting to his feet.

"That won't be necessary."

Despite her protestations, Lockhart followed her from the room. Gilbert rose, wished Lil a good night with a small bow to her retreating back, and returned his attention to Babs.

When Babs entered their rooms just after four o'clock in the morning, Lil was sitting up waiting for her.

"What have you done?" Lil asked her sister, knowing full-well what Babs had been up to.

"I've been having fun. You should try it some time." She smiled at Lil to soften the implied criticism. "And now I'm going to bed."

It was telling that neither Lockhart not Gilbert made any mention of the fact that China in 1912 was in turmoil, with the collapse of the Qing Dynasty, the return of Sun Yat Sen, and the establishment of a republic.

Presumably, they didn't want to upset the romantic mood of the evening by discussing the chilling reality of life for foreigners in China at that time. The sisters were aware of the unrest—it was impossible not to be, but foreign politics had nothing to do with them. In fact, as they drank champagne and danced, the country was teetering on the brink of civil war, a civil war that would leave no inhabitants untouched, not even innocent young foreign entertainers. Both men were fully aware of the precariousness of their position and that of the British interests. And what of Tom? Was he so wrapped up in his new role as international theatrical impresario that he was impervious to the seismic shifts in the political landscape, and the dangers they presented to him, his common-law wife, and two young half-sisters? Although none of his letters and postcards to Frank made any mention of the turmoil, the answer must presumably be yes.

Babs' impulsive acceptance of the Englishmen's invitation to dinner had far-reaching consequences for both women. The flirtatious first evening with Sidney Gilbert flourished into a full-blown affair within days. In keeping with her nature, Lil was more circumspect when it came to Lockhart. She spent more time with him, almost by default, as Babs' attention was fully occupied by Gilbert. Over time, she came to appreciate his quiet, considerate ways. Where Babs threw herself recklessly into her affair, Lil drifted into hers. When Walter Lockhart's Far Eastern tour came to an end at the beginning of 1914, and he prepared to return to England, she experienced an unexpected sense of loss. She was shocked by the realization that Walter Murray Lockhart was what she had been looking for, but, at the age of 29, had abandoned hope of finding. Now, having found him, she was about to lose him. When, three weeks before his departure, he took her to dinner and asked in his diffident way if she would be prepared to accompany him on his return to England, she had no hesitation in accepting. His look of delight mixed with mild incredulity and surprise indicated to her that he had half expected rejection.

Lil's decision to accept Walter's offer spelled the demise of the Price Sisters. It presented her with the opportunity to retire gracefully from the stage, something she had wanted to do after their first season in Shanghai. Tom and Ann had returned to Australia, so there was no pressure from that quarter, either to remain in China or on the stage.

Walter and Lil were married at Fulham, Middlesex on May 24, 1914, almost four weeks to the day before the shot in Sarajevo that reverberated around the world, triggering off hostilities that became known as the Great War, and the War to End All Wars. By then Walter and Lil had moved to Port Sunlight in Cheshire where Lever Brothers, Walter's company, was based. They were to live in and around Port Sunlight for the rest of their lives, although Walter's return to Lever Brothers was interrupted by his military service. One of two surviving photographs of the couple taken some time later in 1914 showed him impeccably kitted out in officer's uniform, looking diffident and duty bound. Lil, who barely reached his shoulder, looked anything but happy at her husband's imminent departure for the front.

The couple were unable to have children. When Walter returned from the war, they adopted a son, Don. The second surviving photo of the Lockhart family show a much-aged Walter. In the pre-service photo, his face was unlined, and he possessed a fine head of jet-black hair. In the post-war family portrait, deep furrows ran down his cheeks, and his thinning hair was white. Thin-lipped Lil stared over the photographer's right shoulder. Jug-eared Don, standing between his parents, had the appearance of a startled forest creature. Each looked as though they bore their own terrible secret. Over the years, Lil made two trips back to her native Australia, the first in the wake of her sister's tragic death, and the second to visit her aging parents. Her own death came in 1943. Walter outlived her by seven years, dying on July 29, 1950 at Clatterbridge Hospital, Wirral, Cheshire.

With the departure of her sister, Babs embarked on a solo career. However, it was not the same. Something had been lost. Babs accepted fewer and fewer engagements and threw herself into Shanghai's social scene. She and Sidney became a well-known pair among the expatriate community. Their extraversion, and Sidney's generosity with money, guaranteed their popularity.

She married the audacious Englishman in a civil ceremony on a Saturday afternoon, followed by a lavish wedding "breakfast" which went on until well after midnight. The following day, the only evidence that the wedding had taken place was the ring on her finger and a raging headache. Sidney brought her champagne in bed to help her deal with the consequences of the previous evening.

They took a large house in what, until the revolution, had been the British and American concession just off the Bund. Sidney's position as Manager of the General Electric Company of China required extensive travel, and Babs had long periods alone. She cultivated a large coterie of other young bored and restless wives and threw herself into spending Sidney's money on lavishly decorating the house. She made several trips back to Australia, where she stayed in Adelaide with her mother and stepfather, and visited her brother Frank in Broken Hill. Frank had married Violet O'Keeffe, one of Bab's childhood friends, and was raising a family. On these trips, she brought with her a large steamer trunk crammed with porcelain, silk, and fine Chinese linen. She left these with her mother along with the instruction that, in the event of her demise, they be divided among her three nieces.

Toward the end of 1924, twelve years after she moved to Shanghai, she fell ill with a malady that could not be diagnosed by the local doctors. She returned to Adelaide to seek further treatment. There she was diagnosed with nephritic syndrome, the most serious and potentially fatal forms of kidney disease. Over the next few months her condition worsened, and in July 1925, the doctors at the Royal Adelaide Hospital decided that the diseased kidney had to be removed, and she was admitted to the hospital for surgery. Due to gross incompetence, the healthy rather than the diseased kidney was removed, and Babs died on 10 July 1925, at the age of 38.

The Barrier Miner, the Broken Hill newspaper that had done its modest best to promote the careers of Babs and Lil provided the following sparse notice of her death.

Death Notice—Gilbert—At Adelaide this morning, of Mrs. Sidney C. Gilbert (née Babs Price) of Tientsin (China), daughter of Mrs. Price Sen., and sister of Mrs. L. Lockhart and Mr. T. J. Price of St. Peter's, Adelaide, and Mr. F. Price, Ryan Street, Railway Town *(The Barrier Miner, Friday 10 July 1925).*(12)[12]

---

[12] *The Barrier Miner*, Friday 10 July 1925, p.2

Chapter 15
The Pursuit

When he was born at Port Adelaide on 27 November 1881, he was registered as Frank Dearmer. Harry Dearmer was named on the birth certificate as the father, even though he hadn't been sighted for well over a year. Frank had no memory of ever being referred to as Dearmer. Despite the name on the certificate, he lived as Frank Price and only in adulthood, did he discover that he had been registered under another name and made Price his official name by deed poll. His mother also lived as Price, even though she and WH never married. Adopting Price as her family name may have been the only nod she ever made to the conventions of the time.

Frank's one and only sighting of Dearmer occurred when he was eight: on the dramatic afternoon in North Adelaide when he had witnessed Harry bursting into their house, shooting Tom, only to be shot, in turn, by his mother. "Don't worry," he had overheard a neighbour reassuring Ann. "He's only eight. In a few months he'll have forgotten everything." However, the events of the afternoon scarred him deeply, and he forgot nothing: not the noise and acrid smell of the gunshots, nor Tom's screams of agony and the look on his mother's face as she fired her bullet into Harry's stomach. (Had Frank been old enough to provide en eye-witness account to the police, the verdict at Ann's trial might have been very different.) The incident left an indelible impression and taught him a lesson that he never forgot: firearms are a powerful means of solving problems. Years later when he used a gun to solve a problem of his own, the repercussions were to have a catastrophic effect on his own life.

One of the photos that survived in his daughter's battered suitcase was a portrait of Frank and Tom that showed a strong resemblance between the two. The resemblance led to whispers about the real relationship between Tom and Frank. However, with a common father in

WH, the resemblance was hardly surprising, and his real paternity would remain a mystery.

In the decade from 1881 to 1889, the family was constantly on the move. Frank got used to having his possessions packed and moving about Adelaide at short notice. From Port Adelaide, they moved first to Unley, a suburb to the south of the city, where Lilian was born, and then to a more substantial stone house on the corner of Mann Terrace and Melbourne Street North Adelaide. It was here that Viola ("Babs") was born and this was the scene of the dramatic shoot-out between his mother and her estranged husband.

After the shoot-out and subsequent trials, the family moved to Broken Hill where they settled at 32 Ryan Street in the house designed and constructed by Ann. In time it would come to be known within the family as the Old House. WH moved from the miner's shanty he had lived in since coming to Broken Hill and took up residence in a bedroom opposite that occupied by Ann and Tom. Frank was happy to be reunited with his father and saw no ambiguity in living under the same roof as WH, Tom and Ann: they were a family after all, weren't they?

It took Frank some time to adjust to Broken Hill. Having grown up in Adelaide, the mining town struck him as dirty and crude. For his first day at the local school, Ann dressed him up in knee breeches and a smart jacket. He stood out like a sore thumb amongst the rag-tag sons and daughters of miners, not only because of his fancy clothes, but also his manner. He looked each of his classmates up and down with a boldness of eye that unnerved them. Despite his diminutive statue, he was never roughed up for being different.

It didn't bother him a bit when, on the first morning, the teacher called him Your Little Highness and the other children laughed. Of course, he was different! He was a Price. He had learned to read by the age of four, and his reading age was at least three years ahead of his chronological age. Despite several years at school, many of his classmates were still barely literate. He was good at numbers, and adept at art—although not as talented as Lil. At the end of his first day at school, the teacher asked him to wait behind until the other children had left. "I don't know what to do with you, Mr. Price. I don't know what I have to teach you."

"You don't have to do anything with me," replied Frank calmly. "I'm perfectly capable of teaching myself."

After that, the teacher allowed him to sit at the back of the classroom in an alcove that served as the school library and, true to his word, Frank got on with his self-education.

Each member of the family adjusted to life in Broken Hill in his or her own way. Tom established a fruit and vegetable business, assisted WH in running the Broken Hill Secular Association, and threw himself into his true love, the world of entertainment. He satisfied his passion for the theatre by arranging various amateur concerts and theatricals to raise money for community causes such as striking miners, the families of workers killed in mining accidents, and itinerant workers such as shearers. Although he enjoyed the amateur performances, Frank was not as committed to them as his sisters. As he grew into adolescence, his real passion was sports. In 1901, he joined the newly formed Barrier League of Wheelmen and began cycle racing, for which he quickly developed a passion. By 1907, he had earned the nickname "Dodger" due to his ability to weave his way between fellow competitors. The nickname stuck, and was even engraved on his headstone after his untimely death.

After he died, Dodger's name was rarely mentioned to younger generation of the family. When it did, the topic was usually about his exploits as a cyclist, and his passion for fast cars. He remained a mystery to those grandchildren who never knew him. As they grew up, they were encouraged to believe that, as a cyclist, he was little short of a national treasure. However, the record tells a different story. Between 1901, when he began competitive racing and 1920, when he retired from the sport, he had moderate success in Broken Hill. However, in countless races in other parts of the country, the best he ever did was a sprinkling of 2nd and 3rd places.

Violet O'Keeffe, the third of eleven children (three of whom died in infancy) was born on the 2nd of February, 1887, in the wheat belt town of Barmedman in the Riverina district of New South Wales. Her father, William Richard O'Keeffe, owned a team of bullocks and made a living transporting heavy farming materials and equipment. In the middle of 1890, O'Keeffe told his wife to pack up the household. Like other rural areas based on agriculture, the Riverina was suffering, having been hit by the twin calamities of drought and the collapse of property prices. The collapse was brought on by the beginning of what was to be Australia's first major economic depression. This, in turn, was due to the collapse of banks overseas and the withdrawal of capital from Australia. "We'll head west," William told his wife. "Into mining country. Droughts don't matter to miners."

And so it was that Violet and her two older siblings were bundled onto the bullock wagon and made the arduous trek to Broken Hill. With three small children, and another on the way, the journey was one of extreme hardship for his wife, and there were times when William's resolve weakened, but he kept pushing west: he had no other choice. For a start, there was no turning back. In fact, there was no back. Just as importantly, he was descended from County Cork stock, an O'Keeffe, to boot, one of the nine royal families of Ireland. The O'Keeffes never turned back.

William may have been right in his assertion that the mining industry was impervious to drought, but it was anything but impervious to economic depression. If anything, it was even harder hit. Who wanted Australia's minerals and ore when there was nothing to build?

For the O'Keeffe family, it would turn out to be a case of out of the frying pan into the fire. Poverty was evident in the towns and hamlets they passed. William learned that civil unrest had broken out across the nation. In the cities, there were strikes on the waterfront. In the country, rural workers and shearers were on strike. In the bush as well as up and down the coast, there was open talk of revolution. Even in the bush, thousands of heavily armed troops were deployed to put down riots and break up the mobs that gathered to listen to firebrands preaching socialist revolution.

By the time they reached Broken Hill, exhausted and at the end of their physical and financial tether, they found that the town had not escaped the industrial unrest. Miners no longer extracted ore from the ground, but formed angry mobs and gathered in Argent Street. William found accommodation at the end of Morish Street in South Broken Hill. The house was the usual corrugated iron structure. The property was large enough to accommodate not just the family, but the bullock team as well. It was also far enough from the unrest in the centre of town to give at least a semblance of security.

In 1891, the miners were locked out by the mining management. Although the lock-out did not last, it was the prelude to a much bigger conflict. When the global price of lead and silver collapsed, the mining companies had no option but to break an agreement they had struck with the unions. The miners were led off the job by the union secretary, initiating a strike that was to last four months, and cause extreme hardship to the townspeople. The New South Wales government swiftly intervened, sending a detachment of troops across from Sydney. With rifles and fixed bayonets, they forced the striking miners out of Argent Street, and secured the centre of town. Peace was only temporary, however. When the mining managers imported non-union labour from Melbourne to break the strike, trouble erupted again. The unionists set up pickets around the mines. When the workers from Melbourne attempted to break the picket, they were turned away with cries of "Scabs!" and worse ringing in their ears. The troops forced unionists back, allowing the "scab" labourers to enter. William, who hung on the edge of the crowd to see what was going on, asked one of the picketers what was likely to happen now. "Don't worry, Mate," was the reply. "The coppers might have got the scabs in, but they won't be getting them out. There'll be no ore coming out, either."

The townspeople organized a march on Argent Street in support of the miners. When they were turned back at the base of Billygoat Hill, they made their way to Central Reserve, an area traditionally dedicated to the expression of free speech. There, one fiery speech followed another, some given by local union organizers, others by socialist agitators from out of town. Earlier in the day, the manager of the Block 14 Mine denounced the miners as nothing better than ruffians, rebels and loafers. He was rewarded by having his effigy burned, and a mock funeral held.

Late one afternoon, a decade after the political and social turmoil of the 1890s had been all but obliterated by the froth and bubble of Federation, Dodger finished his fruit and vegetable deliveries to the local stores and returned to 32 Ryan Street. It was a pleasant, mid-spring afternoon, and, as he was about to enter the house, he noticed his younger sister Babs sitting in the shade of the creeping vines that formed an Arcadian retreat in the lee of the enclosed passageway that united the kitchen area with the front of the house. His eyes were drawn, not to his sister, but her companion, a girl about his sister's age, who had a face of such translucent beauty that it stopped him in his tracks. She returned his gaze without flinching or changing expression. Finally, he turned away, entered the house and went to the alcove that served as an office. Instead of drawing up the ledger with details of the day's transactions, he poured scotch into a tumbler and sat at the desk, doodling with a pencil on the large square of blotting paper wondering what just happened. Later, when Babs entered the house, he asked about her companion. "That's Violet," replied Babs. "She's my friend from school."

Several weeks later Violet was sitting in the parlour of her married sister Ethel's house in South Broken Hill. So fully occupied was she with the task of darning a rent in her favourite cardigan, that she failed to notice her sister entering the room. Sensing her sister's presence, she turned with a start. Ethel handed her a postcard.

"This came for you," she said. On the front of the card was a studio portrait of Dodger taken by Tom. The card was postmarked Kadina, South Australia, where Dodger was taking part in a bike racing meeting, and dated October 11, 1903. He was twenty-two, she sixteen. The postcard carried a simple message penned in Dodger's floral hand, but its intent was clear: *With love to Vi from Jack.*

"Be careful, Vi," said Ethel. "You're of that age."

"I know what I'm doing," replied Violet. She put the card face down on the occasional table where she kept her sewing kit. She said nothing more to Ethel. She wasn't going to give herself away. If Jack wanted her, he would have to prove to her that he was worthy. Like his family, she referred to him as Jack. She thought that Dodger, the nickname bestowed on him by his cycling friends, was undignified and was the sort of name that might be given to an undesirable character. She had read the Dickens novel *Oliver Twist*, and remembered that the Artful Dodger was the member of a juvenile street gang. No, Dodger would definitely not do for one of the more prominent members of the local business community.

She spent increasing amounts of time at the Old House, and although she tried to maintain a certain distance, was clearly considered part of the family by the Prices. She admired Jack for his hard work, and adored Uncle Tom, as everyone did. Babs remained her closest intimate, although she was less and less frequently at home as she and Lil toured Australia along with the Rickards Troupe and began to venture overseas. Ann treated her as another daughter. From Ann, she received instructions in cooking and running a household, although, as one of a dozen siblings, she had acquired most of these skills at an early age. She was no fool, and it was clear that Ann had an eye on her as a possible match for her beloved son. Ann was grooming her in the skills she would need if she were to make Jack a suitable wife.

His position as a partner in T. J. Price and Son required Jack to travel a lot, not only making deliveries presenting invoices and collecting money around Broken Hill and District, but also traveling to Adelaide, sometimes with Tom but more often than not alone for meetings with their East End Market suppliers. His passion for cycle racing also took him to meetings all over South Australia, Victoria and New South Wales. When he was away from Broken Hill, he sent Vi postcards and letters most days. Missives written in Broken Hill would sometimes arrive bearing an Adelaide postmark. If he were in Broken Hill and Vi was visiting relatives or family friends in Jametown, Moonta, or Kadia, he would continue to barrage her with correspondence. In his missives, he documented the pedestrian incidents of daily life in the town: shooting kangaroos with Tom at the Pinnacles, a strange clump of hills south of Broken Hill, visiting Violet's family and describing her newly-arrived baby sister Monica, nicknamed Monney, as "just the ticket," or "just the thing." Within eighteen months, there was a deeper level of intimacy in the postcards, Dodger signing off in various ways: "Fondest love from yours truly, Jack," "Yours lovingly, Dodger," "Heaps of love to you. Your loving boy, Frank."

Shortly before Christmas 1907, the haberdashery business in Argent Street where Violet had worked since leaving school went out of business along with a number of other establishments. The financial downturn was occasioned by a fall in ore prices on the international market. Violet lost her job along with the other store assistants. It was not the most exciting position in the world, but young, unmarried women were expected to contribute financially to the family, particularly when the family was a large one of modest means. Jack promised to ask around among his business contacts. A week later, he told her that he had secured an interview for her as a sales assistant at *The Alma Fruit, Confectionary & Wine Palace*. She knew the store, which was located in Patton Street a few blocks from her sister Ethel's house. She never shopped there herself. There was no need as Jack kept the O'Keeffe family well supplied with fruit and vegetables at wholesale rates.

The Palace proprietor was a quiet young man called David Steinberg, a well-respected member of the community, who kept largely to himself running his grocery business with his sister and two female shop assistants. One morning, when Jack arrived to make a delivery to the store, Steinberg joined him in the street. As his assistant unloaded sacks of potatoes and onions, and crates of late season tomatoes, Jack and Steinberg chatted about the fall in ore prices, and the effect this was having on both their businesses. When the goods had been unpacked, and the paperwork completed, Steinberg mentioned to Jack that one of his girls had left and he was looking for a replacement. "I told him I had just the person," Jack informed Violet that evening. "I told Steinberg that Miss O'Keeffe was a highly respectable young woman and friend of the family who had experience in the retail trade. He would like to interview you tomorrow at the close of business. That's if you're interested."

Late the following afternoon, she left Ethel's house and walked to the Steinberg emporium. When she saw that the blinds had been drawn, her first impulse was to turn away, but she tried the door and it yielded to her touch. The tinkle of a bell set above the door frame announcing her presence. With the blinds drawn, the interior of the emporium was dimly lit. Dust motes swirled in the shaft of light that was admitted by the open door.

Assuming that for whatever reason she had decided not to keep the appointment, Steinberg was about to rise from his desk and lock up, when the doorbell rang. At first, she was nothing but a silhouette against the afternoon light, but as she came towards him, he saw her more clearly.

At his first sight of Violet O'Keeffe, David Steinberg's reaction was similar to Jack's. He was transfixed by her face: her large eyes and prominent cheek bones gave her a look of startled innocence. Her skin was translucent. She had an air of vulnerability that touched some place deep inside him. Jack's first impulse at that initial sighting in his mother's garden had been possession. Steinberg's was protection.

"Miss O'Keeffe." He extended his hand to shake hers, but her own hands remained clasped.

"Mr. Steinberg."

Steinberg asked her what she knew of ledgers, invoices and inventories. "I have much to learn," she replied. He showed her around the shop, the stockroom, and the private residence at the rear, which he shared with his sister. She offered her references, which he took, but set aside on his desk without inspecting them. She accepted his offer, and agreed to begin in the New Year.

Violet enjoyed her work at Steinberg's "emporium," as he called his suburban store on the dusty outskirts of the town. It was a short walk from Ethel's house and not far from her parents' place in Morish Street. Steinberg was embarrassingly attentive to her, and his sister was kind. When Jack made his deliveries, he chatted with Steinberg while his men unloaded the goods and, if it was late in the afternoon, took her back to Ethel's place or to the Old House for a meal.

The contrast between Jack and her employer was stark. Jack exuded a confidence bordering on arrogance. From the first time their eyes had locked in his mother's garden, he had pursued her, either in person, or by bombarding her with postcards and letters. She, by nature, was quiet and reserved. As their relationship developed, she fended him off by calling him Mr. Price, partly to tease him, but partly to protect herself. It was a cooling counterpoint to the enthusiasm of his "Your loving boy," a subtle indication that her heart was not to be taken lightly, and that she would have some say in the momentum of the relationship. When she failed to respond to his enthusiasm as he wanted her to, he was bewildered. Surely, she must love him. He was a brash, confident, snappily dressed man, six years her senior, from one of the most highly respected families in the town, and she the daughter of a bullock team owner. Clearly, in his mind, not loving him was unthinkable.

Her employer was a man of a very different nature. Also successful in his own way, he was as diffident as she in his dealings with others. He was as polite and deferential to her as to his customers, and never referred to her as anything other than Miss O'Keeffe. "It's time for your tea break, Miss O'Keeffe," he would say, even though her tea break was not due for another twenty minutes. One afternoon, hearing her cough, he insisted that she take the afternoon off, even though she only had a slight cold. When Jack called on his delivery round or to pick her up, Steinberg sat quietly at his desk, at the rear of the emporium, and watched as Jack boisterously teased her. He noted her resistance and the way she chided him for his foolishness.

As the months passed, she detected a subtle shift in Steinberg's attitude towards her. She felt his eyes following her as she went about her work. One quiet afternoon, he called her to his desk and announced that they would close early. It was several days before the end of the month, a time when the miners' wives who relied on their husbands' wages had to tighten their belts. Only those with an established line of credit could afford to shop as the month drew to an end. After she had drawn the blinds and hung up the "closed" sign, he invited her to take afternoon tea at the tea room down the street. His sister could stay behind to finish up. The invitation surprised her. Despite the egalitarianism of the town, it was highly unusual for a person in her position to take tea with her employer. Although there had never been an official announcement or a formal betrothal to Jack, it was widely known, certainly among family and friends, that she and Jack were keeping company. Her married sister and her parents lived nearby, and tea with Mr. Steinberg was unlikely to go unnoticed. In the end, she agreed, simply because she didn't know how to say no, and, if the truth be told, she wanted to go.

As it happened, the event passed off without anything being said. After an initial awkward silence, Steinberg told her how he established the emporium, and the long hours that he and his sister had to work to make it a going concern. She sipped her tea and was emboldened to ask him why he chose the profession of shopkeeper. He took his time answering, and finally said, "I didn't have much choice."

"Why is that?" she asked.

Options for Jews are limited—in this town and elsewhere."

"Oh, I had no idea," she said.

"Don't worry," he replied, "it isn't catching, not like tuberculosis or leprosy." He laughed lightly but she sensed bitterness behind the words.

"I didn't mean…" she wasn't sure what she meant and left the sentence dangling. She was raised a Catholic and accepted their rituals as the natural religious order of things. Of Judaism, she knew next to nothing. It took time to come to terms with the resolute secularism of Jack's extraordinary family. Jack and his sisters didn't have a great deal to say on the subject, but when Uncle Tom was in full flight, he was likely to go on for half an hour or more, laying bare an argument she found bewildering.

She had always respected Steinberg for his quiet compassion and fairness. Now she warmed to him. After the revelation of his religion and the effect it had on his position within the community, they chatted more easily about the events of the day. The box of eggs broken by the new girl. Mrs. Haggar's habit of turning up to do her large weekly shop just as they were closing up for the day. The difficulty of extending credit during mine lockouts or strikes. She became less reserved in his presence, and after several more visits to the tea shop, almost came to see him as a friend. His gentle nature and consideration for others touched a part of her that would have been beyond Jack's comprehension.

For most of 1908, her life was uneventful. Despite the lack of a formal engagement, the unspoken assumption on the part of their respective families was that Jack and Violet would eventually marry. Then, early in October, an event occurred that shattered the uneventful rhythm of her life. The seismic shift was preceded by a rumbling that occurred on the evening of Tuesday, October 6. On that evening she and Jack attended a charity concert. It was a last-minute decision on her part to accompany him. The evening was cool, and she was suffering from one of her frequent colds. Jack, however, was insistent. He had arranged to take her to supper after the concert, so she reluctantly agreed. The concert received a lukewarm reception from the audience, whose expectations had been raised over the years by events arranged by Uncle Tom and the Price Sisters. Lilian and Babs rarely returned to Broken Hill, although Babs was shortly due to visit the family following a tour of the Far East with the Rickards Troupe.

On leaving the theatre, they encountered Steinberg, who had also attended the concert. She was surprised to see him. He was a serious man, and during their outings to the tea shop, conversation was limited to small talk about his business. There had never been the slightest hint of any interest on his part in light entertainment. He and Jack shook hands, and he raised his hat to Violet.

Although surprised to see him, she was also pleased, and couldn't resist teasing him. "What a surprise to see you, Mr. Steinberg," she said with the easy familiarity that had developed between them. "I thought you would be home slaving over your accounts or tucked up in bed with an improving book, not enjoying the theatre.'

He smiled. "People are not always as they seem, Miss O'Keeffe," he replied. "No, I'm not much for this sort of stuff, but it was for a good cause."

During this brief encounter, Jack shot Violet a quizzical look but said nothing apart from reminding her of their dinner engagement.

"Please don't let me detain you," said Steinberg.

Jack steered Violet across the street. During the short walk to the Palace Hotel, he was uncharacteristically silent. However, once they were seated and drinks had been ordered, he turned to Violet.

"So," he asked. "What was all that about?"

"What was all what about?" she replied, genuinely puzzled.

"What's going on between you and Steinberg?"

"Going on? Jack, I have no idea what you're talking about? He's my employer. He's a very nice person."

"Oh, Vi, you're so naïve, so trusting."

"There's nothing to it Jack," she said, coldly. "Nothing to it at all."

Was she imagining it, or had Stenberg's mood changed? Since their chance encounter at the theatre the previous Tuesday, he seemed to have withdrawn even further into himself. She no longer received the shy little smile on entering the shop in the morning. Gone were the invitations to take tea with him. He seemed locked into some kind of inner struggle. Then, late the following Saturday afternoon, after the other assistant had gathered her things and departed, Steinberg asked her to remain behind.

There was something he needed to say to her. Despite the fact that it was the Jewish Sabbath, he had no choice but to keep his emporium open. He locked the front door, drew the shutters, and then indicated that she should follow him into his private quarters. As soon as she entered the residence, he turned on her and took her in his arms. Too shocked to speak, she struggled to free herself. "Oh, Violet," he said. "Oh, Violet." Terrified, she grabbed one of his fingers and twisted it until she heard a sharp crack. He cried out and let her go. She stumbled into the shop, gathered her things with trembling hands, then stumbled towards the front door. Steinberg was close behind. "Violet, dear Violet, please forgive me. Please don't mention a word of this. Not to Jack. Not to anyone. On Monday, I will tell you all. Please wait until Monday." Shaken by the assault, she hurried into Patton Street, disregarding the curious stares of the people on the pavement. There would be no Monday.

When she got home, using the excuse that her cold had freshened up, she shunned the members of her family and took to her bed. That evening, when Jack called to take her to dinner at the Old House, as was his custom on a Saturday night, she refused to see him. Her mind was in turmoil, and she needed to be alone. Although Steinberg had begged her not to tell Jack, it was unavoidable. There was no way she could return to the emporium, and Jack would want to know what had happened. She experienced an unaccountable emptiness at the thought that she would never see Steinberg again, not in the way to which she had grown accustomed. She had always assumed that she could choose her emotions, but in this case the emotions chose her. She had been shocked by the suddenness of Steinberg's actions and what they forced her admit about the true nature of her feelings.

The following morning, she remained in her room listening to the family stirring and readying themselves for church. After they had departed, she made herself a cup of tea and returned to her room. At 10 o'clock, she heard Jack's car draw up at the front of the house. She stayed in her room. Surely, with the family away, not even he would have the nerve to enter the house. No soon had the thought entered her head than she heard the front door creak and steps in the passage. Then the knock on the door, which she ignored. The door opened, and he entered. It was highly improper, but Jack had never been one for propriety. He crossed the room, sat on the edge of the bed and reached for her hand which she immediately withdrew.

"You need to tell me what's going on, Vi," he said in a low voice. "It's Steinberg, isn't it? Tell me what he did to you. Tell me all, or I'll wring it out of him."

Her silence told him everything he needed to know. He stood up.

"Please don't hurt him, Jack," she said.

"I'm going to end this affair once and for all," he replied, and left the room.

She had to get away. She needed time and space away from Jack. Away from the Hill. Away from the claustrophobia and gossip of small-town life. She had friends and relatives in various parts of South Australia, but what excuse could she give for her absence?

A solution presented itself in the form of a wire from Bill Connolly, a family friend in Adelaide. Mrs. Connolly was to be admitted to hospital for a major operation. Would it be possible for her to take time off from work to look after the children as she had done on a previous occasion? Not only was it possible, it was imperative.

After his encounter with Steinberg, instead of returning to Vi, Jack went back to the Old House. There, he kicked off his shoes and threw himself on his bed. Vi would be anxiously awaiting his return. He would not fulfil her expectations. He would let her suffer for encouraging Stenberg's ambitions towards her, and for her betrayal of him. He had been so sure of Violet's innocence and fidelity it was inconceivable that she could allow another man into her life. As he wrestled with his thoughts, he grew apprehensive. Was his pursuit of her an exercise in futility? The contrast between their backgrounds and upbringing was stark. He had been born out of wedlock and raised as an atheist in one of the least conventional households in the land. She, in contrast, had been brought up a staunch Catholic, one who only missed Sunday Mass in the most extreme of circumstances. Jack was nothing if not persistent. He was used to getting his way—and his women. Violet's betrayal was unexpected and infuriating. He sighed, levered himself off the bed, pulled on his shoes, checked his wallet to see that he had sufficient cash for the evening, and made his way to a pub at the north end of Argent Street where he spent the night with a young woman of his acquaintance.

The following day, he decided that he had made Violet wait long enough. Besides, he was desperate to see her. When he had finished his rounds and caught up with some bookwork, he changed into a clean shirt and hurried to Patton Street. He was flabbergasted when Ethel informed him that Violet had left that afternoon for Adelaide to stay with the Connellys. It was an unexpected trip, said Ethel. Mrs. Connelly was being admitted to hospital for an urgent operation and Vi had gone to help look after the children. Doing his best to hide his disappointment, he pinched the baby, Monica, on the cheek, then returned to Ryan Street where he poured himself a scotch and sat at his desk. He took a blank postcard and dipped his pen into the inkwell, but instead of writing to her, he doodled on the blotting sheet. How dare she go off without so much as leaving him a note! If she wanted to hear from him, then she would have to be the first to write.

He felt vindicated when her letter arrived towards the end of the week, However, his smugness evaporated when he read the note. There was none of the anticipated contrition. What he got was a brief note in which she addressed him as "Mr. Price." She hoped that he was well. He learned that the Adelaide weather was cooler than Broken Hill, and that Mrs. Connolly had come through her surgery as well as could be expected. He attempted to reply in kind, addressing her as "Violet" rather than "Dearest Vi" and signing off, not as "Your loving boy," but "Yours Truly, Jack."

> *Ryan St, Railway Town.*
> *Dear Violet, Got your letter today, just finished my round. We are all well. Hope you are the same, lovely day today, will write again tomorrow, will let you know all the news. What do you mean by Mr. Price? I will go to train & post this because I don't go out at night, so goodbye my little love & don't worry about me & others, think you wrote in a hurry. Yours Truly, Jack.*

He was unable to maintain the façade of cool indifference at her absence. Two days later, he wrote:

Ryan St,

Dear Violet, Just before I go to the Pinnacles I will drop a P.C. to you.

I suppose you will be nurse girl when Mrs. Connelly comes home, she knows how to get around you. Well, dear, I don't want to worry you about her. I sent a P.C. last night so you would have something before Monday. I am sending another P.C. You can send it to your mother, she might like it. Well, love, hope you are happy & enjoying yourself. Will write on Sunday to you. Take care of yourself & look out you don't get run over. Wish I was down there with you to take you about, I suppose you see everything there is to see. Well, I must go. Goodbye, my little dear. Your loving boy, Frank xxxx.

Her abrupt departure from Broken Hill continued to bother him. As each day passed, the urge to see her grew ever stronger. He was also curious as to why she had left without informing him. Was her trip as innocent as she maintained? There was an Adelaide Wheelmen bike meet the following weekend which would provide an excuse for turning up in the city. However, no sooner had he sent her a postcard forewarning her of his intention to visit than Tom announced he would be in Adelaide that weekend for the South Australian Secular Association Annual General Meeting at which he would be the invited speaker. Jack would have to remain in Broken Hill to mind the business. Instead of going to Adelaide, he had to settle for writing to Violet to inform her that his plan to visit her had been upset. He complained about the severe dust storm that had settled over the city several days before and refused to dissipate. He said that Tom would be in Adelaide in a few days and expressed the hope that Violet would see him. He was taking a risk. Once before, he had made a similar suggestion which Violet had dismissed out of hand, replying that it would be silly for her to call on someone she knew. He saved the real intention of his letter until the last sentence, writing, *I think the sooner we get married the better. You worry me a lot & I am fed up with being away from your love. Yours Truly, for a life time, Dodger.*"

No sooner had he consigned the letter to the mail than he regretted having written it at all. Tom had once told him in relation to contentious

239

business matters to write a letter if he felt impelled to do so, but to leave it in his pocket for twenty-four hours. Tom's good sense had been hard won through his own impetuosity as a lovestruck young man. It was a lesson that Jack had yet to learn. He had mentioned marriage to Vi on one previous occasion but had quickly turned it into a joke when it was clear that she was in no mood to entertain the notion. Her coolness, sometimes bordering on remoteness, left him feeling rudderless. Was there something about him she distrusted or disliked? He had been raised to take pride in himself and his talents. He was a Price, after all: he repeated the mantra as he mulled over his situation. There was no need for false modesty. A good-looking, monied, man-about-town, he had never suffered rejection. Was she less naïve than she appeared? Did she know his claim that he "never went out at night" was patently untrue? He had been a fool for admitting that she "worried him a lot." It put her in a position of power. When she returned, he would have it out with her.

But when would she return? They were now well into their second week apart, and there was no sign of her returning. She had sent him a brief note that Mrs. Connolly's convalescence was taking longer than anticipated and her return to Broken Hill would be delayed. To what extent was this true? Once the worm of doubt had worked its way into his head, it was impossible to dislodge. From his own experience, Jack knew the ways of men and was not fooled by Steinberg's persona of diffidence and introversion. Yes, in their confrontation on Sunday afternoon, he had been furious with the Jew. Jack was unapologetic about his behaviour in the emporium: not for berating and bullying Steinberg, and not for terrifying his timid little sister. He would not take on trust Steinberg's promise never to contact Violet again. He would enforce the promise. He resisted the impulse to rush to Adelaide and drag her back to Broken Hill. Let her dwell on the mistake she had made and return of her own accord. When she realized he was her best, in fact her only option, she would come to him. And when she did, it would be on his terms.

On arriving in Adelaide, Violet busied herself with the Connelly children and looking after their mother who was convalescing after her hysterectomy. Despite the demands of the family, she had time to think, and she had a lot of thinking to do. The request for her presence in Adelaide provided her with the perfect opportunity to escape for a time from the difficult situation that had developed in Broken Hill, a situation that had, ironically, been created by Jack in bringing her and Steinberg together in the first place. Even in Adelaide, she was bombarded by Jack's daily missives, and was greatly relieved when he was forced to abandon his plans to visit her there. As much as she liked Tom, she had no wish to see any member of the Price family, and had no trouble deflecting the suggestion that she visit him. Each day, Jack's letters became increasingly desperate. He raised again the question of marriage. Of his encounter with Steinberg, there was no mention. On several occasions, she had seen flashes of his jealously and his temper. Had the meeting turned violent? She desperately hoped not. The self-effacing and gentle-natured Steinberg would have been no match for violently jealous Dodger.

Then, at the end of her second week in Adelaide, a letter arrived that provided her with an answer. It had been addressed to her at Ethel's place and forwarded by her sister. Immediately recognizing the handwriting, she retreated to her bedroom with the letter which she opened with shaking hands. It confirmed all of her fears and threw her into even greater distress than she had suffered to this point. She learned that Jack had not resorted to violence in his confrontation. But it did confirm what she suspected: that without doing anything other than living and breathing, she had broken the heart of a gentle creature who had committed no crime.

The Alma Fruit, Confectionary & Wine Palace
166 Patton Street, South Broken Hill
D. STEINBERG
PROPRIETOR
October 13th 1908.
Dear Miss O'Keeffe
With much pain and sorrow I take pen in hand to write a few lines. I can hardly do so for my hand trembles as though I got the fever. I am heart-broken every time I come back from Adelaide, have not had a day's rest, nor could I sleep at night. As long as I live I'll

curse the day I went to the fortune teller.

Yes, Violet, I loved you ever since I have known you, from the very first evening you applied for the job, my heart was yours.

God knows how I have battled against it but I could not help it. You cannot go against nature—it will have its way.

For nine weary months I have suffered. Nothing but your image was in my mind, day and night your face haunted me. Oh! Heavens have mercy on me. What have I done that I am punished so hard? Never in my life have I wronged anybody, and not likely either. You have been long enough with me and I believe you know me well. Have I ever said a word out of place to you? Have I ever maltreated you? Have I ever told you of my love to you?

I think not.

Would not my religion be against me I would have tried my level best to win your love, I would not spare any money, I would work with all my might and brains to be loved, had I deserved it!—for what is life worth living for if not to have the girl your heart desires. But alas, my luck has gone out, everything is lost to me everything is against me.

Why did you not spare me, Violet? Have I not promised you Saturday night that I will tell you all on Monday? Why did you tell Jack?

But never mind, I am glad it is all over now. I have told Jack all, and if he is the Gentleman I believe him to be, he'll have no ill feelings against me as I have none for him. All I can do is to wish him good luck and a happy life which I'm sure he'll have by marrying you.

Do not misunderstand me, Miss O'Keeffe. It is not a love letter I am sending you; it is the only reason you and I had to part. I could not see my way clearer, for being together with you and loving you as I do it only means ruin and the madhouse to me.

I have deeply wronged you, Miss O'Keeffe, and it is your pardon that I am seeking. I could never rest unless it is granted. Have pity on me, Violet, and say that you forgive me.

Cheer up, little girl, and do not worry. As for me, I'll try to forget you. I have nobody engaged yet and do not want to for a time.

I am very lonely and miserable, and must have plenty of work to do to keep myself occupied. I'll try to manage things by myself. I'll work every morning from 4 till 8. All the same I cannot sleep. It'll make no difference.

I have wired to the West for my Cousin and the Wretch won't come, so all my hopes of going away for a time are lost too.

It is now later than two o'clock in the morning and my sister has been singing out to me to go to bed. I am weary and tired but I do not feel like sleeping. I won't be sorry when the morning comes and I can work again.

What have you done to my finger on Sat. night? It is so sore I cannot use it. What happened to me? I don't remember.

Expecting an early reply I remain yours –

David Steinberg

Farewell, Violet, farewell!!!

(Excuse me calling you Violet. I know I have no right to, but I cannot help it.)

Kindly let me know if anyone owes you money that I do not know of and I believe that Mrs. Dunn paid you. It is not marked up in the book. Did she pay right up? If so let me know.

One last favour, Miss O'Keeffe: Jack has promised me not to mention anything about this affair to anybody. Will you promise too?

This is the first and last letter you'll have from me I shall never trouble you again. Please destroy this as soon as you have read it.

DS

She read the letter through several times, then folded it and sat for a long time on the edge of the bed, the letter in her hand. Tears might have brought her some relief, but she was beyond tears. She felt nothing but a profound sadness, and finally admitted to herself what Jack had instinctively known: her feelings for Steinberg were more, much more, than affection for a kindly employer. The possibility of loving more than one man had never entered her head, and it made her wonder about the depth of her feelings for Jack. But Steinberg was right. The notion of a life together was an impossibility. For good or ill, Jack was her destiny. When she eventually summoned the strength to move, she returned the letter to its envelope and put it in a safe place at the bottom of her suitcase.

If Jack thought that Violet would return to Broken Hill filled with contrition and remorse, he was badly mistaken. One of the first topics he raised was marriage. She brushed it aside. It was not an outright rejection. "The time is not right," she said. Would there ever be a right time? he wanted to know. She had no idea. All she knew was that now was not the time. She moved back into the room that Ethel kept for her, although much of her day was spent at her parents' house in Morish Street, where she helped her mother with household chores and attending to the younger children. Jack collected her each evening at the end of his working day and took her either to Ryan Street or in to town. He had recently been admitted to the Broken Hill Club and liked to take her there to show her off. One evening, she accompanied him to a meeting of the Secular Association where Tom gave a lengthy address on the hypocrisy of Christianity. Their Bible teaches them the equality of humanity, he told the audience. Love thy neighbour as thyself. We agree wholeheartedly with this sentiment. It is one of our central tenets. Except, that is, unless you happen to be black—or a woman. The fathers of our Federation established just a few short years ago, Christians to a man, built the country on principles of inequality and hypocrisy. The rot begins at the top. Alfred Deakin, our revered Prime Minister, fervent Christian and devoted family man, is as guilty as the rest of them. Not only are they guilty of discriminating against the original inhabitant of this country, they engaged in the heinous practice of blackbirding— kidnapping innocent natives from the islands to our north and setting them to work as slaves in the cane fields on which they built their fortunes.

There were murmurs of dissent at this attack on Deakin who was no stranger to Broken Hill, and generally admired in the town despite the fact that he fell on the opposite side of the political divide from the working-class populace. Undeterred by the disquiet from several members of the audience, Tom pursued his theme of the equality of all people, regardless of race or sex. He concluded his speech by repeating an assertion made by William Symes at a speech in the Broken Hill Town Hall some years before. "The great lie of the Christians is that only they can live the moral life. Nothing can be further from the truth."

This last sentiment received enthusiastic applause from most of the audience. Violet did not join in, but sat with her hands clasped firmly in. her lap. For some time, Jack had embarked on a not-so-subtle attack on her own religious beliefs. This didn't bother her. Her faith in organized religion had come under serious question as a result of her friendship with Steinberg. Their mutually incompatible faiths rendered impossible anything but the most superficial of relationships. Only one faith could carry the seed of truth. Was it Judaism or Christianity? Listening to Tom, a third possibility occurred to her. They could both be fictions.

Ten days after her return, she announced to Jack that she was going away again the following day. Mrs. Olive Flugge, a distant relative on her mother's side had heard that Violet was available as a companion and household help. Could Mrs. O'Keeffe spare her daughter for a week or two? She could. And so Violet packed her bags and set off for the Flugge household in Jamestown in the Mid North of South Australia. Jack did his best to hide his annoyance at what he saw as capriciousness and defiance. As usual, he barraged her with postcards and letters filled with the trivial occurrences of the day and ended with the inevitable reminder that he remained "her loving boy." She ignored his assertions that in her absence he didn't go out at night but spent his evenings at home except when attending meetings at the Secular Association. Broken Hill was a small town, and rumours of his doings inevitably found their way back to her.

It would be another two years before Frank Price, the lukewarm infidel from Welsh stock, and Violet O'Keeffe, the Irish Catholic girl, gifted to Australia from County Cork, exchanged marriage vows. Naturally, the wedding took place, not in a church, but in a secular ceremony at 32 Ryan Street. Her parents, while paying lip-service to their Catholic roots, raised no objection. While her mother remained devout, her father's faith had weakened over the years. The marriage between Jack and Violet cemented a relationship between the two families that had developed over almost a decade. Tom, Ann and Dodger were frequent visitors to the O'Keeffe household, as were the O'Keeffes to the Old House. Jack was a good catch. The Prices had money and were solidly middle class. They were well-respected within the community, particularly for their active involvement in charitable causes. Their secularism was no great impediment to their standing. Most of their acquaintances either overlooked or were unaware of their unconventional lifestyle. Only their close friends knew that Tom and Ann were unmarried. Despite publicity at the time, their chequered past—the trials, abductions and shootings—were known to relatively few in the town. Many of the inhabitants had colourful pasts. Broken Hill was a place where you could reinvent yourself, and that's exactly what the Price family had done. Little did they know that, years into the future, ghosts from the past would emerge to rupture the family.

Chapter 16
Having It All

Violet was no stranger to the Old House. During her school days, she would walk hand in hand down the dusty street with her best friend Babs. They would sit at one end of the long kitchen table drinking sweet tea and eating rock cakes slathered in butter. On some weekends, she would sleep over, sharing a bed with Babs, while Lil occupied the other.

And now, the Old House had become her permanent home and her nocturnal partner was Jack. The Old House would be her home for the next forty years, her incumbency interrupted only by the scandal that was to tear the family asunder and impel her to abandon both husband and home and flee to Adelaide.

It was in the Old House that she carried and gave birth to her three children—all daughters. The first, born on July 9, 1914, was Lilian Viola, named after her two aunts, and, like her Aunt Viola, was known throughout her life as "Babs." After two miscarriages, her second daughter was born on September 16, 1919. She was named Eunice Rebecca, but was known by the diminutive Betty. Yvonne Olga the third, and last, was born on April 4, 1923.

Several events shook the world in the years during which Jack and Violet created their family and Jack consolidated his position as a prominent local businessman. Principal among these was the War to End All Wars, which was declared three weeks after Lilian Viola was born. Although the Great War played itself out in theatres far from Australian shores, it had a profound effect on those families whose sons and daughters served overseas and never came back. It had very little impact on the Price family. Dodger's secularism and singular lack of interest in contributing to the war effort were no impediment to the development of his business. Outward respectability came in the form of appointment as a Justice of the Peace.

Economically, the war was a mixed blessing for the mining industry.

The Broken Hill Proprietary Company was establishing itself as a major mining and industrial force in Australia, extracting rich ore-bearing rock from beneath the township. With the outbreak of hostilities, it was no longer possible to send ore overseas to be refined: it had to be treated locally. The three major mines, the North, South and Zinc Mines, combined their resources to take over the Port Pirie lead-smelting plant, renaming it the Broken Hill Associated Smelters Pty. Ltd. By the end of the war, it had grown to be the largest lead and zinc smelter in the world. BHP's presence was felt across South-eastern Australia, with steelworks in Newcastle and Port Kembla, a shipbuilding yards at Whyalla and ironstone and limestone quarries at Iron Knob and at Rapid Bay, south of Adelaide.

Ironically, the closest the Great War came to Australia was on a small rise in the landscape to the west of Broken Hill. In a bizarre incident on New Year's Day, 1915, two local members of the Afghan community, Gool Mahomed, an ice-cream hawker, and Mulla Abdulla, the local imam and halal butcher, ambushed a train carrying local residents to nearby Silverton for a picnic. Standing next to Gool Mahomed's ice cream cart, which flew the Ottoman flag, they opened fire on the holiday-makers. Although the rifles they used were ancient, they were effective enough. One of the first to be hit was seventeen-year-old Alma Cowie, who took a bullet to the head and died in her boyfriend's arms. She was the first Australian to be killed on home soil by an enemy combatant. As the open-top train chugged slowly past, the 1,200 passengers were sitting ducks. Three were killed outright and a further seven wounded. The two assailants then fled from the scene to a rocky outcrop about a mile away where some hours later they were discovered and surrounded by a hastily assembled militia consisting of police, civilians and army personnel. In the ensuing shootout, one policeman was wounded. Mulla Abdulla was shot dead. Gool Mahomed's attempt to surrender were ignored. He received sixteen bullet wounds and died on the way to hospital.

When word of the "Battle of Broken Hill," as it came to be known, spread across Australia, it set off a wave of xenophobia with violence targeted at Muslims and Germans. In Broken Hill, the German Club was burned to the ground and a lynch mob descended on the Camel Camp, as the neighbourhood housing the Muslim community was called, determined to run the residents out of town. They were only deterred when confronted by a line of troops with fixed bayonets. Nationally, the Attorney General, Billy Hughes, used the attack to intern all "enemy aliens" for the duration of the war.

Shortly after the birth of Eunice Rebecca, Dodger and Tom established T.J. Price & Son Wholesale Produce Merchants at the East End Markets in Adelaide. Tom ran the Adelaide end of the business. He was well-known at the East End Market, having worked there as a young man, and had maintained his contacts there throughout his life. Dodger was in charge of the Broken Hill end of the business. There were some whispers around town when his delivery trucks appeared with "T.J. Price & Son" rather than "The Price Bros." painted on the driver's side door. Was this, at last, a tacit admission of his real paternity?

During the "Roaring 20s," in the aftermath of the Great War, and the settlement of a crippling mining strike, Broken Hill boomed, and Dodger's financial and social fortunes soared. He became one of the most recognizable identities in town as he strode down Argent Street, a carnation in his buttonhole, a silver-topped cane in his hand, and a small black-and-white terrier at his heels. When not on foot, he drove around town. One always knew where to find Dodger. His Chrysler would be pulled prominently into the curb in front of his chosen watering hole. And the woman by his side as he took his whisky and water was very rarely his wife. Never one to socialize, Violet preferred the comfort of home and the company of her family along with a few close friends, several of whom thought it curious that she had chosen to marry the flashy Dodger.

Although by the early 1920s, Dodger had retired from bicycle racing and exchanged his love of bicycles for fast cars, he maintained an active interest in the sport. In 1922, he was one of the founders of the Burke Ward Cycling Club and acted as its handicapper. He also helped organize charity races to raise money for causes such as the construction of a War Memorial to those who had fallen in the War. In 1928, *The Barrier Miner* published an article documenting his business acumen and lauding his achievements as a champion cyclist. (Six years later, the same newspaper would report on a court case that scandalized the town and turned Dodger from local hero to villain.)

The article introduced him as Mr. Frank Price, well known in Broken Hill as "Dodger" and rehearsed his early life: born in Port Adelaide, but moving with his parents to Broken Hill, where he had resided in the "Silver City" for over 30 years. There was no reference to the ambiguity of his parentage. The "parents" he had moved with to Broken Hill were Tom and Ann, WH, the putative parent, having moved there some years before.

The article then went on to report that on leaving school, he assisted his elder brother Tom in a retail fruit and provision business. In 1920, this business was disposed of and the brothers established a wholesale fruit and vegetable business, Tom supervising the buying, packing and dispatching of produce in Adelaide, and Dodger attending to the ordering, and supply in Broken Hill.

The article concluded with a summary of Dodger's career as a cyclist. He is described as "one of the best the Barrier has ever produced," appearing in road races all over south-eastern Australia, and that his "prowess" was so well recognized that in the first Sydney Thousand, he was only given an 85-yard handicap. Unfortunately, his prowess did not extend to actually finishing the race, as he "met with a mishap early." In fact, the only wins the article mentioned were success in the Barrier Caledonian Wheel Race, an event which he won on three successive occasions.

In this, and various newspaper articles about Dodger that appeared in the 1920s, he is portrayed as a respectable, solidly middle-class businessman. Along with his half-brother, he had created a successful business in a physically, financially, and culturally taxing environment: He was a sportsman of some repute, although the evidence of his prowess is patchy. He consolidated his respectability by becoming a Justice of the Peace in both NSW and South Australia.

After their years in Shanghai, Tom and Ann had settled comfortably in Adelaide, ironically in the bluestone house in St. Peters in which they had had a brief tryst many years before. Tom rose early each morning and drove to his office in the East End Market. He parked in his usual spot in front of the market. The spot was not reserved for him, but the market workers and local shopkeepers all knew that this was Uncle Tom's parking space, and woe betide anyone else who had the temerity to park there. On the stroke of twelve, he rose from his desk, and made his way around the corner to the venerable Botanic Hotel, an imposing Italianate structure that had been built during the boom years of the 1870s. No expense had been spared in its construction. A corner table was permanently reserved for him at the rear of the elegant dining room. Sometimes, Ann would join him for lunch if she had shopping or business to attend to in the city. Now and then the resolutely teetotal William, who knew his brother's habits well, would turn up. On most days, however, he dined alone, reading or making notes for an upcoming address to the Secular Association or penning a letter to the editor of the *Advertiser* on a political or civic issue that had caught his attention.

One day, he was putting on his coat and pondering whether to have the steak and kidney pudding or the fish for lunch, when a young man appeared in the doorway of the office.

"Mr. Thomas Price?"

"Yes. How can I help you?"

The young man advanced into the office and extended his hand. "Joe Prendergast," he said.

Tom grasped the extended hand. "What can I do for you, Mr. Prendergast?"

"I'm down from the Hill. Work for *The Miner*. I'm doing a series of articles on prominent locals. In fact, I did one on your brother a few months back."

"Oh, yes," said Tom, "Jack showed me a copy when it was published. So, you're the chap who wrote the piece."

"I am indeed. I'm down in Adelaide visiting family, and thought while I was here, I might take the opportunity of interviewing you for the series."

"That's very nice of you, but I haven't lived in Broken Hill for some years."

"But you made a great contribution to the place when you lived there."

"And when would you propose doing the interview?"

"Would now be convenient?"

"Well, I'm just on my way to have my lunch. Twelve noon, on the dot. I've become a creature of habit in my old age, Mr. Prendergast."

"I wouldn't want to keep you from your meal. Would you allow me to buy you lunch?"

"What a splendid suggestion, but it won't be necessary. I'm happy to give you an interview, but I do have one requirement."

"What is that?"

"I would need to see the piece before it's published."

"Hmm, that's a little irregular, but I don't see why not."

Storytelling was one of Tom's gifts, and over lunch, he kept Prendergast entertained with stories that ranged from his charitable work to his adventures in Shanghai while Prendergast scribbled away in his shorthand notebook. He received a detailed treatise on secularism, and the ills wreaked on society by organized religion. The meal and the interview completed, Prendergast pressed on Tom a second whisky and water. As a rule, Tom only allowed himself a single glass during the day, but yielded when Prendergast's insisted. The reporter then accompanied him back to East Terrace. They shook hands and parted, Prendergast to attend to other business, and Tom to nod off at his desk until it was time to go home.

True to his word, Prendergast sent Tom a pre-publication copy of the article. In it, Tom was portrayed as an astute businessman and a contributor to the lifeblood of the Broken Hill community through his fundraising efforts for various worthy causes. His lifelong embrace of secular humanism and his contributions to the Secular Association were reported by Prendergast with no hint of judgment or sarcasm. Abandoning a business career to manage a vaudeville theatre in Shanghai at a time of great civil unrest in China was reported as the act of an adventurer rather than that of a foolhardy or eccentric individual.

Tom tugged at the waxed tips of his moustache and smiled quietly to himself. He had very good reason for wanting to vet the article before it was published. While in no way ashamed of his early adult life, he did not particularly want certain scabs pulled off his past. He was therefore relieved that there was no mention of his abduction of a young girl during his former life as a schoolteacher, nor of the double shooting in North Adelaide which almost cost him his life. While he was shot, or shot at, more than once in dramas involving members of the opposite sex, there was no evidence that he ever shot anything other than kangaroos and rabbits. Tom allowed himself a self-satisfied smile as he finished the article. It would have taken an investigator more astute than Prendergast less than an hour in the archives of *The Adelaide Advertiser* and *The Register* to draw Tom's skeletons out of the closet. As is was, Tom's efforts at reinvention were not threatened by the article.

In July 1924, Dodger returned from Adelaide with extraordinary news. Having defied social and moral conventions by living as an unmarried couple for 35 years, Tom and Ann announced that they were to tie the knot. The ceremony would take place on August 7, 1924 to coincide with Ann's 69th birthday. Tom was 64. Dodger was stunned at the news. Tom and his adored mother had first met when Tom was a schoolboy, and she was working for William Henry. Dodger's personality and worldview had been conditioned by his upbringing in this unconventional family in which nothing was impossible. With the right frame of mind, you could have anything you wanted. "Never forget that you are a Price," was a constant injunction in his formative years. "And never let anyone else forget it." Tom was a nurturing presence in his life, an amalgam of loving father-figure and protective elder brother. Although she had never divorced Harry Dearmer, Ann had lived as Ann Price since 1880.

Dodger was bemused by his mother's decision to marry Tom so late in life. What had prompted the decision? Certainly not to avoid embarrassment, or inuendo from outside the household. When questioned, she said that it was an affirmation of her adoration for Tom. "We're doing it for ourselves and no-one else," she said. In the early years of the relationship, marriage was out of the question as she was still married to Harry Dearmer. Living as a common-law wife might have been frowned upon, but it was not a crime. Bigamy was. By 1924, Harry had neither been seen nor hear of for many years. Then came rumours of his death in New South Wales, so at last they felt free to marry. "Who knows how many years we have left?" she said.

And so, on a cold, blustery evening in early August, Dodger left the business in the capable hands of his foreman, packed the family into the car and set off for Adelaide. Babs and Betty sat in the back, Violet in the front with the baby Yvonne in a basket at her feet. Mintie, his black-and-white terrier, rode in his customary place on the running board, questing the freezing air with his nose.

Dodger preferred making the twelve-hour trip at night when there was little other traffic on the road. Leaving after dusk minimized the possibility of hitting one of the kangaroos that emerged as the sun went down to feed on the verge bordering the road. As usual, he pushed his car to the limit, ignoring Violet's entreaties to slow down "for the sake of the children." Getting him to pull over for a toilet stop was also next to impossible. They almost came to grief in the Thackaringa Hills, which formed a natural border between New South Wales and South Australia. A big red came from nowhere, bounding out of the scrub into the path of the car. Dodger was forced to brake and swerve so sharply that the dog was dislodged from the running board. The car came to a halt at a right angle to the road. "Now will you slow down?" asked Violet.

Deep into the night just short of the railway township of Terowie, Babs woke from a bad dream and looked out of the window. "Father," she called out. "Mintie isn't with us." Dodger immediately turned the car around and headed back towards Broken Hill. After several miles, the car headlights picked up a black and white speck in the distance, kicking up puffs of red dust as he belted towards the oncoming car as fast as his legs could work. He must have run for miles, because when they lifted him into the car, he died from exhaustion in Dodger's arms. Dodger wrapped the warm body in an old towel and placed it in the trunk alongside their suitcases. "We'll bury the poor little thing in Mamma's garden," he said. After the wedding he would acquire a replacement Mintie from the pet shop in Gouger Street, the source of all his Minties.

When they arrived at St. Peters, the girls jumped out of the car and ran up the steps to the front door. After the interminable drive, they were full of pent-up energy. Ten-year-old Babs pulled vigorously at the doorbell, while Betty banged on the door. "We're here, we're here," both girls called. After allowing themselves to be kissed and cuddled by Uncle Tom and their grandmother, they ran on through the house and into the back garden where, despite the cold, they played happily until called in to breakfast. Mid-morning, Dodger drove the family to Glenelg, known as the Bay, a favourite destination for Hillites. Although there was plenty of room at the St. Peters house, he didn't want to disrupt the wedding preparations, and had taken a cottage just off the beach. The intention was to stay a week and have a family holiday—their first in several years.

When Violet had dressed the children, they drove from the Bay back to St. Peters, where they left baby Yvonne with the housekeeper. They then proceeded back across the river and through the city to Wayville, where the wedding was to take place at the residence of the Reverend G. E. Hale. The girls chatted excitedly: this was to be their first wedding. Violet warned them that the ceremony might be boring, but they had to sit quietly and not fidget. Afterwards, they would return to St Peters where there would be a wedding breakfast. "Breakfast?" asked Babs. "But we already had breakfast. Won't it be time for lunch?"

"That's what wedding feasts are called," she replied. "It doesn't matter what time of day. I don't know why."

"A feast," said Betty. "Will there be cake?"

"There will be lots of cake. But you mustn't eat too much and make yourself sick."

She remembered her own wedding at the Old House twelve years before. It had been followed by a lavish breakfast prepared under Ann's supervision. The event had given her mother-in-law an opportunity to give full rein to her culinary imagination. She remembered little of the ceremony itself, being too full of apprehension at the thought of the night to come.

The Reverend Hale, a friend of Tom's, was a minister of the Unitarian Church. Violent thought it odd that the couple were united by a minister of religion, but Jack explained to her that the Unitarian Church was no regular Christian establishment. In fact, most of its beliefs were regarded as heretical. Although its members subscribed to the existence of a deity, it rejected the notion of the Holy Trinity—that God consists of three entities: the Father, the Son and the Holy Ghost. While it accepted the existence of an historical person called Jesus, it maintained that he was a regular human being whose beliefs and actions were inspired by the deity. Other concepts they rejected were original sin, predestination, heaven, hell, and the literal interpretation of the Bible. Tom and Ann got to know the Reverend Hale through his work as an outspoken pacifist, and his views were very much in line with their own.

Ironically, it would turn out that in getting married, Tom and Ann had unintentionally committed bigamy. At the time of the wedding, her husband Harry was still alive and living in rural New South Wales. Records show that he died in the township of Young in 1927. His remains reside in the Young cemetery in a grave marked by a headstone which reads: *In Memory of Henry Dearmer, died 23 October, 1927, aged 75 years.*

Dodger's passion for fast cars was one he pursued for the whole of his adult life. It was a passion that would ultimately bring about his end. In 1928, he acquired a six-cylinder Chrysler Roadster, a gleaming monster that attracted admiring glances, as it was supposed to do, as he cruised down Argent Street with the latest version of Mintie perched on the running board. Designed for the Manhattan and Long Island fast crowd, it was hard to imagine a car less suited to the dusty, corrugated tracks that passed for roads outside the township. Dodger modified the vehicle to suit the conditions. He fitted a custom-made, sixteen-gallon fuel tank, special oversized tyres, and a four-wheel hydraulic braking system. He kept the car in mint condition. Johnny, a fifteen-year old simpleton who swept out the office and storeroom in Beryl Street was deputed to dust down the car each morning with a feather duster, and to wash it once a week.

One evening as he was having his customary whisky and water in the Broken Hill Club, a refuge for the professional elites in the town, he entered into an animated discussion with three of his drinking companions about the merits of an American-made vehicle. The other members of the club all drove British cars. One, Gordon Brooking, owned a Jaguar in which he had been the first to drive to Adelaide in under twelve hours, a record which still stood. After a second whisky, a wager was struck. Dodger would break the record in his flashy American vehicle. If he succeeded, Dodger would take possession of Brooking's Jaguar. If he failed, he would give Brooking his beloved Chrysler. The challenge would begin the following Thursday evening at 6 p.m. Dodger would leave from the Sulphide Street railway station. Rather than a starter's gun, the whistle of the overnight express train to Adelaide would signal the start of the race. As a further incentive, the other men who were party to the wager each put one hundred pounds into the hands of the barman. If he beat the train to the Adelaide Station on North Terrace, he would pick up the cash. If he failed, he would give a hundred pounds to each of the punters. That night, when he informed Violet of the race, she shook her head. "You're determined to kill yourself, and I don't know why. Where did the death wish come from Jack? It's not why I married you."

"You just don't understand," he replied.

Isolated showers fell throughout district that day—enough to settle the dust, but not enough to turn the Barrier Highway, as it was called, into a hazard for Dodger's attempt on the record. Despite being impeded by the movement of some mining equipment near the Burra copper mine (the "Monster Mine" his father had helped establish), he easily broke the record, completing the 328 miles in a little over eleven hours at an average speed of around 30 miles an hour. Over the next few years, as automotive technology evolved and the state of the road improved, the speed would come to seem positively risible. Dodger would continue to improve his time, and he held the record until well after his death.

In the year following Dodger's motoring feat, a bleak economic wind began blowing across the Australian landscape. It was a wind that was to blow far harder and far longer than anyone anticipated. As in the 1890s, the global economic downturn hit Australia harder than Europe or North America because it was at the financial mercy of the more developed economies of the Northern Hemisphere. Within Australia, the pain was not evenly distributed. Although unemployment rose to around thirty per cent and stayed at that level for years, it was the working class that suffered most. Broken Hill, a largely working-class town, was particularly savaged. Many men were forced to leave the town. Husbands abandoned their families, mounted their bicycles, and rode east in search of work. Some made it all the way to Queensland. Riding a bike across the unforgiving interior of Australia was hazardous. However, it was quicker than walking, and less hazardous than jumping a freight train.

How did the Price family fare? Solidly middle class, they did better than most, particularly given the nature of their trade. Hairdressers and haberdashers struggled. You could get your wife or sister to cut your hair and patch your coat so it would last another year. But while you could reduce your intake of fruit and vegetables, substituting them with bread and dripping, you couldn't do away with them altogether. So, while T.J. Price & Son saw a reduction in their business, the business survived. Uncle Tom and Ann retained their substantial stone house in Adelaide. In Broken Hill, Dodger had no trouble maintaining his fancy cars. Along with a reduction in the volume of trade, they had to deal with those who bought their goods "on tick," as credit was called. It wasn't long before many of his debtors failed to open their doors to Dodger on collection day.

Tom, a committed humanist with a longstanding record of supporting charitable causes, argued that they should forgive the mounting debts as far as possible. Dodger, a reluctant humanist at best, had other ideas. From 1931 to 1934, court records show that Frank Price, Justice of the Peace, on behalf of T.J. Price & Son, recovered debts from non-paying customers by taking them to court.

In 1934, the Great Depression was close to its nadir. However, in that year, litigation by Dodger abruptly ceased. The reason was simple. In that year, Dodger's litigious spirit was curbed when he found himself on the other side of the law.

Chapter 17
The Fall

On Friday, 29 June 1934, in the depths of the greatest global depression the world had ever experienced, *The Barrier Miner* was focused on more local issues. Its front page carried the following bold headline:

Shooting with intent to Murder...Charge Against F. "Dodger" Price... Accused remanded on Bail.

The headline was followed by this paragraph:

A sensation was caused in the city today by the appearance in the Police Court of Frank "Dodger" Price (56), a fruit merchant, and well-known resident of Broken Hill. He was arrested at Railway Town last night following an alleged shooting at North Broken Hill *(The Barrier Miner, Friday 29 June 1934)*. [13]

Of Dodger's three daughters, Babs, the eldest, was the sporty one. She was an attractive young woman with an upright bearing who played several sports. Tennis was her passion. Her build, poise and ball sense suited her to the game. Although he had long since ceased to be an active sportsman himself, Dodger was proud of his daughter and took a keen interest in her progress as a tennis player. In contrast to Europe and North America, where it was an elite activity, in Australia, tennis was an egalitarian game, popular as a competitive sport as well as a social activity, and one played by all social classes. Even the smallest country town had at least one tennis court. Broken Hill, whose population continued to grow despite the depression, had many. Because of the harshness of the climate, there were no grass courts: the surfaces were either bitumen or clay. All of the public parks in town had courts, and these could be used free of charge by anyone with a racquet, regardless of its vintage, and a ball that retained enough bounce to clear the net. Because of its popularity and the egalitarian nature of the game, for

---

[13] *The Barrier Miner*. Friday, 29 June, 1934, p.1

several decades Australia became dominant as a tennis-playing nation. In Broken Hill, it was also popular with churches of every denomination: most had a hall on one side for social events, and a tennis court or two on the other.

In 1931, at the age of 16, Babs reached the finals of the women's doubles championship. As the tournament progressed, it dawned on her that she had caught the eye of a newcomer to the club. His name was Arch Cashman. Tall and athletic, with a receding hairline, he was a contender for the men's singles final. Recently arrived from Sydney, he was employed as a clerk by the NSW Public Works Department. At thirty-one, Arch was almost twice Babs's age. Despite the difference in their ages, by 1932, they were regularly partnering one another in mixed doubles. The duo had moderate success, reaching the final stages of a number of tournaments over the next couple of years. Babs's doubles partners included former schoolfriends Maisie Inman, and Joyce Nunan. "Archie's keen on you," Maisie said to her one hot afternoon as they sat in the shade drinking lemon squash.

"Oh, don't talk nonsense, Maisie," replied Bab. "And what does it matter if he is? I'm not keen on him. There's nothing to it."

At or about the time that Babs caught the eye of Arch, Maisie Inman, caught the eye of her father, and Dodger's eye for women was finely honed. The thirty-year-plus gap in their ages was no impediment to his appreciation for the way her long legs carried her about the court. The more seemly, spoke in whispers about Dodger's propensity for "paying attention to young ladies;" the less so joked openly about his habit of chasing skirt.

It flattered the impressionable teenager from a working-class home to be the object of attention of one of the town's most prominent businessmen. However, Dodger's audacity in pursuing his daughter's best friend was to be his undoing. Trouble began when Maisie's sister warned their father of the Dodger's interest in his younger daughter.

Late one evening, as Dodger was making his way to his car, which was parked at the rear of the Royal Exchange Hotel, he detected movement in the shadows. The man was upon him before he could reach the security of his car. He was grabbed roughly by the collar and spun around. He tried to back away but was pushed up against the side of his car.

"Price," said his assailant, breathing alcohol into the older man's face.

"Get your hands off me," replied Dodger. In response, the stranger pulled him forward, and then slammed him roughly back against the car.

"If it's money you want..." began Dodger, but was cut off by the stranger.

"You stay away from my daughter, you hear me. I'm telling you once. I won't tell you again. You, you with the fancy clothes and the fancy car. I know your type."

Dodger twisted free and fumbled for the keys to his car, but Inman wasn't finished. The first punch caught Dodger in the eye, the second bloodied his nose. Dodger raised his hands in an attempt to fend off a third blow, but Inman swept them aside and caught him in the temple. When it came to fisticuffs with Inman, Dodger was on a hiding to nothing. Inman worked on the mines where he operated the winding mechanism that lowered miners underground in cages. At 6 feet 2 inches tall, he towered over the diminutive Dodger who stood at a mere 5 feet 4.

"This is just a taste of what you'll get if you approach my daughter again," said Inman before turning and disappearing somewhat unsteadily into the night. Badly shaken, Dodger climbed into his car, and retrieved a whisky flask from the glovebox. He took two strong pulls to steady his nerves before driving the short distance to the Central Police Station and reporting the assault. He identified the assailant as one Inman, first name unknown, of William Street North Broken Hill. When questioned as to the cause of the assault, Dodger replied that he had no idea. "It was completely unprovoked," he said. "It was clear that he had been drinking at the time. He seemed to have contempt for someone who dressed well and could afford a decent car."

As he drove back to Railway Town, Dodger reflected on the dramatic end to what had been a pleasant evening with business associates in the dining room of the Royal Exchange. If Inman thought a roughing up would deter him, he was mistaken. He would do his best to avoid the man, but Maisie was too sweet a prize to be so readily abandoned. If Inman came at him again, he would be ready.

The feud between Dodger and Inman came to a head on the evening of Thursday, 28 June, 1934 at a Church of England Sunday school hall in William Street North Broken Hill. Maisie worked as a shop assistant at a shoe store in Iodide Street a short walk from Dodger's storeroom and office in Beryl Street. She took her lunch hour at one o'clock in a café between her workplace and his office, and when he wanted to arrange a meeting, he would pass her a note as she entered the café. On the afternoon in question, he brushed past her as she approached the café and dropped the note into her coat pocket. Despite the care he took, he fooled few of his friends with his subterfuge. He and Maisie were seen in tea shops and the parlour bars of hotels away from the centre of town. His keen interest in the local tennis scene was also noticed, as was the way in which his eyes followed Maisie about whether she was on or off the court.

Once she had ordered her lunch, a ham and egg sandwich and an orange juice, she fished Dodger's note out of her pocket and read it. That evening, a charity dance was to be held in the William Street church hall. He would make contact with her there at 8 o'clock and take her driving. He had something he wanted to tell her. Dodger realized that he was taking a risk. The church hall was diagonally opposite the Inman house, but it was a convenient place to pick her up and whisk her out of town.

At 7.45, Dodger parked his car in a side street where he could see the entrance to the church hall. He smoked a cigarette and took a pull on his hip flask to steady his nerves. His plan for the evening was to take the next step in Maisie's seduction. His stomach fluttered at the prospect. Although he was getting on in years, he still felt a tingle at the prospect of the hunt. At 8 o'clock, he watched Maisie cross the road and enter the hall. He got out of the car, crushed the cigarette with the heel of his shoe, and made his way to the hall. He stood in the shadows at a side window attempting to spot Maisie and attract her attention.

Inman was sitting in his kitchen drinking beer, smoking a cigarette and thinking about a mishap that had occurred at the end of the day shift when the winding mechanism jammed, trapping in the cage the men he was bringing to the surface. His eldest daughter came into the kitchen. "He's over there," she said, jerking her thumb in the direction of the church. "The old geezer that's been paying attention to our Maisie. I saw him through the front window." Inman leapt to his feet, and without bothering to change out of his carpet slippers, rushed across the street.

Dodger was lurking near a knot of young men who were smoking and chatting at the entrance to the hall when he noticed Inman crossing the street. In an attempt to avoid detection, he crouched behind the younger men. He was aware it was undignified, but so was receiving a thrashing in public. Inman brushed aside the younger men and swung a fist at Dodger who turned away. He caught a glancing blow to the side of the head and rose unsteadily to his feet. "I'll shoot you, you bastard," he shouted. Backing away, he drew a revolver from his overcoat pocket, fired a shot at Inman that missed, then turned and ran towards his car. Inman took off after him but was reduced to a shuffle by his slippers. Breathing heavily, Dodger locked himself in the car and fumbled for his keys. He got the car started just as Inman reached it and began tugging at the driver's side door handle. Dodger engaged the gears and drove away, tearing the handle from Inman's grasp. Once clear of Inman, Dodger's panic subsided. He knew that Inman would go to the police and that they would come after him. However, he figured he had a good hour to do what needed to be done. He continued down William Street crossing the train tracks of the Silverton Tramway Company and turned left towards the Old House. Rather than entering the house, he made his way toward the kitchen garden. Less than two minutes later, he returned to his car and drove back into town. He stopped at a pub at the far end of Argent Street just short of the town limits. It was one of several pubs that never shut. There, he drank several long, slow scotches and constructed a narrative that he hoped would sound convincing when the police caught up with him. He knew that nothing would save him from the quiet fury of his wife who for years had endured private humiliation and abuse. Public humiliation she would not endure.

As Dodger had predicted, Inman returned home, changed from his slippers into his work boots and pulled on a shabby gabardine coat. Maisie, pale and shaken, came into the house as he was leaving. "Get to your room, you," he said. "I'll deal with you when I get back." He rode his bicycle to the nearby North Broken Hill police station and reported the shooting. As attempted murder was a serious charge, the desk sergeant called the Central police station in Argent Street, and two plain-clothed officers, Detective-Sergeant Duckworth and Detective-Constable Sutherland, were dispatched to investigate the case. They interrogated Inman and then went to the school hall in search of Price who had long since gone

An hour and a half after the drama, Dodger left the Great Northern Hotel, got into his car and headed home. He made no attempt to stick to the back streets but proceeded up Argent Street. As he was approaching Billygoat Hill, he noticed the lights of a patrol car following him. He crossed the train tracks into Railway Town and was proceeding down Wills Street when the patrol car drew parallel with him and pulled him over. The uniformed officer in the passenger seat approached him and shone a flashlight in his face.

"Mr. Price."

"How can I help you, Tom?" asked Dodger. He was no stranger to the courts. Most members of the constabulary knew him, and he knew them.

"We need you to follow us back to the station."

They drew into the parking lot behind the Central police station. When he got out of his car, he was asked if he was in possession of a weapon. "I am not," he replied.

"Do you have any objections if we search you?"

"None whatever."

The officers searched both Dodger and his car, but found no weapon. He was then taken to an interrogation room and asked to wait.

"Detective-Sergeant Duckworth wants to have a word with you."

When Duckworth entered to the room, Dodger, who remained seated, asked, "What's this all about?"

"I want to see you about that affair with Inman at the school hall tonight."

"He assaulted me," replied Dodger calmly.

"Inman says you fired at him at close range."

"I did not fire any shot: I have no revolver; search me. Inman would say anything against me."

"There are witnesses besides Inman who saw a flash and heard a shot."

"I did not fire a shot," repeated Dodger. "It was I who was assaulted by Inman. Now if there's nothing else, I would like to go home. It's getting late, and my wife will worry."

Despite his assertion that he was the victim in the altercation, Duckworth informed Dodger that he had no option but to charge him with shooting at Inman with attempt to murder.

"Then I will answer no further questions without the presence of my lawyer."

Dodger's solicitor, a prominent local lawyer called Hudson, was summoned and Dodger was taken to a cell adjacent to one occupied by a couple of noisy drunks to await Hudson's arrival. When the lawyer arrived, Dodger was inspected for evidence to support his claim of assault. Small amounts of blood were found on his shirt, overcoat and handkerchief. Growing increasingly agitated, Dodger said, "Every time Inman sees me, he attacks me. Why worry about this nonsense about me attempting to shoot him? Next time, I'll bring him down to his own level."

"Don't say any more, Jack," cautioned Hudson.

He listened, impassively, as the charge was read. They might well have been addressing a stranger. Hudson was telling him that at this time of night, it was impossible to arrange bail, and that he would be kept in custody until morning. The lawyer departed, and Dodger was returned to his cell. A short time later, Duckworth came to the cell to inform him that he and his colleague, Detective Sutherland were going to search 32 Ryan Street. Was Mrs. Price at home? He assumed so. Was the garage locked? It was not.

Foremost in Duckworth's mind was the imperative to find the weapon. Without it, he knew that a conviction was unlikely. The few neighbours who were still up at that late hour peered through their curtains as the police car pulled into the front yard of the Old House. What were the Prices up to now? When the police made late-night visits to a miner's house, it was always to bring bad news. But Dodger was no miner. Duckworth, a senior member of the constabulary, was well aware of the reputation the Price family had around town. Despite the work of his father in establishing Broken Hill as a global mining presence, and his step-father in championing good causes, Dodger was not particularly well-liked. A general view prevailed that the Prices, particularly Dodger, thought themselves a cut above regular townspeople. When Dodger brought shopkeepers struggling through the Depression before the local magistrate for failing to pay their bills, word spread quickly, as it always did in isolated communities. Forgotten were Tom's charity events which he organized as a young man. In Dodger, they saw a man with fast cars and flash suits who did not have a charitable bone in his body.

Violet knew about his wandering eye and his philandering ways, and had been disturbed when his eye led him in the direction of Maisie Inman. Nevertheless, she was shocked when Duckworth and his colleague knocked on the side door and informed her that a fight had occurred earlier in the evening between her husband and Maisie's father. It was alleged that Dodger had discharged a shot in Inman's direction, and had been charged with the attempted murder. They wished to search the house and garage for a possible weapon. Duckworth observed that her left arm was set in a plaster cast and supported by a sling and asked what had happened.

"We do not discuss such things," she replied.

Pulling her gown around her, she accompanied them to the garage. When the search proved fruitless, she led them into the kitchen. As they had no warrant, she refused them access to the front of the house where her daughters were sleeping. "Wait here," she said. She disappeared in the direction of the bedrooms and returned a few minutes later with a revolver which she handed to Duckworth. Then she showed the officers to the door and retreated to her room where she spent a sleepless night. How had it come to this? she asked herself as nocturnal creatures fought small wars on the corrugated roof above her head. How on earth had it come to this? When dawn broke, she rose, lit the Aga range in the kitchen, and waited for the arrival of the housekeeper.

At nine o'clock, Duckworth, who had had little sleep himself, confronted Dodger with the revolver. Dodger inspected it calmly and then asked whether it had been fired recently as all of the chambers were loaded.

"No, not recently; I'm not suggesting that it was used last night."

"Well, you can see I have been telling the truth about it," said

Dodger. Then he added, "That revolver doesn't belong to me."

"So, how do you account for it being in your house?"

"It belongs to my wife."

"Your wife? What would Mrs. Price want with a weapon?"

"The wife has had it hidden away lately: I suppose she thought I might shoot her," he replied, enjoying the look of shock on Duckworth's face.

"You mean she kept it for self-defence? Against you?" asked the astonished detective.

Deciding that he had probably said too much, Dodger chose not to reply. Handguns, rifles and shotguns had been an integral part of family life. As an eight-year-old, he had witnessed the dramatic shootout between Harry, his putative father, Tom, his half-brother cum stepfather, and his mother. From this incident, he learned that a firearm was essential when defending oneself against a larger aggressor.

"I think it best that I say no more until Hudson is here."

Hudson was late, as lawyers usually are. When he finally turned up he told the officers that he needed to have a word with his client in private. When they were alone, he informed Dodger that he had been detained by an unexpected visitor—Dodger's wife.

"What the dickens was she doing in your chambers?"

"She wanted a restraining order taken out against you."

"She wanted what?" Uncharacteristically, Dodger lost his composure, smacking his forehead with the palm of his hand.

"Take it easy, Jack. You have enough problems right now. I told her that, as I was being retained by you, I was unable to act for her. I sent her up the street to McLeod."

Dodger was stunned. A restraining order would prohibit him from coming within speaking distance of her and his children. He would not be permitted to enter his own house, the house that had been lovingly constructed by his mother. He had always been able to sweet-talk Violet into forgiving him. Filled with remorse after beating her, he would lavish her with jewellery, Bohemia crystal vases and other gifts. But with a restraining order in place, he would be unable to buy his way back into her good books.

After bail was posted, and he had been released from custody,

Dodger moved into the Grand Hotel in Argent Street opposite the Post Office a short walk from the Police Court. He was offered a large, high-ceilinged room at the front of the hotel, but took instead a smaller one at the rear containing a single bed and a view of the hotel car park. A laneway divided the car park from a row of backyards enclosed by corrugated iron, fencing wire supported by rickety posts, or nothing at all. In the yard directly opposite half a dozen chickens scratched at the dust in search of worms while keeping one eye on the blue heeler chained to the laundry at the back of the house.

He stood motionless by the window for several minutes before drawing the curtains. Then he perched on the edge of the bed, and wrote a note to Hudson listing the clothing, papers, books and other possessions he would need. Could one of Hudson's clerks fetch these from the Old House? When he had finished, he summoned the housekeeper, gave her the note for delivery to Hudson, and instructed her to have an office desk and swivel chair, comfortable lounge chair, stationery, decanter of whisky, soda syphon, and two crystal tumblers delivered to his room.

The housekeeper, stony faced, noted his instructions. She, along with the manager and most of the bar staff had known him for years. As a regular, a big spender, and a generous tipper in a town where no one tipped, he was always warmly welcomed. Now she treated him as a stranger. "Will there be anything else?" she asked.

"Yes, he replied. "I need exclusive use of the bathroom at the end of the corridor. And I will take all of my meals in my room. "He dismissed her with two large bills from his wallet. She looked disdainfully at the notes but took them and shoved them into the pocket of her pinafore.

When his sister had returned from Shanghai for the life-saving kidney operation that killed her, she had said to him, "We spend so much time anticipating the future that we don't know how to live in the present. When the future is taken away, we have nothing." Shortly before returning from China, she had been granted a visit to one of her husband's British associates who had been condemned to death by the provincial governor, a local brigand in cahoots with the Chinese Communist Party, newly formed in the Shanghainese French concession by Chen Duxiu and Li Dazhao. Rather than being executed immediately, as was the Chinese way, he was kept alive for several days. "This is my real punishment," he had told her. "Execution will be nothing." It was only now that Dodger realized the significance of her story. Babs, the eternal optimist, suspected her time was up even before she set sail from Shanghai. Now, almost a decade later, he realized the implication of the story for himself. Without an acquittal, there would be no future for him.

As the later afternoon sun filtered through a gap in the curtain, Hudson himself delivered the items he had requested. They drank whisky and Hudson outlined his strategy for the trial.

Violet and the girls were devastated by the events, and it left a permanent mark on all of them. Betty and Yvonne, the two younger daughters, were still attending school, and had to endure whispered conversations that took place between their school friends as word spread of the shooting and its cause. Babs, somewhat reluctantly, accepted the solace offered by her tennis partner Archie Cashman. As an outsider from the East Coast, he had no truck with the gossip of the locals, although neither did he have any sympathy for Dodger. A devout Catholic, he rejected the misguided views of these atheists, although he never discussed religion with Babs. Violet suffered the pity of her friends and acquaintances in silence. She would rather have been despised than pitied. Several days after the alleged shooting, on a whim, she walked into the grounds of St. Mary's Catholic Church in Railway Town and asked to see the priest. Undeterred by his whisky breath, she made a general confession and was received back into the arms of the Church.

The formal proceedings to determine whether Dodger should face a trial by jury began on Tuesday, 3 July before Magistrate Donaldson. The defendant and plaintiff made an odd couple sitting adjacent to one another in the dock: diminutive, dapper Dodger in his hand-tailored suit, collar and tie alongside the rough-hewn miner, sitting stiffly in a borrowed jacket that was too small for him. The magistrate and Duckworth, who represented the Crown, also made an interesting contrast. Donaldson had plump, smooth jowls, and the satisfied look of a man who thought himself high in the legal pantheon, whereas in reality he was nothing more than a rural magistrate sitting on a hard bench in the middle of nowhere. Duckworth was tall and bent. He had a large hooked nose, and thinning hair which was combed straight back from his forehead and kept in place with hair oil. His general demeanour was of one who had seen too much.

Interest in the case was high, and the public gallery was packed. However, the proceedings only lasted a few minutes. After Detective-Sergeant Duckworth had read the charge, Hudson moved that his client be further remanded until the following week, to which the magistrate agreed. However, the following week, as soon as Price's name was called a solicitor from Hudson's chambers moved for a further adjournment. When the magistrate asked for a reason, the solicitor replied, "It will suit both parties." Duckworth concurred with this enigmatic reply. The police had still been unable to locate the revolver, and a further delay would increase their chances of the weapon turning up. His failure to find it was both a mystery and an irritant. He didn't believe for a second Dodger's assertion that there was no weapon. If Dodger had flung it from the car or put it into a street bin in the time between the altercation and his arrest, it would have been handed in. Two thorough searches of Ryan Street had proved fruitless. Violet, given her anger at the humiliation brought on the family by Dodger would certainly have turned it in. It was clear she thought that a spell of incarceration was nothing less than Dodger deserved.

Hudson's motives in seeking a further adjournment were twofold. He was not delaying the inevitable, but trying to arrange a reconciliation between Violet and Dodger. Her presence in court in silent support of her husband would play well in the court of public opinion if not in the eyes of the law. Her absence would indicate to the jury that she considered Dodger guilty. Although he had no intention of calling her as a witness for the defence, he was also trying to get further details from Maisie Inman on the exact nature of the relationship between her and Dodger. Any admission that Dodger's pursuit had culminated in a full-blown affair would spell the end for him in the eyes of the jury. His hope was to get a statement from Maisie that there was nothing of a sexual nature to the relationship, that it was she who had approached Dodger at a tennis tournament in the hope that he might assist her to find employment: a long shot, admittedly, given Dodger's reputation. Despite the fact that it was common knowledge, the best outcome would be to have any information about the affair kept off the public record.

After two false starts, the committal hearing finally got under way on Friday, 20th July, 1934. Dodger rose before dawn and laid out his clothes: white shirt, sombre suit, and waistcoat. He debated on the choice of a necktie, standing by the window with a polka dot bowtie in one hand and a rather funereal regular tie in the other. Eventually, he rejected the bowtie, suggesting as it did, a degree of flippancy that he certainly did not feel. He took a long bath, dressed and waited for the chambermaid to deliver his breakfast. At nine o'clock, Hudson arrived and accompanied him across the street to the courthouse.

Despite the delays, interest in the case remained high. *The Barrier Miner* reported that "A crowded public gallery, in which many women occupied prominent seats, listened to the evidence given today in the shooting with intent to murder charge preferred against Frank 'Dodger' Price (56), a well-known local fruit merchant."[14]

The gallery, overflowing with women accompanied by knitting and shopping bags, underlined the fact that in the public eye this case was not about a physical altercation between two men who had taken too much liquor, but a salacious tale of the seduction of a young woman by an older man. While a case of this nature involving sex and violence was always going to attract attention, there was another reason for the public interest. They anticipated the fall of Dodger Price, and wanted to be there when it happened. Dodger did nothing to downplay his image. He simply didn't care what the common townsfolk thought, these miners who came off shift work with dirt behind their ears and on their hands, who wandered down Argent Street in blue workmen's singlets and shorts. Why shouldn't he wear tailor-made suits and insist on wearing a collar and tie? Why shouldn't he drive the fanciest and fastest car in the district? He was proud of what his family had achieved, emerging, on one side, from the Welsh valleys, and on the other, from the back-blocks of Aberdeen, to achieve a high degree of public prominence. He was the son of one of Australia's best-known mining engineers, the half-brother and step-son of an internationally celebrated impresario. He had been to

[14] *The Barrier Miner*. Friday, 20 July, 1934, p.1

the Far East and to Paris, while most of the townspeople were lucky if they had been to Adelaide once or twice in their lives. He had built a successful business, and yes, he *did* have a fast car. And he knew how to drive it.

The first witness for the prosecution was the plaintiff, Edward Francis Inman. After swearing to tell the truth, the whole truth, and nothing but the truth so help him God, he was led by Duckworth through the events that occurred on the evening of the 28th of June. During pauses in his narrative, he glared angrily at Dodger. When he was finished, Hudson rose and conducted an aggressive cross-examination, the main goal being to establish that his client had acted in self-defence.

Inman admitted that he had attacked Price and said that he would have given him a "a damned good hiding" if he had been able to catch him after the shooting. When Hudson attempted to establish that there was a history of violence on Inman's part against Price, the following exchange occurred.

"I believe you once hit Price in the eye near the Soldiers' Hostel."

"Yes, under provocation."

"Answer my question."

"Yes, I hit him."

"And made his nose bleed?"

"I made something bleed."

"Did you threaten Price at a tennis tournament, and did a Mr. Edwards ask you not to make a scene?"

"I had no intention of making a scene."

"When questioned by Detective-Sergeant Duckworth, did you say, 'This was what I was waiting for'?"

"I cannot recollect using those words to Detective-Sergeant Duckworth."

"Tell the court what happened on the night in question."

"I was about 15 yards from the door of the church hall when I saw Price. I got home about 7.40 pm from Railway Town. I intended going to the hall to see how things were going. I had no other reason."

"You didn't go because you knew Price was there?"

"I had been told that Price was prowling around my house that night. That was not why I went to the hall. I was told about Price some time before I went to the hall. It was common gossip."

"I don't want common gossip. Who told you?"

At this point, Inman turned to the magistrate and asked if he was compelled to answer. When the magistrate reminded him that he was under cross-examination, he replied that his daughter Gloria had told him. Hudson then continued with the cross-examination.

"Was that not the reason why you went to the hall?"

"No. I wanted to see how things were going. I also intended to see if Price was there. I wanted to see what he was doing there. I did not attempt to assault him until he crouched behind those young fellows."

"You intended to have words with him?"

"I was going to ask him what he was following my daughter about for. I first spoke to Price in a quiet manner. Price was in a crouched position and was evidently trying to hide his identity. Price was still in a crouched position when I struck at him. From the time Price said, 'Get out, you cunt,' until the time I struck at him, only a moment elapsed. There was nothing to prevent Price from standing up straight. Price made no move to defend himself. I never called Price a cunt. I chased Price and intended to assault him, because there was every justification, after what he had called me. I never got near enough to strike him. I may have given Price a hiding, or I may have spoken to him."

"You would have given him a damned good hiding?"

"I may have, if he had not given me a satisfactory explanation. I intended to ask him what he meant by following my daughter about."

"I suggest you chased Price 75 yards."

"No. I ran about 15 yards. I stopped because my slippers were coming off, and I could not get any closer. I had stopped when the defendant turned with the gun in his hand."

"What do you mean by saying that you felt something whizz past your left side?"

"I mean that the senses of the body caused a ripple in the muscles of my left thigh. The body being so sensitive, the shock of the bullet going past would cause that. The muscles sensed the danger of the bullet."

"But for the rippling of the muscles of the left thigh you would not have known the course of the bullet?"

"I also heard the hissing noise. I was only five yards away. The sound of the gun going off did not deaden the noise of the passing bullet. I suppose the report of the gun going off was a shock. It was not a loud report. It was like the crack of a whip. The people at the hall could have heard it."

Duckwoth, representing the Crown, summed up the events of the evening based on the statement he had taken from Dodger. He repeated the defendant's insistence that he had not fired a shot, and didn't even have a weapon, this despite the fact that witnesses had heard a shot and seen a flash. He also reported that no gun was found at the scene, in the car or anywhere else. He also told the court of his visit to 32 Ryan Street and of Violet turning over a pistol to him, although there was no evidence of that weapon having been fired that night. The gallery gasped when he repeated Dodger's statement that his wife might have hidden the revolver because she thought he might shoot her. Hudson attempted to have this statement struck from the record, but the magistrate deemed it pertinent, given the charge his client was facing.

"Was he making a joke?" the magistrate asked. Duckworth shook his head. In light of the seriousness of the charge, there was no indication that he might have been joking, nor that it was just an idle remark. Attempting to counter this damaging piece of evidence, Hudson asked whether the attitude of the defendant from the time he was arrested until he came before the court was of a man greatly worried, to which Duckworth replied that he did not appear worried but sat calmly in the interview cell. There was certainly no laughing or joking, not in Duckworth's presence.

Hudson then turned to the assault by Inman on Price some months earlier. When Duckworth said that Inman had assaulted Price to warn him off his teenage daughter, Hudson immediately rose to have this comment struck from the record. "I submit it is irrelevant," he told the magistrate.

Donaldson agreed, saying, "I think that is irrelevant too. Further examination in that quarter will not be of any use and is not admissible."

Clearly pleased with this ruling, Hudson replied, "Certainly not. The charge has to be proved, and that is that a shot was fired and not things that happened months ago."

Despite the fact that the ruling was odd given that it went to the heart of the ongoing feud between the him and Inman, Dodger was relieved to hear these words. Without a motive or a weapon, the prosecution case would rest on the statements of those witnesses who claimed that a shot was fired. However, his affair with Maisie was a matter of public record, and if the case went to trial it would be impossible to empanel an impartial jury.

The magistrate's ruling failed to deter Inman. He was called back to the stand to be questioned by the detective. He changed the story slightly about his motive for going over to the hall, admitting that when he heard Price was lurking around the hall, he had gone across to check on Maisie. When Duckworth asked his daughter's age and Inman replied, "Nineteen," Hudson immediately rose to his feet.

"I object. It is irrelevant." He was again supported by the magistrate.

"I won't admit it. We don't want the age; just the fact that his daughter was there." Because of the heavy case load on the court, the trial was then adjourned to the following Friday.

When the hearing resumed, the local press again mentioned the preponderance of women in the courtroom, noting that, "Many of the women in the public gallery seemed to have combined shopping with interest in the case, for some entered the court with parcels." The first witness for the Crown was Kelvin Henderson Wilson who gave his occupation as electrician.

Wilson provided the following statement to the court. "On June 28 last I went to St. John's Church of England hall at the corner of Williams and McCulloch streets. After being in the hall some time I went to the front and then walked to the north side of the hall. I returned to the northeast corner and saw Price there. He was walking towards the north window. A little later I saw Mr. Inman come from the front to the side of the hall with a man named Jenkins. Price was then trying to look through one of the windows. I heard voices but did not hear what was said. Price turned his face towards Inman, and then I saw a struggle, but it was not clear. Price broke away and tried to run but was impeded by his overcoat. Inman followed and then they were struggling, but I could not distinguish whether any blows were struck by Inman. Later I saw a flash and heard a report. Then I heard an exclamation like 'Oh,' by Inman."

In his cross-examination, Hudson sought to establish a personal relationship between Wilson and Inman, and possible collusion between them in Wilson's evidence. Wilson admitted that he lived a short distance from the Inmans, he had known the family for about six years, had been to their house on numerous occasions and knew Inman's wife and daughters. He said that he had been interviewed by the police on the evening of the alleged shooting and admitted that he had spoken to Inman after the adjournment of the hearing the previous week. He had never spoken to Dodger, but knew him by sight, as he was a well-known local identity. He then provided the court with his recollections of the alleged murder attempt. He had been smoking on the corner of the street with about a dozen other men when the fight broke out between Inman and Price. He admitted that when Inman had first come across the street, he and the other young men expected that there might be a fight. The bad blood between the two men was common knowledge. Although street-corner fights were common in the town, they rarely occurred at the church hall, a respectable place. Inman passed the group without saying anything. He was clearly looking for Price. When Hudson asked him to name the others in the street corner group, Wilson hesitated and looked at the magistrate. Hudson said, "Come on, you have to tell. You're under oath." After further hesitation, he named Allan Bent and Clyde Millstead, and then continued with his recollection of the altercation. Inman spoke to Price, and then swung a fist at him. Wilson repeated what he had already told the court. Price broke away and fumbled in his overcoat. He then saw a flash and heard a report. Assuming it was a revolver, he said to the group, "I'm getting out of here." The group broke up and then headed into the hall.

"Did Inman and Price seem to be quarrelling?" asked Hudson.

"They were, judging by the language they were using."

"What do you mean by language? When men are shouting at one another, they are not good friends, are they?"

"No."

"You can distinguish Inman's voice from that of Price?"

"Yes."

"Well, if Inman said he did not speak to Price he would not be telling the truth?"

"Yes."

"Assuming that Price had a gun, it would not be pointed at Inman if they continued in the direction you said they were going, would it?"

"No."

"You said you saw a struggle. What do you mean by that?"

"I saw two figures moving about for a few seconds before the flash and report."

"If Inman said he stopped five yards from Price, would he be telling the truth?"

"I could not say. I could not tell what distance separated them."

"How did Price and Inman leave the hall?"

"At a very quick walk."

"Would you say Price was trying to avoid trouble and keep out of Inman's way?"

"Yes."

"That Inman was looking for a fight?"

"I would not say that. Mr. Inman does not strike me as a man like that."

"How long have you known Price?"

"I have never spoken to the man in my life. I have seen him driving about in his car."

At this point Duckworth approached the magistrate and suggested an adjournment. Hudson agreed to the suggestion, satisfied that he had establish several key points: Wilson was a friend of Inman and his family, Inman was the aggressor, the men in the neighbourhood who know him were expecting a fight, and Dodger was trying to avoid trouble. However, he could not shake Wilson on the issue of the gunshot. He and the other witnesses were adamant that Price had produced a pistol and fired a shot at Inman. If this were the case, where was the weapon?

When the hearing resumed the following Tuesday, the final witness for the prosecution, Bertram Lawrence Hall, was called. Hall made the following statement:

"About 8 pm on June 28 I was at the Church of England hall at North Broken Hill. I was outside on the north side looking through the window. Price walked around the side of the hall from the front. Price came and stood alongside the window. Inman came along and walked up to Price. I did not hear any words spoken, but Inman struck Price with his hands.

Price backed away and Inman followed. I then turned and looked through the window. I could not say how far they were from the window when I looked back into the hall. I glanced round and heard a shot and saw a flash. They were about 30 yards from me. It was dark. I could not see properly."

Hudson then cross-examined Hall. He began by asking if he knew Price. He did. He'd known Price for about five years but had never met Inman until the court hearing began on June 28. Yes, the church hall window was up, and if Price had spoken to Inman, he would have heard. In asserting that Price had sworn at him prior to taking a blow, Inman was not telling the truth.

The cross-examination continued. "Inman followed Price after he turned to go?" asked Hudson.

"Yes."

"Despite the fact that Inman followed Price you turned around and looked into the dance room?"

"Yes."

"Does dancing make more appeal to you than two men having a fight?"

"Yes."

"Did you turn at the very moment you heard the shot?"

"I just happened to turn, and I then heard the shot and saw a flash."

"When did you see the figures in the distance?"

"After I heard the shot and saw the flash. I could recognize the men by their size. Price was almost behind Inman."

"You told Sergeant Duckworth that you could not see Price. Was what you told the sergeant untrue?"

"Yes."

"Was any of your other evidence untrue?"

"No."

"Could you say whether Inman and Price were there still?"

"They were."

"You are still going to say that you looked back into the window after you saw the first blow struck?"

"Yes."

"How long were you at the hall that night after the fight?"

"I could not say. I have no idea."

"Why are you afraid to answer that question?"

"I am not afraid. I told you I have no idea of the time."

This exchange ended the prosecution's case. Magistrate Donaldson ruled that a prima facie case been made and committed Frank "Dodger" Price to a trial by jury at the Court of Quarter Sessions on August 21, on the charge of shooting at Edward Francis Inman with intent to murder. In response, Hudson submitted that the case was not one for the defendant to be committed for trial. "The basis of whether Price is to be sent to trial is whether a jury would convict," he said. "In the case of a major charge the prisoner is generally committed, and the Crown Prosecutor left to decide whether to file a bill. In this case Price comes as a married man, a Justice of the Peace, and a prominent business man with a good reputation. The charge is one of intent to murder. You have to take his actions to determine whether he intended to commit murder when he fired a shot at Inman. It is required to show that firstly a revolver was fired, and secondly it was fired at Inman with intent. I submit that in the whole of the evidence there is none, apart from Inman's, that can establish even whether a revolver was fired, and that it was fired at Inman. You will notice that the only evidence that Price stopped and turned and fired was given by Inman himself. I submit that on this evidence there is not a jury that would convict a man on the charge." Donaldson, however, was unmoved.

Speaking directly to Dodger, he said, "I think that a prima facie case has been made out. I am not able to say that it is highly probable that a jury will not convict, and therefore I deem it a case to call upon you. Frank Price, you are now charged with having on June 28 shot at Edward Francis Inman with intent to murder."

Asked if he had anything to say, Price replied: "I am not guilty, and I reserve my defence."

Prior to his appearance before Judge Coyle in the Court of Quarter Sessions, Dodger learned that the Crown Law office had reduced the charge against him from attempted murder to shooting with intent to do grievous bodily harm. At the trial, which took place on 28 August, Dodger was again represented by his friend Ernie Hudson, and pleaded not guilty to the lesser charge. The jury was empanelled, and witnesses for the prosecution, including Inman, repeated the evidence that they had given during the committal hearing.

The final witness, Joseph Blight, a labourer, was called by Hudson to make a statement on behalf of the defence. He said that he was near the hall on the night of the shooting. "I saw two men run a distance of about 75 yards. One man was behind the other. The big man was following. I heard a sort of a crack. Both men were running. The front man had his back to the other man. The smaller man did not stop after the report but kept running."

The Crown Prosecutor cross-examined the witness about the distance between the two men, and how far they were from the hall. He then said, "No further questions, Your Worship." This closed the case for them.

As Tom had done in Adelaide many years before, Dodger refused to swear on the Bible as he did not subscribe to Christianity, or any other religion. He then made a statement from the dock that caused a mild sensation. Changing his story, he admitted that, yes, he had a pistol and had fired it at Inman. Given the number of witnesses who had testified to this effect, Hudson convinced him that he could not do otherwise. Speaking directly to the jury, he said, "On the night in question I was in the car and went to North Broken Hill. I went down Chapple Street and the lights came on in a hall. I went to the taxi terminus, and then I went to the hall later and stood in front. I looked round and saw Inman. He came at me, swung at me and said, 'You bastard, I have got you now.' I ran 50 yards and he came after me. I tried to get away. I had a pistol in my overcoat pocket, and while I was still running, turned and fired into the ground to frighten him. What was I to do? I was at his mercy on the Common. Look at him. Look at the size of him. Inman had said on the Common 'I have got you now, you bastard.' But the pistol shot had the desired effect, because he retreated to the hall. That is all I have to say. I am in your hands, gentlemen."

The foreman of the jury asked, "Do we understand that Price fired into the ground?"

"Yes," replied Judge Coyle.

"What of the revolver?' asked the foreman. This was a question that everyone in the court wanted to know, but the Judge quickly dismissed the question. "You can't ask questions, gentlemen," he replied. And so the question as to what Dodger did with the pistol was never answered: certainly not in the court on that day. Many years later, long after the principals in the drama were dead and gone, for reasons of safety the well at the rear of the Old House was drained. There, buried in the mud and silt that had settled at the bottom of the well, was a pistol that could only have belonged to Dodger. In the time that elapsed between the shooting and being apprehended by the police, Dodger had returned briefly to the house and tossed the weapon into the well.

The trial concluded with a lengthy address from Hudson. He emphasized the fact that Inman was the aggressor and that his client had fired a warning shot in self-defence. "If Price had been intent on murder, why would he have only fired once? Why did he fire on the run, rather than standing his ground and taking a steady shot?" he asked rhetorically. The prosecutor, Captain Storkey, then gave a much briefer address before Judge Coyle informed the court that he would give his summing up the following morning. At this point the foreman of the jury asked if the jurymen could confer in the jury box. Permission was granted, and the court waited wondering what the jury was up to. The foreman then rose and announced that they had reached a unanimous verdict. "How say you?" asked the judge.

"Not guilty, Your Worship," came the reply. And so, the hearing and trial that had kept the town entertained ended suddenly with an outcome that disappointed many in the public gallery. Dodger was discharged. There was paperwork to be completed and arrangements to be made for the return of his bond but that would be sorted out by the clerks from Hudson's chambers.

Outside the court house, Hudson suggested that they walk around the corner to the Broken Hill Club, to celebrate the acquittal. The Broken Hill Club was favoured by mine managers, the professional classes, businessmen and the whisky priests. It was about as genteel a place as you were likely to find this far into the bush. It was also discreet. Here he would be spared the stares and whispers that were sure to pursue him into the regular watering holes about town. Dodger, however, shook his head. He had things to attend to back in the hotel room that had been his home and sanctuary since his ordeal had begun. Besides, he told Hudson, he was not yet ready to face the public. He may have been exonerated by the jury, but the court of public opinion would have a reached a very different conclusion long before a single piece of evidence had been tendered. He sat long into the night, alone with his thoughts and the decanter of whisky.

His desire, to return to his home at 32 Ryan Street, was not an option as the restraining order was still in place. In any case, he knew he'd find no sanctuary there. Violet had attended neither his arraignment, nor the subsequent trial, and he was well aware of the public shame she would have endured during the trial. Although he had not touched her since the broken arm incident, he knew that she was afraid of him. During the trial there was also the telling incident of the pistol Violet had produced for the police. He had told Duckworth it was his wife's weapon, and she kept it hidden for fear that Dodger might shoot her with it. At this point, Hudson had asked Duckworth whether he had any knowledge of the relationship between the defendant and his wife? "I know they are not on too friendly terms," replied the detective, to which the magistrate responded, "That means you know that they are not on very friendly terms."

She had adored him in the early years of their relationship, before the domestic violence had begun. He certainly pursued her with a passion, bombarding her with letters and postcards. Typical of many men, after the marriage, he became a controlling presence in her life. Although his own interest in secularism was lukewarm at best, after they married, he had insisted that she abandon the Catholic Church. He had no doubt that she would be dismayed when the news reached her of his acquittal. And what of his daughters? None of them had been to see him. Babs would be as judgmental as her mother, and Betty would be filled with shame, but what of little Yvonne, his secret favourite? Removing the silk handkerchief from the upper pocket of his jacket, he dabbed at his eyes, then refilled his tumbler.

Several days after his acquittal, Dodger came to a major decision. Despite the fact that the jury had ruled in his favour, he knew that his reputation had been badly damaged by the revelations that emerged during the trial. If his hometown was going to shun him, he was not going to stick around to be humiliated. On 28 August, the following brief notice appeared in *The Barrier Miner.*

> **Mr. F. Price** to reside in Adelaide…Mr. Frank "Dodger" Price left yesterday for Adelaide where he intends to reside. In Adelaide he will work with the firm of T. J. Price & Co., with which he was associated in Broken Hill. The Broken Hill work of the firm will be carried out by Mr. R. S. Coates. *(The Barrier Miner, Tuesday 28 August 1934)*[15]

[15] *The Barrier Miner,* 28 August, 1934, p.1

Chapter 18
Reunited by Death

Meg, the daily help, brought her a cup of tea and a plate of digestive biscuits. Violet ignored the biscuits and stared at the China cup while the tea grew cold. In the laundry, Meg thumped away at the freshly laundered clothes with an iron. A loose sheet of roofing iron flapped in the wind, which whipped around the back of the house. The thought came to her: August is the cruellest month. When she shared her plan with Father Kenny, he said that the earliest it could happen would be October. By then, the first hot breaths of summer would be tormenting the seedlings in the kitchen garden. Babs would have to take instruction before being received into the Church, but that was contingent upon her agreeing to Violet's plan.

She would have to pick her moment. Her daughters differed considerably in nature and temperament: Betty, timid and introverted, Yvonne, the fun-loving extravert, and Babs, so certain in her convictions that she needed no facts to support them. They shared one character trait: an obstinacy that at times took the wisdom of Solomon to counter.

It was Archie who had sown the seed: kindly, clever Archie, ever the gentleman, even when he had taken drink. His feelings for the eldest Price girl were evident, and there was no objection from that quarter when she put the plan to him. Less certain was the extent to which they were reciprocated. A devout Catholic, he made a single request: that the ceremony take place in the Cathedral on the hill. She had no argument with the request. In fact, it had been her intention all along. This would not be a quiet affair at one of the little suburban churches dotted about the town. She might be leaving, but she wouldn't be slinking away, she would see her daughter married at the Cathedral, and then depart with dignity.

The conversation was every bit as difficult as she had expected.

"I'm not in love with him," was her daughter's immediate response.

"What's love got to do with it?" replied Violet. "It doesn't last. If you marry for love, you'll be disappointed."

"And you're speaking from personal experience."

"Please do not be offensive, Babs.'

"You want to marry me off to get me out of the way."

"I'm moving to Adelaide, and I'm taking your sisters with me. I cannot and will not remain here. You have a choice. You can give up your job and your friends and your social life and your tennis and come with us—or you can marry Arch. It's your choice. You can't find him too objectionable, you're playing in the tennis finals with him."

"There's a big difference between a tennis partner and a husband."

In the end Babs agreed, but made it clear she was doing so reluctantly. Her close friends were envious. Archie was a fine catch: an older man still with a reasonable head of hair, and a profession. He would take her back East, away from the dust storms and dreariness of desert life. The best they could hope for was life with a shoe salesman or a bank clerk. Babs's only response was to pull down the corners of her mouth and mutter that the marriage was not of her choosing.

The issue decided, there was much to be done. In addition to the usual arrangements—drawing up the guest list, ordering wedding gowns, organizing the wedding breakfast at 32 Ryan Street—there was the major issue of taking instruction from Father Kenny and being received into the Church. Father Kenny had kindly agreed to instruct Babs at home. He suggested that Betty and Yvonne also be baptized. As bridesmaids, it wasn't strictly necessary for them to be received into the Church, but it would be better in the long run if they were. Betty raised no objection. Yvonne muttered that it was "nonsense," but she, too, went along with the suggestion. Ironically, of the three, Yvonne would be the one to embrace the Church with an enthusiasm that surprised her mother. Later, when Violet and the younger daughters had moved to Adelaide, Father Kenny's suggestion turned out to be remarkably prescient. The only available school places in Adelaide were in a Catholic convent in Glenelg. Had they arrived in the city as atheists, their chance of being admitted to the school would have been little short of zero.

Invitations for the union of Lilian Viola Price and Archibald Leo Cashman were sent out to friends and relatives. The ceremony was to take place at 2 p. m. on the 6th of October 1934 at the Sacred Heart Catholic Cathedral, Lane Street, Broken Hill. It would be followed by a wedding breakfast at 32 Ryan Street. It fell to Betty, who had inherited her grandmother's passion both for cooking and gardening, to oversee the breakfast. Several of Archie's sporting friends sent their regrets. The day clashed with the Victorian Football Association's Grand Final between Northcote and Coburg, and they had made a commitment to travel to Melbourne for the game to support the Northcote team which included two players from Broken Hill. Had it not been for the wedding, Archie might have gone with them, although, coming from the east coast, he was no champion of Australian Rules football. North of the Victorian border, Rugby League was sporting spectators' opiate of choice, and it was Archie's preferred code. In later life, Saturday afternoons would find him at Brookvale Oval supporting his beloved Many Warringah Sea Eagles.

Included on the guest list were Uncle Tom and Ann as well as Uncle William. While Violet got on well with them, particularly Uncle Tom, it was with some trepidation that she added them to the list, and only did so at Bab's insistence. "They are my grandparents, for heaven's sake," she said. After the turmoil of the preceding months, Violet wanted the wedding to be trouble-free. Once Dodger, who was lodging with his parents in St. Peters, learned of the impending nuptials, trouble was likely. And trouble there was. Dodger immediately called his friend and lawyer Ernie Hudson demanding to know why he had been excluded from the event, although the answer must have been obvious. "Tell my wife that I have every right to give my daughter away, and I intend to exercise that right." Hudson drove to 32 Ryan Street to deliver the message. Violet was silent for a minute and then said quietly, "Remind him that he is still under a restraining order. If he turns up at the church, where he is not wanted, he will be violating that order and will ruin his daughter's wedding."

Betty, who was drawing up shopping lists at the end of the dining table and mulling over the dilemma of flowers for the event at this early time of the growing season, was troubled by the conversation. Although, like her mother and sisters, she was disgusted by Dodger's behaviour and the shame it had brought upon the family, she loved him. On the day of the wedding, she rose before dawn, and began arranging the flowers she had cut from the garden along with the ones that had been delivered from the florist the night before. When Meg, the housekeeper and her sister arrived, Ann appeared in the kitchen in her dressing gown and immediately took charge, issuing instructions to Meg on what was to be done while the family was at the wedding ceremony.

As she assisted her grandmother, Betty thought about Dodger. What was he doing? What was he thinking? Once the dust had settled from the wedding, and they had relocated to Adelaide, she was determined to bring about a reconciliation between her parents. It would be no easy task, but she was determined to give it a try. This was supposed to be a joyful day, but the only one likely to experience any lightness of heart was her soon-to-be brother-in-law. With the back of her hand, she brushed away tears that had appeared unexpectedly, clenched her jaw, and got on with what had to be done. Although still coming to terms with the fact that life was not meant to be easy, she was determined to find one spark of joy in the day, no matter how small.

As first light broke, Dodger was navigating the curves through the Thackaringa Hills. He had driven at speed through the night and was now a few miles short of the town that he had once called home. If his wife thought that she could prevent him from being with his daughter on her wedding day, she could think again. He drove past the cemetery where his father lay buried in un-consecrated ground, proceeded up Williams Street, turned into Bromide Street, and pulled up at the rear of the Pig and Whistle Hotel. The pub was one of a number of early openers, catering to miners coming off night shift. Ignoring the state licensing laws, Broken Hill pubs set their own opening hours. Some stayed open into the small hours of the morning to serve those who finished the afternoon shift at midnight. Others, like the Pig and Whistle, opened at dawn. There were several scattered through the township that never shut. Opening hours were never advertised. Shades in windows facing the street were pulled, and the front door was locked. To all intents and purposes, the publicans were obeying the law. But locals knew the hours, and which back door would yield to their touch.

Dodger pulled a Gladstone bag from the back seat of the car, and entered through the screen door that led on to the rear verandah. The mine whistles signalling the end of the night shift were yet to alert the town that the weekend had begun, and at that hour, Dodger had the bar to himself. "Anyone home?" he called.

A tousled head appeared in the doorway that led to a kitchen of sorts.

"Hello, Piggy," said Dodger.

"Cripes, Dodger. You scared the shit out of me. What are you doing here? You were the talk of the town—none of it very flattering. Then you shot through and the chatter stopped."

"Give me a whisky, please, Piggy. Your usual generous pour. Here's something for your trouble." He placed a bill on the bar. "Put the change in the tip jar, or in your pocket."

"Gee, thanks, Dodger. You always were a generous bloke. I never let anyone say a word against you—not in this bar."

"Yeah, yeah. Now where's that generous pour?"

Armed with his whisky, Dodger retreated to a table in the far corner of the bar. When the mine whistles echoed through the town, he finished up the tumbler of whisky and left. He had driven through the night for one purpose, and one purpose only and it was not to engage in idle banter or endure the scrutiny of the miners coming off night shift.

Consecrated in 1905, the Sacred Heart Cathedral sits on the highest hill in Broken Hill with commanding views across the central business district to the towering line of black slag heaps that defined and dwarfed the town. At the conclusion of the ceremony, the bride and groom, followed by family and guests exited the main doors to the Cathedral to have photos taken on the front steps. The first sight that greeted Betty as she followed the newlyweds from the church was her father sitting in his car under a majestic eucalyptus tree on the other side of Lane Street. Although he had driven all the way from Adelaide to be with his daughter on her wedding day, he kept his distance, the restraining order an insurmountable barrier between him and his daughter. Although he was some distance away, Bet could see sadness etched on his face. He gave Babs a long look, and then drove away. Clearly, it had broken his heart not to walk Babs down the aisle, but then he had done heart-breaking of his own.

Shortly after the wedding, Violet moved to Adelaide with her two younger daughters. With Hudson's law firm acting as intermediary, she allowed Dodger to repossess the Old House. In return, he agreed to pay the rent on a cottage she secured on Brighton Road, Glenelg. It was far enough from St. Peters, where Tom and Ann lived, to enable her to keep her distance, but close enough for her to be in touch if required. Bet spent most weekends with her grandmother and Uncle Tom and was able to carry news between St. Peters and Glenelg. Apart from that, contact between the two branches of the family was minimal. One Saturday afternoon as she was helping her grandmother roll pastry for a steak and kidney pie, she heard a car draw up outside. The front door slammed, there were footsteps in the hall, and then Dodger appeared in the doorway. Dropping her rolling pin on the table, she rushed to embrace him. It was her first physical contact with him since before the night of the shooting.

"Come back to us, Father," she said when she could speak.

"The time is not right," he replied gently. Tragedy would reunite the family, but that would not happen for another year.

Late one August afternoon in 1935, Violet received an unexpected message from her sister-in-law, Lilian Lockhart, the elder of Dodger's two sisters. The younger sister, Babs, who had died tragically a decade earlier through an operation gone wrong, had been Violet's best school friend in her teenage years, and it was through Babs that she had met Jack. She and Lilian, her senior by three years, were never close. Despite her life as an actress and vaudeville artist, Lilian, like Violet herself, was quiet, and somewhat reserved. After marrying Walter, she had settled in Port Sunlight and rarely left England. This was the first trip back to Australia since the scandal involving her brother the previous year.

The message from Lilian arrived in the form of a handwritten note, brought back from St. Peters by Bet. Lilian had arrived in Australia to visit her parents. Her mother, now eighty, and her stepfather, seventy-six, were in reasonable health for their age, but were not going to live forever, and she had travelled from England to spend time with them. Could she pay Violet a visit? Of course she could. Violet dispatched Bet to St. Peters with an invitation for Lilian to come for afternoon tea the following day. She had forgiven, if not forgotten, Lilian's perfidy following Babs's death, of removing to England the collection of fine china, the hand-embroidered tablecloths and elaborate silks which Babs had brought back from Shanghai—treasures which had been promised to Violet's own daughters.

Lilian had aged considerably in the decade since they had last seen each other. Violet, on the other hand, had weathered the years remarkably well considering her difficult marriage and the traumatic events of the preceding year. Her features were as unlined as they had been in her twenties.

Once they had greeted one another and were comfortably settled in the front drawing room, Meg served them tea and biscuits, and then withdrew to the kitchen. Once the pleasantries had petered out, an uncomfortable silence descended. Then, without warning, Lilian reached across and took one of Violet's hands. "How long are you going to make Jack suffer?" she asked.

Violet jerked her hand away. "Please do not speak of such things," she said primly, her lips a thin slash in her face. Unlike her extraverted and long-dead sister, Lilian was a withdrawn and non-confrontational individual. She would have infinitely preferred to be sitting at home completing a watercolour painting than carrying out this mission. "You may not wish to, my dear Violet, but you must."

"I loved Jack in ways you can never imagine. In some ways I still do, despite the things he did to me. Despite the fact that he destroyed my family." She rose to her feet. "And now that you have delivered your message, I think it is time that you should go." Without waiting for a response, she proceeded to the front door, which she held open while Lilian gathered her things together and departed.

The following day, Violet was just about to begin her lunch when Bet, plump and red-faced from exertion, burst into the room. "You have to come, Mother, you have to come right now!" She began pulling at Violet's arm.

"What are you doing? I'm having my lunch, dear." She was unsettled at the evident distress of her normally placid daughter.

"It's Uncle Tom."

What's happened?"

"Can you please just come?" She stood by the door, her cheeks shiny

290

with tears, as her mother gathers her coat and bag. On the street, at Betty's insistence, they hailed a taxi. There was no time to wait for a bus or tram to the city

The house on Eighth Avenue was a classical Adelaide bluestone villa fronted by a return verandah in the comfortable middle-class suburb of St. Peters. The street, quiet at this time of day, contained more than its usual quota of cars. Lilian greeted them at the front door. The words that had passed between the previous day were forgotten. She led them to the bedroom where Uncle Tom in his street clothes lay on the bed. A doctor stood on one side of the bed checking his pulse. Ann sat on a high-backed wooden chair on the other holding his hand. She neither looked at nor acknowledged Violet.

In the kitchen, Lilian explained what had happened. They were on their way to the city on a shopping expedition. In Rundle Street, right next to the East End markets, where he had spent much of his life, Tom became short of breath and complained of chest pains. Lilian, who was driving, immediately turned the car around and returned to St. Peters, where they got Tom into the house and called for the family doctor.

At 2.55 p.m., on Monday, the 23rd of September 1935, Thomas John Price was pronounced dead. On hearing the words, his wife uttered a single anguished moan, rose from her place by his side and staggered into the lounge room where she collapsed onto the sofa.

"Where's Jack?" asked Violet.

"He's on his way from Broken Hill," said Lilian. "I called him as soon as Tom collapsed, and he left immediately. He'll be here soon."

The doctor left to complete the necessary formalities and to contact a funeral director. As Tom died in the presence of the doctor, who certified the death, there would be no need for an autopsy.

Betty took the place of her grandmother on the high-backed chair next to the corpse of her beloved uncle. It was her first direct experience of death, and her brain was numbed by its finality. This gentle man, who had been a permanent part of her life, was irrevocably gone. Yvonne joined her briefly but was too overcome by grief to remain. Time passed, and the shadows lengthen into evening. She had no idea how long she had been sitting there. She dozed off but was roused by a commotion in the living room. She heard her father's voice and went to the door.

Dodger was bent over his mother, who hadn't moved from the sofa since collapsing there some hours before. Her eyes were closed. Dodger was shaking her by the shoulders and entreating her. "Mamma, Mamma, wake up. It's Jack. Please Mamma, wake up." But there was no response from Ann, who remained completely comatose. "Get the doctor back," Dodger called to his sister.

While they waited for the doctor, Dodger continued to shake his mother intermittently, gently begging her to respond. But there was no response. When the doctor arrived, he examined Ann, and then put a hand on Dodger's shoulder. "There's no hope," he said. "Don't make immediate plans for Mr. Price. This will be a double funeral."

And so it was. Ann Price died of a broken heart at the age of eighty just after midnight on Tuesday, 24th September. Both bodies were laid out side by side in the Eighth Avenue house they had occupied for the last years of their lives, and it was from here that the funeral cortege left two days later for Payneham Cemetery where they were interred in the same grave as their daughter, Babs. Next day, the following obituary appeared in the newspaper. It made no mention of Tom's successful career as a businessman and impresario. It did refer to Ann's charitable work and ended rather bizarrely with an account of her eccentric habit of meeting and greeting famous aviators of the day.

The remains of Mr. & Mrs. T. J. Price, of Eighth Avenue, St Peters, who died within a day of each other, were buried at Payneham Cemetery yesterday. Grief, following the collapse of her husband a few hours earlier of a heart attack, is believed to have hastened the end of Mrs. Price, who was aged 80. At the request of Mr. & Mrs. Price, the burial service was not denominational. It was conducted by Miss A. Lennon, who is the secretary of the Rationalist Association in South Australia. During the service, believed to be the 1st of its kind held in this State, Miss Lennon eulogised the services rendered by Mr. & Mrs. Price, who were supporters of a free-thought movement. Mrs. Price, who was born in Aberdeen, Scotland, collected much money for charity during the war. She placed one of the first bricks in position when the Broken Hill Town Hall was built. One of the chief interests of Mrs. Price in recent years was to shake hands with leading aviators. She had met James Melrose, Campbell Black & Scott, Sir Kingsford Smith, Sir Keith & the late Sir Ross Smith & Amy Johnson. She had received letters from the mother of the noted airwoman. Mr. Price, who was born at Burra, collapsed on returning from a shopping expedition with his wife and daughter on Monday. His wife became ill seven hours later and died without regaining consciousness. She was unable to speak to a son, who had arrived for his father's funeral. *(Barrier Miner, Thursday 26 September 1935)*[16]

Some years before his death, a more considered appreciation of Tom's life had appeared in *The Barrier Miner.*

We were privileged within the last few weeks to publish a short article and photo of Mr Frank Price of Broken Hill. In this week's article it is our pleasure to show our readers the smiling features of his elder brother Tom, who looks after the Adelaide end of the business of T. J. Price.

Mr Price was born at the Burra in 1860 and in his boyhood attended St. Peter's and Prince Alfred Colleges. Prior to going to Adelaide for his education, Mr. Price recalls many incidents of life at the old copper mines of the Burra where his father, Captain W. H. Price, was employed as a mining engineer in the smelters. The headmaster of St. Peter's during his sojourn in that institution was Canon (afterwards Archdeacon) Farr, while Mr. John Hartley was in charge of the Prince Alfred College of Learning.

At leaving Prince Alfred College, Mr. Price joined the South Australian Education Department as a pupil teacher, afterwards graduating as a headmaster, and as such was in charge of nearly all the model schools in Adelaide and the leading country centres.

Recognising that the scope for advancement in the government service was very limited, Mr. Price in 1891 relinquished his position in the Department and came to Broken Hill to commence in business on his own account. After enduring the usual vicissitudes of Barrier

[16] *The Barrier Miner,* Thursday, 26 September, 1935, p.4

life, he decided that in opening as a wholesale produce merchant there would provide greater opportunity of enjoying life to the fullest, and in 1920 went to Adelaide, where he is now permanently residing, attending to the Adelaide end of the business and the junior partner, Mr. Frank Price, looking after the Broken Hill end.

Mr. Price's father will be well remembered as one of the early managers of the old Potoal, Rising Sun, and South Extended Mines. He, prior to that time, was manager of the Talisker Silver Lead mine near Cape Jervios, and the Aclare in the Adelaide Hills near Callington.

During the early part of his sojourn on the Barrier, Mr. Tom Price was the foremost figure in the amateur theatre world, and it was to his credit that a considerable amount of financial assistance was provided to necessitous causes particularly during industrial depression. From this source the Price sisters received their early theatrical training which culminated in their joining the Rickards Circuit in tours of Australia, New Zealand and the Far East. Viola Price was billed as the first and only lady conjurer of Australia and in this capacity toured Australia, New Zealand and Tasmania. She was afterwards joined by her sister Lillian (sic) and subsequently they both toured the East as the Price Sisters, dancers and entertainers.

Nowadays, Mr. Price is always pleased to see old Barrierites on their visits to Adelaide, and has the latest sample of theatrical witticisms for the telling. His histrionic powers are by no means to be despised, and if anyone desires a short history of the Australian stage, he cannot do better than to seek out our subject at his offices in the East End Market. *(The Barrier Miner, Thursday 2 August 1928)*[17]

This rosy portrait is full of inaccuracies, exaggerations, and overstatements. He was never a headmaster, and was certainly never in charge of "nearly all the model schools in Adelaide." It is chiefly of interest for what it does not say—that he left the profession under a cloud

---

[17] *The Barrier Miner* Thursday, 2 August 1928

as a relatively junior country teacher after kidnapping a teenage girl and a high-profile trial following her brother's attempt to murder him. Also airbrushed out of the picture is the fact that he took up with his father's common-law wife, probably fathered at least one child with her, and was involved in a shootout with her estranged husband.

The deaths and double funerals of Tom and Ann had one positive outcome: it brought about a reconciliation of sorts between Violet and Dodger, although they never lived again as husband and wife. In the wake of Tom's death, Dodger threw himself into keeping both ends of the business afloat. He installed a manager to control the buying and dispatching of goods at the East End market, and shuttled constantly between the house in St. Peters in Adelaide and the Old House in Broken Hill. Death notices for Tom and Ann named him as Mr Frank Price of Broken Hill where he spent the bulk of his time. Violet and her daughters continued to reside in the cottage in Brighton Road for several years, returning to, and re-establishing themselves, in the Old House at the end of the decade.

Almost as soon as Australia had struggled out of the most severe depression in its short history, the dogs of war began to bay once more in Europe. Despite their proximity to Asia, most eyes were on Europe. They were soon to learn that this far-sighted view was woefully short-sighted. However, the mood was far different from that which preceded the Great War. "Please God, not again," muttered those who had seen that war at first hand. In 1914, country boys had jumped on their farm horses and piled into troop ships, to take part in the "glorious adventure." None of the horses returned. At the end of the campaign, the Australians, who were under the command of the British, were ordered to surrender their horses. To spare the animals from ending up in a glue factory in England, or pulling bread carts around London, the Australians shot them. One in five of the 400,000 men who went to war failed to return. Many of those who did come back were never the same again, having been wounded, gassed, taken prisoner or blown up.

While Dodger was of serviceable age during the First World War, he was too busy building his business with Uncle Tom to even contemplate enlisting. Leave it to those who had nothing better to do than shoot at Huns and Turks at the behest of the British. By the start of the Second, he was far too old, and far too busy still. Since Tom's death, the burden of running both ends of the business had become increasingly stressful. Although the inclination had never died, it probably also left him with too little time or energy to indulge in chasing skirts.

On the morning of 1 July, 1941, while the thoughts of many were with their loved ones serving abroad, Jack's were firmly rooted on the busy day ahead. He shaved with the heirloom, cut-throat razor, inherited by Tom from William Henry, and then passed on to Dodger. He kept it as sharp as a gurkha's kris, honing the blade each morning with a heavy leather strop. Then he dressed in the outfit he had laid out the previous evening. As he and Violet no longer shared a room, and hadn't done so for years, he was able to use the spare bed in his room for laying out his clothes. He tugged at his tie in the dresser mirror, slipped his silver cigarette case into the inside pocket of his jacked, and adjusted his gold watch and fob.

Violet was in the kitchen shoving bits of redwood into the Aga range. It had been a cold night, below freezing judging by the way the frost crackled on the roof as the sun came up.

"There's fresh tea in the pot," she said, although she did not offer to pour him a cup. "Jane just made it."

"No time," he said. "I'll get something in town."

"Will you be home for lunch?" He often took an hour out of his day to come home for lunch, and when this happened, she had to alert the girl.

"Not today. I have a delivery to make out the south, then I have to put the car in to have a new set of tyres fitted. They're overdue, and I'll need the car in good nick for the run to Adelaide tomorrow." These were the last words to pass between them. Plucking a small posy of flowers from a vase on the kitchen sideboard, he headed for the garage.

It was cold, definitely the coldest morning of the year, and the temperature continued to dip as the sun came up. As he left the house, a thin drizzle began to fall. All in all, it was a miserable day, a good one to stay indoors, which is what he planned to do once he had made a couple of urgent deliveries and had the car seen to. Minty followed him to the garage, and, ignoring the drizzle, jumped onto the running board after Jack had climbed into the car, arranged the flowers in the vase that sat on the console beside the driver's seat, and pulled the door shut. The engine faltered as he pulled on the starter, but eventually caught. He let it idle until it began to purr. "Telling me it's ready," he said to himself. He reversed the car out of the garage and pulled onto the road. Railway Town was beginning to wake up. Several miners on day shift, crib bags clipped to carriers, pedalled slowly toward the mine shafts that stood like sentinels dividing South Broken Hill from the rest of the town. The milko had already completed his round, the only evidence of his passage being the occasional pile of steaming horse dung on the side of the road. Several times, he felt the car slide on the wet tarmac. It was definitely time to have new tyres fitted. He would attend to that once he had completed his morning deliveries.

Rounding the bend at the top of Wills Street, Dodger crossed the tracks separating Railway Town from the rest of the city, turned left and pulled up at a goods siding where trucks and other vehicles sat waiting to receive the produce being unloaded from the overnight goods train from Adelaide. One of the trucks still carried the name T. J. Price, Fruit and Vegetable Merchant on the driver's door. Two men were unloading crates of fruit and sacks of potatoes and onions. The burly one, bent double under the weight of the sack of potatoes, dropped his load onto the flatbed tray of the truck and straightened up, grappling hook in hand.

"G'day, Boss," he said.

"Morning Len," Dodger replied to his foreman. "Is the consignment all correct?"

"We're missing a crate of apples. That's about it, as far as I can see."

"I'll follow up in Adelaide tomorrow. Mark it on the delivery note and leave it at the warehouse. I'll pick it up later on this afternoon."

Len and his offsider loaded the Chrysler with boxes of produce that had to be delivered to several stores in Railway Town and South Broken Hill that required the goods at opening time. Once the car had been loaded, Dodger retraced his route down Wills Street. He deposited several boxes by the delivery door at the rear of the Service Stores before turning left into Gypsum Street. Passing the Hillside Hotel, he changed gears to accelerate over the low rise that preceded the steeper climb up

South Road Hill. As he crested the rise and began the descent toward the line of lode the car picked up speed and plunged down the hill. Alarmed, he stepped on the brake, causing the car to slew sideways on the wet road. As the car began to roll, he flung the door open and attempted to leap out, but only made it halfway before the car rolled onto its side, crushing him between the door and the body of the car. The car came to rest on its side against a wire fence, the horn playing a monotonous and mournful elegy as the spinning wheels slowed, and then stopped.

The next day, the morning newspaper, *The Barrier Daily Truth*, carried the following account of the accident.

Mr. Frank "Dodger" Price (62) of 32 Ryan St., was killed instantly yesterday when the car which he was driving in Gypsum St. swerved on the road and turned on its side. Mr. Price was well known in the city, for many years having been a wholesale fruiterer. There were no witnesses of the accident and Mr. Price was the only person in the car, a Chrysler sedan. The police theory of the accident is that Mr. Price met his death when making a desperate effort to jump from the car as it was about to turn over on its side. The injuries through which Mr. Price died instantly, revealed by the post mortem examination conducted yesterday by the Government Medical Officer, Dr W. E. George, support this theory. The post mortem examination revealed nine broken ribs, punctured lungs, and damaged vertebrae. It is believed that when Mr. Price saw that the car was about to turn over he opened the door on the driver's side and attempted to jump clear, but was only halfway out of the door when the car turned on its side, closing the door on him. The accident happened at about 9 a. m. yesterday morning at a spot about 25 yards south of the railway line that crossed the extension of Gypsum St. into the Zinc Corporation. Marks on the surface of the road indicated that the car swerved suddenly to the left and was almost on its side as it left the bitumen, coming to rest on its side against a wire rope fence. It was raining lightly at the time and the road was wet, this apparently contributing to the cause of the car skidding. Mr. Price was on his way to South Broken Hill to deliver fruit and vegetables, which he had taken delivery of at the Railway Town railway station.

Frank Stranley Edes, of 205 Mercury St., was the first on the scene. He saw the car lying on its side when he reached the top of South Hill when he was going to the city from the South. Soon after he reached the scene, several motorists arrived. The ambulance, which was at the South Mine, was summoned and also Dr George, who pronounced life extinct and the body was taken to the Morgue. An inquest will be held at the Court House this morning at 10 a. m. *(Barrier Daily Truth, 2 July 1941)*[18]

A report in the rival afternoon newspaper, *The Barrier Miner*, indicated that Dodger was formally identified by a Constable R. Ashton. The newspaper also speculated on the whereabouts of Mintie, Dodger's constant companion. There was no sign of the dog at the accident scene or in the vicinity: no mangled body, no black-and-white terrier sitting patiently by its master waiting for him to wake up. The little creature had vanished and was never seen again.

At the morgue, after the post-mortem examination had been carried out, the body was released to the funeral directors Fred J. Potter and Son who prepared it for burial. Dodger then made his last trip back to 32 Ryan Street, where he was laid out in the same room as his father, William Henry, after his death in 1891. The funeral took place the following morning. Bearers included members of Violet's family. No other details of the funeral or burial exist, apart the fact that he was interred in a plot in the Church of England section of the cemetery. While Dodger's atheism was neither as deep-rooted nor as informed by reading and thought as were his father's and Uncle Tom's, he was not tempted to stray into the path of Christianity. Allowing his remains to be interred into the consecrated ground of the Church of England was an act of charity that Violet's own church refused. Death notices made no mention of whether there was a graveside oration, and it must be assumed that there was none.

There was one occasion when Bet spoke to her son of her father's death. It was just before his eleventh birthday. While secreting in her wardrobe

---

[18] *The Barrier Daily Truth*, 2 July 1941, p.2

the gifts she had bought for his birthday, she came across a long-forgotten box of her father's possessions. She had just removed a battered and stained silver cigarette case, when he opened the bedroom door, no doubt hoping to catch her in the act of hiding the gifts.

"What's that?" he asked.

"Well, it isn't one of your presents," she replied, rather tersely. Then, more gently, "My father was carrying this when he was killed."

"Who killed him?'

"No one killed him. His car rolled over on South Hill early one morning."

"Are you sad, Mum?"

The possibility had never occurred to her. She was surprised to catch herself nodding.

"Can I see it?"

She handed him the case. He rubbed a forefinger across the stains. "Is that his blood? I bet it is." Of course, for an eleven-year-old it *had* to be blood. She took the case from him and returned it to the box that also contained the cuff links he had had been wearing on that inhospitable morning.

It was Violet who had said out of the blue one evening as they sat by the fire a week after the funeral, "Yes, but what about the fob?" The fob! The gold watch of which he took such fastidious care, winding it each morning and adjusting its time by the grandfather clock in the corner of the lounge. At the time, none of the family had given a thought to the fob. Somewhere between the death site and the morgue it, like the dog, had disappeared without trace.

"What are you thinking about, Mum?"

"The morgue."

"What's that?"

He was too young to be hearing this, but she said it anyway. "I had to identify his body. The newspapers said it was some police officer or other, but it was me. After they broke the news, they made me get dressed and dragged me off to do the identification. I was Sensible Betty. Mother and Yvonne were in no state." She shook herself. "Anyway, isn't it time for you to get yourself off to footie practice?

Chapter 19
No Regrets

Less than an hour after her husband has put Bet and the children on the train, the excitement of the adventure has evaporated, and the whining begins. "Are we nearly there yet?" Little Paul wants to know.

"No, not yet. We have a long way to go. Now play with your cars." She had splurged: two new books for David, her elder son, and a miniature car set for her younger. But he is already bored.

"Don't want to. I already played with them."

David looks up from his book. "How long, Mum?" A slightly more mature request, but no easier to deal with.

"I'm not sure," she says. She knows very well: another eight interminable hours at the very least to Parkes. Longer, if there are hold-ups, break-downs or other delays.

"I've finished my book."

"Read your other one."

"No, I want to save it up." (Another hopeful sign of maturity.)

"Get your pencils and write a story."

"The train's too bumpy."

He is right. The train sways and rattles across the plain.

"Look out of the window. You might see a kangaroo?"

"Where's the kangaroo?" demands Little Paul, scrambling onto the seat. "Want to see the kangaroo."

"I said might. You *might* see one."

But there are no kangaroos. Just unrelieved monotony: red earth punctuated by scrubby acacias and occasional evidence of human habitation in the form of a tin shed, or a windmill. When three emus appear from nowhere and pace the train, before wheeling off into the scrub, she says nothing. The elderly woman sitting on the other side of the carriage gives her a sympathetic glance and a wry smile. Been there, done that, is written all over her face. Yes, her stoicism is nothing short of heroic, but there will be no medals at the end of this campaign. When

Babs called with the news, it was clear she would have to make the trip. Yvonne offered to look after the boys. The trip would have been much more manageable with only the girl to care for, but she was not leaving the boys to run wild at the Old House.

When the train pulls into Menindee, the younger boy bounces excitedly on his seat, crying out, "We're there, we're there." This wakes the girl who has been sleeping with her head in her mother's lap.

"We're not," she says sharply. "Now look what you've done." She lifts the girl into her lap and offers her a bottle.

"Can we go for a walk along the platform?" asks David.

"Absolutely not. The train only stops for a short while. If you get left behind, it won't come back to get you. Then what would you do? Go and live on the river with the aborigines?"

The carriage begins to fill up. Four jackaroos occupy the seats in front of them. Little Paul blinks at them through his glasses. One of the jackaroos winks at Paul. "Got your hands full there, love," he says to her. She acknowledges his comment with a smile.

"Goin' all the way to Sydney?"

"Newcastle."

"Long trip."

When the train pulls out of Menindee, the conductor comes through and announces that the dining car is open. The jackaroos immediately leave their seats and make their way back through the train.

"I'm hungry," says David.

Thinking that an excursion along the train will distract the boys, she straps the girl into her stroller and says, "Let's go along to the dining car." She could do with a mug of tea. She hands David a brown paper bag containing egg sandwiches. "Can you carry these for me?"

By the time they get to the dining car, the jackaroos are already on their second can of West End. She settles the children at a table away from the men, orders a cup of tea and hands each boy a sandwich.

"Look," says David, "A kangaroo." Sure enough, a big red is bounding along, pacing the train, before peeling off into a rise of sand dunes. Paul swivels to face the window, but the big red has already disappeared behind the dunes. "I didn't see it," he cries. "Make it come back." His lip quivers and he drops his sandwich.

"Now look what you've done," she says. The cook brings her tea. "Sorry," she says, pointing to the mess on the floor.

"No worries, love. I'll clean it up in a minute." He distributes to the jackaroos plates of steak, eggs and chips, along with more beers. The steak smells delicious. She hands Paul another sandwich. He crams it into his mouth and is promptly sick. She sighs and cleans him up. The day, which had begun with little promise, is not improving.

Back in their seats, the sun strikes through the glass, heating the carriage. Drowsy, the children nod off. At last she has a little time to herself. Hour after hour, mile after endless mile, the train rattles and rolls through a landscape of spinifex, red sand dunes and the occasional line of hills. The monotony is broken by brief stops at railway sidings with incomprehensible, alien names: Kinalung, Kaleentha Loop, Beilpaiah, Matakana, Euabalong West. Almost imperceptibly, the desert scrub gives way to grazing pastures and fields of wheat.

She thinks what her life would have been like if she had allowed herself to follow her heart rather than her head. Her most persistent suitor had been voted Broken Hill's most eligible bachelor by the other barmaids at the Royal Exchange Hotel. "That Reg Livesley," they would say. Dashing, with a touch of the arrogance that often accompanied impossibly good looks. She was the one his wandering eye had lit upon. When he was shipped off to the war, they kept up a constant correspondence—as constant as was possible under the circumstances. They drew closer through the correspondence. Occasionally, he would enclose a small black and white photograph— "snaps" they were called back then. One day, a letter arrived informing her that he was on his way home. It also contained a proposal of marriage. In a letter that arrived a week later, he broke the news that the wedding (to which she had not yet agreed) would have to wait. The troop ship he was on had been diverted to Japan where he and his fellow soldiers would meld with the Allied Forces, bringing an end to the war in the Pacific. The final letter she received contained a snapshot of Reg crouching on the scorched earth of Hiroshima. It had been taken shortly after the city had been devastated by the atom bomb that finally prompted the Emperor to capitulate. Bronzed, bare chested and dressed only in slouch hat, khaki shorts and boots, he looked back over this shoulder at the camera with an expression of insouciance and smugness. He might well have been personally responsible for bringing the Pacific War to an end.

They never did marry. On his return, while declaring eternal love, he admitted that there would be other women in his life. Devastated, she coldly informed him that this was not good enough for her. Closing her ears to his entreaties, she turned and walked out of his life. However, like her mother, she could not bring herself to destroy the wartime letters and photographs. Half a decade would pass before she finally married a man eleven years her senior on 15 January 1949.

As dusk descends, and after interminable stops, the Silver City Comet draws into the Central West township of Parkes, its silver shell mottled by red dust. It has arrived at this drab outpost from beyond the back of beyond—not quite as alien as a silver spaceship from Mars, but not far off. It is an hour at least before the train on the opposite platform is due to pull them through the night over the Blue Mountains, and down into the conurbation on the coast: an urban growth that crawls malignantly away from the eastern seaboard. A porter trundles their suitcases across the platform to the connecting train, one of an earlier generation from the sadly misnamed Comet. The boys, fascinated by the monstrous, hissing steam engine at the head of the train, want to follow the porter, but she herds them into the café where they sit, tired and fractious, on metal chairs and refuse the last of the egg sandwiches. Paul has spotted the Choc-ice advertisement on the wall behind the counter and, diminutive as he is, is more than capable of causing massive disruption to the microcosmic café if one is not delivered to him instantly. Not a massive drinker, all she craves at that moment is an ice-cold beer in the bar next door. Unfortunately, it lacks a ladies' lounge and the children would not have been admitted if it did. She rifles through her purse and hands David a ten-shilling note. "Don't drop the change," she says.

She has taken a sleeping car for the overnight leg of the journey, an extravagance, she knows, but spending the night slumped on cracked leather seats in an economy carriage is out of the question. Thrilled at the prospect of adventure, the boys scramble like monkeys up the detachable wooden ladder and claim the top bunk. She and the girl will share the bottom bunk. All three children are fast asleep before the train hisses and grunts its way into the night.

Despite her exhaustion, she sleeps fitfully, abandoning sleep altogether as dawn breaks and the train descends onto the Sydney Plain. The children continue to sleep as the conductor brings her an industrial-strength mug of sweet tea and a Scotch finger biscuit. After chugging through incomprehensible miles of identical brick bungalows, the trip terminates at the Central Railway Station, a cold, cavernous, alien place. On the platform, the children, still groggy with sleep, cling to her like chicks. Another cafeteria and another lengthy wait for the Newcastle Flyer. She fetches plates of bacon, eggs and toast for herself and the boys. Paul pushes his plate away. "This egg is raw," he says.

"Eat it," she hisses at him. He shovels several spoonfuls into his mouth then promptly regurgitates the lot onto the table as well as himself. "This is all I need." She turns to her elder son. "Look after your sister." Then she drags the younger one off to the washroom to clean him up. When she dumps him onto the toilet bowl he complains, "But I don't want to go.'

"You'll sit there until you do. If you don't get a move on, I'll leave you here."

The Newcastle Flyer is silver and sleek, modern after the steam train. Exhausted, she nods off, the girl still in her arms, then wakes with a start and gazes at the thickly wooded bushland and inky inlets. Finally, a day and a half after their departure, they arrive at their destination, are greeted by Babs and Arch and driven to a solid, suburban brick house that will be their temporary home for the next two weeks.

The asylum was constructed on the edge of Lake Macquarie, the largest saltwater lake in the Southern Hemisphere. It was officially opened in 1909 to relieve pressure on the overcrowded Sydney lunatic asylums. Over half a century later, when the Price sisters had their mother committed, it held over 1,000 inmates. On the day of their first visit, the Lunatic Asylum Morisset, looks more like a retirement village than an institution for the criminally insane. The expansive lawns are dotted with family groups. The benign sun and light breeze set the water sparking. While Babs disappears into a sandstone building on the edge of the lawns, Bet keeps an eye on the children. A small wallaby limps around on the grass near a line of trees totally unafraid of the proximity of humans. Paul spies the wallaby, and runs toward it, but as he approaches, it hops unhurriedly away, keeping just out of his reach. Arch retrieves a picnic hamper, tartan rug and folding chairs from the trunk of his car. He spreads the rug on the grass to mark their territory and then reclines on the grass.

Bet is shocked at the wasted, fragile figure on Babs's arm. "Oh, what have they done to you, Mother?" she whispers to herself. She hastens across the lawn, takes her mother's other arm and pats her on the hand. "It's Bet and the children, Mother, come all the way to see you," says Babs brightly Reaching the rug, they get Violet settled on a chair. She sits passively with her hands folded in her lap and looks confused when the boys are summoned to give her a kiss. "I don't want to kiss her. She smells," says Paul, his mantra from the days when she lived with them. "She doesn't remember us," says David, echoing something his cousin had once said.

Turning away, she helps Babs unpack the hamper. As always, there's enough food for a football team: curried egg sandwiches for the adults, and Vegemite for the children, cold meats, tomatoes, a block of cheddar cheese in plastic wrap, biscuits, a custard tart, a chocolate cake, a bottle of cordial, and a thermos of tea. The boys comply with her second directive to kiss their grandmother, then, a sandwich in one hand and a chocolate biscuit in the other, run off to see if they can interest the wallaby in Vegemite. Too soon, they return to the rug and begin whining to leave. The plate Bet has loaded with food sits untouched on her mother's lap. She doesn't speak, but nods from time to time when spoken to. And then visiting hour is over and it's time to return her to the asylum. "Can you keep an eye on the boys, please, Arch?" she says to her brother-in-law. "Don't let them go near the water." She and Babs shepherd their mother back to the building. Over the next week, and a half she, Babs and the girl make three more trips to visit Violet. The boys are left in Newcastle in the care of their considerably older cousin. She makes her last visit two days before they are due to return to Broken Hill.

After they are settled on the train, her son asks to her, "Doesn't Aunty Babs love us anymore?"

"Of course. Why do you say that?"

"I hear what she said to you are the station.'

"What was that?"

"She told you not to come back."

Unaccountably, she leans across the seat and squeezes him to her. "She was talking about something else."

When the trunk call comes, neither the call nor the rush of conflicting emotions it triggers, are unexpected. She has to admit that the profound sadness is accompanied by a sense of relief. Guilt is also a constant presence. As Violet's condition worsened, the rambling Old House with its many exits and dangerous nooks no longer offered the sanctuary she needed. Her own house was smaller and more secure, so she agreed to take her mother. Violet's condition continued to deteriorate, and she soon realized that this had been a mistake. It was like adding a fourth child to the family, and one who was more difficult to manage than the other three. Violet refused to cooperate. She would neither be bullied nor coaxed. Getting her to eat, never an easy chore, became next to impossible, and cajoling her into the bath could take an hour or more. Babs arrived from Newcastle with a solution. Snapshots and the brochure presented a benign portrait of the place with lawns sloping gently to the water and extensive gardens. There was even a swimming pool. What the brochure did not show were the rooms where electro-convulsive shock treatment was standard practice, not only for the criminally insane, but throughout the hospital. Only later did Morisset Hospital become notorious for the extremity of its treatment measures, including the use of powerful tranquilizing drugs. At the time, the only thing that gave her pause was the name of the place: The Lunatic Asylum Morisset. But Mother isn't a lunatic, she said to herself. To Babs she said nothing.

On Sunday morning, she calls her elder son as he is about to ride off to early Mass. She stuffs an envelope containing a one-pound note into his pocket. "Find Father in the sacristy and give him this," she says. On the front of the envelope, she has written "Dear Father Leonard, Please have mass said for Violet Price (nee O'Keeffe) late of 32 Ryan Street Railway Town."

Later that morning, she removes from the bedroom wardrobe the few pathetic threads that were left hanging in the wardrobe when Violet had been bundled off to the asylum. They can go to St. Vincent de Paul, or the Salvos, if they take such things. If they don't, the clothes can be consigned to the backyard incinerator.

She is more concerned with what to do with the suitcase. She rummages among the shoe boxes at the bottom of the wardrobe and hauls it out. Being made of leather, it remains sturdy, despite the battering it has taken over the years.

In a moment of lucidity, Violet had insisted that it be left behind. "There are... there are... things in there," she said, before lapsing back into a mindless present. In the months since her death, Violet's little suitcase had languished in the wardrobe that was pushed up again the bedroom wall, the bedroom that is now occupied by her daughter.

In the kitchen, she fiddles with the clasps, and finally resorts to a sturdy carving knife to spring them open. She has no idea what to expect. Forgotten trinkets? Bottles of her favourite scent, purchased in bulk to see her out? The first thing she comes across delights her - a manila envelope crammed with dozens of photographs. Her beloved Uncle Tom and Ann in their garden on Ann's 80th birthday; a second of Ann on the same day, resplendent in a satin gown sitting on the verandah of their home, a cake with 80 candles in her lap; her parents, Yon and Aunt Lil on the deck of the ship that is to carry Lil back to Walter in England; a bare-chested Dodger flexing his muscles like a showground strongman; a dashing Walter in army uniform and Lil with a fox fur draped around her shoulders; three family portraits, one of Tom, Ann, Lil, and Babs, one of Tom and Dodger, and one of Murray, Don and Lil. There are sheaves of postcards and letters as well as newspaper cutting. The bulk of the postcards and letters are from Dodger. The newspaper cuttings also concern Dodger. Then, at the bottom of the case, an envelope containing a letter that stuns her—a wrenching message to her mother from a David Steinberg in which he lays bare his broken heart. The revelation of a rival for Dodger comes as a shock. That Violet kept the letter all these years despite Steinberg's instruction to destroy it is telling, as is the fact that she left the letter for her daughter to find. She returns everything to the suitcase apart from the newspaper cuttings, and sorts these into two piles.

The larger pile consists of reports on Dodger's trial. After all these years, they still have the power to wound. The smaller pile contains accounts of his death and funeral along with an earlier complimentary story about his achievements and contributions to Broken Hill life.

Leaving the suitcase on the table, she returns to the bedroom, and retrieves from the wardrobe a shoebox containing her own more modest collection of snapshots, letters and postcards. Back in the kitchen, she sorts through these, putting to one side the benign items—letters from an adolescent pen-pal in Paris, photos of her children and nephews in the garden of the Old House, and newspaper cuttings of social events in which she had been involved. To the newspaper accounts of Dodger's trial, she adds the letters and photos that had arrived during the war. Only one item is saved—a snapshot of a digger crouching in the dust and ashes of Hiroshima.

Then she crosses to the Aga and consigns the incriminating newspaper cuttings, letters and photos to the fire, prodding them with a poker until they are bits of black ash. Satisfied that she has expunged all evidence of her father's shame, she makes a pot of tea and returns to the kitchen table. Little could she know that many years hence digital versions of the evidence she had so meticulously destroyed would be retrievable in minutes with a few quick finger strokes.

Over a cup of tea, she re-reads the cuttings she has saved from the fire. The rosy newspaper appreciation piece creates a portrait of the father she wanted to remember, although she carried in her heart the scars that had been carved there by the scandal he had wreaked upon the family. As a cyclist, he proved "one of the best the Barrier has ever produced." He stood out as a businessman, and managed a wholesale fruit and vegetable concern that "monopolized the fruit market of Broken Hill." The article concludes with his love of fine fast cars, and his assertion that the "Chrysler" was the finest vehicle on the road. His beloved Chrysler, she thinks, the possession that brought him to an untimely end.

The photo accompanying the piece shows a middle-aged man with a vigorous head of hair, high forehead, penetrating eyes and a wry smile. Justice of the Peace in two states, he was every bit the upright community leader before the fall.

Putting the cutting aside she recalls, not Dodger's cruelty to Violet, but his kindness in later years. Living out his life as an apology. She remembers one incident in particular. Babs, Arch and the children had travelled from Newcastle to spend Christmas at the Old House. She had vacated her own large bedroom to accommodate them. One evening before dinner, his granddaughter Patsy took him by the hand. "Come, Grandpa," she said. "It's time to say our prayers." Patsy and her little brother Frank were being raised as Catholics by their devout father. Her and Yvonne's offspring would also be raised as Catholics although their own husbands were decidedly less than devout. Her own wedding day was jeopardized by an angry altercation between the officiating priest and her husband-to-be who refused to sign an undertaking that their children would be raised within the Church. "I will allow it even though it's a lot of hooey," Bill had told the priest. "But I will not sign the paper. If my word isn't good enough for you, then you can forget the wedding."

Although Dodger, the lukewarm infidel, had never uttered a prayer in his life, he obediently bent his head, clasped his hands, and muttered meaningless phrases as his granddaughter chanted her way through the Lord's Prayer.

Her own path into the One, Holy and Apostolic Church had not been smooth. One day, after morning prayers at the school in Glenelg, Sister Mary Margaret summoned her to the office. "Your family is heathen," she said without so much as a preamble, or a hint of Christian compassion. "Heathen?" she asked. "Infidels, every one of them. All except your dear mother. You are so fortunate, my child. You were raised a heathen, but the good Lord intervened. You mother was brought back to the Church, and as a result the Church accepted you. You and your sisters were saved by the grace of Our Lord Jesus Christ."

Her family members were infidels? Grandma? Uncle Tom? Uncle William? Her father? Well, her father had been called lots of things, particularly after he had brought shame upon the family. But Uncle William believed in God.

Sister Mary Margaret had tilted her head and given her a pitying smile: one that smelt trouble. "Do you know what an infidel is, my child?" She shook her head. It rang in her ears like a sentence of death. Worse than cancer. An infidel, she learned, was someone who has no religion. The headmistress spoke in a kindly voice, but her double chin trembling beneath her veil. And did she know what happens to people who had no religion? She had no idea, but suspected she was about to find out. She wasn't wrong. They would never get to Heaven, she learned. Far worse, they would go to Hell, where they would burn for eternity. She knew better than to raise the issue of Uncle William and his religion. He had it tattooed on his wrist. Would a simple tattoo save her from damnation? She suspected that Uncle William's brand of religion differed from Sister Mary Margaret's brand. A non-Catholic brand, and therefore a corrupted version of Christianity. Although she and her sister had been at the Catholic school for less than a year, they'd had it drummed into them. There was only one true form of Christianity, and that was Catholicism. All the rest were fake.

She survives her husband by seventeen years, living a largely solitary life, tending her beloved garden and keeping a watchful eye out for the one small pleasure that would mark this day as having been worth living: a visit from the grandchildren, bringing back to life a potted plant her neighbour had thought beyond rescue, a modest vermouth and soda at sunset, signs that the recalcitrant potted bay tree had survived transplantation to the bottom of the garden. "Every day brings one good thing," she would tell her neighbour over a cup of tea. "Sometimes even more than one."

After the shock of the diagnosis, her practical side takes over and she sets about getting her affairs in order. She makes lists. She buys a roll of masking tape and a marking pen. Armed with these, she traverses the house bequeathing fading framed replicas of iconic paintings, silver-plated chafing dishes and bits of furniture to those offspring and relatives she thought might appreciate or have use for her possessions. First names suffice—there is no ambiguity in her mind as to the intended recipients, and so there should be none in theirs.

The possession she agonizes over most is the battered antique suitcase. While its contents have next to no monetary value, and are of no practical use to anyone, to her its sentimental value is worth more than all of her other possessions combined. Lifting the lid on the suitcase, she goes through the contents one last time: the bundle of letters and postcards secured with twine with which her father had wooed and eventually won her mother; Uncle Tom's journal; photographs, some dating back a century, the stiff poses and unsmiling faces demanded by the technology of the time concealing the loves, desires, passions, crimes and misdemeanours of those whose images the camera had captured. Common sense tells her to consign the contents of the suitcase to the kitchen trash can. That is surely where they will end up when the time comes for her children to dispose of her possessions. But she can't bring herself to commit an act of such brutality. To discard photos of her beloved grandmother and Uncle Tom was beyond her. Lost in thought, she sits for a long while clutching the 80th birthday snap in her crippled hands, remembers Uncle Tom, schoolteacher, entrepreneur, alleged kidnapper, promoter of the arts, painter, photographer, philanthropist, secularist, unwitting bigamist, half-brother, then step-father, to her father and aunts. And her grandmother, a bundle of contradictions—tough, tender, diminutive, dismissive of convention, pipe-smoking, and gun-toting. The old lady could not have been more different from her, the most timid and conventional of people. She had craved the anonymity of respectability. Her grandmother had no truck with conventional morality, which she saw as middle-class hypocrisy. Despite their very different natures, she adored Uncle Tom and Ann. No, she would not, could not, consign them to the dustbin.

There is no doubt that she had been born into an exceptional family. While intensely proud of them and their achievements, she regrets that she had not been raised in a more conventional one. Despite her grandfather's gifts and talents, his role in developing the Australian mining industry, and his lifelong involvement in the Secular Society, accounts of his exploits were scant. No books had ever been written about him. From what she had learned about him from Ann, he had no interest in self-promotion. Her grandmother, aunts and uncles had devoted themselves to education and the arts: specifically, to photography, painting, writing, singing, dancing, conjuring and other vaudeville entertainments. Apart from Babs and Lil, none rose to public prominence, and all that remained of their artistic and literary output was a single volume of Uncle Tom's journals: "*Special Lessons* by Thos. J. Price" inscribed in copperplate on the opening page. Lifting it off the table, she cautiously thumbs through the brittle pages, some of which had come adrift. She struggles to decipher Tom's copperplate hand, his words penned in fading black ink ending in extravagant whirls and curlicues. The contents reflect the extraordinary range of Tom's interests: poems, ranging from sonnets and longer poetic forms to doggerel and limericks; plays, finished and unfinished; the table of contents for a book provisionally entitled "The Ocean"—the different oceans of the world, their physical features, waves, tides, winds, and value to humanity; an essay on how the body is nourished; the Latin derivations of key terms such as mastication, being provided in a glossary; a treatise on the crocodile; another on the human heart, this accompanied by the only piece of artwork in the journal—a cross-sectional pen and ink illustration of the human heart. She pauses a long while on this page which demonstrates his creditable if not exemplary draughtsmanship, and regrets that none of his other journals, nor any of his or Ann's artwork survived. "There is nothing quite so disappointing as a great unrealized potential," she had once heard it said. Could this epithet be applied to her forebears? Had they been overlooked by those who mattered for refusing to acknowledge the conventions of the day? Or had they simply not cared?

And of her own offspring and those of her sisters—the fourth generation of the family. Would any of them rise to prominence in the arts, science or entertainment? She thought not, and was thankful for it. On the surface at least, they were living out the typical respectable middle-class lives she herself had craved. And after her mother's death, she had done what needed to be done to ensure that the shameful events of the past would never see the light of day.

She returns Tom's journal to the suitcase, snaps the lid shut, and attaches to it a piece of masking tape on which she scrawls the name of her daughter. She would face what future is left to her with the stoicism and quiet dignity that has characterized her life.

32 Ryan Street, Broken Hill, the house that Annie built

Ann Price, eightieth birthday

Ann Price's eightieth birthday

Ann, Viola, Tom and Lillian (seated)

Frank Price, Betty Price, Lilian Lockhart (Price) Yvonne Price, Violet
Price October 1935

Frank 'Dodger' and Violet Price

Frank 'Dodger' Price as a teenager

Frank 'Dodger' Price with Minity, his faithful companion

Murray and Lil, Shanghai

Thomas John Price and stepson, Frank Price

Viola Alice (Babs) and Lilian Therese Price, on the stage in Shanghai

Violet and Lil boarding for Shanghai

Afterword

The point of departure for this narrative was that notoriously unreliable instrument—my memory. During the ensuing five years and seven drafts, I drew on the equally unreliable memories of my relatives. I will excuse my sister Margaret from the accusation of unreliability—she has a mind like a steel trap. Once a fact is locked in, there is no escape. Without the Internet, that repository of almost everything, this story could still have been told, but it would have been an emaciated version of the account appearing here. Newspaper archives were invaluable, particularly those of the following newspapers: *The Barrier Miner, Barrier Daily Truth, Adelaide Advertiser S. A. Register, Melbourne Herald, West Australian, Melbourne Herald,* and *Sydney Morning Herald*

Monographs and websites consulted in the course of writing this account included the following:

Arnstein, W. L. (1965). *The Bradlaugh Case: A study in late Victorian opinion and politics.* Oxford: Oxford University Press. Aslan, R. (2013). *Zealot: The Life and Times of Jesus of Nazareth.* London:
   The Westbourne Press.
BBC. (2008). The Welsh in Australia.
   http://www.bbc.co.uk/wales/history/sites/themes/society/migration
   _australia.shtml
Blainey, G. (2013). *A History of Victoria.* Cambridge: Cambridge
   University Press.
Brett, J. (2017). *The Enigmatic Mr. Deakin.* Melbourne: Text Publishing.
Butlin, N. (1962). *Australian Domestic Product, Investment and Foreign
   Borrowing, 1861 – 1938/39.* Cambridge: Cambridge University
Press.
Cervero, R. (1998). *The Transit Metropolis: A Global Inquiry.* Chicago:
   Island Press

Curtis, L. S. (1908). *The History of Broken Hill, Its Rise and Progress*. Adelaide: Frearson's Printing House.

Dale, G. (1981). *The Industrial History of Broken Hill*, Melbourne: Fraser
and Jenkinson.

Favenc, E. (1888). *The History of Australian Exploration: From 1788 to 1888*. Sydney: Turner and Henderson.

Garrett, R. (2018). *The Peak: An Illustrated History of Hong Kong's Top District*. Hong Kong: Blacksmith Books

Ginswick, J. (2017). *Labour and the Poor in England and Wales*. Abingdon, Oxon: Routledge.

Grose, P. (2009). *An Awkward Truth: The Bombing of Darwin, February 1942*. Sydney: Allen & Unwin.

Graham, T., King, B., & Trotter, B. (2014). *The Search for HMAS Sydney*.
Sydney: UNSW Press.

Greenwood, G. (1955). *Australia: A Social and Political History*. Sydney:
Angus and Robertson.

Gruhl, W. (2007). *Imperial Japan's World War II*. New York; Transaction
Publishers.

Johnston, M. (2007). *The Australian Army in World War II*. Oxford: Osprey Publishing.

Karskens, G. (2009). *The Colony*. Sydney: Allen and Unwin.

Lakoff, G., & Johnson, M. (1980). *Metaphors We Live By*. Chicago: University of Chicago Press.

Lakoff, G. & Turner, M. (1989) *More than Cool Reason: A Field Guide to Poetic Metaphor*.

Hazlehurst, C. (1979). *Menzies Observed*. Sydney: Allen and Unwin.

Howard, J. (2014) *Lazarus Rising*. Sydney: HarperCollins.

Howard, J. (2014). *The Menzies Era*. Sydney: HarperCollins.

Leffman, D. (2016). *The Mercenary Mandarin*. Hong Kong: Blacksmith Books.

Leigh, W. H. L. (1839). *Travels and Adventures in South Australia 1836 – 1838* London: Smith, Elder and Co.

Montgomery, M. (1980). *Who Sank the Sydney?* New York: University of

  Columbia Press.

McLean, D. (1966). *Broken Hill Sketchbook.* Adelaide: Rigby Limited.

South Australian Mines and Energy Department. (1993). *Talisker Silver-Lead Mine: A Guide to the Historic Mining Site.* Parkside S.A.: Mines and Energy.

Mullard, B. (2002). *Iron Horse and Iron Bark: History of Morisset and District.* Marrickville, NSW: Southwood Press.

Nunan, D. (2012). *When Rupert Murdoch Came to Tea: A Memoir.* Seattle:

  Wayzgoose Press.

Nunan, D. (2018). *Other Voices, Other Eyes: Expatriate Lives in Hong Kong.* Hong Kong: Blacksmith Books.

Payton, P. (2005). *The Cornish Overseas: The Epic Story of the 'Great Migration.'* Fowey: Cornwall Editions Ltd.

Price, T. J. (1904-07). *Special Lessons.* The Unpublished Journal of Thos.

  J. Price, Private collection.

Scholes, A. (1958). *The Sixth Continent: The Discovery and Exploration of*

  Australia. London: Allen and Unwin.

Sinclair, W. A. (1976). *The Process of Economic Development in Australia.* Melbourne: Cheshire.

Stilwell, G. (1976). Charles Grant Tindal (1823 – 1914) *Australian Dictionary of Biography* (Vol. 6). Melbourne: Melbourne University Press.

Wallace, M. (Ed.). (2010). *Realizing Secularism.* Sydney: Australia and New Zealand Secular Association.

Webster, M. (1958). *John McDouall Stuart.* Melbourne: Melbourne University Press.

Wood, M. (2016). *Australia's Secular Foundations.* Melbourne: Australian

  Scholarly Publishing Pty., Ltd.

Printed in Australia
AUHW010322171120
337090AU00003B/3